Without Mercy

Without Mercy

COLONEL DAVID HUNT
AND R. J. PINEIRO

A TOM DOHERTY ASSOCIATES BOOK
NEW YORK

This is a work of fiction. All of the characters, organizations, and events portrayed in this novel are either products of the authors' imaginations or are used fictitiously.

A Forge Book
Published by Tom Doherty Associates
175 Fifth Avenue
New York, NY 10010

www.tor-forge.com

Forge® is a registered trademark of Macmillan Publishing Group, LLC.

The Library of Congress Cataloging-in-Publication Data is available upon request.

ISBN 978-0-7653-8260-3 (hardcover)
ISBN 978-1-4668-8827-2 (e-book)

Our books may be purchased in bulk for promotional, educational, or business use. Please contact your local bookseller or the Macmillan Corporate and Premium Sales Department at 1-800-221-7945, extension 5442, or by e-mail at MacmillanSpecialMarkets@macmillan.com.

First Edition: March 2017

Printed in the United States of America

0 9 8 7 6 5 4 3 2 1

To those who gave their lives in the global war against terrorism, to those who continue to fight this noblest of fights, to the victims of cowardly acts of terror, and to their families.

ACKNOWLEDGMENTS

Being authors is a bit like being astronauts. There is a large support structure behind a space mission but only a couple of names make the headlines, or in our case, the book cover. We are particularly grateful to:

Robert Gleason, the finest editor in the business, for coming up with the concept for this book, for bringing us together as coauthors, and for pushing us to hammer out the best possible story we could. We are also appreciative of all we have learned from your considerable research and wisdom on the topic of nuclear proliferation, as well as from your nonfiction work, *The Nuclear Terrorist*.

The rest of the staff at Tor/Forge, especially Tom Doherty, Linda Quinton, and Elayne Becker. It's always a pleasure working with such pros.

Matthew Bialer, super agent at Greenburger Associates, for twenty-five years of guidance and friendship.

Bill O'Reilly and Judge Jeanine Pirro of Fox News, Peter Kostis, friend and professional golf instructor, and Howie Carr of Boston's WRKO *The Howie Carr Show* for your support of this project and for your unflagging friendship. A special thanks goes to Bill Shine and Dianne Brandy of Fox News, and Rob Guralnick, producer.

Colonel Ralph Peters and Ward Larsen, who gave up time from their busy schedules to review the manuscript.

Alicia Vidaurreta, for your timely review of the proof.

And last but not least, our families, and especially our wives, Angela Hunt and Lory Pineiro.

We will not prematurely or unnecessarily risk the costs of a worldwide nuclear war in which even the fruits of victory would be ashes in our mouth.

—JOHN F. KENNEDY

Without Mercy

PROLOGUE

The Hand of God

BAGRAM, AFGHANISTAN

They moved swiftly and decisively, with the quiet confidence of knowing one's fate and being prepared to face it. Jamal was in charge, but he was not in front; he was coordinating the night raid from the rear of the assault force racing toward Bagram Airfield with speed and abandonment.

His Jeep Wrangler's thirty-two-inch off-road tires bit into the uneven terrain, kicking up dirt and gravel, the road noise deafening. Sweat rolled down his forehead and into his eyes, stinging them.

Blinking it away, Jamal tightened his grip on the steering wheel while crossing a shallow ravine. The Wrangler bounced, going airborne for a second, before landing hard on all four tires, slamming the suspension. Jaws clenched, he kept his hands taut on the wheel to avoid setting off the fifty pounds of Semtex explosives secured to the rear seat. His demolition expert had designed it to detonate with a spring-loaded trigger strapped to his left hand or by the digital timer fixed with Velcro to the dashboard. Initially set for five minutes.

And counting.

Twenty-foot concrete walls surrounded the airfield's western perimeter. Outward-facing floodlights pierced the massive cloud of dust trailing the collection of 4×4s ahead of him.

His force consisted primarily of the rugged UAZ-469, the Soviet's version of his Jeep. It was appropriately nicknamed *Kozlik*, or Goat, because of its ability to handle rocky hills. Left behind during the Soviet Union's 1989 retreat, Jamal's deadly herd of refurbished all-terrain vehicles sported fat sand-grabbing tires and overhauled engines.

He silently cursed the damn lights giving those guarding the compound the unfair advantage of seeing better and farther than his group.

But it would not matter.

Jamal's answer to their technology was not to fight it but rather overwhelm it and deceive it, and those who depended on it. Every four-wheel-drive racing across the desert hauled a similar load of Semtex, all double-rigged like his.

Four minutes.

He eyed the red LED counter directly in front of him and then the pressure trigger as the desert rushed past him and the tan-colored wall grew larger in his windshield. An eight-foot-tall chain-link fence topped with barbed wire stretched around the compound twenty feet in front of the wall, forming a perimeter road used by patrolling Humvees.

But tonight there were none in sight.

Yet.

The plan was simple: hit the airfield hard and fast in multiple sections along its western border.

If they broke through, great, kill everyone they could.

If the defenses held, no problem, the real mission was already in progress three miles on the other side of the base.

And nothing on Earth could stop that attack.

Jamal's diversionary force of thirty-four drivers had rehearsed, prayed, and rehearsed again. They had accepted the inevitable outcome of their actions. Some yelled, some cried, some sweated, some were calm, and some even chanted. But they all charged as one across the sand toward their certain ends.

Three minutes.

Two dozen Chinese-made 107mm rockets zoomed overhead, launched by twelve-tube launchers towed behind UAZ-469s hidden a thousand feet behind him.

Armed with white phosphorous incendiary heads, the projectiles arced toward the base, drawing the attention of the two west-facing Phalanx Close-In Weapons Systems.

Originally designed as a last line of automatic weapons defense to protect U.S. Navy ships against incoming missiles, the venerable Phalanx CIWS now guarded Bagram. Their deadly accurate 20mm Vulcan Gatling guns would have decimated Jamal's ground attack before it got near the base.

The computerized systems, however, prioritized the rockets, pivoting the guns toward the night sky. Thundering to life, they painted walls of self-detonating tungsten rounds directly in front of the incoming rockets.

Nearly half the 107s exploded in midair or were knocked off course when colliding with the radar-guided bursts of explosive shells. The rest stabbed the base, detonating inside the perimeter with distant thumping sounds accompanied by flashes of orange light.

Another volley of Chinese projectiles shot across the sky, keeping the Phalanx systems occupied as Jamal's team pushed closer to its target.

Two minutes and thirty seconds.

Gunfire erupted in many places along the top of the wall as interior forces reacted to the ground attack. Their sporadic fire suggested momentary confusion. Bagram Airfield had been hit in the past by rockets and mortars as well as by the occasional car bomb, but never in such large and coordinated force.

But soldiers were soldiers, and many in that base were hardboiled veterans with three and four combat tours. Within a minute, over two hundred soldiers from the closest barracks joined those on perimeter duty to hit the incoming wave. They were a mix of Special Forces, the 82nd Airborne Division, the 1st Cavalry Division, and the Military Police—all in various stages of deployment and job rotations.

Jamal frowned as bullets zoomed overhead, raining down from a dozen wall-top defensive posts packed with soldiers. An instant later, headlights pierced the night around the front of the base a mile away.

Humvees, Jamal thought, giving the distant trucks armed with .50-caliber Brownings a quick glance. They accelerated in tandem down the narrow patrol road between the chain-link fence and the concrete wall.

But it won't matter.

The lesson would be taught yet again: when fighting against someone who did not care if they lived or died—the fanatic eventually succeeded.

Another volley of 107s whistled toward the compound. The Phalanx systems thundered, spewing ridiculous amounts of ammunition. Some rockets sparked in midair, others spun out of control. A few detonated inside the base.

Two minutes.

Helicopters took flight across the compound, distant red and green lights rising in the night sky. Their rumbling blended with Jamal's engine, with the surrounding gunfire.

But it also would not matter.

Five hundred feet ahead of him, the dozen jihadists of his initial wave crashed through the chain-link fence and slammed into the base of the wall.

A combined two thousand pounds of Semtex tore into reinforced concrete, breaching the airfield with maddening force in several places. Bursts of fire, cement, chain link, and rebar stabbed the night. The one-ton blast swallowed soldiers, floodlights, and Phalanx systems, turning perimeter defenses into piles of smoldering rubble.

The powerful shock wave reverberated across the valley. It rattled his seat, the steering wheel, and even his own teeth. But Jamal kept his focus on the detonator, keeping it compressed against the steering column, his knuckles turning white.

The second wave, just three hundred feet ahead of him, drove into the gaps punched by the first wave, massive tires scrambling across mounds of debris. Explosions boomed seconds later from within as his warriors detonated their charges beyond the breached wall, triggering fireballs that licked the sky and fueled the confusion.

The shock wave caused larger sections of the wall to collapse outward, crashing over the chain-link fence almost in slow motion, slapping the desert floor, and ironically creating entrance ramps. Two of his men managed to ignite their Semtex after reaching the power generating station adjacent to the infringed wall, throwing the entire base into the twilight of emergency lighting.

One minute.

Jamal pressed on, along with eight other jihadists. They formed the final wave as gunfire momentarily subsided after the back-to-back detonations. Steering the Wrangler to the closest breach, he felt the aluminum and steel chassis tremble as he drove it up a collapsed slab of concrete. All four tires spun furiously, their deep thread propelling the Jeep into a war-torn compound.

Fires burned everywhere, thanks to the combined effects of the truck bombs and the 107s. To his right the power station vomited sparks and fire. To his left heaps of unrecognizable and sizzling waste blocked the streets.

Backup generators came on, engulfing the compound in lights, providing a clearer view of the magnitude of the destruction. It was impressive. Everything within a hundred feet of this section of the western wall was gone, replaced by craters, smoking rubble, and fires.

He floored the Wrangler straight ahead, toward a row of tan-colored shipping containers stacked two and three high, five hundred feet away. It was marked by his intelligence source as a U.S. Army weapons depot.

The digital timer on the dash ticked below forty-five seconds, red LED numbers counting down the final moments of his life.

Jamal's vision tunneled on the containers at the end of a field flanked by buildings on fire, his mind visualizing the magnitude of the blast he could create.

But he never reached them.

Defenders quickly regrouped. A dozen Humvees surrounded him, followed by at least a hundred soldiers from the nearby barracks of the 82nd Airborne. Their desert camouflage uniforms flickered in the pulsating glow of neighboring fires.

Three Boeing AH-64 Apache attack helicopters also approached the kill zone with haste and determination, their downwashes scattering billowing smoke.

One of them fired a Hellfire, but not toward him. The projectile shot at blinding speed to his far left. It trailed bright light for a fraction of a second before demolishing a black UAZ-469 just clearing the wall. The blast tossed the Soviet chassis up and sideways against the front of a Humvee.

Another Apache killed two more of his Goats in rapid succession, one with a Hellfire and the other with guns.

An instant later the Brownings mounted on the Humvees' rooftops came alive with muzzle flashes pointed at him. Bullets tore across his hood, ripping through the Jeep's engine, steering, and tires.

Spinning out of control, Jamal saw soldiers, Humvees, and hovering Apaches swapping places amidst gunfire and flames. Somewhere in this spinning and blazing world of his own creation, a .50-caliber round hit him squarely in the chest, slamming him against the seat.

And he lost his grip on the steering wheel, releasing the pressure trigger.

Near the foot of the mountain overlooking the eastern sector of the base, Mohammed gazed down at the distant explosions. They painted the sky in splashes of red and yellow-gold, momentarily washing out the stars. Gunfire and more detonations echoed across the valley.

Above it all, a silvery moon in its third quarter hung immobile against the mountain range at the opposite end of the Panjshir Valley, as if stabbed by its jagged peaks.

His small group had negotiated over half a mountain of rough terrain in a pair of UAZ-469s before continuing on foot down a winding goat path that Mohammed remembered quite well from his youth.

Floodlights along the top of the wall protecting the eastern perimeter shone outward, illuminating the clearing between the foot of the mountain a few hundred feet below him and the base. Their shafts of light reached the sparse vegetation, casting the ragged shadows that Mohammed favored as he led his three handpicked warriors in this historic mission.

All wore dark pashmina shawls over traditional *khet partug* garments.

Pashmina, the fine hand-spun and woven cashmere wool draped around their shoulders, protected them from the bitter cold. The *khets*, heavy tunics made of cotton, matched the dark color of their *partugs*, the loose pants secured with strings around their waists.

Everything, down to the dark army boots and camouflage cream, had been carefully selected by Mohammed to help them blend with the murky surroundings under their last star-filled night in Central Asia.

Mohammed paused, kneeling by a clump of boulders as a hairpin turn skirted a ledge overlooking the base. Setting down his weathered Kalashnikov, he pressed the rubber eyecups of his Russian binoculars against his face, fingering the focusing wheel while his men fell in behind him.

His vantage point a couple hundred feet above the valley allowed him to see clearly over the wall and into the base. Explosions and gun-fire reigned on the opposite side of the complex. The blasts reverberated across the desert as his brothers and sisters carried out their jobs, helping to guarantee the ultimate success.

God willing, he thought.

Bagram Airfield, the largest U.S. military base in Afghanistan, forty miles east of Kabul and sprawled between the Panjshir and the Kuthesda mountain ranges, covered six square miles. It encompassed two long runways and a control tower to manage heavy military traf-fic. A-10 Warthogs and F-16 Falcons shared the tarmac with Apache and Pave Hawk helicopters, a collection of Reaper and Predator drones, and lots of transport planes, from the C-130 Hercules to the colossal C-5 Galaxy.

Mohammed shifted the night-penetrating binoculars over the metal roofs of dozens of hangars, brown with a tint of red to match the surroundings. They faced a vast tarmac covering twenty-three acres of planes and helicopters—all bathed in yellow light.

Beyond them, he inspected the countless forty-foot shipping containers—as many as there were stars in the night—stacked two and three high, converted by U.S. Army Engineers into living quarters. Resembling low-income apartment complexes, they formed the core of multiple housing zones spread across two square miles in support of the citylike base's inhabitants. At its height, Bagram accommodated as many as forty thousand people, primarily U.S. and international troops and contractors. But in recent years, the base's population had shrunk by nearly half as the U.S. withdrew from the region.

Surrounding the lodging zones stood hundreds of wooden struc-tures used as office space, mess halls, Laundromats, rec halls, movie theaters, and shopping centers—all creating another two square miles of tin rooftops. Off to his far right, a large water treatment plant stood adjacent to a sewage and waste management facility. Barriers made of concrete or sandbags formed large partitions between housing areas and other structures to isolate and absorb the damage caused by ar-tillery and rocket strikes.

The well-lit compound, with its endless grid of blacktop roads and walkways connecting living spaces to working areas, incorporated all branches of the U.S. military, a variety of government contractors, and some NATO forces. There was also a detachment of a thousand soldiers from the Afghan National Security Forces being trained to take over the facility in the not-so-distant future.

There was a rhythm to the place, set primarily by the constant sound of large and small planes—jets, props, drones, and helicopters—landing and taking off.

That rhythm was now broken by Jamal's attack and would be forever changed by what Mohammed prepared to do.

Originally built by the Soviets during their ill-fated occupation in the 1980s, which had orphaned him, Bagram Airfield was expanded after the American-led invasion of 2001. For the past decade, it had been the place where men and women arrived alive, full of promise and fear, and left different, changed.

Or worse.

And that included prisoners, such as Mohammed.

He inadvertently tightened his grip as he panned across the roofline of the Parwan Detention Facility, surrounded by double perimeter fences topped with electrified barbed wire, dominating the southern end of the military metropolis.

And home to over three thousand of his fellow Muslims.

Breathing deeply, Mohammed ignored the anger raking his gut while he stared at the place where he had spent so much of his youth, entering a naïve goat herder and exiting two years ago a man scarred to his soul.

But tonight he had come home.

And he was ready—all of them were.

The journey from Islamabad had been long and tiring, with multiple refueling stops across endless desert and mountains, first aboard helicopters and later in the Goats.

A couple miles north of the facility, a safe distance from the attack, stood his hometown, the city of Bagram, dating back to the days of Alexander the Great. It was now an assortment of mud-brick structures and wooden roofs connected by twisted pathways amidst bullet-riddled façades that served as evidence of decades of street fighting and mortar attacks.

He had stared at those weathered rooftops from his jail cell while reminiscing about his former life as months turned into years. But tonight Mohammed surveyed his hometown systematically. He followed the alleyways that led to a mosque, the tallest structure in the ancient city. Slowly, he shifted his narrow field of view toward its topmost window.

There, a candle burned bright, its flickering light outlining the half-round window opening.

It was time.

As he set down the binoculars, Mohammed's gaze landed on the Pakistani brothers, Qadeer and Hamid. They were orphans, like him, but not by the Soviets' hand. The brothers had lost their parents to an American bombing raid in 2005.

They knelt by the one-hundred-pound chest they had hauled from one of the Goats. The siblings were big and strong, as Mohammed had once been, before muscular atrophy overwhelmed youthful vigor during those sessions in the Parwan Detention Facility's infamous Black Jail.

He inhaled deeply at the thought of the secret prison within the prison run by the Defense Intelligence Agency and U.S. Special Operations. The place was designed to break their spirits—and their bodies—through a nightmarish brew of sleep deprivation, stressful positions, waterboarding, and beatings.

But the bastards didn't break him.

If anything, those grueling years only served to transform the boy into a hardened man, extinguishing his humanity, his compassion, pouring and solidifying the foundation of his jihad mentality.

And tonight, he planned to break *them*.

Mohammed stood, ignoring the pain stabbing his knees from being stuffed inside the crippling Black Jail coffin-like enclosures that prevented full leg extension for weeks at a time. But he had learned to walk again following his release, albeit not without the limp that would haunt him for the remainder of his short life.

The Pakistani brothers also stood, picked up the heavy trunk by the side handles—just as they had drilled endlessly in the prior weeks in order to build their endurance—and followed him.

Yasser, the fourth man in the team and a native of the tribal areas, brought up the rear, armed with an AK-47.

Mohammed ventured down the goat path, silently giving thanks to the star-filled sky—and his ISIS leaders—for this opportunity to strike back against the forces that had invaded his nation and destroyed his way of life. His small group, in sharp contrast with Jamal's large overt assault team, would use deception and surprise to carry out its mission.

The trail widened as it reached the foot of the mountain, as vegetation thinned, limiting the number of shadowy areas where they could hide from the floodlights.

He looked for patrols along the eastern perimeter, where reinforced concrete walls towered over the desert as high as thirty feet, lessening the need for the armored vehicles guarding the exterior in other sectors of the base. And besides, any nearby patrols should have already been redeployed to reinforce the western wall.

Or so he hoped.

He paused again, this time nodding toward Yasser, the educated one in the group. An engineering graduate of the Quaid-i-Azam University in Islamabad, Yasser had worked for the esteemed Dr. Atiq Gadai, custodian of Pakistan's nuclear program.

Yasser, who had lost his wife to a drone attack several years ago, set down his assault rifle and dialed the combination of the trunk's digital lock, breaking the protective seal.

He lifted the lid, which was lined with a film of lead even though the combined sixty pounds of weapons-grade uranium-235 at the heart of the gun-type device posed only a negligible radioactive threat in its current state. But Dr. Gadai had wanted to avoid even the slightest chance of sickness before they reached their goal.

None of that mattered anymore, however. From now on a higher power would guide them as they began the final leg of their journey to paradise.

Together.

While Yasser worked the unit's digital screen, Mohammed inspected the hollow cylindrical shape that made up the projectile, or bullet, built from a dozen rings of fissile material stacked together. It rested inside one end of the six-inch-diameter gun barrel pressed against a charge of conventional explosives. Once triggered, the explosives would fire the bullet to the other end of the tube, impelling a target uranium-235 cylinder. The latter also consisted of stacked rings, but of a smaller diameter that allowed it to fit perfectly inside the hollow section of the projectile—forming the required mass to achieve fission.

Yasser's fingers moved with practiced ease, powering up the embedded computer and keying the activation code. Lighting the digital fuse.

Mohammed placed a hand on the engineer's shoulder. The world had called Yasser's wife collateral damage, and then it had just moved on. The world had forgotten about the blast that had dismembered her—forgotten how she had bled out in his arms, forever scarring Yasser's heart.

But the young scientist never forgot, and neither did Mohammed nor the Pakistani brothers.

And tonight they would remind the world.

With fire.

At precisely four in the morning, the final volleys of Chinese rockets in the wake of Jamal's attack prompted the twin Phalanx systems guarding the eastern perimeter to shift to the west.

As dictated by their well-rehearsed plan, Mohammed and his team left the protection of the waist-high shrubs the instant the gun systems opened fire at the distant 107s. The group began their final sprint toward the compound less than a quarter mile away, four figures shifting across the sand, facing a wall of blinding light.

The Phalanx 20mm Gatling guns vomited fire toward the west, thundering across the desert. Mohammed and Yasser, AK-47s at the ready, rushed ahead of Qadeer, Hamid, and their precious cargo.

It didn't take long, even at this carefully selected hour and while chaos reigned at the opposite end of the compound. Alarms blared amidst screams and warnings from the top of the wall, but Mohammed could not see the enemy, only those glaring lights.

Ignoring everything, the group pushed on as fast as they could, getting closer to their objective. The device beeped loudly, marking their final moments.

Gunfire blasted down from the compound, muzzle flashes pulsating an instant before sand erupted to their right in clouds of glittering light.

Mohammed and Yasser shifted left while lifting their AK-47s and firing toward the flashes, spraying the top of the wall. The staccato gunfire echoed against the concrete barrier soaring over them.

Reloading while running, Mohammed emptied a second magazine directly at the floodlights. The Russian assault rifle vibrated in his calloused hands.

Brightness dimmed as glass exploded above the rim of the wall, and a priceless island of darkness suddenly emerged to their right.

Mohammed and Yasser cut toward it, followed by the Pakistani brothers, stepping away from the light and rushing forward within the confines of their temporary cover.

But it didn't last. A spotlight panned over to them. The fire raining down from the walls became fairly steady but not necessarily accurate. Unless properly and constantly trained, guards at night would typically shoot high, over their heads, confirming Mohammed's intel report handed down from his ISIS leadership. Afghan guards who lacked the training of NATO personnel protected this side of the wall.

Mohammed and Yasser fired another volley against the closest defensive positions, their rounds peppering the top of the wall, before reloading and—

Yasser's head snapped back and tore from his torso.

He collapsed on the sand, blood splattering everywhere.

Hamid and Qadeer jumped over Yasser's body and continued running behind Mohammed while he emptied another magazine into the beams in short, measured bursts. He took out more lights, creating another patch of darkness, but once again, more spotlights converged on them.

And he fired the Kalashnikov into those lights as well, buying them time. Every second that passed allowed them to bring the device closer to the wall—and closer to the cowards hiding behind it.

Humvees appeared in the distance, headlights piercing the night, racing toward them from the front of the compound.

Mohammed ignored them while inserting his final magazine, cocking the weapon, and lifting it back up.

But he never got to fire another round.

His shoulders and chest burned from a barrage of bullets piercing him, bursting through his back, and peppering the sand behind him.

Mohammed dropped on his side, unable to breathe, as the Pakistani brothers leaped past him, running side by side into a fusillade while clutching the trunk between them. Their dark silhouettes cut left then right, just as they had practiced.

He blinked and watched them kick up sand as they advanced another hundred feet. The fire intensified from above and also broke out from the incoming Humvees. Tracers from their .50-caliber Brownings drifted toward them as gunners adjusted their fire.

And that was the last image his mind registered: their tall outlines approaching the wall as sand exploded all around.

Before the flash enveloped them.

Terrible and all consuming, it was breathtakingly beautiful yet overwhelming in its completeness—the hand of God and the finality of death in the same arch of time and space.

The air heated to a temperature close to that of the center of the sun, vaporizing Mohammed, his team, and the nearing Humvees while unleashing vast amounts of thermal energy absorbed by the cratering desert floor.

The chain reaction sparked an incandescent spherical mass that lit up the night sky and was visible for a hundred miles. It rapidly morphed into an expanding fireball the size of a football field, engulfing several hundred feet of the perimeter wall. It incinerated several dozen Afghan soldiers and fused tens of thousands of tons of sand, concrete, rebar, and rock.

The airburst crushed everything in its path that had not yet been consumed by the blaze, from airplanes on the tarmac to hangars and service trucks, reducing to eighty psi within the first few hundred feet. It further dropped down to five psi after a quarter of a mile, before turning into a sandstorm, spreading debris across the remainder of the airfield and the nearest housing zone.

Morphing its original spherical shape into the traditional mushroom, the powerful updraft sucked millions of cubic feet of cold air into the stem—along with sand and pulverized concrete and rock. Propelled upward, the radioactive cloud blossomed higher and higher over the region, fueled by swirling hot gases while forming highly radioactive particles as altitude condensed the vaporized fission.

The vertical thrust continued for a couple of miles, before gravity, humidity, and cooling temperatures slowed the rising column as the atmosphere put up a fight. The reaction finally stabilized at a height of fifteen thousand feet before it bowed to the prevailing winds, spreading out laterally, away from the air base, sparing its inhabitants from the toxic fallout.

Bagram Airfield relied on its concrete walls as its first line of defense against the hostile environment surrounding it. Now over two hundred feet of them were completely gone and three hundred more were crumbling on its eastern side, plus multiple smaller gaps on its western perimeter.

By dawn, however, thirty-foot-deep barriers of Czech hedgehogs—static obstacles made of metal I-beams and capable of stopping tanks—bridged every gap in the wall. Behind them stood lines of bumper-to-bumper Humvees, their Kevlar-wrapped .50-caliber turrets aimed at the desert and manned by soldiers in hazmat suits working thirty-minute shifts. A third line of defenses a safe distance from the radioactive perimeter set up M2 Brownings on tripods surrounded by sandbags.

Although a nuclear device with a yield of 3.1 kilotons hit Bagram Airfield—a third of the size of the bomb that leveled Hiroshima—initial casualties were limited to 269 American soldiers and 183 Afghan troops. And most of those took place during the fight with the jihadists deployed by a man standing on the rooftop of the mosque overlooking the base.

Ibrahim al-Crameini, leader of the ISIS caliphate in Afghanistan and Pakistan, had used the nuclear explosion as the backdrop of a video destined to become the most viral in history.

1

Vaccaro

"How did we let this happen? And what are we going to do about it?"

They were simple questions that the newly elected president tossed down the thirty feet of conference table in the Situation Room to guide the outcome of this emergency meeting.

Every black leather chair was occupied this early morning. Each faced a thirteen-inch mobile computer, a sparkling crystal water glass, a white coffee cup adorned with the White House seal, and one very pissed-off commander in chief.

Wearing a dark blue skirt suit, President Laura Vaccaro rested her palms on the table and looked around the room. She weighed 120 pounds, with a slim frame. Short dark hair framed her narrow face, partially covering a fine scar traversing her left temple and cheekbone, earned a lifetime ago in Afghanistan.

Those physically present included the secretary of defense, the secretary of state, and the directors of the FBI, the DIA, and the National Intelligence Program. The White House chief of staff, John Wright, sat to Vaccaro's immediate right, next to National Security Advisor Lisa Jacobson, the vice president, the secretary of Homeland Security, and the head of the National Nuclear Security Administration. They formed a mixed group of men and women of varying ages. Some she had brought along, like John Wright and Lisa Jacobson. Others she had retained from the prior administration, like the secretary of defense and the heads of the FBI and the CIA.

For now, she thought. *Let's see how they handle this mess.*

The Pentagon feed on the large screen at the end of the room showed all seven members of the Joint Chiefs of Staff. They sat stoically shoulder to shoulder along one side of a black table facing the camera. The chairman and the vice chairman occupied the middle seats, flanked by the chiefs of the army, naval operations, air force, and the National Guard Bureau, and the commandant of the Marine Corps. They formed a unified wall of chiseled faces, starched uniforms, ribbons, and shiny medals.

A pair of sixty-inch TVs on each side wall depicted images of Bagram from various feeds, including the Department of Defense, the National Reconnaissance Office, and two networks.

Even with the sound muted, the videos were hard to watch. Body bags lined the floor of a hangar. Hundreds of wounded overwhelmed the base's hospital. Rubble and debris reigned across the airfield. Fires raged on the tarmac from countless wrecked planes and helicopters. Soldiers in hazmat suits guarded the gap created by the blast while others began the cleanup process. Meanwhile, demonstrators were out in numbers across the Middle East, dancing and chanting in the streets. In northern Iraq, black-clad militants hung out of cars and trucks waving their AK-47s while parading down the streets of some village. In Tehran, hundreds of American flags were being burned in celebration of the attack.

Vaccaro contemplated the Stars and Stripes in the corner of the room under a single spotlight before calmly looking over at her chief of staff. "Go ahead, John."

Wright was a former U.S. Marine captain who'd served three tours in Afghanistan before working the Pentagon and then Capitol Hill as a military liaison. He was slim but firm, with penetrating hazel eyes and a full head of blond hair, trimmed very short. He wore a tight gray suit and spit-shine black shoes. Everything about the man was shipshape, from the way he'd led his teams back in the day to his golf game, and especially the manner in which he ran the new White House administration.

Perching a pair of reading glasses on the tip of his aquiline nose, he looked at his computer screen and said, "We will start with a fifteen-minute brief from the DoD, followed by another fifteen minutes from the NNSA, since this clearly deals with nuclear proliferation. Then ten-minute briefs from the counterterrorism divisions of the DIA, the CIA, the FBI, Homeland, and the NSA. An open discussion will follow for exactly one hour. Our goal this morning, ladies and gentlemen, is to formulate a clear plan of action by eleven hundred in response to that." He pointed at the TV screens. Then he added, "That will leave exactly two hours to prep for the presidential address scheduled for thirteen hundred hours."

Producing a digital chronometer, Wright looked over at Charles Grandville, the secretary of defense, and started the timer.

Shipshape.

Grandville leaned forward to start his brief, but the president spoke first.

"How many people work inside the Pentagon, Mister Secretary?"

The man blinked, considered the question, and finally said, "Over thirty thousand, Madam President."

"Specifically, there are thirty-six thousand three hundred and twenty-seven in that building."

General Grandville, a heavyset man who cut his teeth in the Baltics before fighting in both Gulf Wars and then Afghanistan, obviously didn't know how to respond to that. So Vaccaro decided to assist him. "Considering all that brainpower, I am looking forward to understanding the facts and our immediate and violent reaction to what I'm seeing on these very large HD screens."

This was combat. She had been in combat, led men and women into battle in some of the worst armpits of the world. She had killed and had witnessed close friends getting killed or wounded.

She had the damn T-shirt.

And the fucking scars to go along with it.

Vaccaro had risen to popularity after logging more than seven hundred combat flying hours in the A-10 Warthog, the armor-plated aerial "tank" built to fly low and protect the backs of ground soldiers. She became one of the first authorized female combat pilots in 1993, when then-Defense Secretary Les Aspin approved it. And she went on to serve, first in Iraq and later in Afghanistan. During her final tour, she'd refused to leave several ambushed marines, even after taking heavy fire and losing an engine. She'd pushed her wounded A-10 to keep the Taliban at bay until the marines were rescued, but got shot down in the process. Vaccaro spent two days fighting her way to an extraction point, getting shot in the face and stabbed twice. All of the marines she had protected were aboard the two Black

Hawk helicopters as volunteers for the daring rescue mission. They had provided the required muscle to reach Vaccaro's hideout in a nearby cave. One of the marines had ignored the cross fire, raced across the clearing, found her in the cave, and hauled her back to the chopper.

His name was Captain John Wright.

Vaccaro returned a decorated hero to her family in Colorado Springs, where a grateful state sent her to Capitol Hill to represent them in the U.S. Senate.

And within a decade, she was propelled to the Oval Office, where everything she said or did was scrutinized under the twenty-twenty lens of hindsight. This was only her third month in office, and the honeymoon was certainly over.

And now the President needed this man who had saved her life in Afghanistan to help her get America through this. Vaccaro needed to trust him completely as her gut told her the nation was about to enter one of its most dangerous times: facing terrorists armed with nuclear weapons.

Unfortunately, Vaccaro never really learned to trust anyone quite completely. And while Wright, as well as Lisa Jacobson, came damn close, the President still lived and died by the old Ronald Reagan quote from his days dealing with the Soviet Union back in the 1980s.

Trust but verify.

Wright waved his chronometer at Grandville and said, "Tick tock, Mister Secretary."

Grandville leaned forward again, and again Vaccaro cut him off. Something on the flat screens had caught her attention.

Stretching an index finger toward the closest LED monitor, she said, "Volume, John."

All turned to the video playing on every TV feed.

A tall and thin man with a prominent hooked nose and a closely trimmed beard filled the screen. He wore all-black, traditional clothes. In a very calm British accent he began to describe what next came into view in vivid color: nuclear explosions from our past, experiments in the Nevada desert, at Bikini Atoll, and views of Hiroshima and Nagasaki.

All had seen them before in various movies and History Channel segments. The voice then described what had just happened in

Afghanistan. The video transitioned from historical footage to the city of Bagram, zooming in on the base during the final seconds before the detonation. The actual blast was shown in high resolution and in slow motion. The fireball engulfed the far end of the base, incinerating soldiers, equipment, and structures. The ensuing pressure wave vaporized a large section of the eastern wall and part of the airfield, tossing massive C-5 Galaxy transports around like toys.

"We wanted no doubts, no illusions, no questions of what has happened and by whom," said the man as the images of Bagram dissolved and the video transitioned to his upper body. "We, the Islamic State, have nuclear weapons. We have the ability to deliver them anywhere in the world. We have followers where we want them. These followers are your neighbors, your babysitters, your bosses, your police officers—everyone and anyone you know and just as importantly those you do *not* know, but will very soon.

"We demand the release of all prisoners from your black sites, including Guantanamo Bay and the Parwan Detention Facility. In addition, we demand the withdrawal of every United States soldier from the Middle East. Go home. Now. This isn't your land. You have no business being here."

The man paused as the camera closed in on his face.

"These demands will be met within seven days. Your God claims to have built this world in those few days; surely our demands are much easier. However, should our demands not be met in the seven days, the next attack will be on *real* American soil . . . not the soil you stole from the Afghan people."

While his voice trailed off, the images that replaced his face reminded Vaccaro of a big-budget Hollywood production. Most in the room did not realize how well done the message was until later, when the shock abated and realization set in.

What everyone in the room knew, beginning with President Vaccaro, was that the four horsemen of the apocalypse had just galloped their steeds into the White House Situation Room and let them crap all over its blue carpet.

2

Monica

FBI Special Agent Monica Cruz spent the first waking hours of her fortieth birthday steering her Ducati 848 precisely four vehicles behind her mark, a silver Cadillac Escalade driving down Connecticut Avenue.

The black-on-black bike wasn't an official FBI vehicle, but then again, this wasn't an official FBI surveillance job, and today she wasn't officially on the clock. In fact, she was supposed to be at the Ritz-Carlton's spa in Georgetown enjoying every penny's worth of the small fortune she had spent as a birthday gift to herself.

Until the U.S. flags flying at half-staff reminded her that terrorists never take a day off.

The SUV turned right onto Seventeenth Street and continued alongside Farragut Square. Monica downshifted to third with the toe of her riding boot before releasing the clutch and twisting the throttle. Leaning into the turn, she never lost sight of the Escalade reflecting the early morning sun forking between high-rises.

The vehicle belonged to Amir Dham, cousin of the Pakistani ambassador to the United States. Amir was also owner of Jasmine Companies, a chain of stores that sold luxurious furniture and assorted high-end imports in Washington, D.C., New York, and Chicago.

On paper, Amir's operation was squeaky clean, down to impeccable IRS records managed by Ernst & Young. Amir's exclusive clientele included several U.S. senators and congressmen. He golfed regularly with White House Chief of Staff John Wright, was a prominent donor at various D.C. nonprofits, and contributed heavily to the Metropolitan PD and the DCFD. Amir had even hosted a large fundraiser dinner for Vaccaro's campaign last year.

Quite the fucking little angel, Monica thought.

Except for the fact that two months ago one of his trucks was used to transport enough weapons and explosives to start a revolution.

Monica had led the joint FBI-ATF-Metro PD operation that resulted in the recovery of two hundred UZI PRO submachine guns fitted with Gemtec MK-9K sound suppressors, Reflex scopes, and twenty thousand rounds of ammo. On top of that, she had seized three hundred pounds of Semtex, a general-purpose plastic explosive. And she was even able to chase down the driver as he tried to flee the scene. The man turned out to be a disgruntled former employee who allegedly stole the truck to commit the crime.

Amir owned over one hundred such delivery trucks across three states. Although he had diplomatic immunity and was well connected, he claimed he had nothing to hide and invited the Feds to scrub his operation. The driver turned out to be an Afghan national with ties to ISIS back home, and hung himself in his jail cell before Monica or anyone else could interview him.

The subsequent monthlong FBI investigation supported Amir's claims and he was cleared of all charges. But Monica's sixth sense told her there was more to this story. Although her superiors had officially closed the case, she made it her hobby to keep tabs on the man.

Amir lived in a multimillion-dollar brownstone up in Dupont Circle and worked at his shiny headquarters in Manassas, Virginia, across the Potomac. But today he was breaking routine, heading in the direction opposite the Theodore Roosevelt Memorial Bridge.

Where are you going, asshole?

The Escalade slowed as it approached H Street, turned left toward Lafayette Square, and continued past the U.S. Department of Commerce. It finally pulled up beneath a large portico supported by four round tapered columns belonging to the prestigious Hay-Adams, a luxury boutique hotel resembling a 1920s mansion.

Monica parked illegally across the street in time to see one of Amir's bodyguards get out and open the rear door for his boss, who stepped out and waltzed into the lobby.

Climbing off and securing the helmet to the handlebars, she flashed her badge at a Metro PD cop signaling her to move the bike. Running across four lanes of traffic, she reached the front of the hotel just as the valet service drove off with the Escalade.

Amir's well-dressed bodyguard trio had just vanished beyond the glass front doors, held open by a bellhop. He was dressed in a tan jacket and trousers, with matching suspenders on a white shirt. A brown bow tie, a neatly folded handkerchief in the jacket's breast pocket, and smart two-tone brogues completed the period look.

As she approached the entrance, the bellhop, a man in his forties with broad shoulders and pristine black hair, smoothly closed the doors and blocked the way.

Smiling politely, he said, "Sorry. No vacancies."

Monica caught her reflection in the glass doors, guessing that her dark riding jacket, black jeans, and boots probably failed to live up to the dress code of one of Washington's premier hotels.

Pulling out her badge again, she said, "One just opened up. Step aside."

Eyes widening, the bellhop complied and opened the door while mumbling an apology. She ignored him and walked into the elegant lobby.

Square columns of dark mahogany rose to meet cream-colored ornamental arched ceilings under the soft glow of crystal chandeliers. Mozart flowed from unseen speakers. The place smelled of flowers.

Looking past the décor, Monica located her mark standing off to her far right, at the opposite end of the lobby. Amir was shaking hands with a man wearing what she recognized from her in-country days with the Rangers as traditional Saudi clothes. They included a *thawb*, an ankle-length shirt made of fine cotton. On his head, he wore a large cotton square folded diagonally over a skullcap. Next to the Saudi stood a bejeweled woman in a shiny black gown wearing perfect makeup and perfect hair adorned with a diamond-studded tiara. She reminded Monica of one of those extravagant Saudi princesses.

Amir's defensive linemen remained a respectful distance from their principal and the Saudi couple, forming a semicircle, protecting the pocket. Monica remembered them clearly from the investigation over a month ago. All three were Pakistani nationals who fell under their embassy's diplomatic immunity umbrella. And all three had treated her with stereotypical Muslim resentment for being a woman crossing into what they considered a man's world.

Monica surveyed the lobby once more and saw no one else, which she found strange, especially for a hotel as prestigious as the Hay-

Adams. Then it dawned on her that the bellhop might have told the truth. There were no vacancies probably because the Saudis, in true form, had reserved the entire damn hotel.

Using the mahogany columns for cover, she slipped close enough to snap photos of the Saudis with her phone, zooming in on their faces—enough to run them through the Bureau's facial recognition software later.

The trio sat down around a cocktail table and seemed to discuss the contents of some brochures that Amir spread in front of them.

Monica snapped photos of that as well, but she had to step away from the column to get a better angle. In doing so, she drew the attention of the bodyguards.

Deciding this was as far as she should go today, she put the phone away and made a beeline for the exit.

But she didn't get far.

One of the bodyguards, who went by Saddam, which she thought fit him perfectly with his rectangular face and thick mustache, caught up to her. The burly Pakistani managed to slide in between Monica and the doors with surprising agility. Dark eyes under thick brows burned her with controlled anger.

Glancing over her shoulder, she noticed the other two Pakistanis standing tall behind her five-foot-eight frame while Amir and the Saudis remained to her far right, looking in their direction.

Amateur hour, she thought. *Never abandon your principal.*

"This is a private meeting. We need to delete those photos, Agent Cruz," Saddam said, extending a hand, palm up.

"Three of you against one of me? Hardly an even fight."

"No one will harm you, and it'll only take a minute," the Pakistani insisted.

"You misunderstand," she said.

Saddam blinked once before frowning.

"The phone, ma'am. Final warning."

"And this is my final warning to you: get the *fuck* out of my way."

Gazing over her, Saddam said, "Take her upstairs. We're doing it the hard way."

"Touch me and it's assault."

"You can't arrest us," he said, failing to contain a slight grin. "Diplomatic immunity."

"Who said anything about arresting you?"

Saddam gave her a bored look and tilted his head at one of his men, who grabbed her from behind, by the wrists.

It happened fast.

Monica simply reacted, turning her wrists ninety degrees and jerking her forearms forward, breaking the handholds. Lifting her right leg, she stomped the closest instep with the heel of her boot. In the same fluid motion, she drove both elbows back, ramming them into the man's rib cage.

The guard behind her moaned.

As Monica shifted right to face the remaining threat, the injured Pakistani staggered backwards, hands clutching his torso, face twisted in pain. He tripped and fell, hitting his head against a column.

One down.

Monica reached for the extendable baton stowed next to the service Glock secured to her left hip.

A flick of the wrist and black steel alloy tubing extended sixteen inches from the top of her fist, friction locking it in place as Saddam and his partner tried to grab her.

Monica dropped to a deep crouch, missing the incoming hands aimed at her throat and lapels. Swinging the baton counterclockwise at knee level, she smashed ligaments and bones, before driving it hard in the opposite direction.

Saddam and his colleague collapsed by her feet.

Monica turned for the double doors but Saddam somehow managed to grab her left ankle.

Seriously?

She whacked his wrist with the tip of the baton.

The Pakistani grimaced and jerked the hand away.

Monica rushed through the double doors but ran into a pair of men dressed like the bellhop but much wider. Earpieces connected to coiled wires disappearing in the suits suggested hotel security.

The men spotted her baton and parted like the Red Sea to reveal a Metro PD officer standing behind them, the same guy from a few minutes ago. He was apparently calling for backup before turning to Monica, a hand on his holstered pistol.

"Officer Uvalde, Metro PD! Put down your weapon!"

"Easy, Officer. Remember me? FBI Special Agent Monica Cruz," she replied, retracting and stowing away the baton before flashing her badge at him again. "Those men in there tried to abduct me. I defended myself."

Uvalde looked past her and frowned. Monica turned around and realized how bad it looked with all three on the floor. One was unconscious while the other two wailed in pain, including Saddam, whose wrist was bent at a sickening angle. In the background, Amir had his phone pointed at them.

"That may be the case, Agent Cruz, but procedure requires that I take statements from everyone."

As Uvalde said this, two patrol cars pulled up under the portico. Now five Metro PD officers surrounded her, plus the two security guards.

And Monica's birthday party went downhill from there.

3

Salma

STAR OF OCEANIA. SOUTH ATLANTIC OCEAN

Thunder and the supertanker's increased rocking awoke her.

Salma Bahmani sat up abruptly as lightning flashed through the single porthole of her stern cabin four levels above the engine room.

But there was something else.

A feeling . . .

She jumped off her bed, landing on the cold tiled floor while reaching for her Beretta 92FS wedged under the mattress.

But her fingers never touched it.

Her cabin door burst open. A bulky figure backlit by the passageway and clutching a pistol fitted with a sound suppressor fired into the bed. The mechanical noise of the semiautomatic blended with the spitting sounds ripping through the mattress, striking the floor.

She rolled away in the semidarkness, surging to a deep crouch next to the door. Cocking her right leg, she snapped it toward the side of the intruder's knee, heel up and toes pointed down.

The side kick connected, but the man was large, strong. He staggered back, regaining his footing, shifting the weapon toward his left and firing again.

Remaining low, the smell of gunpowder tickling her nostrils, Salma pivoted on her left foot, shifting out of the way. Two rounds struck the wall where she had been a second before.

Whirling toward him at waist level, she tightened her right fist, uppercutting his groin. Surging to her full five-seven height, she followed with a palm strike to his solar plexus.

The man screamed, dropping the weapon, a black Makarov, and sending it skittering under the bed.

Bent over, he stumbled back into the corridor, tripping over Fahkir, the guard she had posted outside her cabin. He fell on his side by the blood pooling around the young Pakistani's head.

Salma rushed through the doorway as the man, whom she now recognized as Viktor, the large Ukrainian cook, managed to get up while unsheathing a shiny knife. He clutched it like a professional, with the serrated blade protruding from the bottom of his right fist.

He turned sideways, grimacing in obvious pain but very much still in the fight, narrowed eyes measuring her.

She also turned sideways, keeping most of her weight on her rear leg, hands in front as they circled each other. The man was a bear, over six inches taller than Salma and twice her weight, arms as wide as her thighs.

He moved first, thrusting the blade from left to right in a wide arc aimed at her neck before driving it vertically toward the abdomen.

Salma shifted like a shadow, missing both strikes, her eyes not on the glistening blade reflecting the overhead fluorescents but on the Ukrainian's torso, which telegraphed his intentions.

Viktor attacked again with the same behead-and-gut double move.

This time she stepped into the strike the instant the tip of the knife rushed an inch past her neck. Her right forearm blocked the offending wrist before he could reverse the thrust and drive it down her belly.

In the same fluid move, Salma grabbed Viktor's wrist with her blocking hand and twisted it, forcing it between her and his body while turning the elbow. She struck it with the heel of her left palm while shifting her weight forward into the blow.

Bone cracked. Cartilage snapped.

The Ukrainian screamed and dropped the knife while stepping back, staring in visible horror at his arm bent backwards, useless.

Salma exploited the distraction. Pivoting on her left leg, she swirled like a ballerina in a deadly pirouette, building momentum to offset her smaller mass. Bringing her right arm around, she chopped his throat with the edge of her hand, snapping the larynx.

Viktor fell to his knees, left hand reaching for his collapsed windpipe, staring up at her in disbelief as his face turned white. He collapsed next to Fahkir, his mouth wide open, gasping for air.

Rushing back into her stateroom, she put on a pair of sneakers and snagged the sound-suppressed Makarov from beneath the bed. Counting four rounds still in the magazine plus one in the chamber, she tucked it in her jeans against her spine. She reached for her Beretta, which she always kept fully loaded, fifteen rounds in the high-capacity magazine plus a sixteenth chambered.

Clutching it in both hands over her right shoulder, muzzle pointed at the spaghetti of pipes and wires layering the ceiling of her sleeping quarters, she stepped back into the hallway and over the bodies. Her narrowing stare landed on the yellow bulkhead at the end of the long corridor. White light shimmered from fluorescents wedged in between more ducts and cables running the length of the compartment.

Salma covered the hundred feet in ten seconds.

The vessel swayed in the storm. Lightning gleamed through portholes. Thunder clapped outside.

She pushed the watertight door designed to seal off this section of the structure in an emergency, and reached the large stair landing.

The commotion one level above her, which sounded like a heated argument, echoed down the structure in between sporadic thunder, making her look up. But her immediate priority was to protect Dr. Atiq Gadai's fission-type bomb in a trunk locked in a supply room four levels below.

She headed that way, down four flights of stairs to the large landing overlooking the cavernous engine compartment, nearly five stories high.

Massive diesels powered colossal drive shafts amidst more pipes, wires, and other machinery. Lights blinked, generators whirred, assorted equipment hummed, inducing vibrations on the metal structure. In the middle of it all stood the control room, a large glass compartment filled with monitors, computers, and other hardware. Three operators in bright orange jumpsuits moved about, turning knobs and keying in commands. One talked on the phone, probably to the bridge amidships as the crew worked in unison to maneuver the vessel through the storm.

And apparently completely oblivious to whatever was happening in her world.

One of them looked up through the glass partition and waved. It was Johan, the chief engineer who had already asked her twice to his stateroom since departing Karachi a week ago. Although the Norwegian was handsome, Salma didn't need complications in her historical mission, delivering a nuclear bomb to Houston and detonating it inside the shipping channel.

But it now seemed like complications had found her.

Hiding the Beretta from view, she forced a smile and waved back.

The smell of lubricants and diesel struck her like a moist breeze as Johan returned to his work and she inspected the scenery. It all looked as it should for the midnight shift, with the added complexity of a South Atlantic storm that she'd heard Captain Sjöberg mention at dinner.

Salma was covertly a nuclear terrorist, but overtly she headed the team contracted by the Norwegian shipping company to provide security for the trip, in particular while cruising down the treacherous east coast of Africa. And that gave her a seat at the captain's table with an eclectic group of seamen contractors, mostly Norwegians plus some Eastern Europeans and a couple of Africans. There she would get caught up with the latest information on their journey. But tonight the incoming storm had taken second seat to the Bagram Airfield nuclear attack and the video released by Ibrahim al-Crameini. It was all everyone could talk about.

She sighed. The realization that Dr. Gadai's devices actually worked only added stress to her situation.

Refocusing her thoughts, she stared at the walkways flanked by guardrails covering the perimeter of the noisy chamber. They connected to lower catwalks through a series of stairwells built into the walls on both the port and starboard sides of the spacious compartment. And they continued all the way down to the main floor of the engine room.

But Salma didn't need to go that far. She stopped just one level below and approached a bulkhead that led into another corridor, this one longer and wider than the one for her quarters.

She inched open the heavy door and froze when spotting the body of Saj, another one of her men. He had been shot behind the head, execution style, halfway down the passageway, near the room he was posted to guard, marked EMERGENCY SUPPLIES.

The bright yellow bulkhead door leading to it was wide open, swinging slightly back and forth as the supertanker weathered the storm.

Controlling the anger constricting her throat, Salma stepped into the corridor, the business end of her Beretta pointed straight ahead. She broke into a run, covering the distance in seconds and tiptoeing past the expanding circle of blood around Saj's head.

I must have just missed the shooter.

Quietly, she peeked into the compartment.

Another Ukrainian cook stood next to a Nigerian janitor. Their backs were to her while they noisily worked a crowbar under the lid of a large metallic trunk chained to a pair of steel columns in the rear of the large stateroom.

She almost fired with her Beretta but opted for the sound-suppressed Makarov. In spite of the storm and the noise in the engine room, she feared the metallic structure might telegraph the reports across the ship.

Retrieving the Russian-made semiautomatic, she aimed its bulky sound suppressor at the Ukrainian. Exhaling, she squeezed the trigger.

The weapon responded with a barely audible spitting sound. The cook fell forward over the trunk while his Nigerian counterpart began to turn around, left hand reaching for the pistol tucked in his pants, by his belly.

But a 9mm Makarov round sprayed his brains against the porthole behind the trunk as lightning forked through it, followed by thunder.

Salma put both guns away, the Beretta tucked in front and the Makarov against her spine.

Shoving the men aside, she inspected the trunk, running her fingers around the edges and over the digital keypad, verifying the bastards had not damaged it.

She entered the access combination, releasing the magnetic locks.

The spring-loaded mechanism slowly lifted the lid, exposing the five-foot-long gun barrel housing the fission material, the trigger mechanism, the embedded computer, and a battery pack good for a month.

She stood there a moment, satisfied that Dr. Atiq Gadai's work was undamaged. Closing the trunk, she gave the dead men another look, noticing the radio strapped to the Nigerian's belt.

Kneeling, she pulled it off, clipped it to her waist, and killed the volume. Locking the room, she double-backed to the main staircase, a hand on the railing for balance. The *Oceania* continued swaying in the storm, thunder roaring outside.

The stairs connected the engine room to a long corridor and the astern upper deck. She scrambled up them, reaching the top and dashing to the bulkhead double doors at the opposite end of the hallway. They led to the ship's galley and dining area, plus a large rec room with a satellite TV, a Ping-Pong table, and assorted gym equipment.

Salma paused, peeking through the small oval windows on the doors.

Five of the six remaining members of her team were on their knees, hands behind their heads, including Azis, the large native from Karachi who was also her right-hand man. He knelt next to Omar, his younger brother.

Four men watched over them, all wielding more sound-suppressed Makarovs. Three were Serbs from the day shift—two engine room operators and a navigator. The fourth man was Benjamin, another janitor from Nigeria, who always kept to himself but who now appeared in charge. He held a radio in his other hand, similar to the one secured to her waist, while ordering the Serbians around. Beyond the group stood the dining area overlooking a set of panoramic windows offering a spectacular view of a South Atlantic gale. Whitecaps raged atop massive waves pounding the hull in explosions of water and foam.

Her mind, however, focused on the storm inside the ship as she wondered who the hell was after her weapon.

And where was Tariq, her last man?

Was he also roaming the ship like her?

If so, she could really use his help right now.

Salma felt certain she could take two of the men in the rec room by firing the Beretta and the Makarov in unison, especially if they were looking the wrong way. But she was staring at *four* armed men and they all faced the double doors.

As she considered her options, a short and skinny man stepped into view, walking up to Benjamin while also holding a sound-suppressed Makarov.

Tariq?

Salma stopped breathing as anger swelled in her gut at the realization that she had been double-crossed by a member of her own damn team.

And what of the rest of the crew? Was Captain Sjöberg in on this? Johan down in the engine room had not given any hint of alarm. What about up on the bridge? Did Benjamin now have control of the *Oceania*? Had they changed direction? Were they still headed for Houston?

Salma forced control over her many questions, and pushed aside the thought of these bastards stealing a weapon four times more powerful than the one used in Bagram. Instead, she fell back on her paramilitary training, realizing the impossibility of overtly attacking *five* armed men.

Slowly, quietly, she stepped away, hiding in a fire station a couple dozen feet down the hallway. Recessed into the wall, it had a clear line of sight on anyone leaving the rec room through the double doors.

She couldn't take them all at once, but she could sure as hell pick them off one at a time.

Reaching for the radio, she keyed the Talk button multiple times, transmitting the international SOS Morse code signal. Three short strokes followed by three long ones and three more short ones.

Turning off the radio and setting it aside, she pulled out the

Makarov, confirmed she had three rounds left, and aimed it at the entrance.

She didn't have to wait long.

Two men emerged, Serbians, pushing the heavy bulkhead doors and running into the corridor, holding their Makarovs.

Salma bided her time, letting them come to her. She verified that the spring-loaded bulkhead doors had closed behind them, isolating her prey from the herd.

From her vantage point, in a crouch peering around the corner, the Serbs looked massive, dressed in the bright orange jumpsuits of engine room personnel, thick beards hiding their features. Their eyes focused on the bulkhead at the opposite end of the passageway leading to the stairs, weapons pointed at the fluorescent lights.

Salma shot them in the face from a distance of ten feet. The gun's mechanism chambered new rounds while ejecting the spent casings.

Their corpses crash-landed on the floor, face down. Blood splattered. Weapons clattered loudly, metal hitting metal as they skittered toward her.

She frowned at the noise, tossed her Makarov and pulled out her Beretta, aiming it at the double doors. And waited.

No one came out.

Putting the Beretta away after counting to thirty, Salma stood, grabbed their sound-suppressed pistols, and verified they were fully loaded. Clutching one in each hand, she returned to the double doors, peeking once again through the small oval windows.

Benjamin now spoke loudly into the radio while pacing back and forth with apparent concern. She could hear him but could not understand, since he spoke not in English—the common language aboard the ship—but in Ebo, a Nigerian dialect.

The tall and skinny African stopped to listen and grew frustrated at the static on the radio.

Her remaining team still on their knees exchanged brief glances, hands behind their heads. But she noticed that their wrists and ankles were not flex-cuffed.

Salma considered that for a moment. She had shifted the odds a bit more in her favor now that there were three of them against one of her. Now she also felt confident that her team would get in the fight the instant she started shooting.

Still, she wanted just a bit more insurance to minimize the chance of incurring more casualties in her already depleted team. So she waited, right shoulder pressed against one of the doors, twin Makarovs cocked and ready, while observing the trio walking around her men. Beyond them, the storm raged. Lightning sparked with ferocity across the horizon, gleaming through the windows, followed by thunder.

Then it happened.

Tariq and Benjamin moved away from the group, stepping toward the dining room at the far end of the rec room, by the panoramic windows, to have a private conversation. In doing so, they turned away from the door, leaving just the Serbian navigator standing a respectful distance from Azis and the rest of her team.

Staring at the guns in her hands, she pushed her way in just enough to have a clear shot. Although she had the option of eliminating Benjamin and Tariq with her first volley, she pointed both guns at the Serb, the most immediate threat to her men.

She fired twice from a distance of twenty feet and scored two hits in the middle of his chest just as Benjamin and Tariq turned around.

Salma switched targets, firing again, wounding Tariq in the shoulder but missing Benjamin as he dropped from view behind tables and chairs. Tariq also dove for cover.

Her men reacted just as she had hoped, rolling away, dispersing.

Salma rushed toward one side of the rec room while Azis grabbed the dead Serb's Makarov and moved to the other side, reading her mind.

Tossing the Russian pistols across the floor toward Omar and another one of her men, Salma reached for her Beretta, finding comfort in the familiar grip.

She raced in a crouch, muzzle pointed at the tables.

The fight didn't last long. Tariq surrendered to Azis and Omar.

Benjamin, realizing he was hopelessly outnumbered, tried to make a run for the galley.

Tracking him in her sights as he scrambled across her field of view, Salma fired twice, hitting him once in the leg. The reports reverberated inside the rec room.

Benjamin tumbled, dropping his weapon, falling on his side while screaming, hands on his bleeding thigh.

Salma was on top of him in seconds, shoving the gun in his face.

"Who are you? What do you want with my weapon?"

Benjamin grimaced in pain.

Salma slapped him while Omar and Azis brought Tariq over to her.

"Why?" she insisted, swatting Benjamin's hands away from his wounded thigh and shoving her index finger in the bullet hole.

The Nigerian urinated on himself while trembling, crying, begging her to stop.

"Tell me!" she shouted in his face, twisting the finger while sinking it to the knuckle, feeling the slug lodged against his femur.

Benjamin squealed, yelling in English, then in Ebo, and back in English.

"Boko Haram," Tariq said, flanked by her men, a hand on his bleeding shoulder. "He is with Boko—"

She snapped her head at the traitor. "I wasn't talking to you!"

Azis smacked Tariq in the back of his head with one of his massive hands.

"Well?" she said, removing the finger, watching the Nigerian breathe deeply before slowly nodding.

"I . . . am . . . with Boko Haram."

Salma pistol-whipped him with the Beretta, tearing a gash across his cheek at the mention of the Islamic extremist group based in northeast Nigeria. Boko Haram also had a strong presence in Chad, Niger, and Cameroon.

"But you are Sunni Muslims!" she screamed, shaking him by the lapels. "Like us! Your leader even claimed allegiance to the Islamic State in 2015. Have you no honor?"

Looking away, a hand on his bleeding face, Benjamin replied, "Your device . . . priceless . . . my people need cash for our . . . cause. The Nigerian government has been fighting back . . . we need more weapons . . . more infrastructure . . . and selling your bomb would have provided us . . . with the funds to—"

She struck him again with the pistol, this time across his temple, knocking him out before slowly turning to Tariq.

"Who else is involved?" she asked, standing while pointing the Beretta at his left knee.

Tariq's chest swelled as he breathed, lips trembling, blinking rapidly, a hand applying pressure to his wounded shoulder, blood trickling through his fingers.

He would not last long without medical help.

"You will die soon," she said, putting the gun away. "But how you spend eternity will be determined by what you say next."

Hesitating, and while surrounded by his former comrades in arms, Tariq dropped his gaze to the floor, blood dripping by his feet. "No one else knows," he finally said.

"What about Captain Sjöberg?" she asked.

Tariq shook his head.

"And what was the plan?"

"Take control of the ship . . . after securing the weapon . . . and killing all of you . . . then force the Norwegians to steer toward fixed coordinates off the coast of Nigeria."

"And?"

He closed his eyes and shook his head before saying, "Rendezvous . . . with a boat . . . transfer the weapon to Benjamin's associates with Boko Haram . . . get paid . . . and disappear."

Salma looked at Azis and then tilted her head toward the galley. "Feed him to the sharks."

"Wait!" he pleaded as the Karachi brothers dragged him away to the back of the ship's large kitchen area. It included a wide chute to dump leftovers overboard to the schools of South Atlantic blue sharks always swimming alongside the *Oceania*. "I told you everything!"

"And I believe you," she replied.

Tariq wailed as they dragged him to the galley and forced him headfirst inside the stainless steel chute. He screamed a final plea as Azis unlatched the hatch and he slid overboard into darkness.

She ordered her remaining team to help her carry and dispose of the bodies the same way, including the unconscious Nigerian plus the ones she had killed in the hallway, in her stateroom, and down in the supply room. They also gave Fahkir and Saj a burial at sea following a short prayer.

They worked quickly, finishing all cleanup tasks by three in the morning, and doing so without alerting the night crew on the bridge keeping the vessel on course through the storm.

Then Azis began to bark orders to what remained of their team, sending the three covering the day shift back to bed, his brother, Omar, to guard the supply room, and another soldier to the engine room. Azis would head up to the bridge to continue scanning the horizon with binoculars, per their contract.

Before he left, Azis asked Salma, "How do you plan to handle the captain in the morning?"

She shrugged. "By telling him the truth."

The Pakistani's dark eyes widened.

She smiled. "African terrorists assisted by Ukrainian and Serbian militants attempted to take control of the *Oceania* last night. But our team put them down . . . just as we were contracted to do by the shipping company."

Azis slowly nodded. "What about the bodies?"

"Tankers don't have a refrigerated morgue, so we tossed them overboard."

"He may want to report it."

She shrugged again. "So let him—as long as he keeps the ship on course."

"Will he?"

"I believe so," she replied. "The infidels only care about money . . . profits. And delivering this oil to Houston—on schedule—is their top priority. That's how Captain Sjöberg and his crew actually get paid: per delivery. They're not going to jeopardize that. In fact, I'll expect them to be grateful that this didn't turn into another *Maersk Alabama*."

She paused, then added, "But, if the good captain starts to get suspicious . . ." She tilted her head toward the garbage chute.

Azis leaned closer to her. "I agree, though I'm beginning to think that perhaps Captain Sjöberg may have already started to suspect something."

She frowned, also recalling a strange feeling she'd gotten when having dinner with the bearded Norwegian captain, especially after the news from Bagram Airfield. At the time, however, she thought perhaps the lonely sailor, like Johan, wanted someone to warm his bed, which Salma was prepared to do if the situation required it. But maybe she had misread him.

"I will handle the captain," she told him. "You just make sure our men are *always* alert. Yes?"

"I am deeply sorry this happened. We will not be surprised again. I swear it on my children," he said.

"Good. And be ready to take control of the bridge and the engine room if your feeling about the captain turns true. Remember, we are trained to operate this vessel, but I'd rather leave it in their expert hands until we get to our target. The next thirty-six hours will be the most critical, as we reach the Gulf of Mexico," she replied, patting him on the shoulder. "Now go, I need to be alone."

Azis bowed respectfully and walked away. Salma watched the giant man duck through the bulkhead while she remained in the galley.

She brewed black tea in a kettle along with a mixture of aromatic Indian spices and herbs to make Masala chai, a popular Karachi drink influenced by the strong local presence of Muhajir cuisine.

Leaning over the kettle, she closed her eyes and inhaled deeply, filling her lungs with an aroma that calmed her down. It brought her back to simpler days growing up in a girls' orphanage on the outskirts of the vast port city. Soon after, the Karachi native was recruited by the ISI, Pakistan's Inter-Services Intelligence, along with dozens of other attractive teenage orphans. Trained to honey-trap Indian businessmen and government officials, Salma became part of an extensive sexual offensive against their neighboring country. Taught English as well as the ancient art of seduction, Salma was flown into Delhi, where she distinguished herself by entrapping her marks and collecting tons of intelligence. She stole secrets of state, confidential papers, high-tech documents, and business plans. Her efforts earned her a scholarship to an ISI advanced training camp outside of Quetta, in western Pakistan. It was there that she met ISI star Malik Darzada, who developed her skills as an operative. He took her on extended assignments to Europe and America to help her understand their enemy. Malik also introduced Salma to his contacts in al Qaeda and ISIS, including Ibrahim al-Crameini and his brother, Hassan.

She stared out the large portholes along the starboard side of the galley, amused that so often people got ISIS and ISI—her intelligence network—confused. But then again, the acronyms were close enough.

The storm was finally subsiding. Somewhere out there, beyond the sporadic lightning flashes and shrinking swells, Malik and his team were aboard a second supertanker headed for New York City. His team also traveled under the clever disguise of being security contractors. The scheme allowed them free rein in the vessel and also the right to carry weapons in case they had to defend the *Oceania* against African pirates.

Or against African terrorists.

Malik had come up with the elegant solution to justify their presence aboard the supertankers. Many shipping companies contracted retired law enforcement or military personnel on a regular basis to provide private security for vessels traveling the dangerous waters off the coast of East Africa. So the powerful ISI chief, Dr. Atiq Gadai, had made a few phone calls and in a matter of days the Karachi Shipping Security Company, Ltd., was born. And in her particular case, the captain and his crew were even getting bonuses for accepting a woman aboard their vessel.

Salma continued staring at the ocean, recalling her last night with Malik in Karachi. She thought of their years together, some enjoyable but most quite violent, deadly, as their profession often was.

The kettle began to whistle.

Salma turned off the fire and poured a steaming cup, sweetening it with a drop of honey.

Stepping onto a large balcony alongside the rec room, she stared at an endless ocean, still unsettled in the wake of the dissipating storm as clouds parted, revealing pockets of stars.

In spite of the close call, the men accompanying her on this mission represented the best that the ISI and ISIS could provide, all hand-picked by Malik from his inner circle in Islamabad. The veteran operative of her country's equivalent of the CIA trusted no one but those who had fought with him in the field. And even then her lover and mentor was wary. If his agency could turn sons against fathers and wives against husbands, the enemy could certainly turn a brother in arms against them, as had been the case with Tariq.

Paranoia is a weapon, my dear Salma, as powerful as your Beretta.

She brought the cup to her lips and sipped the infused tea. Silver-crested waves crashed against the double steel hull of the Norwegian supertanker sailing under the Panamanian flag.

Silently, she prayed that they had chosen their vessels wisely.

Malik and Salma—along with Dr. Atiq Gadai and his scientists back in Islamabad—had scrubbed all possible venues for smuggling the tube-shaped devices into America. They had considered using small boats, driving them across land borders, flying them in small planes, or simply hiding them in shipping containers. Each method carried its own set of risks, including discovery by authorities using a variety of detection devices. It was common knowledge within the merchant shipping industry that security measures at major ports couldn't effectively monitor the movement of goods. And especially those inside the millions of garage-size shipping containers moving in and out of ports weekly, thereby allowing exploitation of the system.

Although the concept of using shipping containers had been appealing, it had also been as predictable as using a small plane or boat, or trucking it across the border. And they felt the risk would increase tenfold after the nuclear explosion in Bagram. Therefore, they had opted to smuggle the bombs inside two supertankers, each carrying three hundred thousand deadweight tons of crude oil.

The United States imported over two million barrels a day from Persian Gulf nations. Detection devices such as gamma-ray radiography systems to scan shipping containers would be of limited use on a supertanker. The systems used cobalt-60 or caesium-137 as a radioactive source and a vertical tower of gamma detectors to create an X-ray-like image. The supertanker's sheer size, thick double steel hulls, and large quantity of crude oil made such methods ineffective. Another detection technique, neutron activation, in which a burst of neutrons was sent into the item to be examined, would also be difficult to use on a supertanker. Neutrons that struck uranium-235 would cause some atoms to fission, releasing neutrons and gamma rays. However, neutrons fired into the oil and any produced by the fission of radioactive materials would be absorbed or simply scattered by the hydrogen atoms in the fossil fuel. Plus the large volume of oil would mitigate any gamma rays produced, defeating this form of detection.

In some ways, their original approach reminded her of the brave men who flew those planes into the American towers and the Pentagon long ago. It worked because it was not expected, at least not by those in a position to prevent it.

And that's why our mission will succeed.

Salma watched the waves still fighting against the *Oceania*'s bow in explosions of foam and surf splashing over the gunwale. They receded to the backwash boiling down the sides of the structure before blending with the ship's wake.

The American public was far more interested in the latest music video, tweet, or post from scantily dressed young whores than the impending reality of another major terrorist attack. And that suited Salma just fine, especially with the way Washington and its politically correct mind-set frowned on profiling any given group. But doing so created more bureaucratic barriers between law enforcement and terrorist cells, enabling their proliferation in recent years.

The time had now come to show the infidels just how helpful they had been with their so-called Bill of Rights, protecting her network's activities by allowing *alleged* terrorists access to attorneys and lengthy trials.

Instead of simply removing their fingernails and torching their genitals, she thought, recalling Malik's way to get an enemy soldier to confess in minutes.

Salma remembered how they had brought the bombs aboard the tankers disguised as part of their piracy security equipment. ISI moles working port security had assisted them. Trained by none other than the U.S. Coast Guard's international port security liaison officers under the U.S. Maritime Transportation Security Act, the moles had approved all of the necessary forms, bypassing crucial inspection steps.

She smiled. The Americans had even *trained* her own people in their port security measures, making it all too easy to defeat them.

Salma's mission called for detonation the moment the *Oceania* reached the Port of Houston's inner canal, within range of shipping container terminals and oil refineries, and before inspection crews could come aboard.

Malik's objective was a bit more ambitious. He would wait for his ship to dock by the Bayway Refinery at the Port of New York and New Jersey. Moles had been planted long ago in the New York/Newark Field Office of U.S. Customs and Border Protection. If their deep-cover agents failed to keep inspection crews from finding the device, Malik would detonate immediately. Otherwise, he would meet up with a local contact to take the bomb to Times Square.

Salma sipped tea and regarded the ocean, but her mind traveled beyond the waves, past the dark horizon, and up the United States Eastern Seaboard. By morning Malik's supertanker would start its approach into the third-largest port in America, and less than twenty-four hours later Salma would reach her target in Houston.

And together, they would set the world on fire.

4

Gun and Badge

I'm fucked.

Monica stared at her reflection in the one-way mirror of a holding room, awaiting her fate.

But she was pretty damn sure what it would be.

This room on the first floor of the FBI headquarters at the J. Edgar Hoover Building on Pennsylvania Avenue was one of several reserved for questioning. She had been ordered here after Metro PD contacted her boss, Gustavo Porter, chief of domestic terrorism and weapons of mass destruction within the FBI's Counterterrorism Division.

Unfortunately, Porter was tied up in a videoconference with the White House on the attack on Bagram Airfield, so Monica was told to wait until he was out.

A pair of detectives, who'd arrived after the uniformed officers, had already taken her statement back at the hotel. As she had suspected, Amir and his Saudi friends had indeed booked all forty-eight rooms. She learned that the cameras in the lobby had been disabled to provide privacy for them. And that meant the only video of the incident was from Amir's own phone. It made Monica appear out of control, smacking everyone with her baton, including striking Saddam when he was already down. She had continued claiming self-defense, but lacking any other video, it was basically her word against theirs. And "theirs" included the bellhop and the two hotel security guards, who had sided with the Pakistanis.

On top of that, all three bodyguards were under diplomatic status, so the incident now involved the State Department. And, knowing Amir's friendship with John Wright, probably even the White House.

And all that meant Monica was, well . . .

Fucked.

She sighed and continued staring at her reflection. Her shoulder-length dark hair stuck to the sides of her face from wearing the motorcycle helmet. It framed a pair of large brown eyes on a dark olive face showing the fine lines from a lifetime of field ops.

The word that came to mind was *damaged.*

Monica gave the mirror a final frown and just paced the room.

When the door finally swung open, Gustavo Porter stormed in holding a manila folder. He was a large man, built like a linebacker, over six feet tall, with broad shoulders. His bull neck always seemed on the verge of popping the top button of his dress shirts.

"Morning, Gus."

"Not for any of us, Cruz, and certainly not for you," he said, walking to one side of the interrogation table and sitting down. "I've heard about your little stunt with Amir. I even got a call from John Wright asking what the hell was happening."

Monica sat across from her superior and calmly crossed her legs.

Porter opened the manila folder. "Three victims, all with diplomatic immunity. According to the ER report from George Washington University Hospital, one has a concussion, cracked ribs, and a broken foot. The other two have bruised knees and one also has a broken wrist. Witnesses include Amir Dham, one Prince Khalid al-Saud, who is on an official visit from Saudi Arabia, and his sister, Princess Lisha al-Saud."

"I guess I no longer need to run their faces through the database," she said, more to herself than to Porter, who closed the manila folder and just glared at her.

"Now, please . . . *enlighten* me."

Leaning forward and resting her arms on the table, she said, "I was tailing Amir and—"

"Amir was off-limits."

Monica paused and just stared at him a moment before asking, "Are you going to let me tell you my side of this?"

He sat back, inhaled deeply, and slowly nodded while exhaling.

Monica related everything in two minutes, leaving nothing out.

Porter looked down at his hands and slowly shook his head. "Cruz, you're one hell of an agent, leading the division in arrests. One of your strengths is your personal commitment, your relentless drive to get to the bottom of each case. And while your approach sometimes tends to piss people off, even your own fellow agents, your heart's in the right place and you *do* deliver results. This time, unfortunately, you may have overplayed that strength."

"Look, Gus, every bone in my body tells me we missed something during our investigation, and I was just keeping an eye on the man from a distance."

He pointed at the report. "That's some *distance*, considering the number of bruises and broken bones."

She slowly shook her head.

"Well, Cruz, it was your day off and it is a free country," Porter said, locking eyes with her before leaning forward and adding, *"As long as no one got hurt."*

"It was self-defense, boss."

"Yeah, well . . . not according to the evidence and the eye-witnesses."

"Okay . . . consider the following: Amir, who, like it or not, was associated with a gun run involving someone with ties to ISIS—"

"Alleged ties."

"Seriously? Please let me finish."

Porter made an apologetic wave with his right hand.

"Alleged ties to ISIS, fine," Monica continued. "Now Amir meets with Saudi royalty, who we all know have been funding ISIS for years, and the meeting is held hours after ISIS detonates a nuke. On top of that, the surveillance cameras in the lobby were disabled during the meeting, and the beef I had with the bodyguards was over the photos I took, because it's pretty damn obvious they didn't want any record of the meeting. Heck, the Saudis booked the *entire* hotel to ensure privacy. That's one too many coincidences, Gus. If it walks and quacks . . . hell, we've pursued cases on weaker leads than this."

Porter waited a few moments, and then pulled out a paper bag. "Finished?"

She nodded.

"Well, while I have to admit there may be something there, Cruz, you went about it the wrong way, and in the process sent three *diplomats* to the emergency room, creating a shit storm in the State Department . . . and the White House."

"So, let's go about it the right way then. Let's do it by the book."

"That ship's already sailed."

"But—"

Porter held up a hand, and she just crossed her arms and sank into her chair.

"Cruz, as much as I hate doing this, until the smoke clears, I need to place you on administrative leave for a month."

"Seriously?"

"Very," Porter said, tapping an index finger on the shiny metal surface of the table next to the paper bag. "Gun and badge."

She rolled her eyes. "We're really not doing this, are we? Just tell Wright that I'm very, very sorry—with sugar on top—to even consider that his golfing buddy could be a terrorist."

"Won't work. You went too far. Gun and badge. Now."

"A terrorist identified as Ibrahim al-Crameini, who we all know heads the ISIS caliphate in Afghanistan and Pakistan—meaning he has to have very strong ties in those countries—releases a video claiming responsibility for nuking our base and you're suspending *me* for tailing one of *his* kind?"

"*His* kind? The Bureau has no tolerance for that kind of racial profiling. Amir Dham is a respected Pakistani businessman, and he was off-limits. You knew it, you still chose to tail him, and in doing so you harmed *diplomats*, triggering an international incident."

"Like you said, it was my day off and it's a free country."

Porter tapped his desk again. "Well, now you get to enjoy your freedom for a whole month *without* pay. And consider yourself lucky. The White House wanted you terminated and thrown in jail."

"I doubt everyone at the White House speaks for Wright. I bet Vaccaro doesn't even know what her little helper is up to."

"Leave the president out of this. I can assure you she's got enough on her plate."

"Well, perhaps Amir should be added to her menu. Main course. The guy's a snake in the grass, and you know it."

"Face it, Cruz. You blew it. You let your emotions get the better of you and went about it the wrong way. And then you let the situation get out of control—and it's all captured on video!"

"So it's the word of a federal agent against the word of Pakistani nationals with ties to ISIS, plus a one-sided video? Seriously, Gus?"

"Stop saying that. 'Seriously.' What are you, sixteen?"

"Forty, actually. Today."

"Yeah . . . well, happy birthday, Cruz. Gun and badge."

"Dammit, Gus, the day ISIS blows up a nuke at one of our bases in-country, the White House—and you, the head of the FBI's WMD—can't think of anything better but bitch about surveillance I've conducted on a *terrorist suspect*."

"Amir was cleared of all charges. He reported the truck stolen the day before the joint task force caught the guy and recovered the guns and explosives. Any of that ring a bell?"

"Sure, since I was the *motherfucker* who orchestrated it and even chased down the driver through half the city. But MPD took all the credit and then let him get lawyered up."

He shrugged. "It was within his rights."

She leaned forward. "*What rights?* The asshole was an illegal alien driving a truck loaded with guns and Semtex! Exactly which part of *that* gave him *any* rights? Except maybe for the right to spend an hour alone with me, a bottle of water, and a hand towel."

Porter crossed his arms, his face blushing. "We don't even *joke* about that."

"Who's laughing?"

"There are other ways to get to the truth, Cruz."

"Like leaving him alone in his jail cell, where he *allegedly* hung himself before we could interrogate him?"

Porter exhaled heavily. "Yeah . . . that was unfortunate."

"Unfortunate for us, but very fortunate for Amir."

"Look, the man paid his fine for the illegal worker and even invited us to scrub his operation."

"Whoop-de-fucking-do."

Porter tapped the table a third time. "Now, Cruz."

"Don't you get it, boss? The president is doing her job. She's operating with the information she has, which is controlled to a fair degree by John Wright, who, by the way, is also doing *his* job: protecting the president. Hell, he's done that since the day he hauled her into that Black Hawk."

"What are you saying?"

"I'm saying that we also need to do *our* job, which is following up on suspicious activities, especially when it comes so damn close to our job description. You know, domestic terrorism . . . weapons of mass destruction? Any of *that* ring a bell?"

Porter didn't reply.

"Look," she added, "let's go with your theory that Amir has a butt-load of trucks and had nothing to do with the guns or the Semtex. That would make him . . . *naïve*, meaning he lacks full transparency inside his own organization. Well, my instincts—combined with the skills I acquired at Quantico of all places—tell me that successful business leaders like him don't get to be successful by being naïve. So, with all due respect to the White House, the odds are stacked against him. Based on that, I'm strongly suggesting here that the Federal Bureau of *Investigation* needs to do its job and *investigate*."

"Now who's being naïve?" Porter replied. "The world isn't that simple, Cruz."

"Oh, but it is that simple, Gus. Do you know why the terrorists are winning?"

Porter sighed and said, "Why, Cruz?"

"Because their strategy is so damn simple."

"And what's that?"

"To them there are two kinds of people, those who believe in their cause and the rest of the world. And the latter needs to die. Period. There is no middle ground. No compromise. And they're willing to do whatever it takes to eradicate nonbelievers from the face of the planet. So, what's *our* strategy?"

Porter remained silent, staring at the damn paper bag on the table.

"My point exactly. Until we also choose to fight fire with fire, even if it means operating outside the purview of laws, we will continue to lose."

"Cruz . . . I refuse to drop down to their level. That is not how we're going to defeat them. And in the specific case of Amir Dham . . . he was investigated every which way but Sunday, and he came up better than clean, from every possible angle. The line was drawn and you crossed it. And for that . . ." He tapped the table again.

Monica stood, removed her Glock, released the thirteen-round magazine, and ejected the 9mm round in the chamber. She caught it in midair, took her badge and credentials, and slammed them on the metal surface. Her movements were smooth and therefore very fast, making Porter jerk back and nearly fall off his chair.

She almost grinned.

Regaining his composure, Porter also stood. "Cruz . . . what the hell's *wrong* with you?"

"What's wrong with me is that I'm suspended while that asshole with *alleged* ties to the same bastards who just deep-fried the Bagram Airfield runs free."

"Sorry," he said, taking her gun and credentials. "We don't have enough evidence."

"What the hell do you think I was trying to do on my day off?" she shouted, slapping the table. "I was trying to catch the dipshit with his pants down so we could nail his balls to his forehead. But instead, you're suspending me!"

Porter waved at her. "See you in a month."

Slowly shaking her head while watching ten years with the Bureau being dropped inside a brown paper bag, Monica replied, "Since when does the White House get to tell the FBI what to do, especially a glorified secretary like John Wright? You need to man up."

"Tread lightly. You're biting the hand of your biggest fan, and frankly, even I'm growing quite tired of your attitude."

"Why don't you try growing a pair instead?"

Porter shook his head. "Last warning. Be very *careful*, Cruz," he replied before pointing at the door.

As she reached for the doorknob, Monica paused, turned around, found his gaze, and held it.

She knew she was pushing her luck, of course, but the circumstances certainly required it. ISIS had detonated a nuke and had made threats that more would follow—and on American soil—unless their demands were met.

"Gus," she finally said, measuring her words. "The day is approaching, and fast, when this country is going to get *exactly* what it deserves for being so politically correct . . . and so *fucking careful*."

She left before Porter could reply and briskly walked straight for her bike, slipping on the helmet hanging from the handle bars. The Ducati whirled to life and she drove out of the garage and onto the street.

She gave the FBI headquarters across Pennsylvania Avenue a final look, suddenly feeling as obsolete as the leaky structure due to be demolished as soon as the new headquarters was completed in a pretty suburb a few miles away.

Out with the old and in with the new.

And that included her politically incorrect views.

She frowned. Nowhere in the oath she had taken three times did it state that she would defend the Constitution of the United States against all enemies . . . *so long as we didn't offend the feelings of any race, religious organization, special interest group, or political party.*

She steered down Pennsylvania Avenue and turned left on Fourth Street to head to the spa. Monica still had a half day left and perhaps a massage, a facial, and a steam bath were just what she needed to help her forget the—

She stopped the bike in front of the DC Veterans Affairs building on Fourth Street, spellbound by the sight. A couple dozen men and women, all in their sixties and seventies, wearing old war uniforms, stood at attention beneath the Stars and Stripes swaying in the midday breeze at half-staff. A military chaplain stood in front of the group, reading from his Bible.

She watched them for a minute or two, until a Metro PD officer signaled her to move. Deciding she didn't need another altercation today with the local cops, she took off while betting that those aging soldiers had probably lived up to that oath more than some people in her building.

And maybe that explained why she'd ended up alone in this world, like the vets, with nothing to show but old, worn-out uniforms . . . or a fading FBI career.

Monica always knew she was different, from the moment she'd enlisted in the military after college instead of following the wishes of her late father—a Mexican immigrant—to take over the ranch alongside her older brothers. But unlike her siblings, who to this day still carried on the tradition started by her father, Monica just needed to get away, see the world. So while she loved her family and the land her father had turned into a profitable cattle ranch, she had packed up and headed to Fort Benning, Georgia, to attend the U.S. Army Officer Candidate School.

And the rest is history, she thought as she accelerated toward the parkway. She wondered if perhaps no one wanted to be with her because few were *like* her, which probably also explained why she never stayed at one place for very long.

Monica became a second lieutenant and a hell of a sniper, with five combat tours, three in Iraq and two in Afghanistan. She was the recipient of a Silver Star and a Purple Heart for events she'd tried very damn hard to forget. But it was those same events that allowed her to become the first woman to make the ranks of the prestigious Los Angeles SWAT team. A few years later, after she'd grown tired of shooting bad guys from sweltering rooftops and of boyfriends intimidated by her line of work, the FBI came knocking at her door.

So, she'd happily traded sunny L.A. for a shot at Quantico.

Now, a decade later, her passion for the Bureau was dwindling.

Maybe this suspension was her wake-up call signaling it was time to move on again.

But where?

She had literally been just about everywhere, from Texas and L.A. to D.C., from the scorching Iraqi desert to the coldest mountains in . . .

Afghanistan.

Inhaling deeply, Monica remembered her last trip to Kabul.

She had joined the FBI's Counterterrorism Division, who sent her overseas for six months to collaborate with the CIA. It was there that she'd worked with an amazing Special Ops team, crossing paths with someone she'd met a few years before at a shooting school in Arizona.

She sighed at the old heartbreak, especially as her biological clock started signaling that she'd likely end up alone. Her chosen line of work had been thrilling through her twenties and her thirties. But there was something about that numeral four rolling to the front of her life's odometer that made her question this life she had chosen.

She glanced at the Ducati's electronic dash as she drove up the parkway's ramp. Call it coincidence, fate, or something divine, but forty thousand miles rolled in just as she approached the parkway's east-west split.

East would take her to the spa for a chance to escape her world, if only for a little while.

Monica steered the bike west, toward the headquarters of Jasmine Companies.

5

Atiq

It was all in the physics of achieving critical mass at the precise moment by shooting one piece of subcritical uranium-235 into another, thus the name: gun-type fission weapon.

Dr. Atiq Gadai made final adjustments to his latest creation, designed using multiple rings of uranium-235 plus a handful of conventional explosives and a digital fuse to control it all. He worked the computer on the lab table and reconfirmed his calculations. The seventy inches separating the projectile and target, combined with the explosive charge, would allow a final contact speed of one thousand feet per second.

He performed one more check to verify that his scientists had packed enough conventional explosives to achieve the minimum speed required to avoid predetonation. The projectile-target combination would actually reach critical mass almost ten inches before coming in physical contact. That meant free neutrons could potentially start a chain reaction before the materials were fully joined. If the hollow projectile was too slow and failed to bring the two masses together before the release of enough neutrons, the device would fizzle rather than reach the desired chain reaction.

Satisfied, he checked the tightness of the plastic rings securing the projectile and target in their precise location inside the gun barrel. Too tight and the added friction would slow down the bullet, risking predetonation. Too loose and the projectile or target could shift and possibly even fizzle during transport if they came in close proximity to each other, incinerating the delivery team.

He programmed the activation code in the unit and paired the

Bluetooth interface to a small remote control, before closing the lid and entering a digital code for the magnetic lock.

The device, like the ones in the hands of Salma and Malik, had been custom designed based on the available materials at the time of assembly. Malik's had a projected yield of 10 kilotons while Salma was in possession of the largest one, at almost 12.5 kilotons.

He carted the compact system he had just assembled—with a projected yield of 4.5 kilotons—next to a second identical device. He planned to ship them via DHL cargo planes loaded with assorted fashion accessories. The devices would be hidden amidst cashmere and leather products, hand-woven rugs, silks and acrylic fabrics fulfilling special orders for Jasmine Companies in Washington, D.C., and Chicago, Illinois.

He had selected flights that were standard between Pakistani export companies and the Washington and Chicago offices of Amir Dham. One DHL flight was scheduled to depart for O'Hare International Airport in seven hours while the second would follow into Ronald Reagan National Airport an hour later.

He didn't expect the devices to make it through U.S. customs at either airport, but it would not matter. An ISIS warrior, trained by Atiq himself, and armed with a Bluetooth remote control device, would accompany each cargo plane.

Their orders: detonate at an altitude of five hundred feet while on final approach—just as Malik, assisted by Amir, smuggled his bomb from the supertanker to Times Square.

And just as Salma's tanker reached the Port of Houston.

With four devices deployed to America, he hoped that at least two would be successful, triggering the desired fear in the hearts of the infidels. But even more importantly, Atiq had transferred all ownership—and the associated responsibility for the attack—to ISIS, severing any direct link to Pakistan.

The terrorist organization was spread across multiple countries, including Syria, Jordan, Iraq, Pakistan, Afghanistan, Kuwait, and even Saudi Arabia. ISIS operated out of dozens of training camps, many disguised as villages or hidden in mountain caves and beneath the desert floor, making them very hard targets for direct reprisal.

And that was the key to combating the evil that was the Americans:

hit them hard at home while denying them a clear country for retaliatory strikes, which typically came in the form of cruise missiles or laser-guided bombs.

Along with their so-called collateral damage.

Atiq sat back and stared at the scar tissue covering the top of his hands.

He had burned them a lifetime ago, along with his arms and chest, while trying to put out the fire that had engulfed his parents and younger sister during an American bomb raid in the tribal areas.

But he had failed them; he had been unable to extinguish the flames of an American *precision* weapon that had somehow drifted from its intended course and had struck his house and several others in his village—with deadly *precision*.

They had burned to death without knowing why, or even by whom, their bodies charred beyond recognition.

But it was their smoldering remains that Atiq swore to dedicate his whole life to avenge as he had fallen to his knees in the sand. The words from the Koran had filled his mind while his neighbors held him back from the inferno that to this day continued to haunt his dreams.

Kill the unbelievers, wherever you find them.

Fight against them until there is no dissention.

Fight until no other religion exists but Islam.

Atiq closed his eyes. For a while the news channels had been filled with the incident. Images of civilian casualties, along with statistical claims by the Americans, had described an attack achieving 95 percent accuracy, eliminating many high-value targets, or HVTs, along with very unfortunate collateral damage.

But soon, other news from other parts of the world came along, and the incident slowly shifted to the second and third pages in the papers, until disappearing altogether as the world changed the channel.

But Atiq never did.

His old friends and acquaintances in his village may have continued with their lives. His country may have focused on more pressing issues.

But he didn't—couldn't.

The images of his family, their agonizing cries, forever etched in his soul, would not release him. The Americans had robbed him of his mother, father, and baby sister—all in a brief flash of destruction.

A brief flash of destruction.

He contemplated the thought of delivering four such flashes, just like there had been four jetliners on September 11, 2001.

Allah had been great indeed on that glorious day, allowing three of the four planes to reach their historic destinations.

Kill the unbelievers, wherever you find them.

Fight against them until there is no dissention.

Fight until no other religion exists but Islam.

The senior director of Pakistan's Inter-Services Intelligence could only pray for similar results two decades later.

And this time, as the world turned its attention to the fields of death across the home of the brave, it would be his turn to calmly change the channel.

Atiq stared at his computer screen. He had two additional actions on his plate this afternoon, before his daughter, Maryam, stopped by for tea. And they both involved deception.

First, he reviewed the latest status of a diversion he had conceived and set in motion a week ago to lure the local CIA men away from his historical mission. Atiq's best honey-trapper in New Delhi, India, had leaked fabricated intelligence to one of her American marks, an embassy staffer. It concerned activities inside the Ministry of Interior in Islamabad guaranteed to get the attention of the CIA.

That should keep them looking in the wrong direction.

Second, he typed a long string of numbers and letters, activating the final part of his plan to ensure that Pakistan was never blamed for the attacks.

Within nanoseconds, a data packet floated in cyberspace like a dust particle drifting in the wind, swirling from ISP to ISP. Ignored by most engines because of its complex encryption, it floated across the vastness of the world's digital highways, dashing across Delhi one instant and Istanbul nanoseconds later.

But it was its transition between two critical ISPs, one in Peshawar, Pakistan, and the second in Kabul, Afghanistan, that instigated a phantom algorithm roaming the region's networks to sample it, creating a replica.

Seconds later, the clone was dispatched, along with thousands of other intercepts, at the speed of light in fiber-optic cables deep under the Atlantic Ocean and into the American continent. There, it caught the attention of the autonomous programs of a server farm that didn't exist. At least according to the public records of the unlikely high-tech mecca that was growing in northeast Ohio.

The DoD's decision to set up shop in a location that was hardly Silicon Valley had been simple: cheap electrical power to feed the thousands of servers as well as a safe and unforeseen environment for the Pentagon to store and analyze information.

Server 987 was located on the second floor of a facility hidden in plain sight as yet another warehouse along the I-80 corridor skirting the southern end of Lake Erie. It picked up the data packet first, grabbing it like a frog snatching a passing fly.

The NGE, or next generation encryption protecting the packet's binary core, a military version of Cisco's latest IOS software IKE—Internet key exchange—was dissected by the powerful system. Unraveling its scrambled fiber, the server retrieved a message that the linguistic engines recognized as Urdu. The English translation was forwarded to a basement office in the Pentagon, where it made it up the chain of command, reaching the desk of the secretary of defense within the hour.

6

Slideware

WASHINGTON, D.C.

President Vaccaro returned to the Situation Room after addressing the nation from the Oval Office. The speech had been short and to the point; just the facts as she knew them, which weren't many, yet.

As she now sat through an onslaught of PowerPoint briefings containing nothing new, she quickly grew to despise the process the previous administration had left in place to deal with national emergencies.

But then again, America had never before been hit by a nuclear weapon and faced the threat of more attacks within a week, so in a way Vaccaro was blazing a new trail here. And that meant all her leadership and combat experience, all she had read, listened to, and learned—all had led to this moment.

She was the first combat-experienced president in a while, the last two being George H. W. Bush and John F. Kennedy. And as such she had read all she could about the men, their lives, and especially how they handled the First Gulf War and the Cuban Missile Crisis, respectively.

For example, Vaccaro learned that in 1962 the White House staff under Kennedy totaled the grand sum of sixty-two people. Since she had been elected, she had yet to get a precise answer as to how many staff there were in the current White House. But John Wright was closing in on the numbers, which already exceeded two thousand.

Hearing and seeing these briefings, she thought each of the two thousand had prepared a slide for today.

Ridiculous and counterproductive, and at the most critical time in recent memory.

How the hell could she trust the information she was getting? How could she *see the battle*? How could she lead and make things happen if she had to work through this massive bureaucracy?

She had learned long ago the major law of all bureaucracies: they were self-sustaining, making work, and always justifying their existence.

Vaccaro needed information now; she needed to make things happen, decisions that would start activity—almost any activity but sitting here for another second listening to briefers, directors, generals, advisors, and occasionally her vice president.

The CIA and the DIA had already confirmed the Ibrahim al-Crameini video as legit. She knew that ISIS was responsible for the detonation as well as the diversionary ground attack. America, Afghanistan, and many other nations had lost sons and daughters. All in the room also knew that the death toll could have been much higher. And on top of all the death and destruction there was the toxic fallout to be dealt with. She found it interesting that in the middle of this terrorist crisis, the only presentation she found informative—and productive—was the one from the EPA administrator. In addition to having already located the precise areas affected by the fallout in Afghanistan and Pakistan, the EPA chief had taken the initiative to dispatch cleanup crews to both countries to work in coordination with local crews to mop up the mess.

Everyone else today had simply told her what she already knew.

The American chief executive strongly suspected that there had to be more bombs out there heading in her country's direction. She knew demands had been made public. She also knew that in order to get this crisis under control, she and her country would have to be nimble, agile, very deadly, and right—most of the time.

Vaccaro stood the moment her EPA administrator wrapped up his pitch, which caused everyone in the room to look at her and stop what they were doing.

She thanked him for taking the initiative, used him as an example of what she expected from everyone else in the room, and announced, "Let's take a fifteen-minute break."

She walked into an adjacent conference room followed by John Wright, her chief of staff, and Lisa Jacobson, her national security advisor.

Wright closed the door and pressed a button that fogged the large window overlooking the hallway.

"John," she began, "we don't have the luxury of time to spoil me up on what the hell I am hearing in there. We need information now, and we need to act on that information immediately. What I'm seeing in that room, with the exception of the EPA, is inertia. Well intended, caring, even competent, but all inertia. We cannot have another second of what we just did—no more talk and no more briefings. This is combat on a world scale and most in that room do not get that."

Vaccaro then turned to Lisa Jacobson, who had ten years of experience with the CIA and ten more as ambassador to a half-dozen countries in the Middle East. She knew the dark corners of both the intelligence and diplomatic worlds.

"Lisa, I need you and John to pull together a team that can provide intelligence on the ground without having to go through *that* bureaucracy. We also need individuals that we can task directly to act on that intelligence. The people we need will have to have presidential authority, tons of money, and the ability to tell government officials to do things. They will need world-class transportation, communications, and the intelligence conductivity to be able to task satellites and move Special Operations units around as needed."

"Madam President," said Wright, "this is a dangerous thing to do. We have a system that works well. We have over two hundred years of combined combat experience in that room. We know how to move people and things to places and blow them up. If you take this power and give it to a few, the checks and balances of our Constitution will be gutted, and your presidency will have a permanent stain on it . . . Why in God's name do you want to do this?"

"I do not *want* to do this, John," Vaccaro replied. "I am *doing* this. By the way, if this leaks, one of us leaked it, and that really means the two of you and whomever you pick. I want everyone in that room to keep doing whatever it is they do, but I want the control stick right here in my hands."

"Madam President," Lisa replied, "no one here or anyone we select will leak this. John and I will have the names in front of you before the end of the day. There is precedence for what you want to do. During the Clinton Administration, the president granted emergency powers to the director of FEMA after the disastrous state and federal response to Hurricane Andrew."

"That's correct," said Wright. "In addition, we will need a separate and secure means of communicating between us and those in the field. Plus we will also—"

Vaccaro held up a hand. "Lisa, John, the world will not care *how* we do it. It will really only care that we actually did it . . . so let's get it done."

Momentarily alone in the Oval Office five minutes later, Vaccaro stood behind her desk looking at the manicured lawn beyond the bulletproof glass of the windows flanked by the American flag and the flag of the president of the United States.

Her gaze dropped to the framed photographs crowding the table in between the flags, staring at the history in those old images while searching for strength; the faded image of her dad and his platoon

buddies on leave in Manila posing shirtless to showcase the matching tattoos over their hearts; her pregnant mother in black at her husband's military funeral at Arlington; Vaccaro in her flight suit and
aviator sunglasses conducting a preflight of her A-10 at Kandahar Airfield; her wedding picture with the strapping Greg Ochoa, the man
who'd managed to sweep her off her feet shortly after she had arrived
at the nation's capital as a newly minted Senator—before cancer
shrunk him to the ghost she buried a year and a half ago.

She ran a finger over Greg's broad smile before staring at her
framed war decorations at the end of the table, including two Purple
Hearts, the Air Force Cross, the Distinguished Service Cross, and
above them, the award that brought back so many painful memories:
The Medal of Honor.

Vaccaro had been in the thick of the fray back then, shot down in
the middle of Taliban country for the sake of those stranded Marines.
But someone, perhaps her father, had been looking down on her, like
a guardian angel, encouraging her through those difficult days as she
evaded and even killed some of the insurgents closing in—when it
looked like the only way out was to follow in her father's example and
fight to the death rather than letting herself get captured by those
savages.

And just when she had seen no option but to press her Colt's muzzle
under her chin, Captain John Wright had battled his way into that cave.

Exhaling heavily, the president turned around, leaving the past in
the past when she heard someone entering the room.

It was John Wright in his tight business suit holding his stopwatch
and his ever-present tablet computer. But for a moment she saw him
just as he had materialized in that cave, dusty and sweaty after fighting his way from the rescue chopper.

"Madam President? Is everything okay?"

If Vaccaro were completely honest with herself, she would admit
that the past would never be quite in the past as long as John Wright
stood by her side.

But she was okay with that, just as she was okay with Wright mar-
rying his college sweetheart after his last tour, or that he had two wonderful young boys—or the fact that the same John Wright was back
in her life as her Chief of Staff.

Those were just the cards that she had been dealt, and President Laura Vaccaro was very okay with them.

Slowly, she gave this man who would always hold a very special place in her heart a slow nod.

7

Gorman

ISLAMABAD, PAKISTAN

"Asshole is late!" shouted CIA Officer Bill Gorman to no one in particular. "I pay this sniveling piece of dog shit a lot of money to do what I tell him! And one of the things I *always* tell him is to be *where* and *when* I fucking tell him!"

Taking a deep breath, Gorman looked past the men standing about him in the warehouse and through the window overlooking the outskirts of this hellhole of a town. For a moment he even considered shooting the jerk in the knee when he finally showed up.

He would never get used to his assets being late, forgetting what they were supposed to do, watch, or listen for. He'd always ingrained in them to be careful, double back as many times as necessary to shake possible tails, and above all, trust no one—all the things that led to successful intelligence operations.

Tonight's op, unfortunately, was rapidly becoming anything but.

Starting a mission by being late usually led to other things going wrong, and then people who were not supposed to get hurt did, while the bad guys walked away.

These were the aggressive and covert operations that many in the press called black ops. But they were really just called special access programs (SAPs). Almost every operation that the forty-four-year-old, twenty-years-in-the-Clandestine-Service Bill Gorman did was a SAP.

And right now his latest SAP was knee deep in a FUBAR—an op that was fucked up beyond all recognition.

Gorman's Pakistani military intelligence contact liaison, Major Muhib Zarmani, was supposed to be here in the storage warehouse meeting with Gorman's special operations group (SOG) team. They were going to go over any last-minute changes and intelligence updates, make final weapons and communications checks, and move out. Then all would be loading into four impossibly small Suzuki SX4 SUVs that were common in and around this town and driving six miles to a release point. They would hit the Pakistani minister of interior's compound, where U.S. aid was being stored before it was loaded onto airplanes headed for ISIS's coffers in banks across the Middle East.

Zarmani had confirmed the intel Gorman had received from the CIA station in New Delhi, India, earlier in the week. There were over 150 million dollars in bags in the house—plus the added benefit of Hassan al-Crameini, beloved brother of Ibrahim al-Crameini, the asshole who starred in the Bagram nuclear explosion video that had gone crazy viral in the past twenty-four hours. Hassan, a high-value target the CIA had wanted for a decade, had moved up several notches in the most-wanted list thanks to his brother's short-film debut.

Glenn Harwich, a bald and medium-built man with beady eyes who never smiled, led the SOG team. He and his team had flown in from the Paris station to assist on this mission. Harwich had been with the CIA longer than Gorman could recall and was also a personal friend. In true form, Harwich stood quietly by his guys, though his stare reflected the concern about a mission that suddenly didn't feel right.

To cover all his bases, Gorman was also employing a group of contractors, all former U.S. military that he had used before. They would keep observation on the target compound and dissuade any reinforcements that were sure to show up.

A former U.S. Army Special Forces colonel named Hunter Stark led the contractor team. He was bald, like Harwich, but with deep blue eyes and scars across his forehead and square chin. A hardened 197 pounds on a six-foot frame, Stark was very bright but also very aggressive, had anger issues, and had studied English and philosophy at Penn State while playing four years of varsity lacrosse. He had six combat tours, three each in Afghanistan and Iraq, and was now on his fourth contract in-country.

Like Gorman—and Harwich for that matter—Stark was scored from his soul to his bones by the brutality he had given and received.

Four former soldiers joined Stark. All had served with him in at least three combat tours. Gorman had memorized their dossiers.

Command Sergeant Major Ryan Hunt had model good looks that many mistook as soft until they spent more than a few minutes with him. Ryan was a former Delta sniper, with over seventy kills, most at over eight hundred yards. He was the very best that any had seen at understanding the nature of the terrorist, figuring out what the terrorist was doing and going to do. And then Ryan had the patience to wait for days for that terrorist to appear in his sights and receive a 660-grain bullet, whose speed was still classified, through his right eye.

Former U.S. Marines aviator Lieutenant Danny Martin was the designated pilot. He flew jets and props of any make and model, taking the crew to their exotic destinations around the world. Plus he was also one heck of a helicopter pilot, from the big Sikorsky models to the fastest Bells and Hughes. If it had a cyclic and a collective, Danny could fly it. He was the smallest of the group, a very fit yet wiry 170 pounds on a good day. The man was always positive, always friendly, and as cold-blooded in a firefight as Gorman had ever seen.

At the opposite end of the spectrum from Danny stood Chief Warrant Officer Evan Larson. The man was just huge—six foot five, 280 pounds of muscle huge. During basic training, because of his size, he was always carrying the radio, which turned him into a communications expert when he volunteered for Special Forces training. He'd developed an affinity for all things electronic during his second combat tour in Iraq.

Gorman's gaze landed on the last man in Stark's team, Michael Hagen. He was the enigma of the group, a former Navy SEAL who Stark met on one of Gorman's CIA-directed raids in Iraq, when Hagen was a member of SEAL Team Two. Hagen saved Stark's life at the door in that mission, as it was wired to explode and Hagen had seen the technique the week before and pulled Stark back. Later in the fight Stark shot a terrorist hiding in ceiling rafters that Hagen could not see, as he was busy with two other terrorists across the room.

There was no greater bond between men than that forged in combat. The very quiet but very deadly and extremely competent SEAL had become friends with Stark for life. They had done and would continue to do anything for each other, to the detriment of almost all other relationships. In addition, Hagen, who had received two years of medical training while in the SEALs, was also the team's medic.

Gorman paced the warehouse for another five minutes, until Major Zarmani finally arrived an hour late and brought with him not Walid Fasser, the agreed-upon guide, but an FNG—fucking new guy.

Gorman was about to go with his initial reaction and shoot them both in the knee, but Glenn Harwich tried to beat him to it. The SOG team leader brought his MP7A1 down tight against Zarmani's groin to separate the skinny Pakistani from his balls. The FNG, a short and stocky Arab with a well-trimmed beard, panicked and took several steps back but ran into Stark, who gave him a shove back in line.

"Ease off, Glenn," Gorman warned as Zarmani's wide-eyed stare shifted from the submachine gun to Harwich to Gorman, and back to the gun. The Pakistani officer in full uniform was visibly terrified.

Harwich raised the MP7A1's muzzle to Zarmani's neck, his jaw muscles pulsating with obvious anger, before whispering, "Say hello to your fucking virgins, you miserable piece of—"

"I mean it, Glenn," Gorman insisted.

Slowly, Harwich took a deep breath, exhaled, and backed away next to Stark, who seemed equally pissed—as were the rest of their respective teams.

Turning to his asset, Gorman asked, "Zarmani, where have you been, where is Walid, who is this fucking guy . . . what the *fuck*?"

Before the Pakistani could answer, Gorman looked at Stark and Harwich, said, "Don't kill them yet," and walked out of earshot from anyone.

Grabbing his scrambled satphone, he called Jack Walch, the CIA station chief in New Delhi, to update him and ask his opinion, which he already knew.

"Jack," he said. "My guy was not just late, he was *very* late, and brought someone with him we've never seen instead of the agreed-upon guide. I want to cancel the op, beat the shit out of him, and put the FNG into a well so deep there's no echo."

"Bill," Walch replied. "It's your call. The intel we got at our end seemed solid, and you cross-checked it with your own asset. But Islamabad is your turf. You've set this up. You have a first-class team, and you have a good chance to recoup some of our cash plus take out the brother of the asshole who nuked Bagram . . . risk versus reward, Bud, risk versus reward."

Gorman stared at Harwich, Stark, and their teams huddled at the other end of the warehouse. They truly looked ready to lynch Zarmani and the FNG.

He replied, "Jesus, Jack, I know that . . . but how come I can hear the damn handsaw on this limb I'm on getting louder?"

He hung up the phone and walked back to where Zarmani stood.

"Tell me why I shouldn't let my friends shoot you where you stand."

The Pakistani major, visibly nervous, said in heavily accented English, "I'm truly sorry, Bill. Walid is very sick but this is Quantir Abdel, a former soldier who served with him. Abdel is a new member of the minister's staff and has agreed to be our guide around the compound. I know him well, Bill. He can be trusted."

Grabbing Zarmani just below the elbow, Gorman squeezed and turned the Pakistani, before clamping his other hand around the man's throat.

Zarmani's eyes widened with the intended fear as Gorman, who was as muscular as Stark, nearly lifted him off his feet, pulled him up to his face, and hissed, "Well, he's not known to *me*, which is the whole *fucking* point."

Zarmani was about to reply but Gorman tightened his grip and added, "I pay you dearly so you can afford your meals, your booze, and your damn whores, and in return you do *what* I say, *when* I say, and with *whom* I say . . . it's called a fucking *relationship!*"

The CIA officer let go of the Pakistani major and left him there, bent over and coughing, while Abdel looked as if he would piss his pants any second.

Gorman then turned to Harwich and Stark to get their opinion. The colonel's deadly quartet continued guarding the Pakistanis while Harwich's SOG team retreated to a corner of the warehouse to await a decision.

Stark said, "Cancel the meet. Abdel is unknown. A bad late change, and we're about to hit a very high-ranking host government official without host government support . . . not a good idea."

Harwich glanced back at his own team, apparently considering what Stark had said, and leveling his stare with Gorman, he added, "I'll go if you go, Bill. But it's a stupid idea."

Stark looked over his shoulder at his men and mumbled, "I knew I liked this guy."

Ryan, the Delta sniper, tilted his face and glanced over at Zarmani. The ominous Evan Larson stood behind him holding his equally impressive Browning M2A1 air-cooled .50-caliber machine gun by its huge top handle with one of his massive hands. The end of the long belt of ammo already fed into the side of his weapon, and Larson wore the rest in a specially designed backpack, not standard but very effective. This monster of a man shifted the heavy barrel of his eighty-pound machine gun as if it weighed nothing, aiming it toward the pair of trembling Pakistanis. But it was Hagen, the former Navy SEAL standing in between Ryan and Danny Martin, his features hidden beneath camouflage cream, who seemed to worry Gorman the most. The man, who had yet to utter a single word since arriving at the warehouse, kept a gloved hand on the handle of a knife that could qualify as a machete. Hagen also kept his very, *very* intense gaze on Zarmani and Abdel, like he was about to go Ginsu chef on them.

Confident that Stark knew how to control his men, Gorman focused on his damn problem, staring at the stained concrete floor for a moment.

Considering the angles, he finally said, "Shit, we're probably never going to get a shot like this again, especially with Hassan. I'll cancel if you both say you won't go, but I'm asking you to help me out."

"I never said I wouldn't go," Stark pointed out. "You're paying me and the boys, so we go where you say . . . but it's a dumb idea."

"Bill, you're the boss and we go way back," added Harwich. "The SOG team goes where you say, but ditto what the colonel just said."

"All right," Gorman replied. "We go."

They made final checks of weapons, night-vision scopes, and communications gear. Aside from Larson's Browning and Ryan's M107 sniper rifle, the team used Heckler & Koch MP7A1 submachine guns.

Stark and Harwich exchanged looks and nods. Gorman knew they both believed in their country and the mission, but they both had men to lead and bring home if at all possible. They tried never to choose between the two, and none of them were about to start now.

The plan was very simple and straightforward, as all good plans were, right up to the moment that the first shot was fired. Then it was instincts, training, and massive amounts of balls with a pinch of luck. Major Zarmani would knock and announce his presence, as this was a prearranged meeting with the minister to transport a rather large amount of American currency. The U.S. aid, intended for schools, hospitals, and water treatment plants, would now fund ISIS. The minister would signal the front gate to let Zarmani in. Once the gate was open the SOG team, led by Harwich, plus Gorman, Zarmani, and Abdel, would assault the compound, grab the money, terminate the corrupt minister and Hassan, and haul ass. All in under a minute.

Stark and his team were on perimeter duty. Ryan was in a sniper perch with direct lines of fire into the meeting area. He reported to Stark and Gorman, speaking into his vibration microphone, to tell them that he was in position.

"Blue is green," Stark said, which meant his team, which was code-named Blue for this operation, was ready, or green.

"Red is green," Harwich said, which meant he and his six-man SOG team were stacked at the back gate of the ministry compound.

Gorman was at the end of the stack, letting his guys establish a secure position for him to come in and evaluate.

Let the shooters do what shooters do and the spies do what we do, he thought. Besides, Harwich and his SOG guys were much better at this than he was. Stark's men were also very good at what they did.

In fact, Stark might be able to do my job as well.

Gorman smiled at the thought.

From twenty-five hundred yards, a 660-grain .50-caliber bullet would hit with enough mass and speed to penetrate an engine block. From fifty yards that same bullet would go through men, doors, posts, glass, other men, dogs, and at least three goats.

Ryan had ten such rounds in the detachable box magazine of his M107 semi-auto sniper rifle, plus one in the chamber. From his vantage point, he saw Abdel bring his MP7A1 up at the exact wrong moment and begin to point it backwards toward Gorman.

Ryan was relaxed, breathing slowly, sight picture perfect. He had taken half of the slack out of his custom-made trigger, saw the wrong movement, informed Stark, and sent the round to its preordained destination.

Abdel's head split in two while Stark and his team continued to search the area for any other issues.

Ryan then observed Harwich shoot Zarmani in the face when the Pakistani major tried to bring his own weapon around. Then Harwich looked back, apparently to see what Gorman wanted to do.

Gorman understood immediately that this was a setup. If he kept going into the compound they would probably be ambushed.

He spoke into his mike. "Sundown."

"*Sundown,*" acknowledged Stark while he and his team continued covering the road, as they were about to leave quickly.

Harwich grabbed the now flex-cuffed Zarmani and headed toward their SX4s.

Ryan saw the flash, followed by a trail of light, as an RPG hit just below and about ten feet from Chief Larson, who was knocked off his feet.

The blast echoed off the tall walls of the ministry's compound. Larson and his .50-cal gun rolled quickly another twenty feet down the small hill, as he was sure what would follow.

Two more flashes, and RPGs crushed the spot where Larson had just been, blinding spheres of fire and shrapnel stabbing trees and the surrounding terrain.

The smell of cordite assaulting his nostrils, Ryan felt the ground shake as he swung his heavy weapon toward Larson's position and began to scan for targets while hearing Stark asking for a situation report.

Before he could reply, Ryan spotted several figures fifty yards to their right. He was about to take them but Larson opened up the

Browning on them. The chief fired for just four seconds, but at a sustained rate of fire of eight .50-caliber rounds per second, he dumped more lead on the enemy than three times the number of bullets in Ryan's sniper rifle. The men disintegrated in an instant.

Still, Ryan spotted many more figures headed their way; saw the headlights of incoming trucks packed with soldiers jumping out, holding AK-47s. The math didn't add up. They had to get the hell out of here, and he informed the colonel of the rapidly deteriorating situation.

Gorman and his men reached the Suzukis when machine-gun fire broke out, muzzle flashes casting a stroboscopic glow on the woods adjacent to the compound.

"Fuck," said Harwich as he gunned the engine of the lead SX4.

"It's going to be close," said Gorman, sitting next to him.

The SX4s rushed to the position that Stark had preselected as an emergency pickup site.

Gorman, Harwich, and three of his SOG guys jumped out armed with MP7A1s and laid down a wall of 4.6x30mm hollow-point steel in the direction from which the RPGs had originated. They also threw several smoke grenades to obscure their position.

However, the problem with smoke grenades was that they could also cause visual problems for the good guys.

The cover fire gave those trying to kill Stark and team a moment's pause—all the former Special Forces soldiers needed to do was fling a few M67 grenades and unleash a full magazine on automatic as they began to pull back to the waiting SUVs.

But it was Larson who finally tipped the scales, buying the team enough seconds to get in their vehicles while he swept the incoming enemy with the Browning. He tore them up, stripping their determination, forcing them to the ground as spent casings rained all around him, the sound deafening.

Trees burst into clouds of splinters. Brick walls crumbled. Troop carriers went up in flames. Men exploded right on top of their hiding comrades, bathing them in blood and guts, triggering panic.

"Chief! Time!" Stark shouted from the side of the last Suzuki.

Larson spat in the direction of the hell he had unleashed before getting in the back, but kept the door open while firing his final burst to cover their getaway.

The Browning was still hot to the touch when they reached the warehouse. Stark patted the chief on the back before walking up to Gorman and saying, "Thanks. You got to us just in time. We were covering your movement, but we probably would not have made it."

Gorman replied, "Sorry about the op going sideways, Colonel, but we got all our boys back to fight another day."

As he watched Stark and his team head to some undisclosed safe house to wait for their next contract, Gorman, Harwich, and the SOG team drove the Suzukis to the American embassy.

He was tired. No, scratch that. He was downright exhausted, having spent the past forty-eight hours planning the damn mission and now dreading the next twelve hours of debriefings. He not only had allowed an asset to deceive him, but it had been a coordinated deception with New Delhi, where one of Jack Walch's assets had also fed him misinformation. And it had all resulted in people getting killed, but at least none of them were Americans. Still, it meant endless questions and paperwork.

But that's the life you've chosen, Billy Boy, he thought, for a moment wondering if he should have followed into his late father's footsteps and stayed in the FDNY, like Victoria, his younger sister, an FDNY paramedic.

Gorman had gone through the training and had just received his probationary status with the FDNY Company 10, also known as the Ten House, when September 11 changed his world. Gorman's wife, Jeannie, worked on the 104th floor of the North Tower and could not be evacuated. Several members of his team clearing the towers never made it out. As he watched his world collapse, Gorman swore to dedicate his life to fighting terror and headed to Fort Benning, Georgia, the Army's Officer Candidate School. He served one tour in Afghanistan and two in Iraq—the last one with Army Intelligence— before the CIA recruited him. He spent a year at The Farm, the CIA training facility in Williamsburg, Virginia, and was assigned to work the New Delhi CIA Station under Jack Walch for a year before Islamabad.

Gorman checked his watch while waiting for Harwich to finish some phone call with his people in Paris.

He inhaled deeply, wincing in painful memory while staring at the stainless steel Rolex, a surprise present from Jeannie at his FDNY graduation. To this day, Gorman wore it as his version of a wedding band, a reminder of the wonderful woman he lost to the same bastards he'd vowed to fight to his dying breath.

Gorman stared at his reflection on the steel door leading to the Secure Compartmented Information Facility (SCIF), the fancy name for a CIA secured facility in country. He frowned at the lines around his eyes. At forty-five-years-old, he wondered how much longer he could realistically keep this up. He was still a fit 200-pound 6'2" man, even with his official desk job, and it was ironic he had Langley to thank for that. The Agency kept sending him way too many damn rookies fresh out of The Farm, forcing Gorman to be more hands on than most Station Chiefs—and also make special requests like flying Harwich and his SOG team from Paris to assist in special raids. No way his rookies could have handled what had gone down tonight on their own.

Gorman looked over at Harwich, tapped the Rolex with an index finger, and got a quick nod in return.

He turned back to the steel door, beyond which no cell phones were allowed, regarding the light-olive skin from his Italian mother's side of the family. Dark hair and a matching goatee allowed him to blend in during field ops far better than most Americans operatives in the region. And he was also fluent in Urdu, though with the accent that Maryam Gadai, his best in-country agent, found entertaining.

Gorman sighed.

Maryam.

He shook his head, wondering if loneliness was what had driven him to break a cardinal rule by becoming romantically involved with one of his key local assets some years ago. Maryam Gadai was an agent with Pakistan's Inter-Services Intelligence (ISI), the American version of the CIA. The beautiful Pakistani had managed to warm Gorman's very cold heart during a joint CIA-ISI mission in Afghanistan several years ago. But it was at times like tonight, after being crossed by someone he had trusted, that made him wonder if she was just using him— honey-trapping him like so many Pakistani female agents are trained to do.

Harwich hung up the phone and walked toward him.

"All good in your neck of the woods?" Gorman asked, powering down his satphone.

Harwich also switched off his phone and nodded. "Well, no crazy ISIS motherfuckers blowing shit up this week . . . so yeah, I guess it's all good over there."

Gorman remembered those attacks in the French capital with as much anger as he remembered Jeannie and everyone else he lost on September 11—events that only served to kindle his hatred for the Muslim extremists.

"All right," Gorman said, keying in the security code into the reader next to the door. "Let's get this over with."

"Yeah," Harwich said while suppressing a yawn. "Hope there's coffee in there, man."

"Yeah," Gorman replied. It was going to be a long night and an even longer morning.

8

Chameleon

MANASSAS, VIRGINIA

It had been a while since she had conducted this type of surveillance, but it had all come back to her in a hurry.

Dressed in her old one-piece ghillie suit from her in-country sniper days, Monica approached her objective an hour after hiding her Ducati in the thicket near the northern end of the Prince William Forest Park.

The ghillie, made from synthetic thread and resembling heavy foliage, broke up her human outline, blending Monica with her surroundings. She advanced slowly across the leaf-littered ground, approaching the perimeter fence separating the park from the woods belonging to Jasmine Companies.

She paused by a towering pine a couple dozen feet from the chain-link fence topped with barbed wire angled outward, designed to deter intruders. Her AN/PSQ-20 enhanced night-vision goggles (ENVG) amplified the moonlight filtering through the thick canopy overhead, painting the woods in palettes of green.

She inspected the fence, failing to see any plastic or ceramic insulators connecting the chain link to the posts, meaning it wasn't electrified. And she couldn't spot any motion sensors that would alert the security personnel to someone trying to scale it.

That leaves cameras, infrared sensors, and ground pressure sensors, she thought, becoming her surroundings, listening for five full minutes without moving.

She scanned the terrain slowly in a pattern of near, far, and farther, always listening, before moving closer, her whole body aware and in a deep crouch. The toe of her leading boot brushed aside the cushion of leaves and felt the ground beneath before shifting her weight forward and pausing; relaxed, slow, and considered movement.

Resembling more a tall shrub than a person, Monica remained completely still except while in transition, making her advance painfully gradual but nearly invisible to the untrained eye or hidden surveillance cameras. Finally reaching the fence, she ran a gloved hand over the wire pattern, fingers feeling the gauge before producing a pair of steel cutters.

She worked an L-shaped pattern close to the ground, bending it just enough to squeeze through and pushing it back, before vanishing in the thick woods again.

Crawling like a reptile, the camouflaged ghillie doing its magical work, she took two hours to cover the couple of hundred feet separating her from the opposite end of the forest overlooking the facility.

Assuming she was in full view of unseen surveillance cameras, Monica made every movement sluggish along the edge of the woods. She finally settled in her ideal vantage point, one that offered a clear line of sight to the rear dock and the surrounding parking lot. She even had a view into the first- and second-story offices and conference rooms on this side of the building. The monthlong FBI investigation had given her ample time to roam the grounds and establish the best location to conduct surveillance if the situation required.

And after her close encounter at the Hay-Adams, there was no doubt in her mind that in spite of her superiors' repeated warnings, the situation certainly called for this level of covert action. Every bone in her body told her that Amir Dham was up to no good, and she was determined to prove it once and for all.

She had brought along her backup pistol, a .32-caliber Walther PPK, and a hunting knife. But her main weapon for this evidence-gathering mission resided in the small backpack she now opened. A 36.3 megapixel Nikon digital camera attached to a powerful 600mm lens with a 200x optical zoom—both camouflaged with green mesh and synthetic fibers.

Monica rested the foot-long telephoto lens on a small tripod for stability and slid the power switch on its side. The unit had cost her a small fortune at one of Arlington's premier camera shops the previous afternoon, after she had ridden in the neighborhood surrounding Jasmine Companies trying to come up with a plan.

The Nikon powered up in a mode that kept the sound muted, the three-inch LED screen off, and autofocus disabled. She had preselected the settings at the store, not only to save battery but also to keep the unit from telegraphing her presence.

Removing her ENVGs and setting them aside, Monica pressed the Nikon's viewfinder against her right eye and manually turned the lens to zoom across the two thousand feet separating her from the parking lot. Panning around, she captured the first images of her mission: a pair of guards dressed in black and armed with what looked like UZI submachine guns.

She frowned. The guards were a far cry from the ones she remembered during the investigation—rent-a-cops armed with flashlights, whistles, and radios.

We're just a luxury imports store, the smooth-talking Amir had explained, *and we're fully insured, so no need for firearms.*

Right.

Monica snapped several shots, zooming in to capture their faces under yellow floodlights washing across the parking lot, mostly empty at this predawn hour.

Upon closer inspection, the men were dark-skinned, like the bodyguards.

Probably Pakistanis, she thought while scanning the lot, taking photos of two other sets of armed guards, and of four men in a conference room on the third floor. She also recorded five trucks coming and going, and the location of the surveillance cameras covering this side of the building.

She counted twenty-three of them, several pointed at the woods where she hid.

That's more than those covering the exterior of the J. Edgar Hoover Building.

Day-shift guards appeared over the next hour, as sunlight beamed over the eastern horizon off to her right. They carried similar weapons slung over their shoulders and took over from the night-shift guards, who walked to their vehicles and drove off.

Monica snapped photos from various angles at a resolution that would be good enough to—

Voices.

Behind her.

Guards patrolling the narrow stretch of woods between the manicured grounds and the perimeter fence a couple hundred feet back, where she had cut through the chain link.

Very slowly, Monica retrieved the camera and sneaked it under the ghillie.

Her mind raced, hoping that the synthetic fibers would continue to blend her with the forest floor as sunlight forked through the woods, as the indigo sky gave way to a clear and bright morning. Had this been an FBI-sanctioned stakeout, she would have had the time and resources to select the correct mix of fibers to best blend with this particular terrain. But as it was, she had simply grabbed her old camo suit and goggles, stuffed them in one of the Ducati's storage compartments, and hoped for the best.

The voices grew closer. Two men talking in what sounded like soft-spoken Urdu, Pakistan's national language. Though she wasn't completely sure because of its similarity to Hindi and Panjabi. But it really didn't matter. She had no earthly idea what they were saying, only that they weren't local and didn't seem alarmed.

She heard their footsteps crunching the thick layer of leaves, pine needles, and dry branches, telegraphing their position, which she estimated at around ten to fifteen feet directly behind her.

At least they're far from the perimeter fence, she thought, deciding they should not be able to see the L-shaped cut unless they walked right up to it, because it was in the shade.

The men continued their noisy patrol, talking and walking past her, until vanishing altogether.

Monica waited a few more minutes before resuming her surveillance. New armed guards now strolled about the parking lot, and the images she captured were far crisper in the sunlight. She also recorded the Jasmine Companies brown trucks loading and unloading by the docks, zooming in on the cargoes, a variety of wooden crates being delivered and just as many heading out.

Time passed; insects crawled around her, some venturing inside the suit.

She ignored the little visitors, just like in the old days. Bugs would annoy and even sting on occasion, but the only way they could kill was if she reacted to them, telegraphing her position.

Surprised at how comfortable she was even though it'd been years, she continued observing and recording. Birds chirped nearby and branches swayed in the breeze, the smell of pine resin and rotten vegetation filling her lungs.

She kept snapping, glad that she had listened to the salesman and purchased the largest flash card he had, 256 gigabytes, capable of storing tens of thousands of high-resolution photos and over sixty hours of HD video.

By ten in the morning the place was bustling with activity. Day-shift employees went about, deliveries and shipments increased. Even Amir made a cameo appearance at ten thirty, accompanied by Saddam wearing a black wrist brace and favoring his right leg as he walked behind his principal.

How's the arm, asshole?

She grinned, zooming in on them as Amir's Saudi associates, Prince Khalid and Princess Lisha, also stepped onto the dock. Based on their mannerisms, they seemed to discuss something related to several crates being loaded into a delivery truck.

But upon closer inspection, she noticed that this particular truck sported a different logo on the sides and back than the Jasmine Company vehicles.

Bright green words against a pretty image of green fields and blue skies read,

SOLAR ENERGY GROUP, LTD.

She frowned, remembering the brochures she had photographed back at the Hay-Adams hotel before getting caught.

Is Amir going green?

She looked around the building, searching for solar panels, but only found thick electric cables running from a nearby tower into the side of the company, where they fed a set of transformers adjacent to the cooling towers of the building's AC units.

Nothing green about that.

Snapping more images of the Saudis, Amir, and the truck, Monica realized something interesting: the truck was being loaded with crates, not unloaded. If Amir's company were indeed going green, then it would make sense for it to be *taking* deliveries of the hardware, like solar cells and transformers. But the crates were going *into* the truck.

Why?

Is Amir importing green energy hardware and distributing it through trucks such as that one?

But what if those crates contained something else?

Could that explain why Amir was meeting with the Saudi—

The blast from the silent round stung her hands, forcing Monica to let go of the camera as plastic and glass exploded inches from her face.

Damn!

She backed away, realizing someone had spotted her, perhaps noticing the glint of glass from her telephoto lens, or maybe—

No time to analyze!

She rolled away as instincts overcame surprise, her training displacing the anger of being forced to abandon the flash card inside what was left of her camera, plus her ENVGs. But her mind confirmed her reaction as follow-up silent rounds fired from an unseen vantage point tore up the goggles and further ripped into the Nikon.

Monica continued rolling, the suit's fabric fluttering around her as she retreated deeper into the woods, vanishing like a whirling shadow. Bullets splintered bark as voices returned to her far left, speaking hastily now, accompanied by approaching footsteps crunching leaves.

She scrambled toward a pine a dozen feet from the edge of the woods and spun behind it, surging to a deep crouch as more voices echoed in the woods but from the opposite direction. Amir's forces were converging on her, tightening the noose.

A glance at the parking lot confirmed the lack of an alarm. Employees walked about the rear dock. Delivery trucks came and went. But in her camouflaged world, suppressed sniper fire flushed her toward sentries closing in, stomping on fallen vegetation as they rushed toward her.

Monica's training once more prevailed, forcing her to trust the ghillie as she shifted from tree to tree quietly, in a deep crouch. She paused when reaching the halfway mark to her exit point on the perimeter fence.

Betting that the sniper had only spotted her camera lens and not her camouflaged suit, Monica stepped into a cluster of waist-high bushes and dropped to her knees with only seconds to spare.

The first pair of guards arrived, clutching what she recognized as UZI PRO submachine guns fitted with Gemtec MK-9K sound suppressors and MEPRO 21 30mm reflex sights.

Like the ones we confiscated two months ago.

She frowned at the stacking evidence confirming her suspicions while staring at the two men scanning the woods with their weapons. They walked about, seemingly confused, mumbling to each other, then to the second pair of sentries that arrived as noisily as the first, before conversing with someone on the radio. Though they spoke in Urdu, she had a pretty good idea what was being discussed. The voice cracking through the static sounded a whole lot like Amir's. It came across harsh, angry, followed by apologies from the quartet for failing to secure the intruder.

Remaining completely still, she observed the way they moved— loudly, their muzzles crossing each other's paths. It was amateurish but working to her advantage because they completely missed her, even as they looked directly at her shrubby hideaway.

Monica tried to relax in spite of staring at the wrong end of submachine guns in the hands of anxious rookies. She told herself that if her camouflage gear and training were good enough to fool al Qaeda back in the day, she should be able to handle these clowns.

Still, she couldn't be too careful, as she had no doubt these characters would shoot first and ask questions later.

She considered reaching for her Walther PPK but decided against it. The eight .32 caliber rounds it held were no match for the barrage of 9mm hell those men would unleash if provoked. Still, she really wanted to get her hands on one of those UZI PROs, including the Gemtec suppressor and the MEPRO scope, and compare their serial numbers to the batch the joint task force had confiscated. Following that successful raid, the FBI had worked with Israeli authorities and discovered that the recovered guns were part of a larger shipment that had been stolen from a warehouse in Tel Aviv six months ago.

So she did the only thing she could: bide her time and wait for an opportunity.

For nearly fifteen minutes Amir's soldiers scouted the grounds around her as the sun rose higher in the sky. Narrow beams pierced the canopy, forming bright islands surrounded by darkness. But none of that mattered to their advanced MEPRO 21 sights, designed in close collaboration with Israeli Special Forces to operate in all lighting conditions.

Two guards stood so close to Monica that for a moment she feared one of the idiots would trip on her. But just then another sentry located the remnants of her camera and night-vision goggles while having more discussions on the radio, before all finally walked away.

Although disappointed that she couldn't steal one of those fancy guns, Monica felt damn glad the bastards didn't spot her. She remained in place for another ten minutes before slowly backing away from the bushes and making a beeline for the opening in the fence.

She moved quietly, avoiding the shafts of yellow sunlight, taking her time, sidestepping fallen branches and other debris that might—

A silent round buzzed past her right ear, stabbing the tree just ahead of her, wood splintering as she shifted left, missing a second bullet by inches.

Cutting farther left, the perimeter fence now visible beyond two dozen feet of woods, Monica remained low, crawling on all fours. She curled behind a wide trunk before clambering toward another one as bark exploded again, but this time a few trees away.

They've lost me.

But not for long.

They would soon reacquire her now that they knew what to look for: the heavy ghillie suit.

Making her decision, she pulled down the zipper from neck to groin, crawling out of the suit, wearing just her black riding gear. Hanging it from a nearby branch, she backed away quietly, toward the fence.

And that's when she spotted them: two figures crisscrossing each other in the semidarkness. Their silhouettes paused, probing the terrain with their UZI PROs' sophisticated optics, waiting for her to make the next move.

Grabbing a stone by her feet, she threw it at the tree next to the ghillie, hitting the trunk, prompting the guards to turn in that direction.

Monica raced toward the fence, masking her hasty retreat with the trampling sounds made by the sentries as they approached the suit and shouted warnings.

Good luck with that, she thought, sliding feetfirst into the fence like a ballplayer stealing a base. She pushed the chain link out of the way with her boots enough to get her legs through, before twisting and turning, wriggling her torso and head out.

The mechanical noise of the UZIs replaced their warnings, followed by the sound of wood being pounded.

She ignored them while racing inside the park, where the trees were taller and closer together, darkening her surroundings as—

A loud metallic clang told her they had fired against the fence, probably after realizing the ghillie ruse and also noticing her escape route.

Good luck with that too.

The opening she had cut was barely large enough for her slim frame, and as she risked a backward glance, she noticed the sentries on their knees trying to pry it open.

And that's how she left them: caught in the fence while she ran as fast as she could, reaching the Ducati exactly where she had hidden it several hours ago.

Donning the helmet, she accelerated out of the park.

Monica was able to escape with her life but little else. She was nowhere in her quest to gather solid proof. And even worse, what evidence she had captured was probably in the hands of Amir Dham.

Assuming the flash card survived the fusillade.

Still, not all was lost. Any remote doubt she may have had about the duplicity of the Pakistani's affairs had been expunged the instant she saw those sound-suppressed UZI PROs with the fancy MEPRO reflex scopes.

Plus the way they had come after her.

Without mercy.

Without remorse.

On top of that, she could now follow up on that green energy company, Solar Energy Group, and how the Saudis fit into all of this.

But once again, she needed more than her word and some speculation before she could go back to Porter.

The problem was one of accessibility. Amir was too isolated, too protected—just too damn unapproachable. Despite her best efforts, she had not been able to get close enough to gather—and actually hang on to—any meaningful evidence, because his operation had apparently been designed to protect him against the likes of her.

As she steered the bike out of the park and back to Washington, however, the thought struck her like the wind whipping her body while she accelerated to sixty miles per hour in the left lane.

Monica could not get to Amir.

But Amir sure as hell could get to Monica . . . if she let him.

All she had to do was dangle the right kind of bait.

9

Maryam

She moved with the crowd, hiding in plain view, flowing with the natural rhythm of the streets that were her home. But it was her eyes, as dark as her hair beneath her light green burka, that separated her from bustling vendors and haggling customers. They constantly checked for motion that broke the natural rhythm of the marketplace.

Goats, ducks, chickens, figs, bread, and milk, along with assortments of silks, cashmeres, and leathers, dominated the negotiations. She kept her pace steady, in control, even though she felt like running, her emotions boiling when Gorman didn't return her text on his secure line.

Where the hell is he?

She pressed her lips together, loathing the need to signal for a meeting this way.

But there was no other choice. The short paragraph she had read completely by accident on her father's computer during a short visit for tea an hour ago forced her to violate protocol, even at the risk of—

Maryam Gadai spotted the tail across the street: the wrong shift of a head at the wrong time, just as a vendor held up two slaughtered ducks, presenting them to his suddenly uninterested patron.

It had been subtle, a glance to check her position.

But it had been enough.

Cutting right into the nearest alley, she raced through a store and swapped burkas, dropping her old headdress and cash in the hands of the surprised owner. She was back out in twenty seconds, cloaked in lavender, swiftly moving down the alley and turning left into another teeming street, then right into a loud food court.

Her mind still in shock at her father's top-secret plan, Maryam zigzagged past crowded tables, slicing through the stifling smell of curry, baked bread, and body odor. She exited at the other end and made three more turns before leaving the market.

Crossing an adjacent park, she vanished in a narrow patch of forest before risking a backward glance. Two men stepped onto the street, one holding a radio to his lips while gazing in every wrong direction. *Amateurs.*

Maryam dropped her thick brows at them, feeling the cold steel of her Heckler & Koch USP .45 ACP pistol pressed against the small of her back. She was glad she didn't need to use the semiautomatic this afternoon. At least not when her father continued to fill the ranks of his internal police with operatives who couldn't cut it in the field.

Maryam left them behind and continued down Isfahani Road, going over the bridge crossing the Jinnah Stream, and turning south on Zhou Enlai Avenue, her eyes always checking her surroundings. Off to her far left stood the Preparatory School of Islamabad for girls, the place she had spent her teenage years before being shipped to England.

Maryam sighed. Her deepest secret—besides how hard she had fallen for Bill Gorman—was her love for the West and the creature comforts it offered, many of them in conflict with her Islamic upbringing. Before leaving that girl's boarding school to spend eight years at Oxford to become a physician, Atiq would punish her for listening to rock music or watching "violent" American TV programs. But Maryam wanted Pakistan to be more like England, the country that opened her eyes, where she became a woman, tolerant to every race and religion. And this secret of secrets, which she kept locked so tightly for fear of being labeled an infidel, made her wonder if the West could help Pakistan achieve that—a thought that had steered her many years ago in the direction of Bill Gorman.

She stared at the boarding school before her eyes followed the Jinnah Stream south to the complex of buildings that made up the Shifa College of Medicine adjacent to the Shifa International Hospital. She had returned here almost fifteen years ago a freshly minted physician from Oxford specializing in emergency medicine. It was there that Maryam practiced her trade for a few years before slowly being lured into the intelligence world by her father. It had happened rather organically, as she used her position at Shifa, combined with her bedside manners and her looks, to gather intelligence for her dad on the wide range of patients that flowed through the hospital.

Sickness and disease are the great equalizers, my dear Maryam.

And her father had been right, of course. Men and women from all walks of life filled the beds of the hospital, becoming targets of opportunity for those in the hunt for human intelligence. Maryam's ability to approach them, gain their trust, and turn them into ISI assets led her to a formal induction into the intelligence network. Her father's connections and her education allowed her to skip the required step for most female ISI operatives to "cut their teeth" in honeytrapping assignments in India before moving up the ranks.

Maryam continued down Zhou Enlai, until reaching a spot precisely across the Jinnah Stream from the American Embassy while producing an inch-long piece of white chalk.

The unimaginable had happened. She needed to tell Gorman what she knew so that he and the rest of the world could better prepare for what was sure to come next.

10

Korai

ISLAMABAD, PAKISTAN

They grew up as friends. Close friends.

They were from poor neighboring families.

They had risen to power by their own efforts, by sheer determination, defying the rules of their country's established social strata.

The young orphan Atiq Gadai had escaped the strong gravitational pull of al Qaeda in the tribal areas and received a scholarship to study physics in Islamabad. His grades eventually earned him an international scholarship to get his master's and Ph.D. from Oxford. Over the following decade, Atiq became one of Pakistan's finest scientists before joining the ranks of the ISI and reaching the esteemed title of senior director.

Vijay Korai's grades had also allowed him to study at his nation's capital before going off to Cambridge, receiving a degree in petroleum engineering followed by an MBA. He climbed the corporate ladder in the Karachi oil industry, becoming a tycoon, one of Pakistan's wealthiest. But he never forgot his roots, sharing his riches with his country's less fortunate. Korai built schools and hospitals, investing heavily in infrastructure. His efforts provided clean water, electricity, and affordable housing to regions long forgotten by his country's leadership—actions that won him enormous popularity, propelling him into politics. He rose from senator in the Pakistani Parliament to becoming his country's newest prime minister, elected into office just eight months ago.

The old friends stared at each other from across the large desk on the second floor of the executive building adjacent to the large Parliament building, and just a stone's throw from Atiq's ISI headquarters.

"So, it has begun," said Korai, sitting back and frowning while looking away from the large TV screens hanging on the right wall of his office, all replaying the same story from the Bagram Airfield attack.

"It appears so," replied Atiq, sipping Masala chai from a fine porcelain cup. "And per the plan, Ibrahim is making sure all blame is being directed to ISIS . . . plus I personally leaked intel into Pentagon servers to corroborate his story."

Korai regarded his lifelong friend, mostly bald now, with an unkempt salt-and-pepper mustache and bloodshot eyes signaling a lack of sleep.

He inhaled deeply and said, "I was never in favor, you know."

"I know," Atiq said.

"My dream for Pakistan has always been one of peace across the land. Seeing a nuclear warhead detonated anywhere in the region is far from that vision."

"Peace comes at a cost, Vijay. And besides, the only lives lost were those of the jihadists who delivered it . . . plus the infidels."

Korai stared into the distance and said, "I've devoted my entire life to helping those in need. I believe that the best way to combat poverty and the extremism that is ISIS growing within our nation's fabric, is through education, through jobs, not by arming them with nuclear weapons."

"But you have to admit," Atiq said, "they did pay us quite handsomely for them—money we are already using to build schools, housing, roads, train systems, even expanding that costly subway system in Karachi."

Korai nodded. The latter project, targeted at solving the massive traffic problems in the port city, was as expensive as Pakistan's Khushab nuclear reactor complex. But it wasn't just about the money they had collected from the terrorist network, at least not to Korai. It was also about distracting ISIS by focusing their energy away from Pakistan. Ever since he'd assumed the position of prime minister, ISIS had been pressuring his government to take definitive action against America or face civil war.

"And besides," Atiq added, "they were going to get their hands on nuclear weapons sooner or later, so might as well control the how, the where, the when, and the whom."

Korai pointed an index finger at him. "But you see . . . the reality is that no one really controls ISIS *but* ISIS, at least in the long run. We may have managed to divert their attention away from our government, at least for a little while, but even then I was never sure which part of ISIS we were really dealing with. Its left hand doesn't always know what its right hand is doing. Any belief to the contrary is just an illusion, an impossibility."

"Well, in that case we may just be achieving the impossible, because so far Ibrahim is sticking to the plan." He turned to face the screen. "No one is blaming Pakistan for the attack. If anything, the Americans are sending scientists from their EPA to help locate and clean up any fallout carried into Pakistan by the prevailing winds."

"They are?" He didn't know that.

Atiq nodded. "Cleanup crews, and their sympathies, are not what they would be sending our way if they suspected us."

Korai also returned his attention to the television. "I pray very hard that you prove me wrong, old friend. I really do. The only way we can elevate Pakistan in the eyes of the world is through commerce and industry, and that requires *education* and *jobs*. And *that* can only happen in times of peace and prosperity, not with nuclear bombs going off a hundred miles from our border."

"And peace we shall have," Atiq reassured him. "That is the beauty of terrorism. It operates outside the purview of nations, making it a much more difficult target to retaliate against. On top of that, I have confirmation that the Internet leak has reached the highest levels in the American intelligence community, especially their Defense Intelligence Agency. And that, combined with the overt efforts of Ibrahim and his organization . . . I'm telling you, Pakistan will come through this unscathed. We have truly achieved the impossible, lessening the pressure that ISIS was placing on your administration by sending them off to kill Americans, and doing so without any downside from either ISIS or the Americans."

Korai stood, walked around his desk, and stood in front of the flatscreen displays hanging side by side on the wall. To him, the answer to Pakistan's long-term survival resided in a combination of keeping ISIS busy outside of Pakistan while finding enough money to invest in his country. He had poured most of his life's effort into Pakistan and then convinced others to do the same, including ISIS, the wealthiest terrorist organization in the world, backed by Saudi Arabia. The decision to accept Ibrahim's generous donation of seven hundred million euros in exchange for the nuclear weapons had not been easy. But like Atiq had pointed out, ISIS was bound to get its hands on the devices sooner or later. So, might as well control it, as well as their targets and the timeline, while also benefiting from an influx of cash to bolster his country's financial position. All across Pakistan new construction reigned, from the Karachi subway system to superhighways and skyscrapers, and this created thousands of jobs. New roads, oil refineries, power plants, water treatment facilities, schools and universities—all the infrastructure a nation needed to elevate its society from decades of poverty.

He firmly believed that each new job represented one less candidate to be recruited by the likes of ISIS and al Qaeda, who preyed on the unemployed. If he could keep ISIS and the other terrorist organizations looking the wrong way for long enough, he just might be able to elevate Pakistan socially beyond their grip. And that included his intelligence network and his military.

Korai sighed, realizing the dangerous game he was playing. One hand secretly collaborated with terrorists to attack the very country that placed billions of dollars of financial aid in his other hand.

A tricky balancing act, he thought, finding it increasingly difficult to play both sides effectively. But what choice did he have? ISIS was deeply rooted in Pakistan, as well as in every other country in the Middle East. They were too powerful to destroy or to ignore, leaving him no choice but to join their cause.

Or at least give that impression.

And he also couldn't ignore American interests in the area when they included such healthy financial packages to benefit his country's infrastructure and his military—especially with hostile India next door.

Korai looked down at the scar tissue covering the tops of his own hands, though not as extensive as Atiq's. While the Pakistani prime minister recognized his own motivation for collaborating with ISIS, he knew Atiq's reasons were quite different, and probably much more personal, given the loss of his parents and baby sister to the Americans. Korai's parents had been away visiting relatives the afternoon the bomb fell, as the two best friends returned from a soccer match to witness the destruction. But what Atiq would never know was that the bomb did not miss its intended target.

The house next to Atiq's family's—Korai's own home—had long been used as a secret Taliban council room and weapons storage depot in their village.

Korai always knew of his father's covert dealings with Taliban leaders—a secret that he would take to his grave.

"I know your suffering," Korai finally said. "I was there . . . I pulled you back from the flames."

Atiq looked away. "I tried, you know . . . tried to save them," he finally whispered.

"I know . . . but they were beyond saving."

"I still had to try . . . even if it was beyond my control."

"And that's my worry, old friend," said Korai, still staring at the tops of his hands. "If this situation gets beyond our control . . . no one may be able to pull you—and me, for that matter—away from the flames."

11

Static Signal

It was all about control: trying to get it, dealing with those who had it, and trying not to lose it.

Control in relationships, politics, coaching, parenting, policing, leadership, and in almost every aspect of spying. In the latter, the very essence of control focused around recruiting, training, and keeping your assets alive and operational. The best intelligence officers had control issues coming out of every pore in their body.

It was in their DNA, and Bill Gorman was an exceptional intelligence officer.

He saw the text from Maryam eight hours after she'd sent it. Cell phones were never allowed inside CIA stations, buildings, or annexes, and certainly not where he had been holed up: a secure compartmented information facility (SCIF). He was still being debriefed on the previous night's activities at the minister of interior's compound and the carnage and failure that had come with it.

But Gorman had needed some air, noticing her text message after stepping out to a courtyard.

Bloody hell, Bill? Where are you?

Putting the phone away, he had walked outside the U.S. Embassy grounds and across the Jinnah Bridge to a nearby market to call her back. And that's when he spotted her static signal: a chalk mark on a telephone pole at the corner of Zhou Enlai Avenue and the bridge.

He stood there a moment, wondering what the hell had happened. Was it related to last night's incident?

Gorman shook his head. Part of his control issues included keeping assets within a country operating completely independent from each other, even one as productive—and as beautiful—as Maryam Gadai.

But to consider Maryam first for her looks would have been a mistake. Her rising to become a physician and then a top ISI operative—all within a society that considered and treated her like a less-than-second-class citizen—was nothing short of heroic. Maryam was forged by her life in ways that Western women could not replicate, let alone understand; she was formidable. Add the intelligent dark eyes set just a bit too close on a narrow face framed by long black hair—plus the dark olive skin of her country—and you had a truly stunning woman.

Gorman had first met Maryam at a typical embassy gathering on a Sunday afternoon. He knew that she knew he was CIA, and she knew that he knew she was ISI. Both had done their homework on the other, and both figured out that dancing around each other, playing games, would be a waste of time. So each decided to be un-spylike and be direct, to the point, and ask for help.

Maryam had walked directly to Gorman, carrying a full bottle of Maker's Mark. He did not try to avoid her. He shook her hand and said, "Well, this is a first for our kind . . . no games."

She kept hold of his hand and said in the British accent from her years studying abroad, "Nice to meet you, Mr. Bill Gorman. Fancy a chat?"

From that moment to today, their relationship had been mutually beneficial, helping both their countries and their careers. Their personal relationship also grew with the intensity of their collaborations, successes, and failures. They became lovers, almost as directly and naturally as that first meeting.

Relationships were hard enough. Add the complication of them being at work, make that work environment within the clandestine service, and then mix all of that up with the clandestine services being with different countries. It was the very definition of drama and destructiveness.

Drama and destructiveness.

Gorman returned to the embassy to set up the meet, but he couldn't help the thought creeping in the back of his operative mind that Maryam's finding would include a hefty dose of both.

12

Team with No Name

After the final briefing of the day, President Laura Vaccaro leaned over to Wright and whispered, "Get a handle on this process, John. We're not sitting through another one of these. What I've learned today is that our administration can produce some magnificent slides . . . that say *nothing.*"

She knew better than to complain to anyone else. Her administration was brand-new. There were relationships and jobs and careers she was not even aware of yet. There were press reactions soon to be dealt with, and public reaction to recognize and confront. Therefore, publicly airing her frustrations with the system she had inherited and that had made sense to someone before her would be the very definition of counterproductive. However, not commenting was one thing; not doing anything about it . . . that was not in her DNA.

Wright asked everyone for a moment. Vaccaro nodded and then Wright got up and moved to a small side office of the Situation Room, where he asked two generals and a state department deputy to clear the space. As they left, Vaccaro stepped in and Wright closed the door and fogged the glass partition.

"Madam President," he started. "Lisa and I have a list of names standing by. I have the order for you to sign here. They'll have a fund site for money, tasking authority to make things happen that reaches across all lines of our government, at least three communications satellites that will have a scrambled nine-bit encryption access, and also dedicated military airlift and ground transportation. We have picked the most talented, most independent, largely insubordinate, totally dedicated, and extremely competent individuals that we could find. The list includes active CIA and FBI, as well as former U.S. Special

Operations men and women, all in the field now. Six in Pakistan; one has a first-class asset inside the ISI. Each one has at least ten years of field and combat experience.

"Madam President, we don't have the luxury of time to get you acquainted with this team of yours. But if you really want to do this—and I still recommend against it, as does your national security advisor—we need to get this directive signed. Then we can turn on the system and notify those involved that we are moving forward with creating a presidential action team, which by the way is a terrible name. Might as well call it the 'Team with No Name.'" Wright made quotation marks with his fingers.

The president's eyes focused on her chief of staff.

"When this operation goes south, which it most certainly could, I want it known that this was my decision, John. So yes, it's a bad name—or no name—and yes, it says exactly what I want it to say," Vaccaro said with a conviction she believed to her core.

"We'll get it done right away, Madam President."

Vaccaro thought about well-known lines from some of her favorite books and movies, but quickly realized that they were make-believe. This was real. So she put her hand on her chief's right shoulder, and simply nodded.

13

Malik

**SEAWISE GOLIATH. AMBROSE CHANNEL.
LOWER NEW YORK BAY**

He had never seen a seal in the wild.

When he was a child growing up in rural Pakistan, his parents had taken him on bus rides to the Islamabad Zoo. He'd developed a fascination for the peculiar mammals sunbathing or diving into the refrigerated waters of their artificial habitat, bellowing sounds that were part bark and part whistle.

Standing on the port side of the supertanker's bridge as the late-afternoon sun blazed off the starboard bow, he pressed the rubber eyecups of the binoculars against his eyes. Slowly, he scanned the coastline of the barrier peninsula known as Sandy Hook. Along with the Rockaway Peninsula to the north, it formed the entrance to the Lower New York Bay from the Atlantic Ocean.

Malik Darzada stared at a large colony of harbor seals beyond the sun glare reflecting off the *Goliath*'s burnished steel deck. From adults to pups, they dotted the shoreline under the echoing screeches of hovering seagulls. For a moment he remembered his parents, his sisters, and his younger brothers—all under a bright summer day, enjoying those captivating creatures.

Seals.

He slowly shook his head.

Later in life, the name had taken a sinister tenor, associated with the dreaded American fighting force responsible for the deaths of so many friends.

And even my family.

Tightening his grip on the binoculars' twin barrels, Malik forced the thought aside.

Carefully, he inspected the horizon beyond the harmless colony in search of the more threatening species of local wildlife: the U.S. Coast Guard, whose station was located near the tip of Sandy Hook.

He shifted his field of view by a few degrees at a time, surveying the waters leading to Staten Island. Zayd, his number one, performed a similar scan on starboard, keeping a watchful eye for any visible threat on the waters framed by the Brooklyn shoreline.

They had traveled far, leaving Karachi over a week ago, sailing across the Arabian Sea and down the supposedly treacherous coast of East Africa. They had even come face-to-face with two separate groups of Somali pirates.

If they could be called that.

Unlike the hijackers of the *Maersk Alabama*, all Malik and his team had to do was fire a few rounds over the incoming boats to send them on their way.

He had even welcomed the attacks, which broke up the monotonous long voyage. Plus they had allowed his team the opportunity to shoot their weapons against moving targets.

But all of that ends now, he thought, feeling the tension mounting between his shoulder blades as they entered the lower part of the bay.

Traffic had increased exponentially, slowing their progress as the captain ordered the tanker's standard FULL AHEAD speed of seventeen knots down to DEAD SLOW AHEAD, or under two knots. And a minute later he had ordered the engines to DEAD SLOW ASTERN, killing the supertanker's forward speed altogether.

They now waited their turn for a harbor pilot to arrive and steer the tanker through a dozen nautical miles in the third-busiest port in the United States.

So close, he thought, fighting the urge to simply take control and accelerate straight into the harbor. A ship the size of the *Goliath* would be unstoppable once it reached cruise speed—at least for the short time it would take to reach Manhattan.

In Karachi, he and Salma had received a crash course from a pair of Pakistani captains. There wasn't really much to it, given the nature of his mission: holding course and speed for a few minutes. Plus he had spent plenty of time on this bridge observing the crew, learning their process. And the captain had even let him hold the controls a few times in the open sea.

But he had to be patient.

According to the agreed timetable, Salma needed another twenty-four hours to reach Houston, and Atiq was transporting the last two devices to the Jinnah Airport in Karachi for their flights to America. Synchronized attacks, like those carried out in 2001, were fundamental to instilling the desired dose of terror.

He had to be patient indeed.

A support team, including an unmarked van—as arranged by Atiq—would be waiting for him the moment the *Goliath* docked by the Phillips 66 Bayway Refinery in New Jersey. Assuming the ISI agents planted in U.S. Customs and Border Patrol did their jobs,

Malik would transfer the device to the van and go through the Lincoln Tunnel and into Times Square, where he would—

"I don't believe African pirates are a threat anymore, my friend! Yes?" The captain surprised him, patting him on the back.

Malik almost dropped the binoculars as he turned around to face the smiling Captain Antonio Giannotti. A native of Napoli, he was a former *ammiragilo di divisione* in the Italian Navy.

Shrugging, he said, "Old habits, Captain. Sorry."

"It is okay!" Giannotti replied, patting him on the back again. "Never apologize for taking your job seriously. I wish everyone did!"

The captain left the bridge with instructions to use the diesels to keep the *Goliath* in place and to wake him up as soon as the harbor pilot arrived.

Malik and Zayd exchanged a brief glance before continuing their surveillance.

He pressed the binoculars against his eyes and fingered the focusing ring. As he brought a pair of distant Coast Guard cutters into view, Malik decided that the good captain had no earthly idea just how *damn seriously* he took his job.

14

Pronto

ISLAMABAD, PAKISTAN

She made six right-hand turns, three more than necessary.

No one—no car, bus, or the ever-present mopeds—made more than one turn with her.

Maryam Gadai looked at everyone and no one while moving with the crowd, the subdued pastels of her *shalwar kameez*, a loose, collarless long dress, blending her with the river of humanity flowing into the market. The noise level grew almost deafening as vendors and consumers engaged in endless barter over the price of goods. Everything was for sale here and everything was most certainly negotiable.

She pretended to inspect a basket of figs while checking the vaulted entrance to the market. It was possible that someone may have made two turns with her; unlikely that they made three.

Maryam went deeper in the market before turning down a side alley, constantly checking her surroundings. Her furtive eyes searched for the telltale signs of surveillance: abrupt movement, a body shifting in the wrong direction, breaking the natural rhythm of the crowd.

Stopping at a small electronics kiosk, she paid cash for a burner phone, and once more joined the mob of people, becoming invisible. She let the masses carry her across the bazaar, exiting at the opposite side and continuing across the street to a park.

Boys and girls ran on a grassy meadow, laughing and towing kites. A group of moms half conversed and half watched over them under the shade of a towering deodar, the national tree of Pakistan.

Maryam observed the colorful variety of shapes rising in the wind at the end of strings as the kids hoisted them with apparent skill.

Pretending to be just another proud mom, Maryam remained at one end of the group, hidden by the deodar's wide trunk.

She pulled out her phone and called a number that changed daily by a prearranged sequence, which also changed weekly.

A male voice answered with, *"Pronto."* Hello.

Maryam responded, "Let's meet for a coffee."

Both hung up.

15

Luck and Skill

Bill Gorman reached the meet after changing taxis three times and walking several blocks in between each ride while also making multiple turns.

He didn't take security but did carry a CIA-issued Beretta 92FS 9mm and a purchased-in-country Colt .45 semiautomatic, plus two extra magazines for each—all concealed under his ubiquitous travel vest.

Gorman changed his course once more, picked up his walk-run pace, stopped short of the meeting spot, and scanned the area.

He walked around back and checked the place, then came in through the kitchen, the smell of curry and freshly brewed tea tingling his nostrils. He approached Maryam without taking his eyes from his surroundings.

Even with all this precaution he knew that the setup and his method for this meeting was against all advice and protocol, especially after the events of last night. His training told him to wait at least a week before considering meeting another local asset. However, Maryam's access, the intelligence she had provided in the past, and their relationship made her worth the risks. Harwich had insisted he let him and his SOG team tag along for protection, but Gorman had declined. He hated personal security details—not the guys who did it but the idea of it. He believed that he was a spy, a clandestine services officer, and should be capable enough not to be followed to a secret meeting.

However, this was a war unlike any other his country had fought, beginning with its length and the many duplicitous relationships all were forced to make and maintain. Therefore, security officers and personal protection teams had become a matter of course. But on this meet and at this moment he chose to count on his skills and some luck . . . well, mostly luck and maybe some skill. And to make matters even more complicated, Gorman had been notified two hours ago directly by Lisa Jacobson that he was now on some special presidential team designed to bypass Washington's red tape. He understood why the president would want such an instrument at her disposal, as it expedited the collection of intelligence, but he was also well aware of the dangers of such maverick directives.

Focusing on the task at hand, Gorman performed a final check of his surroundings. Maryam had chosen the third table in the back. It had access to two exits, complete view of the room, and there were no other patrons at the two tables on either side. She had ordered two chai teas, and was sipping one when Gorman sat across from her.

It really didn't matter how long he had been intimate with this woman. Every time he saw Maryam he had to stare into those intelligent, catlike eyes. Her natural grace, down to the delicate way in which she held that cup of tea to her lips, made him question why they had not disappeared to his place in Maine already.

Why keep risking our lives like this?

They each had put in two decades of clandestine work. Maybe the time had come to let the new generation of CIA and ISI operatives pick up their torches.

Gorman made a mental note to bring that up. But first . . .

"Hey, not really protocol," he said, looking about him.

Maryam set her cup of tea down, and that's when Gorman noticed the very slight shake of her hand.

This was serious.

Damn serious.

She was not smiling when she replied in her British accent, "There is never a good time for protocol on the day after the bloody detonation of a three-kiloton nuclear device at an American air base, *love*."

Gorman had difficulty controlling his poker face. He realized this was beyond serious, as she never called him that unless they were alone.

Leaning closer, she whispered, "I have learned that my own network assisted the Islamic State in the attack at Bagram Airfield."

Gorman took a deep breath, his mind playing through the implications. If the government of Pakistan was indeed involved in—

"I also know they have *four* more bombs," she added.

Gorman was seldom surprised anymore, not with the life he had lived. But Maryam had just managed to shock him to his core.

"*Four?* Are you shitting me?"

"And they are all heading west—but I have no bloody way of knowing for certain the final destination of all of them . . . but I believe I may know where one is headed . . . and I think I also know how it will be delivered, plus a loose timeline."

Gorman reached over the table and put his hand on the shaky right hand of his asset and lover. "Tell me everything you know, then tell me everything you *don't* know."

They departed by different exits, having spent exactly thirteen minutes together.

Gorman reached the embassy in another ten minutes and was headed for the communications room to contact Washington, but first he needed to make a quick private call.

He stopped in the hallway just past the marines barracks and dialed his satphone, checking to see what time it would be in New York.

Just past midnight.

"Gorman," Victoria Gorman replied after the third ring. There was a lot of noise in the background—car horns, distant sirens, and dozens of undistinguishable loud conversations. His sister was working the late shift again.

"Hey, Vic."

"Bill! Oh, my God! What a pleasant surprise! Are you stateside?"

Gorman looked up and down the hallway, hating having to talk about this in an unsecured area, but mobile phones were not allowed inside CIA stations.

"I'm good. And no, still in-country."

"Oh, what's wrong? Are you hurt?"

"No, no. I'm fine. Listen, I can't talk long. Just wanted to pass along, for your ears only, that you need to take a holiday. Get out of the city."

Silence, followed by, "What are you talking about?"

Gorman checked the hall again and said, "I'm talking about it not being a good idea for you to be in the city for the next few days."

"What the fuck, Bill? Are you saying what I think you're saying?"

"I've already said too much, Vic. And I need to go."

"Are we going to get hit?"

"Go upstate for a few days and—"

"Bill, honey, I'm a fucking *paramedic*. If something's going to happen, the city is *precisely* where I need to be."

Just then Harwich walked through the door leading to the CIA station. Gorman shook his head. Vic and Harwich had had a thing going many years ago, when he was stationed in New York after September 11. But it didn't last long.

"Gotta go. Remember, for your ears only."

"Bill, I—"

He hung up the phone as Harwich approached him. He was wearing the same clothes from last night, plus a Red Sox baseball cap.

"What was that?"

"Nothing important," Gorman replied.

"Fine. Then talk to me about something important. What the hell happened out there?"

"Inside," Gorman said, powering down the phone while looking up and down the corridor for a third time.

"Bullshit. Inside I get the official version. I want the *unofficial* one," he replied, blocking the secured door. "That's the price for ditching me."

Gorman sighed, but they were out of earshot of anyone, and this was, after all, the American embassy. And besides, he wanted to get Harwich's opinion before pulling the five-fire alarm in Washington.

Leaning closer to his longtime friend, Gorman gave him the sixty-second version.

"Holy shit, Bill," he hissed. "We need to brief Langley immediately."

"Yeah," Gorman said while entering the security code in the keypad next to the access door, disengaging the magnetic locks. "But first I have to call this other number."

"What number?"

"Ah . . . I'm on some special team, it seems, and this is the kind of intel they don't want to get lost in translation."

"*Special team?* What's the name of this special team?"

They entered the CIA station, went inside one of the secured rooms, and Gorman dialed the encrypted phone on the conference table. "That's the thing, Glenn. It has no name."

16

No Blood, No Foul

National Security Advisor Lisa Jacobson had been around the block with the Clandestine Services and diplomatic circles more times than she cared to remember. She'd first handled assets and then run embassies across the Middle East before being tapped by President Vaccaro to join her cabinet.

Lisa had seen firsthand in Yemen how competent and totally dedicated—and more than a bit cowboy—was Bill Gorman. It happened during her term as U.S. ambassador to that country.

He had saved a member of Lisa's staff who had taken a wrong turn in the market in Sena and was being thrown in the back of a van to begin her new life as a hostage.

Gorman, who happened to be in the same market buying his favorite coffee, had recognized the staffer. He'd kept an eye on her, seen her take a turn she should not, followed her, and broken the nose of one terrorist. He'd shot another through the throat, and the third square in the chest. Gorman had then grabbed the staffer and moved her back to the embassy.

Lisa was even more impressed when Gorman did not make a big deal about the incident and allowed her to handle it through her own channels. He wanted no credit. Also, he did not have a security team with him, yet again, and figured . . . no harm, no fault.

Or if you were from Chicago, no blood, no foul.

So Gorman had been an obvious choice for the national security advisor to put on the team with no name. She had called him directly to tell him about being a member of an organization that was just formed by the president to circumvent his own Agency's intelligence apparatus. And within a few hours Gorman had called the special number she had provided to him, but the process had not been ironed out and it took almost a full thirty minutes before she was notified.

"Bill, this is Lisa," she said. "Sorry about the confusion. Brand-new mechanism. What have you got there?"

"Lisa, well, this is a bit out of the box. I'm here with Glenn drafting the official field report for our people in Langley . . . but what the hell," and he back-briefed her on what he had been told.

"Bill, sorry to ask, but this contradicts what we've heard directly from ISIS and also from the Pentagon, which intercepted an encrypted message confirming that they alone were responsible for—"

"Lisa, I get it, but my source has been impeccable and has no reason to lie to us. I trust the information and the source . . . with our lives."

"I am briefing the president now," said Lisa, realizing that this would also test the theory that the regular system was ponderous to a fault. However, this new way did not allow for checks and balances, which could lead to disasters. The president had a good sense of what was necessary now and was willing to take the political risk to make things happen. The threat to the nation was never greater and all had to be up to task to have any chance of succeeding.

17

Angler

SILVER SPRING, MARYLAND

Her father had taught her the intricacies of fly-fishing—what he called the three Ts—a lifetime ago back at their ranch outside of Eagle Pass, Texas.

Tackle, technique, and timing.

He believed that was what separated an angler, or fly fisherman, from someone standing on the shore looking like a dumbass.

Monica remembered the hours each weekend, knee-deep in her waders, casting her line across the mild rapids of the Rio Grande as it skirted the southern end of their property. She would let her tackle marinate, or drift, long enough to allow brown trout to come close enough for her to hook them.

Which was precisely what she intended to do at this late hour: hook herself a trout—of the Paki variety—along with some of their fancy Israeli hardware.

If she could capture someone that could be linked to Amir, plus an UZI PRO with serial numbers matching those from the shipment the Israelis lost . . .

Monica sighed as she lay on a thick branch of the massive oak across from a decrepit one-story house off of Watson Road. It backed into Sligo Creek Park, a large wooded area on the northwest edge of town, and ten miles north of the capital.

The place was in dire need of renovation. Gustavo Porter had purchased it as an investment during the last market crash, for forty cents on the dollar. But he lost it to his wife during their divorce last year—along with their main residence in nearby Bethesda—after the economy had rebounded and home prices soared. He'd often talked about flipping the place for a profit. But now his ex owned it, and it just sat boarded up until she could collect enough alimony to work on it, while Porter made do in an efficiency apartment across the river.

Tonight Monica thought to assist her boss's ex-wife with that first crucial step in the renovation process: demolition.

The night was star-filled and cool, with a steady breeze sweeping in from the Chesapeake Bay fifteen miles to the east. Monica adjusted the Leupold scope of her old and trusty M24A2 sniper rifle to compensate for the wind while checking her range to target from her vantage point.

Two hundred yards; a walk in the park, she thought, even with the Phantom M2 QD sound suppressor capable of handling the ten 7.62×51mm NATO rounds in the box magazine fired in rapid succession.

Fully concealed halfway up the tree and with a clear line of sight to the front of the house, Monica briefly closed her eyes and enjoyed the calm before the shit storm headed her way. Though this time she was bringing a tad more hardware than her Walther PPK peashooter and a hunting knife to an UZI PRO gunfight.

She had no doubt that the tackle she had cast that afternoon with the click of a button from a burner phone was guaranteed to instigate a reaction even from a slippery fish like Amir Dham. The question, however, was how *big* of a reaction.

The images in that flash card are in the cloud waiting to be released. How much are they worth to you?

It had been a simple question, but one that made sense.

Amir had pressed every conceivable charge against Monica, leading to her suspension and perhaps even her eventual termination of current and future government employment. Which meant she might soon be on the street in need of cash.

And of course, the photos were not in the cloud, even though the Nikon had the capability to upload them—at least until it was destroyed. But Amir didn't know that.

An hour later she had received a reply on another burner phone.

Will half a million and dropping all charges make the problem go away?

Certainly, she had replied.

She had then provided this address to make the exchange, quite certain of the only currency Amir would bring to the party: hollow-point rounds.

By replying to her directly instead of alerting the FBI, Amir had pretty much proven his guilt. The man obviously didn't want his friends in Washington learning that his guards carried the same weaponry that had been confiscated from one of his very own trucks.

And stolen from the Israelis months before.

But it was still a desperate plan, and she knew it. However, the situation was nothing short of desperate. ISIS had detonated one bomb while making threats to detonate more, and this bastard—and possibly even his Saudi associates—were involved. Somehow.

I just need to prove it.

So Monica just lay there, line cast, bait marinating, waiting for the trout.

Tackle. Technique. Timing.

When the catch of the day finally arrived shortly before midnight, however, it wasn't the expected silver Escalade or any of the other high-end vehicles in Amir's motor pool. An old and dark Buick sedan with Michigan plates pulled up in the driveway and six hooded men jumped out, armed not with sound-suppressed UZI PROs but with basic MAC-10 automatic pistols.

Her heart sank at the sight of the wrong weapons, which the group proceeded to fire at the house without warning. The staccato gunfire rumbled down the peaceful street, their collective muzzle flashes stroboscopic.

While three remained on the driveway, the rest shot the front door and kicked it in before storming the place with paramilitary discipline. They threw grenades ahead of them, the detonations visible through every window as they apparently went room to room.

Resting the side of her face against the top of her M24A2, she aligned the closest target in the Leupold sights, exhaled slowly, and squeezed the trigger.

The high-speed round stabbed the intruder's chest, exploding through his back and punching a hole in the sedan while nearly turning him around. His comrades tried to react, but she had already chambered a second round, scoring another hit. The third man tried to make a run for the side of the house but never made it, though it took her three rounds to put him down.

And again she waited, the feeling of omnipotence from back in the day returning with unparalleled clarity as her senses became one with the rifle. Her hands and fingers rested on trained locations, her breathing steady, her body relaxed. From this vantage point and with a suppressed weapon she was invisible.

The men in the house realized something was wrong and came out shooting in every direction. And that was actually the only risk she faced: a stray bullet.

Luckily, none came even close.

She let each figure come into her crosshairs, firing systematically, eliminating two in six seconds.

The last one had enough time and perhaps some sense to figure out the general direction of the threat and dive for cover behind the sedan. But he didn't have enough sense to realize that, from her perch, Monica could fire down through the windows of the vehicle. Her rounds carried enough energy to punch right through the sheet metal of the opposing doors.

Momentarily spotting the top of his head just behind the driver's door, Monica fired twice into the vehicle through the front passenger window, striking the inside of the driver's door.

The hooded man jerked back on impact, landing on the lawn faceup, hit by both rounds, one in his upper chest and the second in his abdomen.

Nine shots. Six kills.

She was certainly out of practice.

Strapping the M24A2 across her back and climbing down—and ignoring the sirens in the distance—Monica rushed across the street.

She removed their hoods while getting her camera ready. She couldn't recover any UZI PROs, but at least she could photograph the bastards.

To her surprise, however, the first three she unmasked didn't look like they were from Pakistan—or anywhere from the Middle East, for that matter.

What the hell's going on?

The men were all white, and two even had blue eyes.

Ditto on the fourth and fifth guys, she thought, photographing them anyway.

But a strange little feeling scratching the back of her throat told her that their images, even if they were in the database, would not connect them to Jasmine Companies.

Just then she heard a moan. The last man she had shot was still alive.

Kneeling by his side on the grass, she removed the hood, revealing yet another white guy.

Selecting the video recording feature on her phone, she asked, "Who are you? What's your connection with Amir Dham?"

The man—a kid really, probably in his midtwenties—stared at the phone, then at her, trying to whisper, but coughed blood instead.

"Tell me! And I'll take you to the hospital!" she insisted. "Tell me about Amir Dham!"

"A . . . Amir? Who . . . is . . . that?" the man replied, blood now dripping from his nose.

"Who hired you?"

"Fifty . . . grand . . ." he mumbled.

"What?"

"Fifty thou," he mumbled again, coughing up more blood.

"Did Amir offer you fifty thousand bucks to kill me?"

"Don't . . . know . . . Amir . . . just contract . . . online . . . for . . . for—"

The man began to convulse, his eyes rolling to the back of his head.

The sirens grew closer as the man died on the grass.

Monica sprinted to the back of the house, jumped the fence, and raced across Sligo Creek Park as police reached the scene, blue and red lights glowing in the street.

But no one came in pursuit.

Five minutes later, she reached her Ducati, hidden behind a playground. She had escaped unharmed, but once more, with nothing else.

Except a price on her head.

She had kicked the bear that was Amir Dham, and that meant that her home and any of her typical hangouts were off-limits. She had no place to run. No Bureau. No police. No safe haven.

But that didn't mean she lacked choices.

Monica disassembled her weapon, stuffing it in a duffel bag she then strapped behind her back.

Before racing into the night.

To do the unexpected.

18

Leadership

WASHINGTON, D.C.

Her life had been one long series of challenges, starting with her decision to follow her father's footsteps and join the military. But unlike Lieutenant James Vaccaro, whose career was cut short by a

Vietcong booby trap in some forgotten jungle, Laura Vaccaro was blessed with a long and distinguished term of service in the Middle East. Politics then followed, along with a marriage to a wonderful man who died of lung cancer shortly before the start of her presidential campaign.

She could have pulled out of the race and no one would have blamed her for it. But the nation needed the kind of leadership that she had demonstrated on the battlefield—and again in the U.S. Senate—as she always faced and overcame staggering odds. But in spite of all her life's accomplishments, her critics believed that she'd won the election because no one dared run negative ads against such a decorated hero and popular senator who'd just been widowed. One leading candidate from the opposite party had tried to smear her name—once—before retiring from public life following a brutal social media backlash.

As Lisa Jacobson and the secretary of homeland security left the Oval Office with their marching orders, Vaccaro walked up to the windows behind her desk and contemplated the manicured lawns and gardens. Her thoughts once more gravitated to JFK, who'd stood right here while handling the Cuban Missile Crisis in 1963. Back then the young president had faced immense pressure from veteran military leaders to invade the island before completion of the installation of Soviet nuclear missile sites ninety miles from Key West. Such a decision would have led to an escalation on both sides, culminating in the unthinkable. So Kennedy had chosen two parallel strategies, one overt and one covert. His right hand worked to find a middle ground with his generals, opting for a naval blockade of the island rather than an invasion. His left hand began a back-channel communications effort with the Kremlin to reach a quick and peaceful resolution before military hotheads on both sides started World War Three.

Vaccaro stared at her own hands, before making fists.

Like Kennedy, she was overtly working with her cabinet and the Pentagon while also secretly organizing a team that had just proven its value by yielding intelligence suggesting at least four more bombs heading to America.

One aboard a ship cruising toward New York Harbor.

On top of that, Lisa's CIA guy in Islamabad believed that the ISI, Pakistan's Inter-Services Intelligence, had collaborated with ISIS in the attack in Bagram and were also responsible for the weapons heading her way.

Vaccaro had been quick to conference in the heads of the New York Port Authority, the NYPD, and the commander of the Coast Guard Station at Sandy Hook. But the intelligence finding lacked the actual vessel name and offered only a loose timeline suggesting that the ship could be approaching the Lower New York Bay in real time. But with hundreds of ships going in and out of the third-busiest port in America every day, there was no practical way to handle such a threat without shutting it all down.

Doing so, of course, could telegraph to the terrorists that U.S. authorities were on to them and perhaps prompt them to detonate the device early. So the secretary of homeland security, along with the NYPD commissioner and the head of the New York Port Authority, had come up with a better short-term solution. They recommended temporarily closing the harbor under the pretext of a collision between two large ships. They hoped that would buy them enough time to isolate all ships with Middle Eastern origin, especially those from Pakistan, and keep them out of the harbor until they could be inspected.

It wasn't a great plan, but it was the best they could come up with given the short notice.

Still . . . her military sixth sense told her she could be doing more.

She pressed a button on her desk and a moment later John Wright walked in through one of the side doors.

"Everything is happening real time, Madam President," he reported, reading from his iPad. "No more ships are being allowed into the harbor and we'll have the list of vessels and their origins within minutes. Then we can prioritize sending harbor pilots to each one, which is standard procedure to enter the harbor, but instead of going in, we'll steer them all out of the way. We've also deployed drones so we can have eyes over the region in the Situation Room. We should be heading down there now."

"There's one more thing, John."

Wright looked up from his tablet.

"Get me NAS Oceana on the line," she said, referring to the U.S. naval base in Virginia Beach.

"Ah, yes, of course. Anyone in particular?"

Crossing her arms, she nodded and said, "The commander of SEAL Team Six."

19

Start Spreading the News

He never could get used to the noise, even after living not far from here as a teenage orphan in a poor neighborhood that at first had denied him the education enjoyed by his country's upper social classes.

He was Pashtun, but he was also brilliant. His grades alone had earned him scholarships to the finest schools here and abroad. Becoming a metallurgist, he pursued a career in the emergent nuclear engineering program at Pakistan's Kahuta facility over three decades ago. There, Atiq crossed paths with Dr. Abdul Qadeer Khan, the force behind Pakistan's nuclear program, and became one of his understudies during the late 1990s.

In time, he'd married a beautiful Karachi woman named Maryam, and for a while, Atiq had been happy. But Allah had once more tested him when his young bride died during childbirth, leaving him alone again—though this time not completely. His scarred hands had cradled his newborn daughter, named in memory of the love of his life, as nurses wheeled her body away.

So Atiq had pushed on, day after day, accepting Allah's will with humility as his technical career blossomed under the guidance of Dr. Khan.

Atiq Gadai reminisced about the years under his mentor with affection. The people of Pakistan would always remember Dr. Khan as the father of their country's nuclear program. But to Atiq, he became not only his counselor and lifelong friend but also the father he had lost long ago to the flames in Pashtun.

Atiq's success in science led him to a revamp of the technical directorate of Pakistan's Inter-Services Intelligence network. He spent two decades modernizing the agency, dragging its old directors—the former ISI senior guard—kicking and screaming into the twenty-first century. He installed server centers, firewalls, high-speed lines, and encryption algorithms. He hired a new generation of officers to prepare the agency to do battle in the age of cyberspace while bolstering the human intelligence division. He even forged secret and controversial partnerships with terrorist organizations for the sake of intelligence gathering. In the process of turning the ISI into one of the finest intelligence networks in the world—second to none but the American CIA—he'd ascended to the highest seat in its leadership.

His technical skills and deep connection with Pakistan's nuclear program, combined with his position with the ISI and the relationships he had cultivated with ISIS, provided Atiq with a unique platform from which to architect his campaign of terror against America.

And it was his unbridled obsession to punish the West that had brought him here this evening, as he waited for his asset while sipping from a cup of Masala chai inside a private chamber in the rear of a bordello disguised as a massage parlor.

The locale was lost in the middle of the bustling shopping center known for its loud vendors, entertaining street performers, amazing local cuisine, and music shops. But it also offered after-dark companionship for lonely hearts, including those far from home.

Situated on the north end of the Pakistani capital, with easy access to four side streets and two wide avenues through myriad alleyways, the lively bazaar offered a safe place to vanish from the ever-resent American surveillance.

Neither foot agents nor drones could handle the hordes of people filling the backstreets and stores at this prime-time evening hour.

Although not a fan of the place, as it reminded him of the depravity of the West, he certainly understood its strategic value to keep his assets safe from predatory American eyes.

And one of those assets had just parted the beaded curtain of a room used regularly for the oldest profession in the world.

The beautiful Nadira stepped into the room. She was dressed in a traditional *shalwar kameez* dress that almost reached the floor, her head and shoulders respectfully draped with a black *dupatta*.

Her features captivated even a veteran spy and scientist like Atiq.

Nadira sat on the bed next to him and just regarded him in silence with those green eyes, a fine-manicured hand reaching for his, inter-lacing fingers.

He recalled the times he'd had her in the beginning, over ten years ago, consummating her training before deploying her to please the infidels. Unlike most honey-trapping agents, who'd required some level of cosmetic surgery, Nadira had been naturally beautiful, mak-ing her a favorite in his network.

For a moment he almost took her, but he controlled the urge. Nadira had comforted the Americans, and before that the Indians. Their filthy hands had forever spoiled her.

As beautiful and desirable as she looked sitting there, softly biting her lower lip, the twenty-nine-year-old had long become damaged goods.

"It is good to see you, *Baba*," said the Sunni Muslim of Pashtun ethnicity, using a tribal term of endearment for a father figure. "It has been a long time."

Atiq set the cup down and placed his other hand over hers, giving it a soft, lingering squeeze. "It has, my dear. But remember that you are doing Allah's work, even in a place like this."

Nadira was fluent in English and Urdu, as well as Pashto and Hindi—making her quite appealing to foreign dignitaries or visiting tribal chiefs. She dropped her gaze. "Yes, *Baba*. But it is difficult. The American soldiers at the embassy . . . they are not . . . gentle. Some-times I cannot walk after one of their sessions."

It truly pained him to think of someone as beautiful as his daughter in the hands of enemy soldiers. But they were at war, and war required sacrifice. This reality forced Nadira, and many others like her, into working here as well as paying visits to the American embassy.

"Soon, my dear. It will soon be over and you would have earned your rightful place in this world . . . and the next."

"Thank you, *Baba*."

"Now, tell me. What is it that required you to break protocol and request this meeting? Did you not trust the handler I assigned to you?"

She looked away for a moment, before gazing into his eyes. Her face still radiated the smooth glisten of youth in a profession that had a way of accelerating the aging process. Most honey-trappers were rel-egated to other duties by their early thirties.

Slowly leaning closer, she whispered, "Three hours ago, in the guest room at the embassy barracks, where the soldiers usually take their turns . . . and after they were finished with me, I overheard two men speaking in the hallway, just beyond the door."

"Soldiers?"

She shook her head. "They didn't sound like marines, no. They sounded older, but I couldn't see them without risking being spotted. But I heard them, and one told the other something he had just learned . . . something that was going to happen . . . in New York."

"New York?" Atiq hissed, inhaling deeply, unknowingly tightening his grip. "What about New York?"

She grimaced, obviously in pain. *"Baba* . . . it hurts."

He softened his hold, kissed the top of her hand, and managed a smile. "I'm very sorry, dear. Now tell me, what did you hear about New York?"

As Nadira spoke, Atiq clenched his jaw in silent anger, realizing there had to be a leak in his organization. Somewhere.

"You were wise to contact me directly," he said, forcing control into his words.

"Thank you, *Baba.*"

"Now, tell me, have you discussed this with anyone else?"

She pressed her lips together and slowly shook her head before replying, "No, *Baba.* I came directly to you."

"Are you completely certain? No one? Maybe you mentioned something to your handler?"

She shook her head more emphatically. "I *swear* to you, *Baba.* Just you."

"Okay," he said. "I believe you."

In a single and swift motion, Atiq struck her larynx using the edge of his hand with enough force to snap it.

Nadira whipped both hands to her crushed windpipe, lips parting as she tried to breathe, eyes widening in fear.

She tried to get up, but Atiq forced her back on the bed, a hand clutching her *dupatta*, forcing her head against the pillow while his other hand pressed down on her chest.

Nadira kicked her legs, parting the *shalwar kameez* as she thrashed over the sheets, revealing her silk-smooth skin, waxed to perfection.

"Don't fight it, my dear," he whispered, her wild stare fixed on him. "It will be over soon, and you will be in paradise."

She struggled for about a minute. Her skin turned shades lighter as she became lethargic, her eyes losing focus.

He waited until all movement ceased before pressing an ear against her chest.

Finally getting up, he calmly rearranged the *shalwar kameez*, covering her legs and draping the *dupatta* gracefully over her shoulders. He lowered her hands from her neck to her lap, leaving her eyes open, staring at paradise.

Taking a final look at his beautiful warrior of Islam, he whispered, "Allah welcomes you into His kingdom."

Five minutes later, Atiq was back in his limousine, rushing toward the ISI headquarters. A large complex of adobe structures amidst manicured lawns, gardens, and fountains, it resembled more a small university campus than the center of Pakistan's clandestine activities.

The driver cruised by the nondescript entrance adjacent to a hospital under blinding floodlights, past a dozen plainclothes officers, a series of gates, and soldiers accompanied by German shepherds. It finally stopped by the steps leading up to the central building, a tall structure in the middle of the well-lit campus.

Atiq raced up the steps, reaching the main entrance, where a guard opened a door for him. He dashed through, the soles of his dress shoes clicking on the marble floors, echoing hollowly in the round lobby beneath a massive ornate chandelier casting a yellowish glow.

"Dr. Gadai?" asked one of his young assistants, a woman younger than Nadira. "Is everything all right?"

Atiq waved her away. He had to get to his computer—had to send out a coded message.

Immediately.

Somehow the Americans knew that a ship carrying a nuclear device was heading into New York Harbor.

Somehow.

But he would worry about the leak later. At the moment, time was of the essence. Although Nadira did not hear a specific vessel named,

Atiq knew that the Americans would keep all incoming traffic from entering the harbor until it could be properly inspected.

He needed to warn Malik and activate the emergency protocol they had practiced for so long off the waters of Karachi.

Precisely for this kind of scenario.

20

Bismillah

SEAWISE GOLIATH. LOWER NEW YORK BAY

Malik should have listened to his inner voice, but he thought paranoia was simply getting the better of him as the ship moved toward his target. Slowly.

Too damned slowly.

They had spent the entire night on hold waiting for the harbor pilot, who had finally arrived at dawn—an hour ago.

He was a heavyset man in his late forties with a full head of dark hair, a blue jacket with the words SANDY HOOK PILOTS ASSOCIATION stenciled on its back, and an all-business assertiveness. It was obvious from the moment he came aboard that he was here to take command of the supertanker and guide it safely to its berth. And he intended to do so by the book. Giannotti and the two crewmen manning the bridge had readily relinquished control of the vessel.

Unfortunately, the harbor pilot had barely made any progress, explaining to Giannotti that the waters beyond the Verrazano Narrows separating the Lower and Upper New York Bay were experiencing excessive delays. Apparently there had been a collision between a cargo ship and a cruise ship a few hours ago that needed to be cleared out.

Until then, all ships—especially one as large as the *Goliath*—could not be allowed in the harbor area.

So Malik had waited patiently, forcing control while listening to the calm conversation between the pilot and Giannotti. Apparently, the Italian captain had done this many times and seemed quite familiar with the process.

But Malik's encrypted phone had just buzzed with a message from Atiq. The Americans were aware of a bomb on a ship heading into New York. However, it was unclear if they knew it was aboard the *Goliath*.

Malik read the message twice, deciding that the Americans probably didn't know which ship carried the weapon. Otherwise the Coast Guard cutters would have already attacked him. At least this explained why the harbor was temporarily closed to incoming traffic. The lie would buy the infidels the time to conduct some sort of inspection.

He considered his next move carefully while observing the captain and the harbor pilot as well as the two crewmen standing by the navigation equipment. None of them were armed—at least not overtly. But then again, weapons and protection were his responsibility as head of the security team.

Malik then wondered if the pilot or Giannotti had been notified of the existence of a bomb somewhere in the area. He guessed they probably were not aware yet, based on how business-as-usual they conducted themselves. And as head of security, Malik felt quite certain that the captain would have notified him already of any potential threat to the ship.

After reading the message from Atiq one more time, he decided he had one of two choices. He could allow the *Goliath* to remain in place and wait for an inspection team to come aboard, risking discovery of the weapon. He was still too far from his target—and in the middle of this damned bay—for a detonation to be of any significance. Or . . .

Making his decision, the ISI operative reached for his two-way radio, pressed it against his lips, and whispered the emergency signal to his team: *"Bismillah." In the name of God.*

Zayd swung his head toward him, eyes narrowed, and nodded once.

Malik returned the nod, reaching for the 9mm Beretta tucked in his jeans, pressed against the small of his back. Zayd did the same.

With practiced synchronization, his number one brought the weapon around and fired into the heads of the two crewmen. Lacking silencers, the guns made a very loud noise. Inside a small metal space like a tanker's bridge, the reports were deafening, masking the sounds of bullets tearing into flesh.

With ease born of years of practice, Malik aligned the surprised harbor pilot in the Beretta's sights. Squeezing the trigger, he fired one round to the sternum and one to the head. Then he turned to the captain, who was frozen in fear, and did the same. The smell of blood and bile combined with gunpowder was overpowering.

"Get everyone to their stations!" he shouted, kicking the dead pilot aside while taking control of the bridge, pointing the bow straight to the center of the Verrazano Narrows, still a half mile away, while reaching for the throttle control. The emergency plan, which they had practiced in Karachi to the point of obsession, assumed that they would have made it at least past the Verrazano Narrows before activating it.

So, not that far off our drills, he thought as Zayd barked orders on his radio to their team dispersed around the ship. A moment later, he received confirmation that the engine room was also under his control.

Malik breathed deeply and focused on the instrumentation in front of him. The older ship he had used for training in Karachi was equipped with an EOT—engine order telegraphy—a round dial twelve inches in diameter with an indicator on its face for the pilot to communicate power settings to engine room personnel. This modern marvel, however, had a direct throttle control that didn't require intervention from the engine room. But it was still critical that his men controlled the engine room to prevent sabotage.

He steadily transitioned the handle from STOP to FULL AHEAD.

The tanker trembled as the massive engines responded with a growl that reverberated through the superstructure, transferring their monstrous torque to the stern screws. Biting into the cold waters, they achieved the desired revolutions in less than a minute, thrusting the ship forward.

Malik stared at the graphical information painted on the flat-screen displays. He scanned the engines' parameters, from RPM and cylinder head temperature to oil pressure and fuel consumption rates, as the digital speed indicator inched up.

The massive hull sliced through the bay. It kicked up a hell of a wake while building the momentum he would need when word got out about the runaway tanker.

"The Coast Guard!" shouted Zayd, pointing to the distant cutters. "They are turning toward us!"

"Just make sure the men are ready!" Malik yelled back while fixing his attention on what lay ahead. A row of tugboats raced to block his way just beyond the Verrazano Narrows.

The tanker achieved ten knots and continued climbing, its massive wake reaching a dozen feet high, wreaking havoc on smaller boats in the bay and pushing larger ships dangerously close to each other. Even the pair of white Coast Guard cutters roughly a mile and a half behind him seemed to have difficulty managing the storm-size swells while trying to gather speed.

"Everyone is in position!" Zayd informed him as one of their men arrived, hauling a .50-caliber M2 Browning machine gun and a backpack of ammunition from their supply room.

It took them less than a minute to set it up on a tripod by the front of the bridge with a clear view of the airspace over the bow and to either side. The initial shots would have to go through the large windows. The location provided the perfect vantage point to fend off any frontal attacks—at least for the minutes it would take the supertanker to cover the required distance.

Zayd thanked his assistant and ordered him back to his post on the starboard side, armed with a similar weapon plus a pair of RPGs.

Thirteen knots and climbing.

Malik narrowed his gaze at the tugboats blocking his way and slowly shook his head. It was a noble effort, but they didn't stand a chance against the colossal tanker measuring over fourteen hundred feet in length and displacing close to a half billion tons.

Atiq had explained that it was all in the physics. The product of mass times velocity equaled momentum, and as the supertanker reached fifteen knots, it became virtually unstoppable.

The tugboat captains must have realized the futility of their effort and tried to get out of the way, but not fast enough.

The collision, albeit loud, barely shook the tanker, which didn't even drop a knot in forward speed.

He watched the surreal sight of a tugboat completely out of the water, almost in slow motion, its port side crushed and its propellers still spinning. It struck the water upside down in an explosion of water and foam somewhere off to the *Goliath*'s starboard, vanishing beneath the towering waves.

Another tugboat floated away cut nearly in half, its crew jumping off the stern and frantically trying to swim away from the supertanker. The massive wake nearly capsized a dozen other tugboats fighting to turn their bows into incoming waves now almost twenty feet high. Two merchant vessels off his starboard collided, their hulls crushing. Then container ships struck each other, their cargos shifting over their decks. Alarms echoed across the harbor.

It was havoc. Madness.

Malik lost them all in the boiling wake as he maneuvered past them, his eyes finding the Statue of Liberty off the port bow . . . right next to a pair of incoming helicopters.

"Eleven o'clock! Two helicopters!" he shouted at Zayd, who swung the M2 in that direction.

The choppers swept over the waters, climbing just enough to clear the bow, their black silhouettes sharp against the morning sun.

"Now, Zayd!"

His feet spread apart for balance, the Pashtun-born warrior squeezed the trigger.

The bridge trembled from the kinetic energy of the weapon as it shattered the glass, spraying the incoming helicopters with a wall of 50mm rounds at a distance of five hundred feet. Ejected casings littered the floor as Zayd kept up the pressure. His body trembled to the rhythm of the heavy machine gun as he used tracers to adjust his aim, centering it on the closest target.

The lead chopper caught fire and dropped from view as the second one cut hard left and climbed out of range.

"Where are those cutters?"

"About a mile behind us!" Zayd replied, reloading the weapon as gunfire exploded somewhere astern, probably another warrior engaging the helicopter or other approaching ships.

An NYC Harbor Police boat, roughly the size of a tugboat, fought the waves head on, coming dangerously close to the *Goliath*'s starboard bow, before turning on a parallel course. Officers aboard pulled out handguns and a couple of rifles and began to fire at the bridge.

A flash of light next to the bridge marked one of his men retaliating with an RPG. It propelled a 105mm thermobaric warhead to a speed of 294 meters per second, striking the police ship in under two seconds.

The vessel went up in orange and red flames, engulfing its occupants. Some managed to jump overboard, before floating away in the tanker's wake.

Malik looked away, returning his attention to the speed indicator as it settled on seventeen knots. He made his final throttle adjustment, pushing the ship from FULL AHEAD to FLANK SPEED, the highest power setting. It squeezed a few extra knots from the already overworked engines. In doing so he forced the RPM dangerously close to the red.

But it wouldn't be for long.

The tanker accelerated to its maximum structural speed of twenty-one knots in another minute. The wake now reached almost twenty-five feet, smashing moored vessels and spreading mayhem in all piers in New York Harbor.

He pointed the bow straight for the tip of Manhattan, still over two miles away. The Coast Guard fast response cutters could reach speeds of twenty-eight knots, meaning they would be almost on top of him just as he reached the island—assuming they could hold their flank speeds through his wake.

But cutters were also armed with missiles and guns that they could fire at any moment.

Malik silently prayed that the Coast Guard captains would refrain from using their weapons with so many ships and the surrounding shorelines packed with docked vessels, piers, warehouses, and lots of tall buildings. And especially against a supertanker loaded with so much crude oil.

It will be close, he thought as the skyline of New York City grew through the jagged edges of the bridge's broken windows.

It will be very close.

21

Unstoppable

President Vaccaro, as well as everyone in the Situation Room, stared at the large screen on the back wall with disbelief.

The supertanker cruised across the harbor, crushing everything in its way while triggering massive waves as the Coast Guard tried to catch up.

"They're too far away, John," Vaccaro said, looking at the cutters' relative speed as captured by the high-resolution cameras aboard a pair of circling drones, which unfortunately were not armed with Hellfire missiles.

"An armed drone will be within range in five minutes. F-22s in ten," he replied while reading on his iPad the update provided from the Pentagon.

Vaccaro shook her head.

That's too late.

But even if they could get there in time and fire on the *Goliath*, she was having a hard time wrapping her head around the ecological disaster that would create. Destroying a supertanker and causing it to spill its load of crude oil in the harbor would trigger an environmental catastrophe.

The *Exxon Valdez* disaster in 1989 in Prince William Sound, Alaska, involved a spillage in the vicinity of half a million barrels of oil. By comparison, the report that Wright had shared with the staff indicated that the *Seawise Goliath* carried over *three million* barrels of crude oil in its colossal tanks.

The situation certainly called for a more surgical approach to the problem.

Turning to Wright, who was sitting next to the secretary of the navy, she asked, "Where are my SEALs?"

22

Patterson

They came in from the south, rotor blades reverberating, echoing across endless miles of beaches. Their powerful downwashes kicked up a sandstorm that enveloped the picturesque Ocean Avenue while cruising at their maximum-rated speed of just under 160 knots, or around 180 miles per hour. The airspace for five hundred miles had already been cleared of all traffic except for these and any others needed for this operation.

Lieutenant Commander Jay Patterson headed the assault in the lead MH-60M/L Black Hawk Defensive Armed Penetrator. The fortified escort and fire support delivery vehicle was designed for Special Ops forces such as his Red Squadron from the U.S. Naval Special Warfare Development Group, or DEVGRU, the official name of SEAL Team Six out of NAS Oceana, Virginia Beach.

Two Black Hawks followed his bird as they hugged the shoreline in tight formation under the confused gaze of hundreds of commuters. In five miles, Ocean Avenue would turn inland shortly before it reached the Gateway National Recreation Area, also known as Sandy Hook.

Minutes ago the *Seawise Goliath* had identified itself by breaking ranks from the rest of the merchant ships still holding for inspection crews.

Somehow, in spite of all of the precautions taken by Port Authority to avoid spooking the terrorists, the supertanker and its millions of barrels of crude oil had now become a weapon of mass destruction.

Even if there isn't a bomb aboard, he thought, glancing at the other two Black Hawks. Each carried a team of veteran SEALs armed with enough weapons and munitions to start a small revolution. He was confident and a little apprehensive, as all leaders were before going into combat.

Was this the right plan?

Was there enough rehearsal?

Did they have luck and the angels on their side?

Patterson narrowed his gaze while staring out the windshield.

The hell with luck.

SEALs made their *own* luck and their *own* odds, and he never bet against himself or his guys. This was what they did, violent and aggressive action, and they did it better than anyone he had ever seen.

Following the call from the president, Patterson had selected his team quickly but also carefully. He chose those who worked well with each other and him, operators with multiple tours in the scariest corners of the globe. Patterson, barely thirty-five but already a veteran, had most of his team alongside him in the last thirteen years of war. Together they had fought in the peaks of Afghanistan and Pakistan and in the sands of Iraq—plus a handful of even darker destinations that would forever be classified. But the places hardly mattered anymore, only the guys, and that most had survived.

Patterson had been a manager of violence. He had set up ambushes and also fallen into them. He had torn the enemy into pieces and had also carried out his dead and wounded. He had fought, blasted, kicked, punched, stabbed, and incinerated his marks with professional precision—all in the name of the United States of America, its war on terror, and the teams . . . always the teams.

The SEALs, like every good unit, took those who made it through a selection process as brutal as the six-month-long infamous Basic Underwater Demolition/SEAL school (BUD/S) at Coronado, California. They were forged in pain and determination, bonded together as only survivors can be . . . for all time. The BUD/S's stories were legendary and all true. No sleep for six days while conducting the most grueling and torturous physical activities, which only former students of the course could devise. And the six-day-without-sleep marathon was just the final test. Getting to that week was actually work. Those fortunate enough to make it through BUD/S were then assigned to SEAL teams, where they had to earn their sacred Trident. Four years on the teams and then they could volunteer for SEAL Team Six, where they had to go through another six months of qualification courses that evaluated and dissected every second of their lives under near-constant combat conditions.

After what seemed like an endless string of operations over the course of a dozen years, Patterson thought he had seen everything. But as he checked his plan and his watch for the hundredth time, something made him wonder if he was about to face a whole new level of bad guy.

"Two minutes," he said into his mike.

He shifted his gaze to the incoming bay as they pushed north at thirty feet, trying to remain out of sight for as long as possible while approaching the HVT, a supertanker sailing under the Liberian flag.

"Red, be advised the target vessel has broken through tugboat barrier. NYPD helicopters and ships have been ineffective. Coast Guard cutters are in pursuit. Drones and F-22s are in the air."

"Roger," Paterson replied. "Red's two minutes out."

Damn, he thought as they cruised over Sandy Hook and entered the Lower New York Bay. *This is what we do.* It was their job. It was what they'd signed up for, trained for, and when they admitted it . . . lived for.

"There, sir!" said the pilot while pointing toward the Verrazano Narrows Bridge.

Patterson knelt in between the pilot and copilot and spotted the runaway tanker well past the bridge with two Coast Guard cutters on its ass.

"That's one big son of a bitch," Patterson yelled. Damn good thing they practiced on these and that the design of these monsters was fairly common. When the bell rang on something this short notice, it was truly come as you are, ready or not.

"Big and slow, sir!" replied the pilot.

Patterson grinned, patted the pilot on the back, and said, "Thanks for the ride."

"Roger that," responded the pilot as they overtook the cutters and dropped below the Verrazano-Narrows Bridge, packed with morning commuters.

Patterson took it all in as the massive stern nearly filled the chopper's windscreen a minute later. The ship was big all right but not slow, dashing through the bay at full speed. It produced an enormous wake, pounding the shore and tossing ships around, prompting at least a dozen collisions already as large merchant vessels were entangled all over the damn place.

It was wreaking havoc on a grand scale, and that was just the tip of this massive steel iceberg.

And it was headed straight for the southern end of New York City and its hundreds of buildings, including Freedom Tower. Its sleek shape dominated the skyline, towering above all other high-rises under a clear sky.

Patterson cringed.

Not again.

That's when he spotted two men against the yellow railing on the tanker's stern, training their large machine guns on them and opening fire.

The pilot released a volley of 70mm Hydra rockets and followed up with the M230 30mm chain gun mounted on the portside stub wing, tearing metal, wood, and flesh.

The Hydras hurtled toward the tanker's stern. And a second later, it all went up in flames, consuming the figures and their muzzle flashes in a soaring wall of fire.

Nice, thought Patterson, as the guns trained on the ship's bridge.

So far all was going as planned, which the SEAL commander knew from experience never lasted long.

23

Twisting Metal

SEAWISE GOLIATH. NEW YORK BAY

The explosions triggered alarms all over the console, along with dozens of blinking lights. But Malik only cared about the digital speed indicator, which continued displaying twenty-one knots.

Nothing else really mattered as long as they maintained their drive toward the target, now less than a half mile away.

"We lost the astern team!" reported Zayd. "Black Hawks!"

About time they showed up, he thought, well aware of the type of Special Forces aboard those helicopters. And he was certain that drones and even fighter jets would soon join them.

Assuming they have the balls to fire on us, he thought, hoping that the massive oil spill on land and on water that would result from crashing the tanker into the island would make them think twice about unleashing their ordnance on them.

Locking the wheel in place as they rapidly approached Battery Park, he looked at Zayd. "Time to go belowdecks!"

Zayd barked orders on the radio while Malik ran to the rear of the bridge and went through the bulkhead. He raced down a long flight of stairs with Zayd in tow, before reaching a landing two levels under the bridge. They met up with the men in charge of the device, which they had already secured to the middle of the platform. A moment later the last three warriors joined them.

"Brace for impact!" shouted Malik.

"Alhamdulillah!" replied his team as they secured themselves and the weapon against steel columns and railings.

The tanker suddenly began to tremble with the sound of twisting metal, but not from an attack. The vibrations came from below as the double hull began to scrape the bay's bottom.

24

Black Gold

NEW YORK BAY

Commander Patterson pushed the fast rope off the side of the Black Hawk as the tanker's bow stabbed the waterfront in an explosion of steel, concrete, and water.

Crude oil began to gush over the bay almost immediately, and also across the park, resembling a black tsunami, staining everything in its path.

The *Goliath*'s momentum shoved almost a third of the superstructure over the ferry terminal, crushing boats, benches, restrooms, and trees. It drenched everything in shiny oil, before coming to a stop near the middle of Battery Park.

25

Judgment Call

WASHINGTON, D.C.

The scene looked straight out of some action movie, only this was real.

Very fucking real.

And it was happening on her damn watch.

The massive ship had run aground, crashing right through the middle of the park, tearing its hull and breaching its tanks. Oil cascaded out of *Titanic*-like gashes from the bow to amidships just as the Black Hawks hovered by the bridge.

"F-22s and drones in position," reported Wright.

"But we don't recommend firing, Madam President," added Rear Admiral Paul Yates, one of the Joint Chiefs of Staff. He sat among the other chiefs along the right side of the Situation Room. Yates was a former Hornet pilot with multiple tours in Iraq and Afghanistan before his current Pentagon appointment. He was a slim man with a slim face and steely eyes. He stretched a finger at the copious amounts of oil raging across the park and flooding surrounding streets like rapids, sweeping people and debris. "It'll be worse than Kuwait," he added.

Vaccaro knew the chief was right, of course. Who could forget those nightmarish oil fires set by Saddam Hussein's retreating army during the First Gulf War?

The time for Hellfire missiles and other large munitions had passed. Firing now would only result in torching the tip of Manhattan and all of the hundreds of people smeared in the spill, haphazardly slipping and falling while trying to get away.

But then again, if there was indeed a nuclear weapon aboard, then destroying the ship, even if it incinerated everyone in sight plus a couple of city blocks, was the lesser of the evils.

Damned if you do and damned if you don't.

Making her decision—and fully realizing that for the rest of her life she would be second-guessed by the world—President Vaccaro said, "Let's give our boys a chance down there. Send them in."

26

The Only Easy Day Was Yesterday

SEAWISE GOLIATH. LOWER MANHATTAN

Patterson stared at the surreal image for a moment, amazed that the collision had not ignited the crude oil. Then he got the green light to start the assault.

His men were tough, but as he stared beyond the side door of the hovering craft, it truly looked as if the devil had gripped the tip of the island and turned it into his damn playground.

Get on with it, Jay, he thought, jumping off the side and sliding down the fast rope using a special seat harness. He braked with his gloved hands in a towel-wringing motion just before his boots hit the deck a hundred feet from the bridge.

Shifting out of the way just as the next SEAL dropped from the hovering chopper, Patterson raised his Heckler & Koch MP7A1 submachine gun.

He led the way, the weapon on single shot, his trained mind ignoring the chaos on Battery Park as police and firemen tried desperately to deal with the mess.

Images of his wife and newborn son flashed momentarily into the front of his mind, but were immediately overcome by the business at hand.

He charged toward the closest bulkhead and headed belowdecks.

Malik heard the enemy approaching—heard their boots clanking loudly against the metal steps as they got near.

Let them come, he thought, holding the remote control in his hand while staring at the faces of his brothers, of the men who had fought alongside him in so many battles. They had readily accepted the chance to fight with him one final time, taking the battle to the heart of the enemy.

"Put down your weapons, brothers!" he commanded as he squeezed the trigger, activating the short countdown. The device responded with a series of beeps. "There is no longer a need to fight back."

Turning to the incoming noise of men beyond the bulkhead, he added, "The end is near."

Patterson raced down a passageway, reached another bulkhead, went through, and came face-to-face with the terrorists gathered in a circle, holding hands. Their weapons were on the ground, next to a large trunk.

One of them turned around and took a few steps toward him, leaving the circle while looking him in the eye. He was a large man, maybe as tall as Patterson, with thick brows and intense dark eyes. He smiled as he lifted his right hand, which held some kind of device.

"No, you don't, asshole."

The red dot shifting to the middle of the big man's chest, the Navy SEAL fired.

Malik stared at the infidel and smiled for an instant before a barrage of bullets swept the metal platform on which he stood, ripping through his chest and cutting down his team.

But it didn't matter. Nothing mattered anymore as he felt his legs give and he collapsed next to his slaughtered team. Most had fallen over the trunk, hugging their ticket to paradise.

As the gunfire subsided, he continued hearing the very faint but very delightful beeps, increasing in frequency, marking the final seconds of the countdown.

Bleeding out, lying on his back facing myriad pipes and wires, Malik let his thoughts turn south, to the Gulf of Mexico, to another supertanker destined to make history. And through the pain and the shivering cold sweeping through his broken body, he saw her face . . . one final time.

"What the hell was that, Jay?" asked one of his men while Patterson lowered his submachine gun, smoke coiling from its muzzle. "Why did they drop their weapons?"

He ignored him and approached the pile of terrorists, including the one who had smiled at him. Blood trickled from his ears and nose as he shuddered on the metal floor. His eyes were steady, focused on the tubes, valves, and cables layering the ceiling. His lips moved, as if he were praying.

"Not really sure," Patterson replied, kneeling next to the dying man, who kept his gaze straight ahead and continued whispering shit he couldn't understand.

"Crazy fuckers," he added, taking a gadget from his hand that resembled the keyless remote control for his Chevy truck back at Virginia Beach.

"What did you take from him?"

Patterson looked at it again. "A remote control . . . probably Bluetooth."

And that's when he heard the faint beeps coming from the direction of the small mound of dead terrorists, whom he now realized had fallen right on their weapons and also over some sort of large trunk.

"That metallic trunk . . . is that what I think it is?" the same soldier asked.

"Oh, shit," Patterson replied, as the beeps merged into a steady high-pitched tone—as images of his wife and son flooded back into his mind before the world caught fire around him.

27

Blank Screen

WASHINGTON, D.C.

They had followed the SEAL team's action through the cameras mounted on their helmets, trembling images painted in hues of green that in some bizarre way resembled some video game.

They had been displayed on the large screen at the end of the Situation Room while the TVs on the side walls provided views from the circling drones as well as from several street webcams. Images of Battery Park from surrounding buildings and light posts had shown the *Goliath* spilling oil onto the tip of the island and across the harbor. The slick mess spread with ferocity down streets and avenues, splashing up steps, draining into subway entrances.

People smeared in black ran, fell, and were trampled by the stampeding crowd. Cars slid across the slippery streets, crashing into each other and over pedestrians.

Vaccaro froze. The images on every screen were difficult to process individually, much less all at once. The SEALs opened fire inside the tanker. Sirens blared outside. Incoming emergency vehicles— police cars, fire trucks, and EMS—rushed to the scene, stalling when reaching the sheet of crude oil. Tires spun in place, vehicles whirled out of control, colliding against each other. People ran and fell. Some were even overrun.

And it was through this chaos, portrayed simultaneously and in high definition, that Vaccaro heard the words that would forever haunt her.

"That metallic trunk . . . is that what I think it is?"

"Oh, shit."

Right before every screen in the Situation Room went blank.

28

The Unthinkable

BATTERY PARK. LOWER MANHATTAN

The explosive charge detonated, accelerating the uranium-235 hollow projectile to a speed of just over one thousand feet per second toward its target.

The combined mass became critical and triggered a chain reaction.

The fission event heated the surrounding air to an incomprehensible temperature—nearly a million degrees Fahrenheit. It melted through layers of steel while releasing a blast of invisible radiation in the initial microseconds.

Milliseconds later, a rapidly expanding fireball exceeding ten thousand degrees engulfed the supertanker and propagated north from Battery Park to Rector Street. It vaporized everything in its path, including the hovering Black Hawks and even the drones circling a thousand feet above them.

Tens of thousands of souls on the crowded tip of the island were incinerated within the first second, followed by an airwave overpressure greater than twenty psi that leveled buildings in the half-mile-radius blast zone. It evaporated the Financial District and propagated north. It converted people, cars, street vendor carts, garbage cans, traffic lights, scaffolds, and even entire sections of buildings into lethal missiles shooting uptown.

The pressure dropped below ten psi as it demolished Liberty Street and down to five psi by the time it reached Fulton Street, but windows were shattered all the way up to Tribeca and Chinatown.

There were no street survivors within the five-psi contour below Fulton Street, and the shock wave triggered the collapse of many subway tunnels, trapping tens of thousands of commuters.

To the south, the blast engulfed dozens of vessels in the crowded harbor, including the Coast Guard cutters, burning everything within a quarter of a mile. It crushed ferries and tugboats with biblical force, capsizing ships as far as a mile out.

At the same time, gamma radiation from the nuclear detonation stripped electrons from atoms in the atmosphere over Lower Manhattan. The Compton effect ionized the air, creating an EMP pulse. Albeit relatively weak because the detonation occurred five stories above ground level instead of at high altitude, it was still powerful enough to induce very high voltages in nearby electronic conductors. Frying all unshielded high-tech gear in its vicinity, it also knocked out the power grid in a two-mile radius.

Commuters on all nearby streets and bridges spared by the fire and the shock wave came to a halt as their cars' electronics ceased to function, along with phones, two-way radios, stoplights, and even pacemakers. Subways came to a stop all the way up to Central Park while underground stations and tunnels that had not collapsed fell into the twilight of emergency lighting.

The groundburst deposited an average of twelve calories of heat per square centimeter by the time it reached Liberty Street, dropping to ten calories by Fulton Street. It inflicted third-degree burns on the bare skin of those who survived the shock wave north of the five-psi contour. Many people exposed to this heat didn't immediately realize they were being fried alive because the burns extended throughout the layers of skin, destroying the pain nerves.

The intense heat triggered superfires similar to those experienced in Hiroshima within its ten-calorie radius, igniting highly combustible materials, dry leaves, newspapers, drapes, clothes, and even hair. Birds burned in midair, fizzled, and vanished. Paint bubbled off many exterior surfaces. Countless rivets popped off metal structures. Asphalt softened in the streets, melting tires and ripping off shoes as survivors tried to run away.

Along with the thermal flash and the air blast, a deadly dose of five hundred rem propagated radially all the way to Liberty Street, dissipating to safe levels by Fulton Street. The invisible wave of radiation silently contaminated the bodies of everyone on the surface still alive. Between 50 and 90 percent of them would be dead from acute effects within a few hours to a week.

About six seconds later, the closest survivors around Fulton Street, already in shock from the blast and burns, were showered with falling glass from dozens of skyscrapers.

Secondary explosions from the deposited heat ignited vehicles' gas tanks everywhere, creating a seemingly endless series of explosions up and down streets.

Broken gas mains erupted below ground, blasting through the pavement like geysers, feeding the combustion materials in buildings and on the street. Infernos sparked above and below ground. Flames propagated down many subway tunnels, hungry for oxygen, incinerating trapped commuters, before bursting through manholes and ventilation shafts.

Close to 40 percent of the initial survivors between Fulton and Chambers Streets—tens of thousands who happened to be either indoors or managed to endure in the streets—perished in the following minutes from exposure to heat and smoke inhalation.

Radioactive debris, mixed with three million tons of fossilized fuel and other vaporized materials from the groundburst, rose in a surreal mushroom cloud into the atmosphere over the tip of Manhattan.

Luckily, the prevailing high-velocity westerly winds in the jet stream carried most of the fallout out over the Atlantic, sparing the island from a radioactive shower that would have turned the area into a quarantine zone for years—if not longer.

29
Ray

LOWER MANHATTAN

One minute prior to detonation, NYPD Sergeant Ray Kazemi had been standing by the front grille of Car 340, parked at the corner of Broadway and Cortland. He was waiting for his young partner, Jenny

Marshall, who insisted on getting a latte. She was a good cop but had expensive coffee taste. They had been partnered now for six months, made seventeen arrests, and had each other's backs. She also had a thing for him. But Ray ignored her. He was already on his second marriage: the first to the U.S. Army and the second to the NYPD. Besides, Jenny, for all her good qualities and great looks, was just too damn young for him.

Ray had joined the force after serving in the army for four years, three on his own enlistment and one being involuntarily extended when the war in Iraq was not going so well. But he did his job and came home with no missing parts, some nightmares, and post-traumatic stress. All in all he got it done.

Ray missed the action, the friendship, and the counting on his buddies. He missed the discipline and the sense of purpose and pride that came with serving his nation, but most importantly, never letting his fellow soldiers down.

He was no braver than anyone else; he just did his job. So applying for the NYPD seemed to be exactly what he needed to do. His service record and ethnicity—he was a half-Italian and half-Lebanese Muslim and spoke both languages as well as his native English—made him a great candidate for one of the best police departments in the world.

Ray felt the vibrations on the street, followed by distant screams coming up Broadway. As he turned south, spotting the distant commotion of people running uptown, he heard the police radio announcing a "ten thirty-three in progress" in Battery Park.

Explosive device or other such threat.

He stared in disbelief at the oncoming mob. It reminded him of the leading edge of a marathon race, but faster and far more chaotic. They rushed north of Cedar Street and reached Liberty Street, just a block away from him. People screamed, trampling each other, running in between cars, on sidewalks. Some cut into buildings or disappeared down subway entrances. The sight prompted everyone on his block to also start running uptown.

What the fuck?

Ray shouted at Jenny, who was still in the coffee shop. She looked up at him and, having heard the same warning on her radio, headed for the door.

As people ran past him, some asking what was happening downtown, Ray's police radio came on again, now announcing a "ten seventy-one."

Citywide emergency.

Neither had received the training, nor seen any sci-fi movie or Internet video game, that could have prepared them for the noise, earth-splitting vibrations, heat, and sound waves that were about to envelop them.

The difference was instincts, fear, and a little luck.

"Get back inside!" Ray yelled at Jenny as she walked out of the coffee shop.

Then he shouted, as loud as he could, "Everyone get down!" before diving between the patrol car and the sidewalk—the latter being about ten inches tall with a large drainage grate.

Jenny came out anyway, looked up, and was no more.

Ray turned his face toward the gutter, fingers clutching the heavy grate. He slid his left foot in the space beneath the grate and the sidewalk, anchoring himself while feeling Car 340 leave as if on a freight train, noise and all.

30

Crisis Response

WASHINGTON, D.C.

She had already made the single presidential phone call that set in motion the FEMA mechanism designed to deal with national emergencies.

Unfortunately, the mechanism was never conceived to handle the magnitude of what had just happened in New York.

"What else do we have besides our standing operations procedure for what just happened?" President Vaccaro asked her stunned audience in the Situation Room, where TV screens now showed images of her worst nightmare, fed by the news crews atop buildings in Midtown Manhattan, Newark, Brooklyn, and Staten Island, as well as a new fleet of drones circling the unimaginable.

Lower Manhattan was engulfed in dark smoke, pulsating with fire and explosions. Nearby chemical and petroleum facilities and other manufacturing operations also appeared severely damaged. Releasing hazardous materials into the air and water, numerous wrecked plants compounded the disaster.

Vaccaro stared at her staff and then at the screen, where one of the news crews panned on Freedom Tower, standing tall, its sleek shape apparently surviving the blast, protruding above the haze and destruction. In the background, the Brooklyn Bridge also appeared undamaged, along with the Manhattan and Williamsburg Bridges.

She continued, her military background keeping her ramrod straight. "What else is there besides the standard United States Crisis Response Plan? Excuse me, everyone, but this is my first nuclear explosion on American soil, so someone here please tell me we have something besides the traditional plan for dealing with natural disasters. I need a workable and ready-to-execute plan to tackle *that*." She pointed at the screen and added, "And New York needs it right now."

John Wright pointed to Lisa Jacobson, the national security advisor, who began with, "Madam President, we have had two nuclear events—"

"Wait," she said. "This has to change. Information and decisions that have to be made at this desk and in this room have to get here faster and without every one of some two thousand of you and your staffs touching it. I know what just happened; tell me what I do *not* know and then recommend to me what I—what *we* have to do about what you just said. Ladies and gentlemen, there is only one wrong answer . . . that we do *nothing* besides the standard response already in flight . . . Now, please continue."

Clearing her throat, Lisa said, "Two events: one in the mountains at Bagram and one on the island of Manhattan. We now know that this wasn't just ISIS but that the Pakistani government—at least at some level—had a direct involvement in both. We are recommending that you talk directly to Prime Minister Korai, tell him of your decision, and send him the video of one of our missile launches. Tell him how the missiles would be directed and when they could arrive. We further recommend that you hold a national press conference and announce your decision and inform the American people what we know and what we are doing about it. Then your next step should be to fly directly to NYC and as close to ground zero as possible without wearing a full protection suit. The country—hell the *world*—needs Churchill, Roosevelt, Kennedy, Golda Meir, and George Patton all at once and right now."

The director of national intelligence began to speak and Vaccaro cut him off as well and said, "Mr. Director, no hedging, no caveating, and *please*, no slides."

Once the president had listened yet again to a series of what had happened, a little of what will happen, and some other insipid noise about possible countermeasures and reactions, she leaned over to Wright and said, "Let's talk, and bring Lisa, please."

As the door closed in the small office next to the Situation Room and the clear glass partition fogged at the press of a button, the president turned to both and said, "Okay, let's try this: I want to talk directly to whomever provided this information as soon as you can arrange it."

"Yes, Madam President," Lisa replied. "His name is Bill Gorman, station chief in Islamabad."

"Good," Vaccaro said. "Also, while I'm considering having a discussion with Prime Minister Korai, given the intelligence we received, I also need a back channel into his government. Let's bring Tristan into our task force with no name." Tristan Lavastede was the United States ambassador to the United Nations.

Wright made a face.

"What is it, John?"

"Well . . . last I heard he was at the U.N. complex . . . in New York."

"Then *find* him and get him here . . . now."

"Right away," Wright replied.

Vaccaro stretched an index finger toward the door. "I'm going back in there and we're going to make some hard decisions."

Before long, on the Situation Room's large briefing screen, center stage in bold and capital letters set to Arial 18, it read:

DECLARE MARTIAL LAW ACROSS THE NATION.

TEMPORARY SUSPENSION OF SPECIFIC CONSTITUTIONAL RIGHTS.

CLOSE ALL PORTS AND INSPECT ALL SHIPS WITHIN 100 MILES OF EITHER COAST.

GROUND ALL DOMESTIC AIR TRAFFIC FOR THE NEXT 24 HOURS. ONLY MILITARY AND RESCUE OPERATIONS WILL BE APPROVED BY THE FAA.

PLANES ORIGINATING FROM THE MIDDLE EAST ARE TO BE DIVERTED AWAY FROM AMERICAN AIRSPACE, PREFERABLY TO THEIR POINT OF ORIGIN—ANYWHERE BUT HERE.

THE NATIONAL GUARD AND THE ARMY WILL NOW BE FEDER-ALIZED TO ASSIST LOCAL, STATE, AND FEDERAL AGENCIES. IT INCLUDES AUGMENTING BORDER PATROL AND TSA AT SELECTED AIRPORTS AND OTHER PORTS OF ENTRY, AS WELL AS AT MAJOR CITIES.

RIOTS AND LOOTING WILL NOT BE TOLERATED. THE NATIONAL GUARD, THE ARMY, AND STATE AND LOCAL LAW ENFORCEMENT ARE UNDER WHITE HOUSE ORDERS TO ENFORCE THE MARTIAL LAW AND USE ANY AMOUNT OF FORCE REQUIRED—INCLUDING DEADLY—TO MAINTAIN THE PEACE.

The last bullet earned her several stares, which she ignored before turning to the secretary of defense and asking, "Where is the strike package for Pakistan?"

Grandville leaned forward and said, "Madam President, I received the request from John last night . . . and, well, the information gathered by my Defense Intelligence Agency over the wire contradicts the intel in the CIA brief. We intercepted an encrypted message indicating that ISIS broke into a Pakistani warehouse and stole five hundred pounds of weapons-grade uranium three months ago. So I wanted to talk with you before making recommendations about attacking someone who should be treated as an ally until proven otherwise. Remember that just a few days ago we deployed a team from the EPA to Pakistan to help clean the radioactive debris that reached their borders from Bagram."

Vaccaro stood, well aware of the long-standing disagreements between the CIA and its military counterpart, the DIA.

Trouble was, over the past decade the DIA had allocated more of its budget to high-tech espionage than to traditional human intelligence, including its expensive server farms in Ohio. It lacked the quality of officers in this situation that the CIA possessed, namely Bill Gorman and his assets gathering the kind of intelligence that would be missed by even the most sophisticated algorithms.

On top of that, nothing bothered the military spooks more than being outshined by their civilian counterparts.

The president said in a monotone, quiet, and yet penetrating voice, "Mr. Secretary, that was *not* a request. Now please leave the room and have your deputy take over."

Everyone stopped, looked at the visibly shocked Grandville, then President Vaccaro, and down at their navels, and did so almost in unison. But that would not do justice to the impact of what had just happened.

Vaccaro understood the impact. This was not her first firing or bloodletting. She had to fire a few soldiers during her military days, and civilians as a senator. There was no question that firing a sitting secretary of defense in front of the assembled staff was unprecedented. But the point had to be made. She was sensing from the beginning of this crisis that her staff, in fact the country if not the world, were not taking this seriously enough.

Two nuclear events, both now with Pakistan's handprints all over their atomic ass, and Grandville wants to talk petty turf wars between the DIA and the CIA? The response to this must be swift and without subtlety.

The newly elected president of the United States knew exactly what the reaction would be, and within the next twenty-four hours so would the entire world.

Because she was going to tell them, while it was happening.

31

Lone Ranger

Monica watched the surreal images on a large flat screen in the lobby of one of the general aviation terminals in Ronald Reagan National Airport in D.C.

Her tribulations with Amir and the contract on her head suddenly seemed insignificant as she stood there paralyzed by the video feed. The unthinkable destruction captured in high definition by news crews in the surrounding boroughs and even from Midtown Manhattan rooftops made her head hurt.

A dense cloud of smoke covered most of the southern end of the island, boiling skyward, pulsating with secondary explosions, before the winds aloft carried the long, dark plume over Long Island Sound.

A section of a skyscraper had collapsed into the East River, adding to the apocalyptic scene across New York Harbor. Many ships had capsized, some on fire. Dozens of clouds of smoke swirled skyward across the harbor, joining the massive haze hovering over the area. The images evoked a diabolic marriage between Kuwaiti oil fires and the destructive power of a Midwest F5 tornado.

Make that a hundred twisters, she thought, arms crossed, struggling to control the rage snaking deep in her gut, raking her intestines. As a scream of fury almost came out of her, she realized she was as angry at her own country as she was at the terrorists.

She'd known something like this would happen sooner or later.

She had warned everyone that the only way to truly fight these bastards was outside established processes and protocols—outside the laws created to deal with the average criminal. The system was never designed to battle fanatics willing to kill themselves for their warped ideologies.

Monica had been chastised, ridiculed, demoted from ASAC to special agent, and was even now suspended for acting according to the oath she took.

The powerful images painted on those screens in vivid color, however, provided a dreadful vindication of her deep-rooted dogma regarding terrorism. The only way to fight these bastards was to be more ruthless, more daring, and certainly more deadly.

Following the shootout outside Porter's boarded-up house, Monica had spent the night parked outside Amir's home in Dupont Circle. She figured that the best way to stay alive was to keep her enemy close. She had followed him to his workplace at dawn and then here three hours ago, where he met up with the Saudi royals. According to a ground crew member Monica had befriended, the Saudis and Amir were scheduled to fly to La Guardia in the prince's massive business jet monopolizing half the tarmac.

All three had headed for the jet, along with an entourage of assistants and bodyguards. But Amir had received a phone call that made him and his protection detail double back and head directly to the executive lounge.

An hour before the bomb went off.

The Saudis departed Reagan but followed an international flight plan taking them to Europe.

When Amir finally emerged from the lounge, he ignored the flat screens that had hypnotized everyone else in that terminal, and made his way to a waiting limousine.

"You knew," she mumbled as he disappeared beyond the automatic doors followed by his team, which included Saddam. "You miserable piece of shit. *You knew.*"

Monica ran to her Ducati, which she had parked in the rear of the lot, away from Amir and his men. Remaining a few vehicles behind him, she followed him back to his house in Bethesda, where he apparently planned to weather out the storm.

Monica left him there and sped to the J. Edgar Hoover Building, her mind going in different directions, considering the possibilities, the implications. She knew she wouldn't be welcomed at the FBI headquarters, but what choice did she have? She had to tell her side of the story again. Perhaps in light of what happened Porter might be more willing to listen. And besides, worst case, she would end up in a holding cell, which was probably a lot safer than in the streets with Amir putting a contract on her.

And that's when she spotted the van following her.

Seriously?

The country's under attack and all you bastards can think of is collecting fifty grand?

"The banks are closed anyway, assholes," she mumbled while gunning the engine, riding in between lanes. The van made an attempt to follow her, but gave up after three blocks.

"Idiots," she whispered after losing sight of them. If there was one thing dumber than bringing a knife to a gunfight it was to use a van to tail a motorcycle in D.C. traffic.

Monica pressed on, riding hard to try to blow off her swelling anger, some of it directed at her superiors for failing to heed her warnings. Instead, they made her persona non grata, suspended, kicked to the curb. However, a nuclear bomb had just been detonated in Lower Manhattan and Monica knew who was at least partly responsible.

Unfortunately, all of her wrath, her rage—her overwhelming desire to exact revenge against those responsible for this cowardly attack—would not let her get past the lobby security checkpoint without her FBI credentials.

She recognized the desk officer.

Monica smiled. He smiled then frowned, dropping to his knees while grabbing his throat.

Monica had an expandable baton out, flipped, tapping the guard just below the Adam's apple, followed by another quick hit to the side of his head, just below his ear. He would be out and have a splitting headache but would otherwise be okay, and, most importantly, out of her way.

She grabbed his pass card and was in the stairwell, knowing that elevators were too easy to stop. She had no time to disable cameras, no time for anything but to get to Porter and convince him of what she knew.

The first two guards coming down the stairs should have had the advantage. They were bigger and traveling at a faster rate. But they were not trained well enough to be violent with a woman in their own building, let alone an FBI agent.

The baton was out again, bruising one knee and another shin, and she was past them, taking the stairs two at a time. The moans faded as she cleared the fifth floor, heading to the seventh floor and the executive suites of the building.

But she didn't get far.

The sheer number of bodies hitting her was crushing. They soon had her cuffed and thrown in the same damn holding room with the one-way mirror. Four FBI agents guarded her—all holding expandable batons.

She ignored them and just stared at the mirror.

The agents locked the door and left her alone.

Monica closed her eyes and took a deep breath, hugging her knees while trying to hold it together. For a moment she wondered if she was better off down here, away from the scorching reality consuming her nation.

Is it even possible to recover from something like that?

By the time she had parked illegally in front of the building and run inside while ignoring two traffic cops, the initial death estimates were north of a hundred thousand. And that figure was likely to grow in the coming days and weeks, as first responders were allowed inside the death zone. With Wall Street incinerated, the financial system had pretty much been shut down. The news was filled with reports from around the country about banks closing their doors until further notice. The president had just shut down all borders and grounded all commercial and private air traffic.

Just like September 11.

Christ. What's next? Martial law? Anarchy? she thought while staring at the door, which didn't stay closed for long.

Gustavo Porter pushed it open and stood in the entryway dressed in slacks, a white dress shirt with the sleeves rolled up to his elbows, and a loosened blue tie. He held a paper bag in his right hand. His face was tight and the veins in his bull neck seemed to be throbbing.

The man was visibly pissed, and Monica couldn't care less.

"Five men with broken bones, the whole building on alert, and if it wasn't for the cameras, you would be dead . . . Who in the *fuck* you think you are?" Porter said. "We are under nuclear attack and you decide to *break* into the FBI headquarters?"

"I'm an FBI special agent trying to do her job," she replied. "You must be the other guy."

"Did your mother drop you on your head when you were a baby, Cruz?"

"I saw him, Gus," she said, standing up. "And he knew about the bomb."

"Who?"

"Amir."

"Dammit, Cruz! Is this why I had to leave a conference call with the White House? To listen to more of your bullshit conspiracy theories?"

She took a minute to explain the surveillance she had conducted on Amir's business, the guns, and how she had managed to escape. She told him how Amir had doubled back instead of boarding his jet to New York. She purposely decided to leave out the shooting last night at his place.

Porter looked away, apparently considering what he had heard.

"Look," she added, "his men carried the *exact* type of weapons we confiscated, UZI PROs with Gemtec suppressors and MEPRO scopes, and the place was guarded like Fort Knox, not with the rent-a-cops we saw during our investigation."

"And you have proof of this? Photos? Video? Audio? *Anything* I can use?"

She shook her head. "Like I said, they shot the camera and I was barely able to escape with my life."

He dropped his head and mumbled, "Christ. So . . . no evidence . . . *again*?" He looked at her with eyes gleaming with more disappointment than anger.

"What about the conveniently timed phone call? Plus the bastard wouldn't even look at the images on TV."

"Well, neither is my wife, Cruz. And frankly I can barely watch them myself. Are you going to accuse us as well?"

"Fine, then fire me, arrest me, or get the hell out of my way . . . but this is total bullshit, Gus."

"Actually," he said, "I didn't come down here to bust your balls. Even though it is a bit enjoyable watching you cut your own throat."

He just stared at her.

"So . . . you're not here to watch me circle the drain," she said while defiantly staring up at this tower of a man. "Then . . . why *are* you here? You need a hug or something?"

"Nope. Current events are leaving us quite short of field agents, plus Amir decided to drop all charges."

She stared at him, stunned. "Amir did *what*?"

"First thing this morning. I guess he decided to be the adult here."

Monica was at a loss for words. The man was truly a master manipulator, overtly making a peace offer while covertly hiring assassins.

It made perfect sense, of course. Amir had just removed himself from the suspect list if she were to be killed.

Porter continued. "The president has intelligence that indicates there may be more nukes—and that info is need to know, by the way. She wants every able body deployed to every last corner of this country to find them before they go off. So, in spite of your insubordination, I'm going to pretend there is a capable agent somewhere inside that thick skull."

"Are you saying what I think you're saying?" she said, walking up to him. "What about the pissant chief of staff?"

"That's the thing," he said. "It was John Wright's idea to get you back in the saddle."

"Well, la-di-fucking-da. Pigs are flying today. I guess it took a nuclear blast in New York City to pull his head out of his ass."

Porter briefly closed his eyes and said, "We need all hands on deck, especially those who think out of the box. The president needs a team of people who believe the rules don't apply to them, and who just don't know how to *fucking* quit, even when ordered to do so . . . know anybody like that?"

Monica wasn't sure how to respond. Porter had just cursed twice inside of a minute—a first in her book. Plus it also looked as if he had just paid her a compliment—another first.

Porter's phone rang. He looked at it, frowned, looked at Monica, and said, "Hold on, it's the ex. If I don't answer then her damn lawyer calls and bills me for the call."

Monica worked on her poker face while Porter listened for a moment. His neck veins began to pulsate again as he hissed, "Gunfire and grenades? Are you certain?" More listening while he closed his eyes and breathed deeply, followed by, "Okay, okay, calm down. I believe you, and yes, I know the chief of police and . . . yes, I'll take care of it."

He shoved the phone in his pocket while mumbling, "The world is collapsing around us and my damn ex-wife is all bent out of shape because some assholes got into a gunfight at this dump I bought to flip a few years back. Now it's all hers—like pretty much everything I used to own. I told her that keeping it boarded up was going to invite the wrong element. Now she wants me to put that incident at the top of my stack . . . believe that shit?"

"Sorry to hear that, boss," she said.

"Forget about it," he said, refocusing. "I'm shipping you off to Houston to bolster our presence down there. Try not to embarrass the Bureau."

Now it was Monica's turn to make a face. "*Houston*? What the hell, Gus?"

"The first bomb came aboard a supertanker, so we're prioritizing all major seaports, and Houston's right at the very top of the list on oil imports. Besides, aren't you a former cowgirl? Probably explains why you like to ride everyone so damn hard."

She smiled without humor and said, "You need to keep me here."

"I don't need to do anything."

"C'mon, Gus. Every asswipe knows that the real action's in D.C., not with shit-kicking cowboys. Besides, the terrorists wouldn't be stupid enough to use the same method twice."

"Want your gun and badge back?" he asked, swinging the paper bag in front of her.

"Heck yeah."

"Then the eyes of Texas are upon you," he said, tossing the bag over.

"All the live-long fucking day," she replied, grabbing it, opening it, and staring at her badge and ID in the leather bifold, before looking up as her jaw dropped.

"Wait a moment . . . this is . . . my old—"

"You're an ASAC again," he said.

Once more, Monica found herself at a loss for words.

"Consider it a battlefield promotion. Hopefully you'll hang on to it longer than the last time."

"Thanks . . . I guess."

"Don't thank me," he replied. "It was Wright's idea . . . No, wait, the *pissant* chief of staff suggested that you would need some level of authority while you were down there."

Monica ignored him while tucking the bifold into the left side of her waist, displaying her badge opposite the Glock in a hip holster. And just like that, she started feeling a little better, even with the contract on her head. Maybe heading down to Houston would be for the best until things cooled down up here. And besides, there would probably be too many cooks in the kitchen up here for her to make any progress.

"When do I leave?"

"A car is already waiting to take you to Reagan. Wheels up in one hour."

"One hour? But my bike's double-parked outside and I need to swing by the apartment and pack a couple of—"

"I'll handle the bike and I'm sure you can find a toothbrush on the way."

"What about Amir? I may not have evidence but I'm telling you that—"

"Relax, Cruz. You've sold me. I will work it . . . but *my* way. Okay?"

"Okay."

"Now, the Homeland Task Force at the Port of Houston kicks off in less than five hours. So you need to get going and report to Special Agent in Charge Roman Dalton. He has full operational authority down there for the Bureau. Clear?"

"Crystal," she said, her mind trying to process everything. "Who's heading the task force?"

He shrugged. "I'm sure Homeland sent someone capable."

"That's what I'm worried about."

Porter shook his head as he said, "Cruz?"

"Yeah?"

"Two things."

"Shoot."

"Keep your damned hands off our security guards. Their job description does *not* include getting beat up by special agents."

"Got it. And the other thing?"

"You're part of a task force now. Try to play well with others, and most importantly, *please* try not reminding me how much of a disrespectful asshole you can be for at least the next two weeks."

32

Point of Failure

Operations seldom went as planned. This was particularly true in the covert world, where the added complexity of orchestrating a multifaceted mission in secret typically resulted in multiple possible points of failure. And each of these potential weak links had the added danger of creating more glitches, multiplying the problem.

The trick was in anticipating, in playing out the possible scenarios and coming up with contingencies that would allow the mission to continue in some acceptable form.

Dr. Atiq Gadai had spent a lifetime working in the ISI doing precisely that.

He'd used mathematics and statistics to improve the odds of a mission's success. He'd simulated scenarios, identifying probable Achilles' heels, and either readjusted the mission parameters to eliminate them or devised viable alternatives should those failures occur.

And that was precisely what he did in the conference room adjoining his office on the third floor of the ISI headquarters.

Atiq was assisted via a secure videoconference link from Karachi by Assar Lari, his best and most trusted analyst. Lari had been instrumental in getting Salma and Malik in the supertankers as well as orchestrating the packages shipped via DHL to Amir Dham.

Together, they brainstormed options to keep Salma's mission alive in the wake of Malik's early detonation.

So far Lari had managed to find Salma, her support team, and the package a way off the supertanker, with covert passage into Mexico.

Now the hard part began: getting her safely to her new target. Washington, D.C.

Atiq had weighed the pros and cons with Lari for hours, trying to decide if they should stick to their original plan and detonate the device in Houston to further disrupt the American supply chain. Or they could shoot for the moon and deliver the weapon to the White House's front door, especially given Amir's contacts in the area.

In the end, they had settled on Washington, D.C.

But Lari had also provided him with dozens of suitable locations along three proposed routes where Salma could detonate if she found herself out of choices. They included Dallas, Oklahoma City, Memphis, Nashville, Atlanta, Charlotte, Raleigh-Durham, and Richmond. All were heavily populated areas guaranteed to yield at least a hundred thousand casualties.

And more importantly, fear.

Once the decision had been made, Lari switched to the identification and activation of the required support cells. His intelligence network, in conjunction with the Mexican cartel and ISIS, had already vetted these support groups based on parameters such as experience, skill set, depth of faith, and proximity.

Atiq worked with Lari through the required monetary transactions. They wired the necessary funds through myriad international connections and banks in a dozen countries. And that included Saudi Arabia, where ISIS held many accounts under a dozen different front corporations. Some of them were funded directly by the Saudis themselves, who did this as a way to keep ISIS off their backs.

Moneys were transferred in and out of them, eventually making their way to accounts in Mexico and into the United States. All were disguised as payments for services rendered by dozens of corporations doing business in the industrial areas of America's southern neighbor.

He left Lari working out the details and stepped back into his office, where two senior ISI operatives from his network's internal police, modeled after Hitler's Schutzstaffel, waited for him.

Ahmed was in his early fifties, with a bald head, a well-trimmed beard, and intense dark eyes under thick brows.

Manish was ten years younger, with a full head of salt-and-pepper hair and clean-shaven face. Both wore business suits.

Atiq settled behind his desk and asked, "Well?"

The agents exchanged a glance before Manish said, "We did as you asked, sir, and placed surveillance on every operative in the city, especially those who have had any contact whatsoever with embassy staff in the prior twelve months. In addition, our IT staff has combed through every e-mail, text message, and phone call."

"And?"

Manish looked over at the older and more seasoned Ahmed, who fingered his mustache before nodding slowly.

Manish cleared his throat and, measuring his words, added, "Our results are . . . conclusive, sir. We cross-checked them. The traitor left chalk marks on a light post for the CIA man, who checked it two hours later. Then the two of them met the following morning. Our IT group also tracked phone calls made to the embassy from a pay phone in a nearby market, and our street cameras picked her up at the same time inside the phone booth."

"Her? Is it one of the honey-trappers?"

The operatives exchanged another glance.

Atiq slapped his desk, startling them. "Out with it, men! Who is it?"

Ahmed stood up and said, "Your daughter, sir."

Atiq motioned for Ahmed to sit back down. They obviously didn't know that Maryam had long been deployed to work the embassy staff. She had made contact with the station chief, Bill Gorman, and others over the course of a few years. And they shouldn't know. One of the ISI's strengths was the compartmentalization of information. But in this case, he felt compelled to share this secret, which he did over the course of the following minute.

The agents traded looks again before Ahmed said, "We were not aware of that, sir. But it still doesn't explain her last conversation with him."

Atiq raised his brows. "Continue."

"We followed her to a meeting with Gorman and used a parabolic microphone to pick up this." Ahmed produced a small digital recorder, set it on the table, and pressed Play.

Slowly, the words flowing from the silver gadget made him realize he had fallen victim to the oldest pitfall in the spy trade: being crossed by a loved one. And in this case someone he had trained from an early age, sending her to the finest schools in London to get a degree in medicine before immersing her in his world.

I watched her become one of Pakistan's top spies.

But she had obviously lost her way. She had forgotten who she was, turning her back on her country by alerting the Americans of the New York bomb, which had forced him to alter well-crafted plans.

Atiq felt a stab in the middle of his chest and realized he had stopped breathing. As he slowly inhaled, the words from the Koran replaced the recorded conversation, filling his mind with the brutal reality of what he must now do.

Kill the unbelievers, wherever you find them.

Fight against them until there is no dissention.

Fight until no other religion exists but Islam.

Family or not, anyone siding with the Americans was against the will of Allah, and against this holy crusade Atiq had masterminded—a cause that had to be protected at all cost.

Slowly, he said, "Bring her in for questioning . . . but quietly. I do not want anyone, especially the Americans, to know that we know."

As the men left, Atiq stood and walked up to the windows overlooking the gardens surrounding his building.

Pinching the bridge of his nose, he took a deep breath, working through the implications, the repercussions. He tried to see this movie through to its conclusion—a grand finale that would not play out well for him if word got out that Pakistan was involved in New York or Bagram.

The whole plan, his grand strategy, which he had managed to sell to enough members of the Pakistani government to get approval, was based on this being solely an ISIS strike. It included the theft of the uranium-235 from a Pakistani warehouse.

Everything had been carefully fabricated—painstakingly crafted—to avoid the sort of retaliation that his opposition in Parliament—as well as Prime Minister Korai—feared.

But now Maryam had betrayed him, and in doing so she had placed not just Atiq but the entire nation squarely in the crosshairs of the United States of America.

She must be found, he thought. *And she must be silenced.*

33

Ghastly Images

It began like the first video.

The images of prior nuclear explosions slowly resolved on the screen, but then came footage from the last days of the Vietnam War, as Saigon fell and the American embassy was evacuated. Somewhere in the background, the tune of "Adagio for Strings," the theme of Oliver Stone's movie *Platoon*, came alive.

Its volume increased as images of injured civilians from the war in Iraq and Afghanistan filled the screen. Burn victims. Amputees. Mothers crying over the mangled bodies of loved ones amidst rubble. Then the images transitioned from Iraq and Afghanistan to New York City, to the recent video feeds depicting the dead, the endless stream of wounded. The screen then split in half. It showed New York City victims on the right and the civilian victims of America's foreign wars on the left as the music hovered somewhere above the ghastly images.

Monica sat in the rear of the FBI jet flying her to Houston, her eyes on the flat screen mounted on the wall leading to the cockpit as her blood pressure rose.

Slowly, the images faded and Ibrahim al-Crameini materialized. He was dressed in a white tunic. He faced the camera, dark eyes staring back at her with deadly intensity.

"For decades, the United States has fought its wars on foreign soil, inflicting pain and suffering far from home. Today the Islamic State has brought the fight to America, punishing the unbelievers for decades of imperialistic oppression. Your country is now feeling the same sting that the people of so many nations have felt for so long . . ."

Blah, blah, blah.

Monica muted the video, not caring to hear the utter nonsense spewed by this fanatic. This wasn't about religion. This wasn't about imperialism or whatever label that clown wished to use on America's government. This was terrorism, pure and simple. This was all about a group of assholes exerting their power, killing innocent civilians for the sake of inflicting terror and fear.

She looked out the window while taking a deep breath, her mind processing everything leading up to this point, including the eerie lack of commercial or private traffic at Reagan. Her jet had taxied straight from the general aviation terminal to the runway, taking off immediately. A pair of F-22s escorted her out of Washington's airspace.

Just like on 9/11.

In the silence of her cabin, as the jet cruised undisturbed above the Tennessee mountains on a clear and beautiful day, Monica did something she had not done in a very, very long time.

She prayed for those who'd died and she prayed for those who had survived.

Then she prayed for the brains and the guts to catch the responsible motherfuckers.

34

God's Children

LOWER MANHATTAN

It had taken him almost an hour to walk two city blocks, crawling past towering piles of rubble from collapsed buildings—some several stories high. It was a man-made obstacle course that evoked images from the days when the Towers fell.

And then he had passed out.

By the time NYPD Sergeant Ray Kazemi came around—two hours later—it was almost dark, and still no one had come to his aid.

Where the fuck is everyone?

Very thirsty and still very tired, he staggered alone for another two blocks before he saw the first signs of life. Two figures caked in ash wandered aimlessly in the shadows of the billowing clouds hovering over the city, obscuring the setting sun's burnt orange glow.

They seemed catatonic, nonresponsive, trembling. But as he approached them, he noticed the burns, the blistering skin, but oddly enough only on one side of their bodies.

"My name is Ray," he said to the closest one, a boy in his early teens who just stared at him with his one good eye before turning his face, exposing facial burns so severe that the sight made him recoil.

Shame on you, he thought. *These are God's children!*

"Come," Ray finally worked up the courage to say, offering a hand, which the kid tentatively took. "Good. You too, sweetheart. Come with me," he added, motioning to the girl roughly the same age as the boy, standing nearby looking confused, in some sort of trance. They seemed unwilling to leave the spot they had been circling, as if protecting something.

Then he saw it: two bodies fused in place amidst a pile of bricks on the sidewalk, statues made of ashes. They stood shoulder to shoulder, arms by their sides, as if shielding someone who was no longer there.

"Parents . . ." the boy mumbled through blistered lips. "Our . . . parents . . . We're visiting from . . . Israel."

The girl, a bit older and not nearly as burned as her brother, dropped to her knees and began to sob by the two figures.

"The fire . . ." the boy whispered. "They blocked it . . . with their bodies."

Ray finally understood, kneeling by the girl and extending a hand. "Come, child. Come with me. Your parents wanted you to live, to seek help. This is why they protected you." As he said this, he wondered why neither one seemed in agonizing pain, but catatonic.

The girl slowly took his other hand without uttering a single word, getting up with him, tears in her eyes, a silver Star of David pendant dangling from her neck.

Tourists . . . from Israel, he thought, by now deciding that the worst of it was to the south, which meant he had to move north.

Ray looked about him, at the incomprehensible destruction projecting in every direction as far as the eye could see. In this wasteland of concrete, twisted metal, broken glass, and fire, God had led him to a pair of Jewish kids who, like him, had been spared . . . somehow. Him by diving to the gutter and them by a pair of loving parents who made the ultimate sacrifice.

And now it's my turn.

"Come, kids," he said in the most soothing voice he could muster, gently nudging them away from their parents, slowly, with compassion.

Together they walked across entire city blocks of rubble, rows of destroyed cars, city buses, food carts, and around the many fires—all covered by a sea of shattered glass that reflected the surrounding fires.

But every step took effort, and now he had the kids holding his hands, pulling him back, and slowing him. Plus he had to constantly look around for any other survivor.

He found no one else in this smoldering wasteland that had been his neighborhood as minutes turned into an hour, as Ray persisted. They doubled back when the rubble blocking the streets was simply too high to climb over, finding alternate routes. They ventured inside half-collapsed buildings, exiting at the opposite end, but always heading north while silently praying for strength, for courage, for wisdom—for the determination that he knew he would need to keep going. These kids would not live long with those burns. They needed treatment, and fast, which meant no pause, no rest.

But the kids could go no farther, their damaged bodies going limp on him. Ray threw them over his shoulders, one on each side, further taxing whatever was left of his stamina.

He was strong. He was muscular. For many years his body had responded well above average to his exercise routine at the NYPD gym. And he now hoped that all of that effort would give him a slight edge.

Step after agonizing step, Ray pushed himself, carrying his half-unconscious survivors, mumbling words of encouragement, of compassion, even of hope. He assured them again that their parents would have wanted them to live—the very reason they had used their own bodies to protect them from the raging flames.

Ray fought on, just as he had combated those extremists in Iraq and Afghanistan who twisted the words of the Koran to serve their evil purposes—the very words that infused him instead with the courage to persevere.

But he felt the end coming, as night descended over the city, as his body screamed at him to stop, to rest.

His shoulders burned from the weight of the kids.

His mind was light-headed, dizzy.

His body demanded rest. Now.

So he silently prayed to Allah for help.

And just as his knees were about to give, just as his vision narrowed, just as his mind grew as dark as the sky, Ray saw lights ahead . . . moving lights.

Vehicles?

Flashlights!

First responders.

Help. Hope.

Invoking all of the strength he had left, he screamed as loud as he had ever screamed, his voice echoing down the street, momentarily drowning all other noises.

He dropped to his knees and with his last conscious effort Ray gently laid the kids on the ground.

Before he collapsed.

35

Bagged

ISLAMABAD, PAKISTAN

Atiq's order sounded simple enough, but as in most things, the devil was always in the details.

The team assigned to the abduction was experienced and ruthless.

Abductions depended on planning, quickness, and violence. The team used three Toyota Hiace vans, the middle one for the actual grab while the other two were blockers. The Hiaces were paneled and white, a popular version in and around Islamabad. Four determined men occupied each blocking van, and two men and two women were in the grabbing van. The women were used for surprise, as no one would see them coming or expect violence from them.

One woman and one man exited the grabbing Hiace about twenty-five yards from Maryam. As a trained operative, she was very aware of her surroundings and had just left another meeting with her CIA handler and lover.

She was even more attuned.

But it did her no good.

The street was packed with shoppers, workers, vagrants, children, motorcycles, scooters, cars and trucks—all trying to go somewhere ahead of everyone else.

The man and woman walked up fast from behind; the woman touched Maryam's elbow.

For an instant, Maryam recognized the face of the man . . . someone she had trained several years back . . . Manish, a young ISI operative who Maryam always thought had a crush on her.

Confused, Maryam turned, but hesitated for a second, which allowed Manish to place a black bag over her head as the woman snagged Maryam's hands behind her back and flex-cuffed her. They yanked her backwards while Manish flex-cuffed her feet.

"Manish . . . what the hell?" she shouted, but just as their training prescribed, no one replied.

The van pulled up, doors open, and someone else got out to help with throwing Maryam inside.

She felt stupid, even embarrassed.

The hands on her she could handle, the spicy breath on Manish was not a problem; all who touched her were very strong and experts at handling people violently yet without breaking any bones. The bruises were hard to avoid.

As they took off, Manish remained with her in the back of the van.

"Hello, Maryam," he whispered, forcing a hand inside her jeans.

Maryam remained still, forcing her body to ignore his intruding fingers.

She was a professional; she was trained to take people just as she was being taken—and as a female operative to take abuse of any kind, especially sexual. She had done it in practice and now it was for real; she was the victim.

Fortunately someone called Manish to the front of the van.

The hand vanished.

How ironic and how helpless—a feeling she had not acknowledged since she was five.

Father . . . you son of a bitch, she wanted to scream from inside the bag, but she knew it would not do any good.

36

Honey-Trapping

STAR OF OCEANIA. GULF OF MEXICO.
ONE HUNDRED MILES SOUTH OF HOUSTON

No one said it would be easy.

But what was necessary hardly ever was.

Salma Bahmani had learned this fundamental truth at a very early age, when the Karachi orphan was inducted into the ISI to serve her country in a most difficult capacity. In fact, Salma couldn't really remember much of her life before the training camps. Before she and the other agents were sterilized in preparation for their upcoming honey-trapping assignments in India.

She remembered that first time, on her sixteenth birthday, the official day when candidates transitioned from girls to women.

Her instructor had been gentle. But it had still hurt.

A lot.

But it had been necessary.

The second time had been easier, as was the third. The many sessions that followed taught her the act of seduction. Motions were honed into a well-practiced ritual, a dance of irresistible sensual beauty on the outside, yet quite procedural in her mind. To Salma it became mechanical, going through movements drilled to the point of obsession to create long-term muscle memory.

And that was the key to achieving the desired state of mental detachment: muscle memory, the ability to disconnect her mind from the actions of a body operating on autopilot. She stimulated without conscious effort, motor skills groomed to perfection, eliminating the need for attention.

Which was precisely what Salma did now, as her body subconsciously pleased the Norwegian captain.

She slid smoothly, going through the muscle contractions necessary to execute the desired task. Hips, limbs, and lips exacted the desired reaction, massaging the precise spots at the precise moments, delivering unimaginable pleasure.

While slowly but steadily taking ownership of his soul.

As Sjöberg shuddered beneath her, Salma thought of Malik, her mentor and lover who had just made the ultimate sacrifice, inflicting terror into the hearts of the enemy. But that attack had been premature, executed before she could reach the Port of Houston and its refineries, chemical plants, and container terminals vital to the American supply chain. Malik had detonated before she could trigger an industrial, commercial, and ecological disaster of unthinkable proportions in coordination with New York.

The blast had occurred while she was still over a hundred miles from her target, requiring adjustments to the mission.

The message from Atiq had arrived via her encrypted satellite phone.

Head south of the quarantine zone, away from the American Coast Guard and the inspection crews.

So Salma had reverted to skills acquired long ago. She had seduced Captain Sjöberg into remaining clear of the large flotilla of merchant vessels accumulating in the quarantine zone, choosing to keep the use of force in her back pocket.

Honey before the hammer.

Salma had given him a little taste the morning after the attack against her team. It had been just a touch. Her hand had brushed his muscular arm as she nudged him away from his crew to relate the events that had taken place the night before. She had kept her face purposely close to him as she whispered, adding intimacy, letting him rest a hand on her waist.

She could have killed him, of course, and fed his body to the sharks, but at the time they had been too far from their objective. And any deviation from the plan only added risk to the mission.

Fortunately, the Norwegian had reacted just as she had hoped. He'd commended her for putting down the mutiny. But most importantly, Sjöberg had agreed to keep the vessel on course to Houston.

Honey before the hammer.

During her years operating in India, Salma had achieved far more by seducing her marks than through the more traditional intelligence-gathering methods employed by ISI's other divisions. And she applied the same strategy here, summoning her powers to manipulate the captain.

She waited for the perfect moment, as she had him completely under her submission.

"I fear for . . . our safety," she mumbled, nibbling on his earlobe.

"Wh—why?" he asked, eyes closed, hands squeezing her thighs.

"As your . . . security chief," she said, rotating her hips and tightening muscles in a way designed to force him to finish, "I think we should . . . stay clear of the crowded quarantine zone . . . especially if there is a chance . . . that one of the vessels near us could be carrying a nuclear bomb."

"I . . ." he started to reply, but instead tensed as he climaxed.

"The risk . . . it's too high, darling," she whispered softly as he shivered, tensed, and relaxed. "The risk is just too high."

Salma smiled her trained smile as the Norwegian opened his eyes and just stared at her.

"I . . . it has never felt like this . . ." he mumbled.

She pressed a finger against his lips, locking eyes with him while her hips continued to work their magic on automatic. It was always the same look—*always*: part surprise, part gratitude, and part please-let-me-have-you-again-and-again.

And that was the key to complete seduction. Salma always left her marks wanting more—much more. She turned them into puppets willing to do anything for another hit of this most addictive narcotic carefully devised by the masterminds of Pakistan's Inter-Services Intelligence.

Gradually, she slid off of him and lay by his side, a hand on his heaving chest, fingers running through his damp hair, waiting for him to speak, just as her training dictated.

"You . . . are correct," he finally said, slowly catching his breath. "It is safer to move south of here . . . and wait to see what . . . transpires."

"I agree," she replied, rolling over him and gently massaging his scalp with the tips of her fingers. "I fully agree."

37

Tristan

WASHINGTON, D.C.

Tristan Lavastede began his career as a war correspondent, first in the Middle East, covering the liberation of Kuwait, before shifting his attention to the Yugoslav Wars. In the summer of 1992, he witnessed the horrors of ethnic cleansing in Bosnia and Herzegovina. The life-changing experience prompted him to resign from his post and launch an international coalition for human rights. He managed to raise tens of millions of dollars for the promotion and protection of refugees. Over the years, he campaigned against human trafficking, for the elimination of child labor camps and the promotion of women's rights in the Middle East, Africa, and Latin America. In the process, he became a top negotiator. He brokered deals with troubled nations and unsavory organizations for the benefit of people typically forgotten by the world. Along the way, he managed to write the Pulitzer Prize winner *A Trail of Tears*, his personal account as a journalist and humanitarian activist.

His international accomplishments caught the attention of then Senator Laura Vaccaro, who asked him to become one of her senior advisors during her long and arduous presidential campaign. He'd become part of the Vaccaro State Department transition team last year. His appointment as U.S. ambassador to the United Nations had been a natural next step in his career. His knowledge of foreign policy and insight into the dirty laundry that most nations wished to keep hidden gained him strong negotiation leverage.

Tristan stood by the top-floor window overlooking Cleveland Park, the historic residential neighborhood in the northwest quadrant of Washington, D.C.—and home to the embassy of the Islamic Republic of Pakistan. It was a three-story structure modeled after the Naulakha Pavilion, a public monument overlooking the Ravi River in Punjab, Pakistan.

Leverage.

Tristan knew where to obtain it and, most importantly, how and when to use it. It always amazed him how the strongest and often most feared political or military figures in the world would crumble in front of his eyes when presented with a truth they could not afford to become public. A mass grave here, a sex slave ring there; rape, genocide, pedophilia, treason, and even embezzlement from drug cartels, industrialists, and heads of state.

The dark rivers of the lowest forms of humanity flowed toward Tristan's estuary.

And today the current was damn strong.

"We have no control over their activities," said Patras Dham.

"So you say." Tristan turned around, regarding the bald and aging Pakistani ambassador to the United States.

Tristan had just flown aboard a Black Hawk helicopter, per presidential orders, from the United Nations complex in New York City to Washington, shortly after the bomb went off.

The official reason: relocating critical U.N. activities until electricity and other basic services could be restored to Midtown Manhattan, where U.N. facilities now stood in darkness.

The real reason: Tristan had been tapped to join a team with no name.

His mission: opening a backdoor channel into Prime Minister Korai's government.

Patras represented the logical first step in that process.

Tristan knew the Pakistani diplomat back in the days when he'd run a couple of missions in Karachi. One was to save orphan girls from being inducted into prostitution. Another was to protect those who turned up pregnant from being stoned to death by the same male-dominated society that turned them into whores in the first place.

Patras had been an assistant to the minister of the interior back then. Tristan had the fortune of catching him embezzling government funds via a mutual bank in Geneva. But rather than exposing him, which would have resulted in Patras's beheading, Tristan had used the information to turn him into an informal asset. He became one of the few sympathizers for his humanitarian mission inside the Pakistani government. Over the years Patras realized the value Tristan's work brought to his country, and their relationship developed into something that bordered on friendship.

"But here's the thing," Tristan added. "I happen to know otherwise."

"Mr. Ambassador," Patras said, "I can assure you. ISIS has acted alone. Just as they did when detonating the device in Bagram, which fallout, as you may recall, actually fell *inside* our borders."

"An unfortunate incident," Tristan replied. "And you almost had us fooled . . . but like I said, we now know otherwise."

"My government had no knowledge of their activities," Patras insisted, and for a moment Tristan wondered if Patras simply didn't know of the connection Dr. Atiq Gadai had forged between ISIS and the ISI.

"Just like in Abbottabad?" Tristan asked, referring to the city in northeastern Pakistan where Osama bin Laden had hidden in a compound less than a mile from a Pakistani military academy.

Patras dropped his gaze.

"But I did not come here today to look back," Tristan added. "I came to engage in a dialogue between our nations that may be of . . . mutual benefit. Does that interest you?"

Patras slowly nodded.

"You see," Tristan continued, "I believe that people like you and I are sometimes caught between doing the right thing and the political needs of the individuals who appointed us to these posts. But I also believe that if men of goodwill, like us, work together, it may be possible to rise above such compromising positions and reach common ground. Does that also interest you?"

Another nod.

"In that case, I have a message for your prime minister."

"A message?"

"It comes directly from the president of the United States."

38

UAVs

ISLAMABAD, PAKISTAN

There can be five different groups of unmanned aerial vehicles overseeing a combat zone, or anywhere the United States needs eyes in the sky.

Groups 1 and 2 fly no higher than thirty-five hundred feet, reach speeds of 250 knots, and are limited to a maximum takeoff weight of fifty-five pounds. The AeroVironment RQ-11 Raven handheld and the catapult-launched Boeing ScanEagle dominate this space, with endurance over the target area of up to twenty-four hours.

Group 3 includes the Boeing RQ-7B Shadow and the larger RQ-21A Blackjack. They operate below eighteen thousand feet with takeoff weights up to 1,320 pounds and rule the midsize UAV world.

Groups 4 and 5 are reserved for the big girls, like the MQ-1 A/B Predator and its larger sister, the MQ-9 Reaper, as well as the jet-powered RQ-4 Global Hawk. The latter has a maximum speed of 340 knots, a takeoff weight of 32,250 pounds, and a range of fourteen thousand miles. It has the ability to remain airborne for over thirty-two hours while operating at a ceiling of sixty thousand feet.

All of these drones, tasked and controlled by different intelligence and military headquarters, sent information to more than one place, and all were invaluable in this war on terror.

Thanks to one of these UAVs, a Reaper circling downtown Islamabad at two thousand feet when Maryam's kidnapping took place, Gorman learned the location where she was being held. And he now sought help to rescue her. He had already enrolled Harwich, who was hard at work planning out the rescue.

Gorman then called Stark on the satphone and told him what had happened.

"Look, Colonel," Gorman added, "I know that you and your team are supposed to be headed home and—"

"Where and when, Bill?"

"Now what?" Ryan Hunt asked, looking up from his game of solitaire, which he played with an old deck of Playboy cards.

Stark hung up the satphone and pursed his lips while regarding his sniper.

The contractor team sat in the rear of a C-21A military transport parked on one side of the tarmac at the Benazir Bhutto International Airport on the outskirts of Islamabad. They waited for Danny to finish the preflight of the military variant of the Learjet 35A before heading to Sierra Leone to deal with a group of blood diamond assholes.

The light jet was originally designed to carry up to six passengers plus the pilot and copilot. Or in Stark's case, five soldiers plus five hundred pounds of violence.

"We have a situation," Stark replied.

Ryan sat next to Larson, who was quietly fieldstripping his Browning. Hagen sat alone opposite them, sharpening his knife.

The veteran colonel owed Gorman for the other night at the money-drug bust gone south. Stark hated owing anyone anything and he suspected that the Gorman-Maryam relationship was more than professional. He couldn't care less but understood the how and why of such relationships and that Gorman was a good man.

Nothing more to say or think.

But getting it done.

Gorman hung up the phone and hit the speed dial for his sister's number, but once again, he could not get through. The phone lines into New York City were pretty much overwhelmed since the blast.

"I'm sure she's fine, Bill," Harwich said, looking up from his laptop. "Vic's a survivor."

"Yeah," Gorman said, putting the phone aside and logging into his computer. "I sure hope so."

39

Enemies of Islam

ISLAMABAD, PAKISTAN

Multitasking: part art, part science, and part experience. The key to its continued success was working by priority.

First he had to finalize the Mexico contingency for Salma. Then he needed to manage the safe return of the containers from DHL after the flights were forced back to Karachi somewhere over the Atlantic Ocean. Finally, he had to deal with his renegade daughter. And while he was at it, Atiq also had to prepare his government for the possibility of American retaliatory strikes.

If Washington chose to believe the intel that Maryam had leaked over the information his agency had so carefully disseminated, corroborating the claims made by Ibrahim al-Crameini in his videos . . .

God help us all, he thought.

But if it really came to that, Atiq hoped that President Vaccaro would live up to his expectations and keep any strike against Pakistan conventional. And even then hopefully limited to ISIS enclaves.

He felt certain that his network, as well as the entire government, was capable of surviving a retaliatory strike as long as it didn't include nukes. And he seriously doubted the Americans would cross that line, especially given their concern for world opinion.

Besides, Pakistan's nonconventional weapons capability couldn't be ignored. His nation possessed over one hundred nuclear bombs in its arsenal. And enough of them lay buried deep beneath the desert, beyond the reach of even the most powerful of their so-called bunker-busting bombs.

He downloaded the latest encrypted reply from Mexico and processed it through a descrambler algorithm. It translated into three lines of text that conveyed the answer from Miguel Montoya, the drug lord that ISI had enlisted to assist Salma.

Montoya was professional, as always, and willing to help, for the right cause—and for the right price, of course.

And sticking it to the Americans was *always* the right cause.

At the moment, his Colombian-born partner was preparing to mount a diversion across the Rio Grande to take advantage of the chaos spreading across his northern neighbor. Then Montoya would personally get Salma into Texas and beyond.

Despite his complications at home, Atiq couldn't help a smile. The situation in America was deteriorating rapidly across all states, and it was only going to get worse.

Much worse.

Closing all ports of entry was a double-edged sword. It did provide the temporary benefit of keeping his other three bombs from entering the United States. But shutting down the flow of goods even for a single day would have a noticeable effect at the consumer level. Turn that into several days, even a week, and the situation would turn critical. Riots would likely follow as people started to hoard goods, forcing the government to declare martial law. Constitutional rights would have to be suspended and soldiers deployed to restore order. And if Salma could reach Washington, D.C., and detonate a second bomb in the middle of all of that, the situation would reach an unprecedented level of horror, of fear, as the public lost faith in its government, triggering anarchy.

But it all came at a cost.

With a single line of text agreeing to Montoya's reassuring yet quite expensive plan, Atiq activated a contingency to achieve precisely that.

He transferred the required funds from banks in Saudi Arabia to Mexico via a mind-numbing set of monetary transactions.

He switched his attention to the DHL planes that had just landed in Karachi, coordinating with Lari to deploy teams to recover and secure their secret cargos until they could be shipped back out. It was unfortunate that the New York groundburst had prevented him from detonating the devices over Washington and Chicago, but at least he had gotten them back for another day.

Many in his network, in his government, and even in the radical ISIS, considered the overall mission already a success—as measured by the images from New York. But the attack could have been so much more than a single strike. And unless he could detonate at least a second bomb, he feared that the Americans would recover from this.

We almost made it, he thought, angry at the realization of just how damn close they had come to cutting off the head of the snake for decades by simultaneous attacks in New York, Chicago, Washington, D.C., and Houston.

But he had been betrayed.

His own flesh and blood had robbed him of his birth-given right to bring the giant to its knees. Maryam had kept him from exacting revenge for the death of his parents, of his sister—and for the scars that to this day continued to disfigure his soul as much as his body. And even worse, in doing so she had involved Pakistan in the strike rather than letting ISIS shoulder the blame.

While many in the government commended Atiq for the Bagram and New York strikes, he believed those same backstabbing bastards would turn against him the instant the American retaliatory bombs began to fall. They would distance themselves, taxing their extensive vocabularies to articulate politically savvy ways to divert all blame to him.

That meant contingencies would be required, damage-control plans designed and ready to be activated should the tide shift against him.

But before that, the time had come for his beloved Maryam to learn what happens to the enemies of Islam.

Kill the unbelievers, wherever you find them.
Fight against them until there is no dissention.
Fight until no other religion exists but Islam.

40

Run for the Border

STAR OF OCEANIA. GULF OF MEXICO.
TWO HUNDRED MILES SOUTH OF HOUSTON

The night was calm, peaceful, and star-filled, a far cry from the explosion of activity inside the American inspection zone almost a hundred miles to the north.

Salma Bahmani stepped inside the bridge and approached Captain Sjöberg, who stood by his pilot behind the vessel's large steering wheel. He reviewed the color GPS map on one flat screen, the ship's vital systems on a second monitor, and live footage via satellite of the New York disaster on a third display.

She walked up to him and stared at the images, harrowing even to her. The death estimate had reached 150,000 and was expected to climb in the coming days.

The news anchor reported that teams of first responders from the National Nuclear Security Administration, consisting of nuclear scientists, engineers, and technicians, were already on site. They were working in conjunction with the Radiation Protection Division of the EPA to set up a safety perimeter from Chambers Street to Battery Park. Although the groundburst had created a handful of radioactive pockets in Lower Manhattan, particularly around Cortland Street, the winds aloft had carried most of the toxic debris over the ocean.

That's unfortunate, she thought, wishing that the fallout had contaminated the entire area, as planned, triggering the complete shutdown of the city for decades, if not forever, given the long half-life of uranium-235.

But still, the damage was certainly unprecedented, even by September 11 standards.

The American Red Cross and the National Emergency Response

Team had already arrived at the scene within the initial hours to provide medical services to the flow of survivors. Firefighter units from dozens of precincts were currently battling the flames south of Chambers Street. The NYPD, assisted by the National Guard and the U.S. Army, maintained order on the rest of the island. The forestry and fire protection departments from New York, surrounding states, and even from Canada were deploying their air tankers to work in conjunction with the FDNY. Together, they were dropping hundreds of thousands of gallons of water and fire retardants over the worst areas to quench the flames.

Using battery-operated radios, rescue crews attempted to make contact with survivors. Military helicopters armed with loudspeakers conveyed instructions to anyone in Lower Manhattan to use the subway tunnels and head to Chambers Street, where radiation cleanup stations were being set up. Meanwhile, voluntary emergency crews wearing hazmat suits ventured south in search of survivors.

In the middle of all of the images, the screen was split in two to replay Ibrahim's stunning message, which had already received over 400 million views online—the most views of any video in history.

"That's one gutsy son of a bitch," Sjöberg commented. "You're from Pakistan, aren't you?" he added while looking at Salma.

She slowly bobbed her head and said, "Karachi."

"Just wondering what your views were. After all, al-Crameini also detonated a weapon that dropped toxic debris over your country."

"We all hope the bastard is caught and executed, and that he rots in hell," she replied, reciting the script that she and Malik had drafted in case the crew of their respective tankers questioned any of them.

"That we agree on," the captain replied, before turning his attention to the navigation equipment.

Salma watched the video in its entirety, until Ibrahim faded away and reporters went on to discuss the latest presidential directives. They included closing down all borders and grounding commercial and private air traffic.

"That is so stupid," Sjöberg said.

"Which part?" she asked.

"Closing the seaports. It's only going to magnify the problem."

"How?" Salma asked, even though she thought she already knew the answer.

"For starters, ninety percent of the world's trade is done via seaports. And to make matters worse, every country relies on a just-in-time supply chain that expects goods to arrive at seaports at precise times. It allows for lower inventory carrying cost and savings on warehouse space. This model is particularly overused in America. By closing all ports of entry, the president will trigger shortages of most goods within a week, from food, produce, medicine, and fuel to basic household needs. America's trucking system will quickly run out of product to deliver across the nation as well as the fuel to do so. What typically comes after that is riots and looting as people fear running out of food . . . compounding the problem."

Salma didn't know it could get so bad so soon, but she liked that.

"I've been in the business for a long time," the Norwegian captain continued, his blue eyes scanning the GPS before shifting his gaze to the horizon. "I was around when the International Longshore and Warehouse Union strike closed twenty-nine American seaports for ten days in 2002. The cost to the U.S. economy was almost twenty billion dollars. With *all* ports closed, it will be many times that, and even more for the global economy. While Wall Street has vanished, which will probably trigger a recession, the president isn't helping by adding fuel to the fire."

Salma couldn't agree more with his logic, especially when the decision was making it challenging to smuggle another bomb.

But that will be rectified soon, she thought, as the Mexican coast loomed in the upper right corner of the GPS.

"How much farther, Captain?" asked the pilot.

"I will let you know," he replied, looking over at Salma, who gave him a slow female wink.

She needed the captain to continue heading south but also veer to the west in a few hours, steering the tanker to the precise coordinates twenty miles off the coast of Mexico.

As instructed by Atiq.

41

Soldiers

There really were only variations of the same option. Once there was a decision to go to war, or retaliate, or bring serious harm to another country, then it simply boiled down to deciding the how and what the consequences might be.

Vaccaro was a soldier first and a politician second. She loved being the first and tolerated being the second. She wanted Pakistan to understand at their molecular level that what they had done would not go unanswered, could never be forgotten, and for the foreseeable future would not be forgiven.

The issue for President Vaccaro was disproportionate proportional response. She wanted the Pakistani government and its people to feel pain, fear, trepidation, hopelessness, and know from whom it came. She wanted the rest of the world to be reminded of the lessons of the first two World Wars: that once truly awoken, the United States of America would demolish its enemies.

The briefer was the new secretary of defense, Leon Ford.

Ford had been a soldier in Vietnam, wounded three times. He had an impeccable reputation and understood immediately what Vaccaro and the nation needed. His briefing with maps and slides of planes, type of bombs, destruction, collateral damage, and safety of the crews was precise and without ambiguity.

It was delivered without emotion.

The recommended strike packages would be specific and simultaneous, executed in collaboration with India and Israel. His plan was designed to cripple Pakistan's military and known ISIS encampments. Plus it included the destruction of Abbottabad, the home of one of Pakistan's military academies, and the place where the Pakistani government helped hide Osama bin Laden. The estimated loss of life in all combined strikes was between six thousand and ten thousand lives—and unlike in New York City, most of those lives would be either military or terrorist in nature.

The president wanted to hurt Pakistan, not destroy it.

Vaccaro looked around the room and said, "Let this decision be recorded—hell, everything in this room is recorded anyway—that I ordered this. I am not asking for a vote, opinion, or advice. The time for all that was before this briefing. Mr. Secretary, proceed with the attack."

"Yes, Madam President. We go live in thirty-six hours."

Turning to Wright, she added, "Meanwhile, John, let's make sure we get every American citizen evacuated from Pakistan before the bombs start to fall."

"Yes, Madam President."

"And get me the Israeli prime minister and the president of India on the phone," she added. "I need to make sure they don't get cold feet."

42

Back Channel

ISLAMABAD, PAKISTAN

It was a work of hybrid art, a classic example of English Palladianism with a touch of Neoclassicism and Pakistan's own Eastern style of architecture. Multiple domes atop columns crowned a structurally complex white façade overlooking Constitution Avenue in the heart of the capital city.

The Prime Minister's Secretariat, official residence and workplace for Vijay Korai and his cabinet, performed the same function as the White House. Its halls included situation rooms, secret passages, and even underground bunker facilities for times of national emergency.

And Korai could not think of a time in recent history that justified the use of every emergency facility at his disposal more than today.

Sitting behind his desk, he contemplated the grim future facing his country. The signs were all there, from the order to evacuate the American embassy a mile away to satellite imagery showing the U.S. Seventh Fleet in the Indian Ocean maneuvering toward the waters off the coast of Karachi. The Americans were certainly on the move, and the worst part was he could not get President Laura Vaccaro on the phone. The radio silence was as bad as any heated discussion—worse, because it meant the situation had deteriorated beyond words.

But then again, Korai was not sure what he could have said to the American commander in chief besides attempting to deny any involvement. He could remind her that ISIS had also attacked Pakistan, at least indirectly, through the toxic fallout from Bagram. But that smoke screen had been most certainly dispersed when Atiq reported a problem with a leak in his organization—a leak coming from none other than his own daughter.

A leak signaling the involvement of our own intelligence network.

So Korai had done the only thing he could do given the circumstances. He had called an emergency cabinet meeting and asked his generals to prepare for an attack. Only he had no idea what such an attack would look like.

Would the Americans retaliate in kind, obliterating a major city with a nuclear missile?

Or would they keep their attacks conventional?

But then, after he had met with his people and set up the best defense plan they could conjure given the nature of facing a much larger enemy, Korai had received a most unusual message via diplomatic channels.

Pakistan would suffer. But if the source of the message could be trusted, the American president had placed control of the severity of the retaliatory strikes squarely in Korai's hands.

43

Goat Rodeo

The Port of Houston, a strategic twenty-five-mile-long gateway to the American West and Midwest, ranked first in the United States in foreign waterborne tonnage, U.S. imports, and U.S. exports. At an annual total tonnage of 240 million tons, it moved nearly twice the tonnage of the Port of New York and New Jersey.

At least as of yesterday, FBI ASAC Monica Cruz thought.

She sat in the rear of a conference room on the second floor of a warehouse designated by the Houston Port Authority to be used as temporary headquarters for the gathering task force. Teams from every conceivable local, state, and federal agency were present, from the FBI, Houston PD, Port Police, and state troopers, to the Coast Guard, the National Guard, the U.S. Navy, TSA, FEMA, and U.S. Customs and Border Protection. Even the local chapter of the International Longshoreman's Union had sent a delegation. On top of that, due to the nature of the threat, there were also senior representatives from the Nuclear Regulatory Commission, the National Nuclear Security Administration, the Nuclear Energy Division of the EPA, and even a couple of safety experts from the International Atomic Energy Agency.

Every agency was under the coordination of the Department of Homeland Security. And to Monica all of that added up to one thing: a cluster fuck.

Monica frowned as she watched the lead of every agency jockeying for position in this massive illustration of government bureaucracy at work.

Everyone had an argument why a particular agency deserved more clout than others. U.S. Customs and Border Protection felt this was a border control issue. The Houston Port Police explained it was their port. The various Texas law enforcement organizations believed this was a Texas resident public safety issue. The Coast Guard tried to convince everyone that they were responsible for guarding the American coastline until a U.S. Navy admiral tried to set them straight. TSA proposed they were the most qualified. FEMA argued they were the most experienced. Each nuclear expert claimed to be more qualified than the others. And to make matters worse, the International Longshoreman's Union rep wanted assurances from everyone that his people would be safe or he would pull them from the harbor. Homeland Security, which oversaw half of the agencies present, was officially in charge by presidential decree with the mission of rallying everyone into a unified team.

Unfortunately, the assigned DHS lead, a deputy undersecretary named Hollis Gallagher, lacked the leadership charisma, experience, and visceral fortitude to effectively manage the powerful egos of this male-dominated crowd. The man looked, smelled, talked, walked, and probably even screwed his neighbor like a typical Washington politician.

Gallagher had no business being here, and for that matter, neither did most of the people in this room.

And that reminded Monica of the goat rodeos in her hometown of Eagle Pass in South Texas. Each agency lead attempted to corral the rowdy herd during his assigned fifteen minutes of shame by parading his team's experience and approach to the massive inspection problem facing Houston.

At the last count, there were close to two hundred merchant ships on hold, and each one would have to be thoroughly inspected before being allowed anywhere near the ship channel. They all had seen the images from New York, and the top goats were at least unified in making damn certain the chaos in that harbor would not be repeated here.

But there has to be a better way.

And the trick to finding it was connecting dots, linking seemingly unrelated observations to spark a working theory, and then adding more observations to either prove or disprove the theory. However, to even start to collect valuable observations, there was an underlying requirement that many FBI agents lacked, or for that matter most bucks in the room: You had to think like a terrorist. You had to ask yourself again and again not what "the manual" directed you to do, and certainly not what established protocols guided you to follow. But what a terrorist would do in any given scenario.

She had spent the past ten hours since arriving here at six in the evening putting herself in the shoes of a potential terrorist trying to enter the Port of Houston. And she tried damn hard to ignore each agency goat bleating on and on while pointing to those PowerPoint slides with those annoying little red lasers.

It was now just past four in the morning, and she suppressed a yawn while fingering her iPad, reviewing the long list of vessels on hold in the quarantine zone. Somewhere in the background the latest government agency presented the latest proposal to solving the gigantic inspection conundrum. It was a basic problem of not enough inspection resources to do a thorough and timely job given the large number of ships accumulating in the Gulf of Mexico. And a quarter of them hauled perishable goods from around the world—goods meant to be consumed by a hungry America, not left to rot a hundred miles offshore. The Port of Houston had some of the best inspectors in the business, and they had already been deployed via Houston Port Authority boats with assistance from the Coast Guard and the U.S. Navy to start tackling the incoming problem. But there simply weren't enough of them to keep the merchant ships from piling up in the gulf.

And what every buck in the corral didn't seem to get was that no amount of presentations or coffee or working into the wee hours was going to solve the fundamental physics of this rapidly growing supply-demand problem. They needed to elevate their thinking beyond business as usual.

Monica smiled while considering getting her old and trusty Elastrator band from her father's ranch to turn these bucks into wethers. Maybe she could improve the herd's collective IQ by separating them from their balls to get more blood where it really counted.

To the group's credit, however, at least they had prioritized the merchant vessels carrying perishable food supplies. But even then there had been heated arguments for nearly an hour before Gallagher finally stepped in and made the call at around midnight.

But sitting through the presentations had not been completely in vain. A U.S. Navy admiral had shared the final words of SEAL Team Six.

What did you take from him?
A remote control detonator . . . probably Bluetooth.
That metallic trunk . . . is that what I think it is?
Oh, shit.

But besides that recording, which the admiral had played three times to make sure everyone remembered it, the briefings had been utterly useless, at least to her.

A representative from the Nuclear Regulatory Commission had stepped up to the podium and droned on about the differences between plutonium and uranium, blah, blah, blah.

Monica scanned through the seemingly endless list of vessels peppering the waters of the gulf. There were dry bulk carriers hauling grain, ore, and other similar products in loose form. There were reefers—refrigerated ships—carrying perishable commodities, including meat, fish, vegetables, fruits, dairy products, and many other foods. General cargo vessels, as the name implied, transported anything from furniture, building materials, and garments to machinery, chemicals, military equipment, electronics goods, and automobiles. Some of the above came aboard the flotillas of specialized cargo vessels like colossal container ships and bulk carriers. There were even a dozen cruise ships in the mix with a combined thirty thousand well-tanned vacationing passengers wondering how the hell they were going to get home. And then there were the oil tankers, over thirty of them from all over the world, though most from the Middle East, and all ordered to the back of the line because of the *Seawise Goliath.*

Monica frowned. She had argued with Porter earlier today that the terrorists wouldn't be stupid enough to smuggle a second weapon aboard another tanker. That would be too obvious.

Unless . . .

She sat up straight and reviewed the list of oil tankers from the Middle East in the past twenty-four hours. It showed nineteen, including eight of the supertanker variety. But one of them, the *Star of Oceania,* had drifted south in the past ten hours.

Monica clicked on it and the satellite imagery software mapped its course from its point of origin at the Port of Karachi over ten days ago. It sailed around the tip of Africa, up the Atlantic Ocean, and into the Gulf of Mexico, before clearly backing away from the inspection zone shortly after the New York blast and heading south.

Where are you going?

She did a quick Internet check for seaports south of the Texas-Mexico border and was surprised by what she found. Next, she pulled up the ship manifests for both the *Goliath* and the *Oceania* and stared at them for a while.

And that's when she read the name of the company contracted to provide security for the two supertankers. A quick Internet check on the history of the security company sent a chill down her spine.

Slowly sitting back, Monica hissed, "Son . . . of . . . a . . . *bitch!*"

The comment drew sideways glances from the half-dozen ASACs flanking their boss, FBI Special Agent in Charge Roman Dalton. He was a husky black man, as large as Porter, with salt-and-pepper hair trimmed short, and very intense gray eyes. Dalton had a military background with multiple tours in Iraq and Afghanistan with the Marine Corps, before getting recruited by the Bureau.

"Cruz?" he whispered. "Anything you wish to share?"

"Can we step outside, sir?" she asked.

"I take it you're not that into the NRC discourse?" Dalton said in a low voice while pointing at the white-haired man standing behind the podium at the other end of the long room aiming a laser pointer at one of several bullets on a PowerPoint slide.

"With all due respect, sir, I think we're wasting our time in this room."

The comment earned her frowns from the other ASACs.

"And why is that?" Dalton asked.

"Because I think this is precisely what the motherfuckers who barbecued New York would want us to do."

"Which is?"

"Sit on our thumbs all night while gazing at PowerPoint presentations. I'd rather shoot myself . . . sir."

While the ASACs showered her with wide-eyed stares, Dalton revealed two rows of glistening white teeth as he grinned. "Porter warned me about you . . . and so did John Wright."

Monica held his gaze while remembering Porter's parting words. But before she could reply, Dalton tilted his head toward the exit.

She followed him under the half-surprised, half-puzzled gaze of the other ASACs, and under the clearly admonishing glare of Hollis Gallagher. Monica ignored him and followed Dalton out of the room.

He closed the door behind them and stood by the entrance to the conference room in a corner of the warehouse. The place bustled with activity, even at this predawn hour. At least two hundred people from too many government agencies forced to work together noisily shared a sea of white folding tables and chairs packed with laptops and printers.

Monica rolled her eyes at so many staff members preparing Power-Point slides for their superiors inside the conference room.

Standing under the glare of a fluorescent light, Dalton crossed his massive arms. "Well?"

"This supertanker," she said, pointing at her iPad. "The *Star of Oceania* . . . it left the Port of Karachi twenty-four hours after the *Seawise Goliath* but with Houston as its destination. Then it mysteriously headed south."

"So it looks like they're not a fan of the inspection zone? Who gives a shit?"

"That's *precisely* what I thought," she said. "Who gives a shit if a supertanker decides to change course? That's one less damn ship for us to inspect, right? Besides, the terrorists wouldn't be stupid enough to try to use the same delivery method twice. Would they?"

Dalton narrowed his eyes at her. "Continue."

"But . . . what if the attacks were supposed to take place at the same time . . . like on September eleven? What if both supertankers were meant to reach their destinations and blow themselves up *simultaneously?* Unfortunately for them, we got the CIA intel from Islamabad while the *Goliath* was still outside New York Harbor, which forced their hand. And now the terrorists aboard the second supertanker realize they lost the element of surprise and are on the run, maybe looking for another way in."

"I like the way you think, Cruz. What else do you have to support this theory of yours?"

She showed him the manifests. "The Karachi Shipping Security

Company provided security for *both* vessels . . . and I have done a preliminary search and can't seem to find that company providing security for any other vessel. Ever."

"Damn," he said, lowering his voice while leaning closer to her. "Don't tell anyone, but so far this is more promising than anything I've heard since I got here."

Not used to being complimented, Monica just stared back at him.

"So," Dalton added. "What do you want?"

"Well, I want world peace, sir, but short of that I'll settle for hopping on a chopper and checking out that tanker. Get eyes on it. Then we'll know for sure."

Dalton rubbed his square chin and said, "You understand you're asking me to devote very valuable, and, as you've heard in there, very *scarce* resources to go chase a ship that's actually cruising *away* from the United States? You realize how crazy that sounds given what we're up against in there?"

"I get it, sir. But let me ask you this: Where is that supertanker with three hundred thousand tons of crude oil going? The only seaport of any significance in Mexico on the Atlantic side is Veracruz, and I just checked it out and guess what? They don't have any oil refineries there. It's a fucking container terminal. And besides, the *Oceania*'s current course isn't even taking it there."

She flipped the screen and pulled out the supertanker's current route. "Look here. It's headed somewhere off the Mexican coast . . . just south of the border with Texas. There's *nothing* there, sir. Not a single port where it can even dock. So, why is it down there?"

"Damn. And if you're right, then trying to contact them by radio wouldn't be a good idea."

She nodded. "It would just telegraph that we're on to them."

"All right," he said. "Stay right here and give me a few minutes to make some calls. I'll get you a chopper, probably Coast Guard, plus a few agents, some hardware, and a satellite phone. You fly over there, land on that ship, check it out, and report back to me. Understood?"

For the first time in a very, very long time, Monica liked her boss.

"But Cruz," he added.

"Yes, sir?"

"Be very, very careful. It'll probably be daylight by the time you get there, so no darkness to mask your approach. If you're right and that ship has terrorists armed with a nuclear weapon . . . well . . ." He raised his brows at her.

"Yeah," she said. "An incoming chopper isn't going to get the warmest of receptions."

Dalton headed outside to get out of earshot from everyone.

Monica stared at the goats walking about, typing on their laptops, talking on their cell phones, and cranking out more slides.

And that's when it occurred to her that she had just signed up to become terrorist target practice.

44

DNA

LOWER MANHATTAN

Ray woke up on an army cot in the middle of what he recognized as Madison Square Garden. He was one of countless wounded amidst an army of doctors and nurses. An IV hung above him, connected to a clear tube feeding his left forearm.

"What . . . what the hell happened?" he mumbled, sitting up as someone checked his pulse. She was a woman in her forties with dark hair pulled back in a tight bun. She wore a navy blue uniform. A stethoscope hung around her neck. A patch on her right shoulder identified her as an FDNY paramedic. Her eyes were bloodshot.

"Easy there," she said, a silver tablet computer in her hands. "I'm Victoria Gorman. I've been looking after you since they brought you in. Here, drink this," she added, offering a bottle of water.

Ray drank it slowly. It was cold, refreshing, soothing his throat.

"How . . . long?" he asked.

Checking her screen, she replied, "About a day ago. You arrived unconscious . . . took three guys to haul you in."

"Sorry," he said.

"Don't be." She pointed at his badge, still pinned to his dusty uniform. "You're a big guy and you look like you take good care of yourself, Officer . . ."

"Kazemi. But please, call me Ray."

"You're lucky to be alive, Ray, especially from the Murray Street area where they found you."

"I actually came up from . . . Cortland."

She made a face. "Cortland?"

"And Broadway," he added.

"Ray . . . there were no surface survivors that far south . . . How did you—"

"I found two kids along the way," he said, slowly coming around, feeling his strength returning.

"Kids?"

"Brother and sister. Tourists . . . from Israel. Boy was around thirteen, the girl a bit older. Both had extensive burns."

"Yes . . . I remember them," she said. "They were airlifted . . . to Walter Reed in D.C., I think. But you, sir, need to take it easy, okay?"

"What's my condition?"

She frowned while checking her screen again. "A specialist—an oncologist—will be by shortly to explain your options."

"*Options?* What the hell, Doc? What's wrong with me."

Looking to both sides, perhaps in the hopes of spotting the specialist, she finally said, "I'm not a doctor. Just call me Vic, please." She pointed at her patch.

"Good, Vic, then you don't have to mince words."

She leaned closer to him and said, "ARS . . . acute radiation syndrome . . . You were exposed to a significant dose of ionized radiation."

"But . . . I feel fine," he said, flexing his arms, stretching, even considering removing the IV.

"For now. But that's why the oncologist needs to speak with you. I'm not authorized to—"

"Look," Ray interrupted, "I get it. But you won't get in trouble. I promise you. I just need to know my condition."

Victoria Gorman stared at him a while, then said, "There's a better than fifty percent chance that you will experience the first symptoms within twenty-four to forty-eight hours . . . probably gastrointestinal—vomiting and nausea—as well as aplastic anemia due to a drop in blood cells. That usually results in infections because of the low white cell count."

"I see," he said, though he sensed the paramedic was holding back the real truth of his condition. "Am I going to die?"

Victoria's eyes betrayed her. Ray had developed an affinity for reading people's faces, a valuable skill in the NYPD.

"I don't know the answer to that, Ray. The radiation caused cellular degradation by damaging your DNA structure, which affects the reproductive ability of cells. As the cells in your body die as part of their normal life cycle, new cells will not be produced to take their place. But in many cases, a treatment of blood transfusions and antibiotics has been known to work . . . but again, I'm only a paramedic. This is beyond my pay grade."

"Vic . . . I appreciate that, but in your professional opinion . . . and off the record," he insisted. "Am I going to die? And please, I *am* a cop but I'm also a religious man. I believe God has a plan for each of us."

She broke eye contact before replying, "I'm very sorry, Ray, but it is really beyond my expertise. An oncologist will be over shortly."

Deciding the good paramedic had already given him the answer, Ray asked the next obvious question. "What . . . what happened out there?"

"You don't know?"

"Well, I saw those people running up Broadway right before the blast. And when I woke up . . . it was a nightmare. Complete destruction. And I now know it had to be nuclear, given your ARS diagnosis."

Victoria frowned, looked down for a moment, before finally meeting his gaze. "You're correct. It was a nuclear bomb. Went off two days ago . . . in Battery Park. It was a terrorist strike . . . ISIS."

"God Almighty," he whispered, trying to process that, before looking about the interior of the massive sports complex under a shower of lights. "How extensive was the destruction?"

The paramedic checked her watch. "I need to keep doing my rounds."

"Please," he insisted. "I need to know."

Frowning again, she said, "What we hear is that everything south of Chambers is, well . . . gone . . . Look, I really need to continue my rounds. But I'll check back on you later, after the oncologist stops by. For now you need to take it easy, okay? You've been through a terrible ordeal and need to rest."

And she was gone, working her way down the long row of patients across the middle of the arena. Most people around him were in far worse shape than him, with extensive burns, broken bones, or limbs missing altogether. It reminded him of old Civil War movies.

And that's when it hit him.

Someone who had real wounds now, not in twenty hours or however long it would take his body to deteriorate, could use the bed he occupied. He believed God had spared him for a reason, for a purpose, keeping him alive through the fire and vicious winds that had leveled his city. And while he wasn't sure what that reason might be, he was damn certain it wasn't to rest here alongside the real victims of this terrible attack.

The paramedic had told him that he needed to take it easy.

Ray Kazemi, however, was nowhere near ready to take it easy.

Swinging his legs to the side of the cot, he inhaled deeply, feeling quite good after sleeping for so long.

Standing up while removing his IV under the surprised stare of a woman with a broken leg and arm occupying the cot next to him, he said, "When the paramedic lady returns, tell her to give this bed to someone who really needs it."

"Where . . . where are you going?" the woman asked.

"To make a difference."

45

End of the Line

No one had touched her in hours—though it was hard to tell time—and Maryam wondered why. Surely her captors, especially Atiq, would want her confession immediately.

Manish and Ahmed, another ISI agent, had removed the bag over her head before gagging her with the same duct tape they'd used to secure her arms, wrists, ankles, chest, and forehead to a large metal chair bolted to the floor of this basement-like room. They had worked in silence, doing a perfect job of immobilizing her.

Floor and walls made of rough concrete glowed under the dim light of a single bulb at the end of an electric cord.

She stared at the rusted metal door directly in front of her, wondering if Gorman knew, and even if he did, would he be able to help her?

Not likely, she thought, well aware of the powerhouse that was her former intelligence agency. Atiq would have taken every possible precaution to make sure no one would ever—

The door creaked open, and Atiq stepped inside. He was dressed in one of his business suits. Manish and Ahmed followed him, also dressed in dark suits. Behind them six men walked in wearing loose black clothing and matching hoods, hauling several bags.

Maryam met his gaze in the twilight of the room.

Father and daughter.

Eyes glistening for very different reasons.

She wanted to tell him that she'd had no choice, that the killing of innocent civilians wasn't the answer. But her muffled sounds were met with indifference.

Atiq raised a hand.

"I don't care to hear what you wish to say at this moment, daughter," he said in a slow, measured voice, before kneeling in front of her and cupping her chin. "Because we both know it will be lies."

He added in a mere whisper, "I will be back tomorrow, after my men have had a chance to . . . properly motivate you. *Then* we'll talk. But before I leave you in their capable hands, you should know that your pathetic attempt to disrupt my plans did not work. New York burns, and another bomb aboard another supertanker is headed for Houston. Lari has worked enough contingencies to see that mission to completion."

He paused, then leaned closer and whispered in her ear, "How could you betray me?"

Maryam wanted to cry out that he was the one who had betrayed her—betrayed Pakistan! But all she could do was swallow the massive lump in her throat.

Atiq pointed to the hooded men. "Maryam, meet my finest work. They will make you wish you were never born . . . and they will do it again and again, every day, for as long as it takes for the truth to emerge from those lips." Then he turned around and left the room, followed by Manish and Ahmed.

The six interrogators made a semicircle in front of her as the door slammed shut and they dropped their dark duffel bags on the dusty floor.

46

Thirty Seconds

They had to think of everything, from deciding whether to use helicopters, trucks, or cars—or a combination—to managing security and observation of the safe house. They had to finalize the communications plan, weapons to use, and the escape route, and then conduct rehersals.

Because once they got Maryam, they would have to be gone and gone fast.

Some of the preparations could be abbreviated but not avoided. Some of the items could be obviated with enough experience. But a couple of things could not be circumvented, like solid communications and observation of the safe house.

Gorman and Stark were painfully aware that the first rule of combat was always true: no plan survived the first shot. Therefore, the plan had to allow for changes, be extremely flexible, and they needed to be decidedly violent in its execution. Then, there was the gotta-go-right-now because the assholes that had Gorman's asset/girlfriend were torturing her before killing her in probably a quite horrible way. So it all felt like a made-to-order shit show of the first magnitude.

Gorman had also recruited his longtime friend, Glenn Harwich, catching him before he hopped on a plane back to Paris. He convinced him to drive the getaway van in front of the safe house at the precise moment when they were supposed to exit the place following the raid.

Then he'd met Stark and his team ten blocks from the three-story safe house where the drone followed Maryam and her captors. He had overhead pictures that were downloaded on his secure tablet, plus floor plans to the building, as his office had long suspected that Atiq Gadai was using the place for intelligence purposes.

The problem was that the house lacked constant surveillance, as Gorman had other priorities. The possibility that tunnels had been dug, or rooms and doors reinforced and booby traps set were among the many questions that Stark and especially Chief Evan Larson were rightfully asking.

All agreed that nothing was optimal; all were told this was a volunteer-only mission. Yes, they would be paid—double—but no one had to go.

Gorman and Stark said they had to go, Gorman because it was his asset and Stark because he owed Gorman. Ryan Hunt looked around and made eye contact with the team, staring Larson, Hagen, and Danny Martin in the eye, before all looked at Stark and nodded.

"What the hell," Ryan had finally said. "Gotta die of something."

The rescue would be straightforward and with no pretense, but with a diversion. Stark's team would come from the top, moving down the interior as fast and as efficiently as the enemy would allow and their training could dictate. The diversion would be a staged accident between a truck and a car, with police sirens and all the noise and confusion possible. The withdrawal would be from the back. Gorman would have his team secure both ends of the street, with Harwich driving the getaway van straight to a road leading to a small airfield. Stark's C-21A jet would take them to Frankfurt, where they would refuel before continuing to Washington, D.C.

Well, that was the plan, anyway.

They approached from the adjoining building. Ryan had set up his sniper's perch with a view of the relevant side of the safe house, his position determined by a heat scan of the building. He would have to move to cover the withdrawal, but limited resources and a come-as-you-are assault plan lacked predictability. Things could go wrong; information could be inaccurate. The enemy had a vote and got to shoot back.

They had decided to do the raid about an hour after Atiq Gadai and his large entourage of armed guards and ISI agents departed the building.

Gorman gave the team of Pakistani drivers the signal to crash and made calls to the police and Pakistan Red Crescent Society ambulance service. This could not be a "go at a specific time" operation. The signal to go had to depend on the crash and the arrival of the police and

PRCS emergency vehicles. Such was the nature of a diversion: you had to give it time to "divert."

They would access the roof of the safe house via a twelve-foot-long plank of hard wood across the expanse between buildings. Larson carried it like a twig, waited another minute until Stark signaled that the diversion was in place, and then quietly lowered it to the other side.

Stark climbed on and ran across in a crouch for balance. His hands clenched a sound-suppressed MP7A1 submachine gun. Hagen followed, similarly equipped, then Danny, and finally Larson, who brought the board across in case it was needed later and also to clean up the access into the target building.

The door inched open to a stairway with one small room on the third floor.

A man with his AK-47 leaned against the wall, smoking a cigarette.

Stark fired twice. The ports along the gun barrel vented gasses into the sound suppressor's chambers, absorbing the reports as the lone figure clutched his chest and went down.

Stark yelled, "Clear and moving!"

Three seconds gone.

Hagen took the lead as Stark paused a moment by his kill at the top of the stairs. The former SEAL moved deliberately, weapon trained down, his dark silhouette blending with the murky stairwell.

Stark, now second in the stack, trained his weapon right while the third man, Danny, concentrated left. Larson continued to cover the rear. All had prearranged and practiced zones; all covered each other with deadly efficiency.

Second-floor stairwell, one man moving up. Hagen quickly put him down with two 4.6x30mm JHP rounds squarely and millimeters apart to the center cavity.

Six seconds.

Two Russian grenades were flung up the stairs from around the corner. Hagen kicked one down but yelled, "Grenade!" and rushed back up, now following Stark, Danny, and Larson scrambling for higher ground.

They rounded the stair corner as the closest grenade went off, followed by the one Hagen had kicked back down to the unseen enemy, the sounds deafening inside the enclosure.

Stark and Hagen endured a blast of plaster and wood fragments on their backs and arms, but otherwise were lucky. Maybe a few small scars . . . nothing but character building.

The team wore light body armor good for stopping up to 9mm rounds. However, they had skipped the titanium plates in the front or back as they slowed them down.

Speed versus safety.

The assault team headed back down with Hagen again at the front of the stack, discovering three dead from the grenade he had kicked down to the main floor.

And no sign of Maryam.

Eighteen seconds down.

She has to be in the basement, Stark thought, as Hagen tossed two sound grenades down the last set of steps, their blasts rattling the structure.

Larson went first now, as prescribed by their plan, letting the big chief with the big gun tear up the basement door, firing down into it to avoid shooting rounds across the room and hurting the hostage.

While Larson battled with the thick metal door, managing to inch it open, Stark tossed a flashbanger through the gap. The acoustic energy nearly ripped it off its hinges.

He stormed the dusty basement, closely followed by Larson, Hagen, and then Danny—muzzles already pointed at their prearranged zones.

The room was large and dusty, with one light bulb, six very disoriented men clad in black, and one bloody woman strapped to a chair in the middle.

Three seconds and all six men were dead.

Using a SOG knife, Stark released Maryam from the interrogation chair, hoisted her over his right shoulder, and moved with the team up the stairs and out the back.

Total time thirty seconds.

————

The rescue team with Maryam drove quickly but not directly to the prescribed airfield. Gorman had arranged for a drone to follow them and to insure he was getting minute-by-minute updates on movements around their escape route. Also he could make adjustments for traffic, which had the potential to stop them or at least slow them down enough that anyone chasing them would have a better chance of catching up to them.

They were in a large Ford van. Harwich drove while Danny kept watch in the front passenger seat. Stark, Ryan, and Larson occupied the center seat. Maryam sat in the rear in between Hagen and Gorman. She seemed a bit out of it—likely due to the combination of the torture plus the concussion grenade.

Gorman and Stark knew that ISIS had entire sections of police, military, and intelligence officers and other government officials either on their payroll or sympathizing with their cause. So the drone was also reporting on police locations.

Stark had Hagen check Maryam for any medical issues.

The former Navy SEAL went to work on her, checking her blood pressure, tending to a bruised cheek, and just making sure nothing was broken.

Maryam quickly came around, eyes half open, panning from Gorman to Stark, who had turned around and now regarded them over his right shoulder.

"I'm . . . okay . . . really," she whispered, blinking, breathing deeply, and grimacing as she huddled into herself, as if she were cold.

At that moment, Maryam looked fragile, scared, but she quickly rose above any self-pity. Hagen took just a few minutes to clear her to Stark and Gorman with nothing more than bruised ribs and a few cuts.

Maryam grabbed Gorman's right hand with both of her hands, mumbled, "Thanks, love," and fell against him.

But an instant later she abruptly pushed back, her dark eyes wide open now, and said in her British accent, "Wait . . . there is another bomb . . . aboard another bloody tanker . . . heading to Houston."

"Houston?" Stark repeated while Gorman and Larson looked on. "Are you sure?"

She slowly nodded. "Atiq told me so before leaving me in the hands of his bloody interrogators. He wanted the satisfaction of me knowing that despite my efforts the attacks would continue. I wasn't sup-posed to leave that room . . . alive."

"Bastards," mumbled Stark.

"When?" Gorman asked.

She shook her head. "That's all he said. I do not know the timing, the route, or any other detail . . . but he did say that he had contin-gencies in place to see the mission to its completion, whatever that bloody meant. I . . . am sorry I do not have more for you."

"That's plenty," Stark said, reaching back and patting her on the shoulder. "That's quite plenty."

Maryam took a deep breath and slowly nodded to the colonel before turning to Gorman without embarrassment and with confi-dence. "I fancied you before you came for me, Bill. Now I am devoted to you. I owe you my life."

Even a hardass like Gorman was stopped in his tracks by what had just happened. He could not look away. "I . . . I have to call this in now," he finally said. "We're getting you out of Pakistan, and in case I don't get the chance to say it later, I also—"

"Will you two get a damn room?" Stark yelled without turning around.

Gorman was dialing the planned number in his satphone with one hand and tossing an empty magazine at the back of Stark's head.

"This is Lax, put me through," Gorman said to the man answer-ing the phone from a basement in a rented office in a secure facility in Crystal City, a suburb in Virginia, just south of the capital.

"She's in a meeting," the man replied in a monotone voice.

"Put her on the phone now!"

The line went silent for a few moments.

"What do you have?" asked Lisa Jacobson.

"There is another bomb on a ship heading for Houston," Gorman began as the streets of Islamabad rushed by while Maryam hugged his right bicep and rested her head on his shoulder.

"How accurate is your source?" Lisa asked when he finished the brief.

"This is from a priority source that has been one hundred percent accurate, and I am only calling this number when I have information like this. We do not have time for me to have to ask to speak to you twice, so if you want to keep this arrangement then either give me access to you twenty-four/seven or tell whomever you have tasked to answer for you that I get put through without delay."

Gorman frowned at the silence on the line, so he added, "C'mon, Lisa. You've been in my shoes before. I'm either in this team of yours or I'm not."

"Thank you for the update, Bill, and here is my twenty-four/seven secure number," she replied, giving Gorman her number before adding, "Now if there is nothing else, I need to brief the president."

"Where . . . where are we going?" Maryam asked as Gorman hung up the phone.

"Small airfield," he replied. "A jet is waiting to take us to Frankfurt. I'm afraid your spying days are over."

Slowly, Maryam shook her head. "But . . . what about the specifics on the third bomb?"

Stark turned around. "What about it?"

Gorman said, "I thought you didn't know the details."

"That's true," she replied. "But I know someone who does . . . someone in Karachi . . . a close associate of Atiq."

"Not a good idea, Bill!" Harwich shouted from the front. "You and your lady friend need to get your ass on that plane."

"He's right," said Stark. "There's a shit storm heading this way, and you don't want to be *anywhere* near here when it hits."

Gorman frowned and shifted his gaze between the back of Harwich's head as he drove and Stark's armor-piercing stare.

The embassy in Islamabad had already been evacuated, as were the consulates in Karachi, Quetta, and other major cities. By midnight there weren't supposed to be any Americans left on Pakistani soil.

His eyes finally landed on Maryam.

What if she is right?

What if there's a chance to find more intel on the third bomb?

But what are our chances without a local support structure?

These questions and a dozen more swirled in Gorman's mind as he looked out the window. The train station was just a few blocks away.

"You sure about this?" he asked Maryam.

"Honey, unfortunately, as you Americans would say . . . *I know a guy*," she said with her best attempt at a half grin.

Making his decision, Gorman screamed, "Hey, Glenn! Stop the van!"

47

Biblical

President Vaccaro demanded to go to New York City.

Every bone in her body demanded it; the American people demanded it. No amount of security concern was going to stop her.

She had a one-way conversation with the head of her Secret Service detail and the head of the Department of Homeland Security, saying the same thing to both. "I am going to New York if I have to walk. I am not wearing a protective suit, so figure it out."

While flying in on Marine One, a Sikorsky SH-3 Sea King helicopter, Vaccaro had a more chilling look at the destruction than the satellite and drone footage had given them. Everyone aboard was fixated on the ground, seeing sections of New York Harbor littered with many ships capsized or in flames. On land, buildings were ruined, parts of everything melted down to their metal, brick, and asphalt skeletons.

To Vaccaro it looked biblical . . . Old Testament biblical—a place beyond recognition; the one time that the phrase "hell on earth" was accurate to a fault.

The Sikorsky landed in Hudson River Park, at the west end of W. Houston Street. A motorcade took her to the edge of the EPA radiation contour by Canal and Broadway.

"I did not prepare a speech," the president began, addressing a crowd of a few thousand people, mostly first responders. She stood flanked by the mayor of New York City, the commissioners of the NYPD and the FDNY, and the governors of New York and New Jersey.

"What I am saying to you now is how I feel, as a human being, a citizen of this great nation, and as president. I know that my coming here is an inconvenience to the state and the city, and I am truly sorry for that, but I had to be here. We are all hurting, all trying to recover, trying to figure out the how and why of what happened. We will find our answers together. My message is simple: We have survived this attack and we *will* rebuild. Every asset at your government's control, plus any and all help being offered from other nations, is being accepted and used. We will not get this perfect, but we will never leave you. There is a hotline available and manned by hundreds to take your calls and react immediately. To those who will play politics with this attack and recovery, to those who will attempt to take advantage of this day, I am telling you now and for all time: we will publicly denounce you, hunt you down, and prosecute to the fullest extent of the law. I have suspended many of our rights as citizens in order to make this recovery as fast as possible and to protect this nation from further attack. I am sorry that I had to make this decision, but I am sure it was the right one to make."

Pausing for a moment while staring at the camera, Vaccaro added, "I now speak to those who perpetrated this act of war. You will be punished on our timetable. We will not be stopped, detoured, or talked out of what is about to happen.

"Thank you for taking time from your day, as you begin to literally rise from the ashes. May God bless you all and may God bless the United States of America."

48

Down to Earth

LOWER MANHATTAN

Since 9/11, first responders in New York City—cops, firemen, and medical personnel—all referred to that day and the heroic efforts and tragic deaths as separate and distinct moments in time. They were never to be touched, forgotten, or duplicated. But as is true in many tragic situations, time, if it doesn't heal, reshapes all wounds.

This event, a nuclear explosion on American soil, was a world-changing event to Ray Kazemi.

But the NYPD sergeant did not have time to contemplate; he only had time to react. His military training had kicked in.

Ray had joined the Army Rangers shortly after that fateful day in 2001. He wanted to be with the best. He was strong and determined and made the grade, seeing combat in both Afghanistan and Iraq. Ray missed Brooklyn, the feeling of home, the smells, the food, and the girls . . . now women. He missed the attitude, his neighborhood, and his friends. He had left a boy and returned a man of blood, surer, less vulnerable, and yet in other ways more gentle and understanding and accepting of others, and a little troubled. His religion helped combat the nightmares, the trauma in his head. He learned what combat veterans learn: all take the war home; some learn to live with it better than others, but all take it home. The decision to become a police officer was easy and natural. Service was a part of him. In this way he could still feel part of something and yet be near his home. Ray had developed into a good man and a great cop.

It was two days since the attack and just two hours since he had walked out of Madison Square Garden.

He, like the rest of the city and the nation, was still in shock.

His senses were upside down, his ears still rang. His eyes came in and out of focus. His balance, sense of feel, in fact his damn bones were sore. However, he was too busy trying to find survivors, starting with his partner, Jenny Marshall. There was no way to explain why some buildings still stood or traffic lights on one corner were blinking. The city block behind him was flattened, with nothing showing but some concrete stairs leading to nowhere, but the buildings just across the street appeared undamaged.

While joining others to search for survivors, Ray literally bumped into a Secret Service agent. There was no mistaking the agent—first, he was clean: starched shirt, earpiece, fresh suit, no dust or grime, and the ever-present sunglasses.

Ray's police-blue uniform was torn, smeared with dirt and grease, and caked in white dust. His shield and weapon were obvious, so the Secret Service agent nodded and continued his duties.

Ray asked, "What's going on?"

"The president is around the corner giving a speech. Me, I'm just doing what I do when the president's around the corner giving a speech," the agent replied.

"Do you like her?"

While looking about him, apparently for a possible threat to the president, the agent replied, "We all like her even though it's not required. She understands what we do. She's very down to earth—hell, she buys us coffee often; the agents and staff who were in the service really like her."

Ray thanked the agent and walked past him, reaching the edge of the crowd in time to hear President Vaccaro's short but extremely appropriate speech.

Damn, he thought. *Sometimes the moment you need real leadership, a leader actually appears.*

Good for her . . . hell, good for us.

49

Summons

ISLAMABAD, PAKISTAN

He threw the phone against the wall, startling his female aide.

Slowly, Atiq Gadai stood, pressing tight fists against the top of his desk, before turning around, arms crossed. His eyes scanned the manicured lawns and gardens of the ISI headquarters beyond a row of panoramic windows.

"Leave me," he said, listening to his aide's hastening footsteps until she closed the door behind her, leaving him to his thoughts.

After all the precautions he had taken to secure his traitor daughter in one of the ISI's most guarded safe houses, the Americans had managed to break her free, murdering a dozen guards in the process. The operation had been swift, executed with military precision. They were in and out in under a minute, leaving nothing but death and destruction in their wake—and, most importantly, no witnesses.

He clenched his jaw, trying to control his growing anger, remembering the brief discussion he'd had with Maryam before leaving her in the hands of his interrogators.

The rescue team had made sure that every guard inside the compound-like facility was executed. Two bullets in the center of their chests and one to the head each, making it far more difficult to understand how they had broken through his security measures.

But seeking understanding would have to come later. At the moment he needed to protect the mission, and that meant protecting Salma, following up with his contacts in Monterrey, making certain that they would live up to their commitments.

So, as enraged as he was at Maryam's liberation, Atiq somehow found the discipline to compartmentalize his ire. Logging into his system, he contacted his allies in Mexico, focusing his energy on making certain that the damn Americans didn't get their hands on another one of his agents.

He finished in ten minutes, before switching tasks, deploying agents after his runaway daughter—assuming she was still in the country. For all he knew, her American rescuers could have her halfway to America by now. He decided to activate the two operatives who had figured out she was a traitor and who later participated in the abduction, Ahmed and Manish. Along with the activation, Atiq wanted to include a clear mission statement: Kill Maryam and Bill Gorman on sight. And don't come back until it is done.

When he was finished, Atiq kicked off another message, posting it on an Internet bulletin board that didn't exist, except to a selected group of bounty hunters. He wanted mercenaries who would stop at nothing to collect the irresistible price he placed on Maryam's head as well as the head of Bill Gorman.

Halfway through the message, there was a knock on the door.

He ignored it, finishing and activating the bounty just as a second knock pounded his door, this one louder than the first.

"What is it?" he shouted, annoyed at the distraction when he had so much to do.

Problems like this fell in a category requiring total concentration. They could not be solved if he kept getting interrupted.

The door inched open and his assistant stuck her head through the gap.

"Dr. Gadai . . . there are some men here to see you."

"Who? I'm busy now," he replied.

His assistant was slowly but firmly pushed aside and six soldiers marched into his office followed by two men in business suits whom he recognized as members of the prime minister's protective detail— and who had been trained by Atiq's network.

Atiq stood, hands on his desk. "You'd better have a *damn* good reason to barge in like this."

"Dr. Gadai," said the older agent, "Prime Minister Korai has summoned you."

50

The Wild West

TWENTY MILES OFF THE COAST OF MEXICO

It began as a mere speck on the horizon, a lone shape against the endless span of blue seas. Its imposing outline slowly loomed on the surface, towering walls of shimmering steel rising two hundred feet above the waterline, glaring and colossal. Longer than the Empire State Building, the *Star of Oceania* seemed at peace bounded by a pristine ocean.

They came in low, turbines propelling the orange and white MH-60 Jayhawk from the USCG at 140 knots. It skimmed the waves, triggering memories from her military days. The splendor of the Caribbean setting—blue skies, turquoise waters, and distant fog-crested mountains—all was lost on Monica as the Sikorsky approached the supertanker from the northeast.

A few minutes ago, Monica had received a call from Dalton informing her that the CIA had reliable intel that there was a third bomb and it was aboard a supertanker headed for Houston.

Her instincts had been correct.

Terrorists were likely aboard the *Oceania*, which now meant a warm reception.

ISIS style.

Focus, she thought, performing a final weapons check, starting with her Heckler & Koch MP7A1 submachine gun and its thirty-round magazine. The MP7A1 had three fire settings, single, burst, and full auto, for firing one round, three rounds, or full automatic, respectively, every time she squeezed the trigger.

Monica selected single fire mode. Real operators preferred single shots, usually two at a time. A burst of three would consume too many bullets, and full auto was for the movies.

Next was her Glock 22, fitted with a GTL-22 attachment featuring a dimmable xenon white light and a red laser. Professional habits kept her sidearm always ready, but the possibilities of combat made her check it again. Her fingers moved automatically, verifying she had a full magazine of fifteen .40-caliber S&W rounds plus one in the chamber. She also wore standard FBI SWAT body armor, which included a vest with pockets loaded with extra magazines for both weapons.

The pilot brushed the ocean while approaching the supertanker from the bow, out of sight from the bridge. He brought the Jayhawk right up to the vessel's hull before abruptly cutting left and continuing along the starboard side to amidships. They stayed low, just above the waves, before suddenly surging skyward.

She fought the pressure in her gut as the pilot pushed the General Electric twin turbines, rocketing the chopper. Monica and her three agents were assisted by the chopper's gunner, manning the M240D starboard-mounted machine gun. It was capable of unleashing over eight hundred 7.62x51mm NATO rounds per minute. They kept their weapons trained on the hull as they rose like an elevator on steroids, reaching the main deck, dominated by the bridge's panoramic windows.

She scanned her arc from left to right, shoulders tense in anticipation of gunfire or the flash of an incoming RPG. She kept her shooting finger on the trigger, ready to reciprocate, shifting sights across the length of the bridge and the surrounding structure area while her teammates scanned their respective arcs.

Silence.

A heavy sinking feeling spread through her heightened system, countering the adrenaline rush as she lowered the weapon and said, "Put us down over there! On that platform next to the bridge!"

The Coast Guard pilot shifted the Jayhawk over to the indicated location with military precision. Monica jumped out first, MP7A1 leading the way, stock pressed against her right shoulder, left hand on the handle beneath the barrel and right hand on the trigger. The gun muzzle followed her shooting eye scanning the gangway, which connected their landing platform to the bridge.

Controlling her breathing, she closed the distance in thirty seconds, kicking in the door to the bridge, and lowering the weapon when spotting the pile of bodies in the rear of the control room.

"Damn it," she hissed, reaching for the satphone while her team passed her up and knelt down to inspect the bodies.

"Still warm," said one of the agents, a black man in his thirties.

"Same here," said another agent, a woman around Monica's age, blond with blue eyes. "Bastards can't be far."

"You three," she told the two of them plus a third agent, another man in his early thirties, all from the Houston office. "Head down to the engine room. Stay alert. There's a chance the bastards may be hiding."

The trio vanished through a bulkhead, accompanied by the gunner. All were armed with MP7A1s.

Monica dialed the phone.

A moment later Dalton's tenor voice said, *"Talk to me."*

"Crew's dead, at least on the bridge. Engines are out. The tanker is just drifting. The team is heading to the engine room now. No sign of the terrorists. I fear they've abandoned ship and are headed inland."

"Looks like your instincts were spot on, Cruz."

"If they were spot on, sir, I would have bagged the motherfuck-ers," she said, staring at the distant coastline, which the Jayhawk's GPS had shown as twenty miles away.

"Don't be so hard on yourself. At least now we know what they're up to."

She nodded. "We need all the help you can get us. Mexico's worse than the Wild West, sir. We also know that any organization that can do what these asswipes have done is receiving lots of support from the locals wherever they go."

"Stay put and stick to the plan. The Coast Guard crew has orders to keep the tanker outside of Mexican territorial waters. I'm calling Washington now and also notifying Border Patrol. Plus tons of reinforcements are headed your way."

A moment later she heard her team through the earpiece coiled inside her vest connected to their ops radio.

"Engine room secured. Crew's dead. No sign of the Tangos . . . or any weapon."

Monica hung up the phone and stepped outside the bridge, anger and frustration boiling into a brew that began burning a hole in her gut as she stared at the seemingly peaceful coastline.

She squinted, for a moment seeing something . . . motion at the edge of her line of sight. It looked like white silhouettes against a ho-rizon bounded by lush mountains with summits buried in banks of foggy clouds.

What the hell . . .

She rushed to the helicopter, ducking under the downward wash, and hopped in the rear. Grabbing a pair of binoculars, she jumped back out before pressing them against her eyes, index finger bringing the coast into focus. Her line of sight, a result of the Earth's natural curvature, was limited to around sixteen miles, preventing her from seeing the actual beach. She could only see the outline of mountains rising in the distance. Unfortunately, whatever she thought she might have seen approaching the coast was now gone.

She climbed back inside the Jayhawk and scrambled to the front.

"Over there!" she shouted at the pilot, pointing at the shore. "I think I saw something approaching land. I need to check it out."

The pilot glanced at the coastline, down at his GPS, and shook his head. "We're just eight miles outside Mexican territorial waters and airspace. My orders are to stay put and take control of the tanker to keep it on this side of the international water line. I can't go in pursuit without permission."

"Hold on," she said, getting on the satphone again to see if Dalton could short-circuit this, but the SAC wasn't picking up.

Probably calling Washington, she thought as seagulls screeched nearby and waves lapped lazily against the side of the tanker. If need be, she was ready to force the pilot to go after them at gunpoint. This was, after all, war.

She scanned the horizon one more time with the binoculars, slowly, methodically, moving left to right in five-degree arcs, and saw nothing but ocean and the outline of distant mountains.

Not a soul in—

There!

She spotted them, two large boats cruising toward the beach, probably no more than ten miles away.

"The terrorists!" she screamed. "They're on boats! Take me over there!"

"Lady, I've already told you that—"

She pointed the Glock at his groin.

"Seriously? You're going to shoot a United States Coast Guard helicopter pilot?"

"Whatever it takes. I'm counting to five and you're never having sex again."

"Are you shitting—"

"One . . . two . . . three . . ."

"All right! All right!" he said, twisting the throttle control and working the collective and the cyclic. "But you'd better know what you're doing!"

51

Margaritaville

The supertanker grew smaller on the horizon as the coastline rose before them. Rows of towering palm trees dotted miles of deserted beaches before the terrain angled toward the foot of the mountains.

Salma had watched the cartel contingent through her binoculars as they had approached the *Oceania* thirty minutes ago. Two speedboats, bright hulls slicing through shallow waves, momentarily disappeared behind explosions of foam and mist, their pilots pushing the vessels with apparent urgency.

They will be here soon, she had thought, remembering the warning from Atiq. The Americans knew about the bomb in her tanker, prompting everyone to accelerate the transfer plans.

Shifting her attention from the incoming boats that Atiq had arranged with the local cartel, Salma stared at her hostages in the rear of the bridge. She kept them all on their knees, wrists zip-tied behind their backs, strips of duct tape over their mouths.

Subduing them had been easy, especially since her team had all the weapons.

Half the crew was up here, including Captain Sjöberg, who regarded her with a terrified blue-eyed stare. The rest, along with two of her men, were down in the engine room, also secured. Azis and Omar were on their way up to the transfer deck with their precious cargo to open the water-level access hatch and meet up with the cartel contingent.

In some strange way, Salma felt sorry for the Norwegian captain, who had conformed to her wishes, even coming up with creative reasons for steering the vessel this far south.

But it was time to move on, and she could not leave witnesses.

Clutching a 9mm Beretta 92FS, she walked up to the four crewmen. Thumbing the safety lever off, Salma cocked the weapon, chambering a round, the sound making two of the men whimper. But her ears were deaf to their muffled sobs as she faced her captives and leveled the weapon at the captain. Ignoring his pleading gaze, his stifled cries, she fired once.

The 9mm hollow-point round echoed inside the bridge. It pierced his forehead between the eyes, exiting through the rear in an explosion of blood, brains, and skull, spraying the control panel behind him.

The other three tried to get up, frightened moans filling the silence after their captain dropped to the tiled floor already a corpse.

She fired a round into each of their heads in rapid succession. Blood spattered on her face, neck, and chest, which she ignored, leaving them where they fell and making her way belowdecks.

Salma joined Azis, Omar, and the rest of her surviving crew huddled by the large oval hatch. Sunlight and fresh air pierced the compartment, washing over them as the boats approached, chrome handrails and fittings reflecting the afternoon sun.

"All good in the engine room?" she asked.

The large Muslim nodded. "No witnesses."

"Good."

The first boat maneuvered toward them. Up close the boats were far larger than she had realized, almost qualifying as yachts. Their decks rose and fell with the waves, making the transfer of men and cargo challenging even in relatively calm seas.

The key was timing, stepping onto the bow deck as the large speedboat rose like an elevator, reaching the short platform projecting beyond the hatch.

They boarded the boats, each manned by two cartel soldiers. One stood behind the controls, expertly keeping the boats neutral with the drifting tanker. The other assisted with the boarding process. All four were tanned, clean cut, wearing sunglasses, T-shirts, long shorts, sandals, and MAC-10 pistols secured in chest holsters.

Salma, Azis, and Omar waited for the second boat, handling the bomb transfer themselves, securing it in a compartment under the bow deck.

"I'm Alfonso Domingo," said the man standing behind the controls in the center of the boat, which she now recognized as a very large Boston Whaler with three outboard motors. He was in his early thirties, muscular. "Don Montoya welcomes you to Mexico."

"Where is he?" she asked, standing next to him, steadying herself by grabbing on to the edge of the windshield protecting the control panel.

"Monterrey," he replied, turning the bow toward shore and steadily advancing the throttles. The large outboards rumbled, propelling them away from the tanker. "Your face, *señorita*. Are you all right?"

"Not my blood," she said.

Alfonso reached under the control panel and produced a small towel, handing it to her.

Salma wiped her face before narrowing her gaze, trying to see beyond the glare.

"Here," Alfonso said, passing her a pair of sunglasses, which she slipped on, relaxing her eyes.

"Thank you," she replied, trying to enjoy the fresh air and the beautiful scenery. Turquoise waters led to pristine sands backdropped by lush green jungles and the mountains beyond.

Just like in the postcards, she thought, closing her eyes while letting the ocean mist cool her face.

And that's when she heard what sounded like a helicopter. She turned around and stared into the distance.

"We'll be fine," Alfonso said. "We're inside the twelve-mile belt of Mexican territorial waters and airspace."

Salma kept looking at the eastern skies, finally spotting a dot just above the horizon.

"No American boats or drones allowed. Plus you're under the protection of Don Montoya now. No one can touch you."

"Well, I don't think that guy got the memo," she said, pointing to the east.

Alfonso told his man to take the control while he reached under the cockpit and pulled out a pair of binoculars, inspecting the horizon before passing them to Salma.

"U.S. Coast Guard."

"How do you know?" she said, panning to the incoming helicopter, white with orange.

"Because it is my business to know that and also that he's not supposed to be here."

"Well, he is, Alfonso. Asshole is coming directly to us. Now what?" she asked, putting down the binoculars.

"We pretend to be vacationing," he replied. "We're just enjoying a beautiful day in Margaritaville."

She frowned.

"I'm telling you. I know these gringos. They're not going to shoot. They will circle us and ask us to stop, but they never shoot first."

Salma looked at the incoming helicopter, then at the trunk, and back at the helicopter. "And if they do?"

The Mexican man smiled while patting the MAC-10 in his chest holster.

"*That?*" she said, pointing at the 9mm gun. "Against *that?*" She pointed at the chopper, now roughly a mile away, glistening in the sunlight. "Please tell me we have more than a bunch of glorified pea shooters for the money my government is paying you guys!"

"Please tell me you have a plan!" the pilot shouted as the boats came in view.

Wearing a set of headphones, Monica had the starboard door already open and her hands on the handles of the M240D gimbal-mounted to the deck, its muzzle trained on the closest of the two speedboats already halfway to shore.

"Come from behind and fly low and very fast alongside them a thousand feet out! I'm going to shoot their engines!"

But she knew it would not be that easy.

The first shots came from the side of the helicopter.

Everyone, even the two boat pilots, instinctively sought cover. But an instant later, as smoke trailed one of the outboards on the other boat plus two on their own, Salma realized the helicopter gunner's intentions.

She stood up first, and her team followed, opening fire in unison with their AK-47s. Alfonso stood up next to her holding two MAC-10s, one in each hand, while his companion kept the bow pointed at the shore.

The staccato gunfire resonated across the waters as the chopper made a low and fast pass, skimming the water, making itself a hard target as it swept alongside them at a distance of around a thousand feet.

Monica unleashed a volley of 7.62x51mm NATO rounds on the sterns of both boats, taking out at least three outboards before the Coast Guard pilot cut hard left as the decks of both boats ignited with muzzle flashes.

The maneuver caught her off guard, throwing her across the deck just as a barrage of bullets ripped into the starboard side of the chopper, precisely where she had been a second before.

Monica rolled inside the Jayhawk as the Coast Guard operator performed some sort of evasive maneuver to get out of the kill zone. She tried to grab on to anything, finally getting ahold of the leg of a metal bench built into the port side.

By the time she managed to stand and stagger back to the cockpit, the pilot had turned the chopper around.

"Almost got them!" she shouted. "Make another pass!"

"No way! We almost got our—"

Monica pulled her Glock out again. "I swear I'm going to fucking shoot you right here!"

The pilot looked at the gun, and then back at the control panel, while swinging the helicopter back toward the boats and shouting, "This will go in my report!"

"Those have to be the craziest gringos I've ever seen!" Alfonso shouted as the Coast Guard helicopter came back after them, its side gunner planted firmly behind the machine guns. Tracers swept over the water, reaching another outboard, which went up in smoke.

Salma waited until it got in range of her Kalashnikov before leveling the weapon at the turbines. "Don't shoot the fuselage, Alfonso! Our bullets can't get through their armor. Shoot the engines!" she screamed. "Aim for the damn engines!"

"Hell!" Alfonso shouted the moment Salma started shooting. "Give them hell!"

Monica swept the sterns again, adjusting her fire. The vibrations of the helicopter and the guns rattled her hands, her arms, her shoulders, even her teeth as she guided the fire, legs spread for balance.

She had a small advantage: the M240D's range. It allowed a few precious seconds of uninterrupted fire before the terrorists could retaliate with their handheld guns.

But the counterattack began soon enough, as another barrage of rounds struck the top of the chopper, just above her head. Several rounds buzzed past as she held her position, keeping the sterns in her sights as she—

Alarms blared inside the Jayhawk and it began to vibrate to the point that she lost her footing again. Falling on the flight deck, she rolled across it once more as smoke filled the compartment. The pilot broke off the attack, shoving the helicopter into a wickedly tight right turn, presenting the armored belly to the incoming fusillade.

Bullets peppered the underside like hammers from hell before they got out of range. She managed to stand and staggered back to the cockpit, realizing the pilot had flown them out of firing range and once more was headed back to the *Oceania*.

"What the hell do you think you're doing? Get me back over there!" she screamed, reaching for the Glock again.

"Can't do!" He pointed at the instrumentation all lit up with emergency lights and annoying sirens. "Starboard turbine is gone and we're losing oil pressure fast on the port turbine! Not sure if we can make it back to the tanker! Much less mount another attack!"

"I'd rather crash on top of the assholes!" she said, once more leveling the Glock at the man.

"Fine! Just fucking shoot me! But I'm taking this helicopter back to the ship!"

"Dammit!" she screamed at him. "There's a nuclear weapon on those boats, and it's headed for America!"

"And I had to shut down one turbine already!" he retorted, pointing at the dead gauges on the control panel. "We have less than a minute before I have to shut down the other one or it will catch fire! WE . . . CAN'T . . . CATCH . . . THEM!"

Monica tried to control her anger, storming out of the cockpit and standing by the starboard machine gun, spotting the trail of smoke behind the boats and loosing another volley. But she knew it would be futile.

Already beyond the range of the gun, they continued undisturbed toward the beach while trailing as much smoke as the Jayhawk.

She silently cursed them.

They stopped firing the moment the helicopter headed back out to sea, smoke billowing from its damaged engines.

Salma ran to the bow and knelt by the trunk, running a hand over its metallic surface, finding no bullet holes. Satisfied it had not been damaged, she glanced at the outboards, all now spewing smoke. But the Mexicans didn't seem to care, keeping them running at full speed.

"Crazy fucking gringos!" Alfonso shouted, still holding his two guns.

Salma shook her head at the man while inspecting her surroundings, probing the skies to the north, to the south, and back to the east, and seeing nothing but blue skies.

Azis and Omar sat on the long benches lining the sides of the stern, holding their AK-47s and staring at the precise spot on the horizon where the chopper vanished. The second boat rode the waves a couple hundred feet to starboard, also trailing smoke. She could clearly see the rest of her team also scanning the skies.

Salma took a deep breath of warm air, suppressing her emotions in the wake of this unexpected firefight. Confidence slowly filled her as they cruised through the breaking waves and approached the beach, where three Toyota Land Cruisers waited by the tree line.

Putting the chopper attack, the tanker, and everything related to it behind her, she allowed herself a moment to enjoy the sun and the refreshing breeze. Her skills and instincts, plus the timely assistance from her network, had managed to get the weapon this far. Even with the Mexican contingent underestimating the enemy's determination.

Salma prayed those same talents, with support from her new friends, would get her through whatever twists loomed in the next phase of her final mission.

"Hang tight," Alfonso said as he steered the Boston Whaler through the surf and straight up the sand. The boat glided over the beach until friction stopped its momentum.

She jumped on the sand and never looked back at the ocean.

52

Special Team

STAR OF OCEANIA. WATERS OFF THE COAST OF MEXICO

They barely made it back. The second turbine caught fire just as the pilot set them down on the main deck, and he quickly shut it off, killing the flames.

Monica jumped out of the chopper and got on the satellite phone to report the attack and request immediate backup. If they hurried, they could still catch the terrorists before they vanished in the jungle and the mountains.

This time she got through, but before she could say a word, Dalton put her on hold—something about being on the phone with Border Patrol.

Considering that for a moment, she dialed the other number that was provided to her when Dalton handed her the special phone back in Houston—to be used strictly for emergencies.

One ring and a pickup.

"I need to talk to her," Monica said to the nameless voice on the other end.

"Give me the message, and I will carry it to her immediately," said the voice.

Before she could reply, the helicopter pilot stepped out of the Jayhawk, ducked under the decelerating rotor, threw his helmet on the ground, and stomped directly toward her, obviously to have words.

Monica pulled out her Glock, fired once over his head, and motioned him out of her way.

The pilot, whose name she didn't even know and who was still wearing his large aviator sunglasses, raised his hands and slowly backed away.

"ASAC Cruz? Is everything okay?" asked the voice.

Holstering her sidearm, she said, "I was told I'm on some special team. Well, I'm not feeling very fucking special right now, and if you do not put me through, I'll hold you personally responsible for letting terrorists armed with a nuclear weapon escape into Mexico . . . so figure it the fuck out."

The Coast Guard gunner, who was running out of the bridge along with her FBI team, joined the helicopter pilot at the edge of the deck a few dozen feet away. She saw the pilot screaming at them while shaping his hand like a gun and pointing it at his groin and then at Monica. Everyone looked in her direction.

She ignored them, and after a long pause, Lisa Jacobson said, "ASAC Cruz, what do you have?"

"What I have is a Jayhawk full of bullet holes from trying to catch the bastards before they reached the coast of Mexico. And now I'm sitting on my sunburned ass with a broken chopper and a pissed-off Coast Guard crew on a stranded tanker while terrorists with the third nuke disappear in the Mexican jungle. When I tried to call the clown you have me working for, he put me on hold because he was on the phone with Border Patrol. Tell you what, send me the Boy Scout troop out of Waco, Texas, for all the help the Border Patrol can give me right now."

"What do you need?" Lisa asked.

Monica took a deep breath while staring at the coastline. "I need world-class operators, Lisa. Right here, right now. Please understand I had the bastards who have the third bomb *in my sights* . . . but I lacked the firepower to put them down, and now the U.S. response is the fucking Border Patrol?"

After another long pause, Lisa said, "We're calling everyone as you and I speak. The president has promised you all the help you need, whenever you need it. So ASAC Cruz, help is on the way. Thank you for calling and for being exactly what your country needs you to be."

This can't be happening, she thought, hanging up the phone and refocusing the binoculars on the dense vegetation covering the mountains.

Somewhere in there, below the triple-canopy jungle, a group of jihadist bastards were being assisted by cartel assholes with a deep-rooted abhorrence for her way of life.

And both shared an insatiable appetite for cutting off the heads of American citizens.

53

Turning the Tables

KARACHI, PAKISTAN

Payback was indeed a bitch.

Maryam led the way, tailing their mark while Gorman followed her every move from across the crowded street.

The decision to stay behind had not been an easy one, but Maryam had been correct, and not because she wasn't ready to start a new life in America with Gorman. She felt her job here wasn't quite done yet, not when there was a nuclear weapon still on the loose and she had enough contacts in the ISI to dig up more intel.

Maryam also knew she was lucky to have lasted this long. When you were involved, even tangentially, in attacking the United States of America with two nuclear devices, the collateral damage would be extensive. She was vulnerable through two avenues: the Pakistani government hunting her down, and the high likelihood of being in the way of American bombs and missiles. One or both were bound to collapse on top of her.

But she had stayed, and so had Gorman, agreeing to part ways with Stark and his men, who headed to the jet waiting for them after the rescue raid. Harwich and his SOG team caught a different plane back to Paris.

Maryam and Gorman had then jumped on a train to Karachi to look for trouble.

But they didn't need to look very far.

Trouble had come to them, as they had hoped, the moment they reached the Karachi train station.

The chase went on for five minutes as they blended with the crowd, following professional habits, their spy senses on high alert.

Together, they were able to turn the tables on the operative that Atiq had deployed—who ironically was one of Maryam's kidnappers, someone named Manish. But they needed to be careful, as someone else, perhaps other agents dispatched by Atiq, could easily turn the tables back on them.

They tracked Manish's movements as he went in and out of stores. He walked through a crowded alley and into a restaurant and back out, his face tight with concern, his movements abrupt, conveying alarm. He knew he had lost them and he would have to explain that to Atiq, a man whom no one in the ISI wanted to disappoint.

The opportunity came a moment later.

A delivery truck stopped in a back alley and the driver jumped out and stacked a number of boxes onto a hand dolly. He hauled them into a restaurant, disappearing through a rear door, but leaving the truck running.

Maryam got behind the wheel and followed Gorman while he continued on foot, tailing Manish for three more blocks. The ISI operative headed back to the same train station where they had first spotted him, probably to report back.

Manish approached a second man, whom Maryam recognized as Ahmed, a senior operative. He held a heated discussion with the older agent before Ahmed got in a car and left Manish alone by the train station, probably as a lookout in case Gorman and Maryam returned.

The grab that followed was textbook.

As Gorman saw Maryam turning the corner and coming down the

block behind him, he stepped up the pace and approached Manish from the side. He palm-struck the web of nerves just below the right ear, triggering a vasovagal episode.

The Pakistani collapsed in his arms as Maryam pulled up, passenger door swinging open. Within seconds they drove off with an unconscious operative between them in the front seat.

With one of their tails disabled and the other driving around Karachi blind, Gorman and Maryam could now continue their planned visit to the port city. She knew an ISI analyst that might be willing to cooperate . . . for the right price.

"Bloody asshole," Maryam hissed before elbowing the unconscious Manish in the ribs twice, hard.

Gorman narrowed his gaze and grimaced when hearing the ribs crack. The man was going to wake up in a world of hurt. "Feeling better?"

"Do you know what this sick bastard did to me in the grabbing van?" she asked, a tear running down her right cheek. "Scumbag had his filthy hand on my twat!"

Gorman cringed at hearing that this asshole had molested her. But then again, Maryam had been damn lucky that had been the extent of the sexual abuse she'd endured during captivity.

"Look, I'm truly sorry that—" he began.

"Phuff," she snorted. "Save it."

"Okay," he replied. "What would you like me to—"

"Nothing. *I* am going to cut off his bollocks after we're through with him," she replied, wiping her face with the back of her hand while steering the van toward the northeast part of town.

"Fair enough . . . I'm assuming you know where we're going?"

"I do," she replied. "Time to visit someone I haven't seen in a very long time."

For some reason, the comment made him think of Victoria, and he hit the speed dial on his phone.

"Whom are you calling?" she asked.

"My sister," he replied, listening to the line ring several times before the same damn recording told him that all lines were busy at this time.

Maryam reached over the unconscious operative and put a hand on his forearm. "I'm sure she is okay, love."

"That's the thing," he said, texting a message, which he hoped would eventually make it through the congested digital traffic in New York. He sent her his own satellite number as well as Harwich's in case something happened to him. "Even if she survived, given the work she does, Victoria is nowhere near okay."

54

A Teachable Moment

WASHINGTON, D.C.

"Mr. Porter, do we have communications with SAC Roman Dalton and his team in Mexico?" President Vaccaro asked the chief of domestic terrorism and weapons of mass destruction within the FBI's Counterterrorism Division.

"Madam President, my report will cover all of the communications briefed by the FBI via SAC Dalton and ASAC Cruz."

President Vaccaro was about to warn the very large FBI man at the end of the conference table of her hatred for PowerPoint slides and vanilla status updates. But Wright leaned over and asked her to give the agent a chance.

So she sat back, arms crossed, and let him get started.

She half listened to him while thinking through other issues at hand, including federalizing the National Guard, the status of recovery and rescue operations in New York City, and the border-closing situation. There was also the preparation of retaliatory strikes, and the priorities of the government from most important to least.

Her chief of staff had stated that only the top four priorities would be discussed today, recovery and retaliation being the two top subjects. He and the president had agreed that they really could only focus on

New York City and the implications of another bomb. One issue was how much of what they knew and suspected should be shared with the public. They both believed in as much transparency as possible but they also agreed that this situation required extraordinary consideration of all that they disclosed.

The press was being relentless; rumors were rampant. The president's speech in New York had a positive effect but it was short-lived. People were scared, angry, unsure, confused, and in dire need of direction and leadership. Everyone needed to be assured that to-morrow would come and that everyone would be safe . . . unfortunately no one could guarantee either.

The issues were overwhelmingly simple: rebuild and insure the safety of the nation—a point in serious doubt. Punish those responsible and deal with the consequences of such action—the subject of continued debate. Keep the nation informed and attempt to have life return to some form of normalcy. There could be no doubt that the effects of the nuclear explosion in New York were devastating to all. But the ability to truly affect what had happened lay in the hands of very few, and those few were in the room with the president and on planes heading to Mexico.

The truth was that everyone still lingered in some state of either shock or denial. Vaccaro's government was barely hanging on and many were having a difficult time getting past both and into acceptance.

How could anyone have stopped this from happening? Really, after 9/11 and over fifteen years of war, you want to be in denial, Vaccaro thought.

Some, including the president, were in kind of group shock and in various stages of post-traumatic stress. Those in charge were not immune to it, and in fact because of their level of responsibilities could have heightened reactions, causing decisions to be delayed, miscalculated, or just plain wrong. The president knew this due to her extensive combat experience. She had witnessed and experienced combat stress that was not just with the pilots and ground operations soldiers but also with the staffs and commanders. Most she had observed, including herself, were in denial; always mission-first, tough-guy approach. It was not until after they had left combat that many experienced the symptoms. The problem with this type of stress, Vaccaro realized, was that the operations were affected and capabilities were diminished.

Porter continued rambling through his briefing on what was happening in Mexico with Dalton, Cruz, and the cartel. He was giving her what was called in the business an "update briefing."

President Vaccaro was having none of it, so she gave Wright one of her I-told-you-so looks before turning to the briefer standing at the opposite end of the long table.

"Mr. Porter, you have unfortunately given me what we used to call in the army 'a teachable moment.' We all need to change how we do business, now and forever. During these meetings everyone is going to give me broad-brush issues and how those issues are being fixed, addressed, and marginalized. In other words, I expect, and the situation demands, that action is being taken way before we have time to assemble here and play this briefing game."

"Madam President," Porter attempted to break in.

Very bad idea.

"Mr. Porter, I am not finished, and another word out of you and *you* will be."

Silence descended once more in the Situation Room. Porter stood there in obvious shock, color coming to his face. His eyes searched desperately for someone to help him out, from the FBI director, who shook his head, to Wright, who simply shrugged.

Vaccaro continued. "We are at war, ladies and gentlemen, with psychopaths under Pakistan's approval and support who have detonated two nuclear bombs, and they have a third one near our southern border. There is nothing more important to discuss or deal with. From now and forever here is how we are going to operate, and yes I said *operate*. I expect independent action. I expect forward progress. I will fire the first individual whose office does not fully cooperate immediately with my request on this issue. We are not used to doing business this way, and I am telling us all that there is nothing usual about this business. Coordinate, assist, be proactive, and take responsibility and blame. The country is in real danger and it is way past time that we all acted like it. First, the retaliation strike on Pakistan is approved. Secondly, we must keep this martial law on a limited basis. We all know the impossible task we have and how it will completely shut the nation down. However, we needed the nation and the world to pay attention; we are deadly serious and we are willing to do anything to regain and maintain our safety and way of life. We might be able to keep martial law for another few days without causing real damage to the nation and before we have armed rebellion in our streets, so I want other options on the table. Finally, I will call President Arturo Gutierrez and ask that he deploy a special forces brigade called GAFE, Grupo Aeromovil de Fuerzas Especiales. I worked with that unit before the war, they are exceptional, with real capabilities."

Vaccaro then turned to her national security advisor. "Lisa, get Stark to Mexico."

55

Deeper Dive

SOMEWHERE OVER THE ATLANTIC OCEAN

Worldwide communications is now an everyday thing, under water, on land, and certainly in the air, and over multiple time zones. With satellites, drones, fiber-optic cable, and the ever-present Internet, cloud, and Wi-Fi, talking to anyone anywhere is something we take for granted.

Stark was old enough to remember when it was not so, and sometimes he wished it still wasn't.

But not now.

He took the call from Lisa Jacobson, who briefed him on the third bomb. SAC Roman Dalton, former marine and veteran FBI hand, was in charge. ASAC Monica Cruz was second in command. She updated him on the FBI's findings, current location, and predicament.

"Lisa, thanks," Stark said. "But I will be needing a much deeper dive on the intel and situation on the ground in Monterrey."

"Already on the way, Colonel," Lisa assured him.

"Hey, Evan," Stark spoke into his mouthpiece after terminating the call. "Tell Danny to divert to Monterrey."

"California?"

Stark almost laughed. "No, Mexico. The international airport. Also let me know when the intel updates hit and do your magic so we can then do a team update and try real hard not to walk into another shit storm without at least knowing all the players."

He recalled Monica Cruz as extremely capable, a serious badass with attitude. He smiled when remembering his former Delta Force sniper Ryan Hunt and Monica having a thing back then.

"Hey, Ryan!" he shouted. "You by any chance remember an FBI agent named Monica Cruz?"

Ryan lifted his gaze and locked it on Stark, and without showing any emotion looked back down at his computer and the intel updates Larson forwarded to the team. Though he couldn't help but notice a thin smile reflected on the screen.

No one who ever met Monica Cruz left the encounter without being impressed. She was smart and touched by the gods with a professional athlete's eye-hand coordination. She also happened to be good-looking, which can be helpful or, as often as not, a hindrance in the male-dominated professions she had chosen.

At the civilian shooting school in Arizona, attended by many in the Special Operations community, Monica and Ryan had been in the same class. The school was famous for teaching reaction, point shooting with and without optics, and aim systems.

Both had spent good time behind a gun and both were at the school to get better. It was there that Ryan, who was already a Delta Force operator, realized that he had a better talent for long-range shooting than he had known. From the school he took two things: an upgrade to his already impressive shooting skills and a friend with benefits in Monica Cruz.

After the first week of training, those who wished to socialize decided to do some bar-hopping in downtown Scottsdale. Monica was always making friends, or at least many of the men wanted to be . . . friends. The problem for most at this school was that the former-soldier-now-FBI-agent was a better shot than most.

Most, that was, except for Ryan Hunt.

Monica was just exiting the ladies' room, which, at the Red Room Bar, was located across from the men's room. The southwest chapter of the Wolfhounds Motorcycle Club was making a piss stop at the bar. Four large, smelly, leather-vest-wearing, half-stoned alpha males came out of the bathroom and saw a very hot Hispanic woman emerging from the door across the hallway.

Zed, the largest of the bikers, said, "Hey, *chica*, wanna see what it feels like to have a very big engine between your legs?"

Monica simply relaxed, moving her back against the wall of the small corridor that led from the bar to the bathrooms, only exposing her left side to the foursome. As Zed moved forward, Monica hit him with her right foot, which was covered by her favorite boot.

Zed's knee caved in. As he fell, Monica backed out of the corridor and into the crowded bar.

Three mobile and one limping all-pissed-off bikers followed her, screaming all manner of epithets.

Monica moved to put her back to the bar and again stood calmly with only her left side facing the incoming angry men. She noticed that one was left-handed and all wore very large rings, which could cut if they hit you but also would damage fingers and knuckles.

As she reached for a half-full bottle of Cuervo Gold at the bar, all of what she was about to do became unnecessary.

The spinning, falling, and crumbling figures of the four bikers were suddenly down and not moving very well.

Standing there looking as if nothing had just happened was Ryan.

The bar went still as the rest of the gang members crowding a table near the entrance stood and just as quickly were sat back down by the six other Special Operations soldiers who were at the party.

Monica, still clutching the neck of the bottle of tequila, frowned, looked at Ryan, and said, "I had this."

56

Sharp Edges

The ride from the beach was long and rough, carrying them over narrow and winding unpaved roads, glorified goat trails traversing the mountain range. They oftentimes were barely wide enough for the SUV convoy—three Land Cruisers that had been waiting for them at the beach.

Salma looked down the precipice beyond her tinted window as Alfonso shoehorned the lead Land Cruiser through impossibly narrow paths.

He hugged towering walls, managing hairpin turns and kicking up clouds of dirt. The Toyota's wide tires bit hard into the gravel, skimming the edge of the road, skirting the abyss. The jerky trip, with its endless twists, gut-wrenching bounces, and Alfonso's skillful yet somewhat reckless driving, even by Pakistani standards, was stupid. And she realized quickly that it was just a macho thing for this idiot of a man.

Salma took her boot knife, knuckles up, and pressed it just hard enough against Alfonso's throat that she had his attention.

"I want you to drive so fast it scares you . . . because none of this will bother me."

"Don't worry, Señorita Salma," he said, left hand on the wheel and right one on the shifting stick. He popped the clutch and slid the four-wheel-drive vehicle into second gear as the road angled up at nearly twenty degrees—according to the clinometer on the dash. "I make this trip twice a week to pick up deliveries from the islands or down south. I haven't fallen once . . . yet. Although to be completely honest, I have not tried it with a knife at my throat." He grinned.

Salma shook her head.

"I think you'll really like Don Montoya," he added as she wondered what would happen if a vehicle came in the opposite direction. "Best boss I ever had."

"What's he like?" she asked. She put the blade back in its place while turning toward Azis. He sat in the back with Omar, returning to a more relaxed pose.

"Well, he isn't a very nice man," he said, glancing at her before turning the wheel just in time to manage a hairpin turn. "But he is fair and values loyalty above all else. Do your job, and you and your family will prosper. Don't—or worse, try to cross him in any way— well . . . that's why they call him El Bateador."

"El what?"

"El Bateador, The Batter," he explained, taking his eyes off the winding road again to look at her for just a moment, but long enough to almost miss the next turn. He cut the wheel at the last minute, almost going airborne.

"The Batter?" she asked.

"*Sí*. He'll kill your entire family with a baseball bat while you watch . . . and then he reserves the best death for you."

"And what's that?"

Alfonso checked his watch, an action that nearly made him miss another turn.

"We might get there in time for you to see it," he replied.

"See what?"

"See what happens to his enemies."

She just stared at the ocean in the distance, becoming increasingly bored with this man and his halfhearted attempt to scare her.

But The Batter? *Come on*, she thought as Alfonso drove them straight up into the layer of dense fog near the summit.

He flipped a switch, and a row of yellow fog lights pierced the wall of white, allowing them to see a dozen feet ahead. It wasn't much. But it kept them in business for the thirty minutes it took to reach the summit and come back down the other side of the mountain range, below the fog.

The view of enshrouding clouds gave way to an immense valley projecting from the foot of the mountain to the edge of a vast metropolis.

"Monterrey," said Alfonso, shifting into third gear as the road began its long and twisting path back down.

It was another two hours before they reached a paved road that connected to a four-lane highway, which Alfonso explained was part of the modern road system of the northern state of Nuevo Leon.

By then, Salma's stomach had long settled down, and she even looked forward to the roadside tacos that Alfonso purchased from one of many vendors flanking the highway under colorful canopies.

"*Cabrito*," he said. "Roasted goat. We will stop to eat and drink."

Salma inhaled two tacos and chased them down with a cold beer. And she enjoyed the final hour to a compound on the northern outskirts of the city, which they reached at dusk.

Floodlights flickered and came on, bathing brick walls topped with barbed wire in a yellow glow as they approached a metal gate. Surveillance cameras slowly whirled in their direction.

A moment later a motor engaged and the gate slid to the side, revealing a paved driveway leading to a modern two-story structure made primarily of concrete and glass. It was beautiful and adjacent to a swimming pool, tennis courts, and manicured gardens. Accent lights illuminated trees, flowers, water fountains, and walkways connecting the main house to a half-dozen other structures. The whole place was peaceful yet heavily fortified, with guard posts along the interior perimeter. A Eurocopter EC135 on a helipad stood adjacent to the house, ready for a quick getaway. A large motor pool included Range Rover and Porsche SUVs, Mercedes and Lexus sedans, a red Ferrari, and two Corvettes. They lined the east wall under a long metal carport.

Alfonso led the Land Cruiser convoy to the front of the main house, past the black helicopter and the pool and tennis courts.

A man in his late twenties, tall and dressed all in black, spoke on a cell phone while walking down the steps connecting the front of the house to the circular driveway. An MP7A1 hung from his right shoulder.

"Welcome, Salma. I'm Danny Montoya. My father is expecting you," he said with a refined British accent while opening the door for her. "Alfonso will show your team the accommodations we have prepared for them in the guesthouse. You will sleep in the main house as our honored guest."

She looked at Azis and Omar, whom she had ordered to never take their eyes off the device—ever. They nodded and began to unload the trunk while she followed Danny up the steps.

The place was just as beautiful inside. Shiny marble floors, high ceilings with exposed wooden beams, and walls filled with modern art, from sculptures to paintings. She thought she recognized a Picasso and a Dali by the steps leading to the second floor.

Montoya's office was large, as she would have guessed, with a great view of the grounds and the distant city beyond the walls, with very tall mountains to the east in the background. They seemed much taller than the ones they had crossed from the coast.

"That's the Sierra Madre Oriental," a deep voice commented.

Salma turned around.

A man worked a small block of ice on a metal tray with an ice pick. He dropped shards into a heavy cocktail glass before pouring a yellowish drink from a liquor decanter on a bar on the right side of the room. Next to him stood a long cabinet housing baseball paraphernalia, including several baseball bats that appeared autographed.

He was ruggedly handsome, tanned, and big though not fat. He looked in his early fifties, like Malik, but without the facial hair, with a massive chest and powerful arms. He wore a pair of jeans, a large Monterrey Sultanes Baseball Club shirt and matching hat, and gray snakeskin cowboy boots. A gold Rolex hugged his left wrist. But it was his eyes that caught her attention. They were the color of emeralds, and they glistened with affection as he settled his gaze on her.

"May I offer you a drink?" he asked.

She nodded. "Whatever you're drinking will work. Thanks."

"Alcohol okay, then?"

"Certainly," she replied. "Why do you ask?"

"Ah . . . because of the Muslim thing?"

"I'm not your average Muslim."

"I'm noticing that," he said.

Using the ice pick to break off a couple of slivers and deposit them into another glass, he looked over at his son and added, "Daniel, please call me when Alfonso is ready."

Danny smiled and backed out of the room, closing the double doors behind him.

Montoya walked up to Salma and handed her a drink.

"I hope you like sharp edges," he said, tilting his glass to her.

She leaned forward automatically, offering a partial view of her perfect breasts while meeting him halfway, touching rims.

"To new friendships," he said.

Salma grinned and took a sip, immediately recognizing the aged scotch. "Macallan," she said. "Which year?"

Montoya's face widened as he smiled, revealing two perfect rows of white teeth. "Nineteen sixty-five. The year I was born."

She nodded. "You look much younger, Don Montoya. Must be the sharp edges."

The large cartel boss stared at her with those penetrating green eyes. "Please, call me Miguel."

He guided her to the windows overlooking the desert valley leading to the city, taking a few minutes to identify the highlights. The massive Mexican flag in the middle of the city; the modern downtown area; the new industrial park; the Monterrey Institute of Technology, considered to be the MIT of Latin America and known locally as the "Tech Monterrey."

Salma gave him an abridged version of her trip from Karachi, including her encounter with African rebels. She omitted sleeping with the captain.

Montoya listened without interruption, his eyes glistening with something that looked like respect or admiration.

They were on their second drink when a knock interrupted Montoya relating a story from his days growing up in Colombia.

Danny inched the heavy door open. "Alfonso's ready for you, Papa."

Montoya gave his son a brief nod before turning to Salma. "I am sorry, my dear, but there's something I need to handle. I will be right back."

"Anything I can do?" she asked.

He frowned. "Thanks, but I think you have been through enough already. This has to do with the . . . unpleasant but necessary side of my business."

"In that case, I insist," she said.

Montoya once more inspected her before slowly extending a hand toward the door.

They went out of the main house, down a narrow path between the tennis courts and the pool, to a windowless concrete structure on the southern perimeter of the compound. Alfonso waited for them by the metal door, which he held open, going in last, and closing it.

The large rectangular room reminded Salma of ISI interrogation chambers, with shackles on the walls and a host of torture devices on tables. A man in his thirties was on his knees, hands tied behind his back. Alfonso and Danny forced a rubber tire over his head, wedging it over his shoulders. A strip of duct tape muffled his cries.

"Meet Arturo Chacón," Montoya said to Salma. "He was one of my best . . . until he became a *rata*."

Chacón slowly shook his head while moaning.

"Have some dignity, Arturo," Montoya said. "You talk to the Federales, you die like the Federales."

Alfonso tied a noose around Chacón's neck and pulled hard on the rope looped through a pulley hanging from the ceiling, forcing Chacón's head up and keeping him from falling over as Raul poured the contents of a gas can inside the tire.

Montoya turned to Salma and said, "It is called—"

"Necklacing," Salma said. "I know the method."

For the third time in less than fifteen minutes the cartel boss just stared at her, before shifting his attention back to the execution in progress.

Alfonso threw a switch on the wall and an overhead extractor kicked in, venting the room through an exhaust fan on the roof.

Danny produced a long disposable lighter and was about to hand it to his father when Salma said, "Miguel . . . may I?"

"You? But . . . why?" he asked.

"Because your enemy is my enemy."

Sighing, Montoya motioned Danny to pass the lighter to Salma.

She walked up to Chacón, looked him in the eye, and set fire to the gas.

The effect was instantaneous. The fuel ignited and immediately enveloped his face as the moans intensified, as the duct tape fell off from the heat, and agonizing screams filled the room. He shook his head violently. Black smoke boiled over him before being sucked up by the overhead system. The smell of torched rubber, singed hair, and burnt flesh filled her nostrils.

She remained there, staring at the man's rapidly disfiguring upper body while Alfonso, Danny, and even Montoya took a step back from the intense heat.

She watched the skin evaporate from his face as Chacón twisted, turned, and squealed to no avail for a couple of agonizing minutes, before all motion ceased.

Turning around, Salma handed the lighter to Danny, who, along with Alfonso, regarded her with a mix of surprise and respect.

But it was Montoya who surprised them all by saying, "You are unexpected and impressive, neither of which I am used to."

57

Amends

ISLAMABAD, PAKISTAN

When Atiq was ushered into the office, Prime Minister Korai was on the phone. He pointed at a chair across his desk, turning around and listening intently for another minute before saying, "Very well. Keep me posted."

Sitting down, Korai rested his elbows on his desk, crisscrossed his fingers, and looked straight at Atiq.

"What is the meaning of this?" Atiq asked. "Summoning me here . . . with *soldiers*?"

"The Americans are coming," Korai said in a very calm, direct voice. "Retaliation is certain . . . and soon. Yet, you assured me—assured *everyone*—that would *never* happen."

Atiq sat back and exhaled heavily. "I . . . we have been betrayed."

"And she will be found and held accountable. But . . . your *own daughter*? How did you not see this coming?"

"I should have . . . the fault is mine, and I am very—"

"Stop," Korai said. "You and I go back too far for apologies. Besides, apologies are just words. What I . . . what *our country* needs from you are . . . amends."

"Amends?"

Korai slowly nodded.

"What kind of . . . amends?"

"The kind that start with the location of the other bomb headed for America."

58

Head on a Stick

MONTERREY, MEXICO

Too many cooks in this kitchen, thought Monica.

There was the entourage of agents that arrived with SAC Roman Dalton at midnight. The U.S. Coast Guard helicopter crews. Plus the deployment of soldiers from the Mexican special forces brigade called GAFE, Grupo Aeromovil de Fuerzas Especiales.

The who-is-in-charge-and-leading-this-operation question is on everyone's mind.

Monica was the only female in sight. Her being there as second in command for the FBI was standard practice. But it was visibly frowned upon by Captain Franco Lamar, the GAFE chief deployed by the governor of Nuevo Leon by direct order from the Mexican president. Lamar was in his late forties, tall, muscular, with a well-trimmed beard, and apparently not a fan of women in law enforcement.

"This is no place for a lady," Lamar said in his thick Hispanic accent, dressed in full paramilitary gear as they huddled around a table in a third-floor conference room in the Monterrey Police headquarters.

"Well, good thing I'm no lady, Captain," she replied, still dressed in standard-issue FBI SWAT gear.

"It's okay, Captain," Dalton said before Lamar could answer. "ASAC Cruz here is the reason we've been able to track the terrorists to your town. My government needs her to be a part of the team."

"I'm sure she is very valuable, Mr. Dalton, but we're not in your country, and down here women have no place fighting against the cartel." Turning to Monica, he added, "If they capture you . . . the things they'll do to you. They will hurt you in ways you can't even imagine before killing you in even worse ways."

"Captain, with all due respect," Monica replied, "I've spent enough years in places far worse than your sunny Mexico. So please, spare me the tough love and let's get on with this. I'm not going anywhere."

"Very well," Lamar replied, before turning his attention back to Dalton. "I need the room cleared. I'm about to share very . . . sensitive information."

Dalton asked all of his agents out while Lamar also excused his men.

"You too, miss," Lamar told Monica when she remained standing next to Dalton.

"The name is *ASAC Cruz*, Captain, and like I said, I'm not going anywhere."

"Captain," Dalton added, "she's my lead in this."

"You better know what you're doing," Lamar said to her. "These people are the worst kind."

"I can handle myself," she replied. "Shall we get on with it?"

Lamar looked behind him to make sure they were alone before unrolling a map of the city over the table. He then looked over to a dark corner of the room.

A man emerged from the shadows dressed in GAFE paramilitary gear.

"This is Lieutenant Alfonso Domingo," Lamar said. "Our last agent inside the Gulf Cartel. His partner was . . . killed last night."

Alfonso stepped into the light and approached the table, nodding politely to Dalton and Monica before standing by Lamar. He was trim but muscular, with short dark hair and a clean-cut face.

"Arturo got careless," Alfonso said in a monotone voice. "Earned him a rubber tire around his neck."

No one said a word, as all were familiar with the gruesome execution method.

"In any case," Alfonso added while pointing to a spot on the northern end of the map, "they arrived here at eight o'clock last night. The place belongs to the Gulf Cartel but it also has Sinaloa Cartel soldiers for protection."

Lamar frowned. "I thought Montoya was at war with them."

Alfonso bowed his head once. "He was, but there has been an alliance forging between the Sinaloa and Gulf Cartels, and they now have contracted Los Zetas for added muscle in the region."

"*Dios mio,*" Lamar mumbled, looking away. "Bastard has Los Zetas *and* Sinaloa?"

"Who is Los Zetas?" Monica asked.

"A group made up of former soldiers, including some from our own GAFE ops, who created a private militia. Funded by Montoya's Gulf Cartel, the group has been instrumental in Montoya's domination of the drug trade in the eastern part of the country, from the Veracruz Peninsula to the border with Texas. And now it looks like Montoya is extending his reach west, to the area long controlled by the Sinaloa Cartel, who has a history of infiltrating the Mexican federal government and military. The alliance, if real, would give them over seventy percent control of all drug trade in Mexico."

"Which is unheard of," added Alfonso.

"Who exactly arrived at this compound?" Monica asked.

"There were six in total, ASAC Cruz," Alfonso said.

Monica gave him a brief nod for using her title.

Alfonso added, "Five men and a woman, their leader . . . goes by Salma. Don't have a last name. They brought along a heavy metallic trunk, roughly one and a half meters long by half a meter wide. Very heavy."

Monica exchanged a glance with Dalton, recalling the final words from SEAL Team Six. If the informant was right, then perhaps there was a chance to catch them before they made it across the border.

"What's our window?" asked Dalton.

Alfonso frowned and looked at Lamar.

"What is it?" Dalton pressed.

"We can't just hit that location," said Lamar.

"Why the hell not?" asked Monica.

Lamar dropped his brows at her and sighed. "It's sensitive . . . and complicated."

"Try me," she said.

"For starters," Alfonso said, "there are no drugs in that compound, which is officially registered to a respectable corporation in Mexico City. We can't just storm any place we want. We need cause, and in this country it means irrefutable proof of drug activity, which we lack because these guys, contrary to popular belief, are extremely careful. I'm sure you have similar regulations in your country, like judges issuing warrants before you can carry out a search or a raid?"

"Yeah, we do," Monica said, "and you can see where that got us. We were hit hard, gentlemen. And I'll be damned if I'm going to give those bastards the chance to hit us again. So, one more time, pretty please, tell me why we just don't blow the place off the map."

Before Lamar could answer, Dalton cut in. "Look, if Alfonso's intel is still fresh, then we have a chance to prevent a nuclear weapon from entering the United States. That trumps any official or unofficial truce or agreement, or whatever the hell you guys have with the cartels to help keep the local peace."

After a long pause, Lamar looked at Alfonso and asked, "How long before they move?"

"Hard to say. Probably no more than a day or so. Montoya and this Salma woman are keeping that intel very close to their chests."

"Then we need to act quickly," Monica said.

Lamar shook his head. "We need permission from Mexico City first."

Dalton grabbed the satphone strapped to his belt. "Look, Captain, you do what you think you need to do. But you should know that a squadron of F-22 Raptors from the First Fighter Wing at Langley just landed in Laughlin, less than a hundred miles from here. My president is trying to work with your president, but please understand that the United States is in a state of war. While we don't wish to violate the airspace of an ally, we will do so if that ally, through inaction, harbors terrorists bearing nuclear weapons destined for our country. Plus an airstrike, as accurate as our weapons are, does come with a percent of error . . . or collateral damage. My preference is to take the place with soldiers."

Lamar paused again and said, "Just . . . hold for a minute, okay?"

Dalton took a deep breath and nodded.

Lamar and Alfonso left the room.

"What are you thinking?" she whispered, leaning close to him while pointing at the two cameras on the ceiling.

Leaning in to her, Dalton replied in a very low voice, "I'm thinking that all of this is a damn charade, Cruz. For all I know these bastards all work for Montoya."

"I think we need drones with Hellfire missiles overhead right now," she said under her breath.

"You think they're stalling us?"

"I'm not sure . . . probably . . . yes."

"Well, Cruz," Dalton said, "I have this feeling scratching the back of my damn throat telling me that if we're not very, *very* careful, our heads are going to end up on sticks while that nuke makes its way north of the Rio Grande."

Before Monica could tell him that she had the exact same feeling, Lamar and Alfonso stepped back in.

"All right, Mr. Dalton. We're in."

"We hit them at midnight," said Alfonso. "When they're least expecting it."

"That's twenty hours from now. Will they still be there?" asked Monica, checking her watch. It was just past four in the morning.

"Yes. I just checked in and they're not moving for at least two days. Apparently, Montoya is still making . . . preparations."

"What's security like?" asked Dalton.

"Two dozen guards in rotating shifts," replied Alfonso. "Not very fancy, but then again, Monterrey is smack in the middle of their territory, so no reason for them to be expecting an attack."

"My people at Laughlin will provide eyes in the sky by dawn," Dalton said. "Don't want any surprises."

"Very well," Lamar said. "So it's settled. We go in at midnight. That leaves us twenty hours to get ready. Alfonso will provide us with a layout of the interior in the next few hours. Then we can work out a plan. Agreed?"

Monica shook her head.

"What is it?" Lamar asked.

"Well, for starters, who will be our eyes on the target between now and then, besides the drones? Also, where is the mock-up of the place we want to hit?"

Lamar and Alfonso exchanged a glance.

"What I'm saying, gentlemen, is that we need to get our collective shit together for what we are talking about. Drones in the air are a good start, but they can be fooled. Eyes on the ground at the target a few hours before the strike, plus a mock-up of the target, are the very basics for any op to have a chance."

As Dalton nodded, her satphone started to vibrate. It was secured to the side of her vest and connected to an earpiece through a coiled wire under her vest.

"Who's that?" Dalton asked.

"Don't know, sir. Only a handful of people know this number, so I'd better take it."

"Outside. Then report back here."

Monica walked out of the room and into a cubicle area, where all of the GAFE, Coast Guard, and FBI personnel waited, including her Coast Guard pilot friend. Ignoring the dozen sets of eyes tracking her, she rushed into the closest empty office and shut the door behind her.

Tapping the earpiece snugged inside her right ear, she was instantly rewarded with a loud background noise that sounded like . . . jet engines?

"ASAC Cruz," she said.

"What's up?"

Monica felt her throat suddenly going dry, the familiar voice triggering a flood of memories from Arizona and Afghanistan.

"Ryan?"

"How you doing, Miss Cruz? In a moment you may confess your undying love and devotion to me, but for now we need to know who you pissed off over there and how we may be of assistance to save your ass once again—and I want credit for not saying 'sweet ass.' "

"What the . . . *fuck* . . . what—what are you doing calling me on this phone? And where the hell are you?"

"Yeah, nice to hear your voice too. Got the number from Washington. We're on a military transport. Caught you at a bad time?"

"Ryan . . . what the heck's going on? I haven't heard from you in *six damn years* and now you're calling me on a government satphone whose number is strictly need to fucking know?"

"We're headed your way."

"What . . . who . . . when . . . slow down. Who's coming here, why, and when?"

"The team, you know . . . the colonel, plus Danny, Mickey, and even Larson, who's pissed at everyone 'cause he nearly got his ass shot off a couple of days ago in Paki."

Monica stood there frozen as memories rushed back. In an instant she recalled the faces, the jokes, the good times . . . and also the death and destruction that led to her request to head back to Quantico before her FBI-sponsored tour was up. She had abandoned that screwed-up part of the world forever, which also meant walking away from Ryan, who wasn't ready to give up that life.

"You still there?"

"Yes, Ryan. I'm still fucking here. Now, tell me what the *hell* is going on or I swear I'm going to shove this phone up your—"

"Looking forward to it. Now hold that thought. There's someone here who wants to talk to you."

The rumble from jet engines intensified for a moment, before a deep but very familiar voice came on the line.

"Cruz?"

"Colonel Stark!" she said. "It's been a while."

"A lifetime for some," he said. *"We're headed your way with an ETA of eighteen hundred local. That's six* P.M. *your time in case you've forgotten. We've been activated to join you in the search for the terrorists trying to smuggle a nuke into the U.S. Based on the intel we've gotten, these bastards are under the protection of Miguel Montoya, and that means that while you're in-country half the people you've already met are on his payroll and the other half don't know they're on his payroll."*

"With all due respect, sir, tell me something I don't know."

"Just the opposite, Cruz. You tell me what you know, what you think you know, what you think you might know, and what you just don't know."

She spent a couple of minutes briefing him.

"All right," Stark said. *"You tell that FBI boss of yours to hold his ass tight until we get there. Don't go anywhere. Don't plan anything. Don't talk to anyone. Don't trust anyone. In fact, just have him sit on his bureaucratic*

ass till we get there. And Cruz: nothing stupid. You need real operators and we're your only game in town. And stay very close to your hardware."

Monica realized she was alone in an office with only the ten rounds in her Glock, which in a place like this was just enough to piss people off. Her MP7A1 and all the ammo and grenades she needed to put up any form of defense were in the conference room.

"Got it, sir. What else?"

"Hold tight, watch your six, and we'll be there by six."

She checked her watch. It was just past four in the morning, meaning she had the luxury to wait, at least according to Alfonso's timetable. Assuming, of course, that he and Lamar could be trusted.

"Got it."

"Remember, Cruz, while in-country you're always just one damn decision away from having your head on a stick."

"Colonel, that's the second time that—"

The phone went dead.

Monica frowned, tapping the earpiece to hang up. She walked up to the window behind the desk overlooking downtown Monterrey.

In the distance a massive Mexican flag bathed in floodlights swayed in the breeze. Off to the northwest rose the modern buildings of the large local university. The city looked quiet under a three-quarter moon, even peaceful.

From a distance.

But deep within, she knew—or at least had to assume—there were forces already hard at work collaborating against her.

She unknowingly placed a hand around her neck.

Dalton and Stark were right. In-country no one could be trusted.

The sooner she finished the job and got her ass home, the better the chances of keeping her head from ending up ornamenting the trophy room of some sick son of a bitch.

59

Holy Cause

Every word felt like a dagger slowly carving the word *TRAITOR* in his heart.

He thought of his parents, of his baby sister, his memories of them forever etched in the scars on his hands and forearms. But Atiq spoke the words anyway, providing his prime minister with the information he had requested.

At least part of it.

In spite of the turmoil of emotions ravaging his mind—caused by everything from his daughter's treachery to his own betrayal of everything he held dear—the spy in him prevailed. He somehow managed to smother all feelings, controlling the information he released.

In the intelligence community, as in most critical negotiations, one never gave everything away on the first pass. He'd learned long ago that the key to thriving in this world of smoke and mirrors was to disclose information only when required.

As much as necessary but as little as possible.

He offered Korai something to go on, enough to gain credibility and remain valuable, but not so much as to lose all negotiation leverage.

As the architect of Salma's recalibrated mission, Atiq knew every detail of her op.

He knew the precise location of Miguel Montoya's hideout.

He knew their exact timeline for the many diversions in store for the Americans after crossing into Texas.

He knew her final objective, and the path to getting there.

He even knew the details behind the activation of several dormant ISIS cells along the way.

But he held most of that back, sharing only Montoya's name as well as the agreed-upon time to depart Monterrey.

And still it was enough to make him want to vomit, resulting in an inner anger that felt almost suffocating. He took a few deep breaths, exhaling, and dabbing the perspiration filming his forehead with a silk handkerchief while Korai stood by the windows gazing outside, arms crossed.

And that's when the sacred words from the Koran came to him, reminding him of his holy cause.

Kill the unbelievers, wherever you find them.

Fight against them until there is no dissention.

Fight until no other religion exists but Islam.

The words—his promise to avenge his family—told him he simply couldn't leave it at that. Although he had released the absolute minimum amount of information, it was still too much, requiring a contingency, something to help level out the playing field.

Slowly, Atiq replaced the handkerchief in his coat's inner pocket, next to his BlackBerry, fingers moving automatically over its keyboard.

While Korai continued gazing out the windows, Atiq pressed seven digits, triggering his emergency code.

In the end, America's punishment had to continue. He had to make every one of its citizens feel the pain that had dominated his life. And that included seeing Salma's mission through to completion—no matter the cost.

Even if Pakistan had to burn.

Like his parents.

Korai turned around and asked, "Very well . . . I have one more question for now."

"Anything," he replied.

"I need the precise location of Ibrahim al-Crameini."

60
Wake-Up Call

Three beeps on her satellite phone awoke her at five in the morning.

Salma sat up and reached for it on the nightstand, blinking to clear her sight before reading the text message on the small amber display.

Bolting out of bed, she grabbed a white silk robe on her way out of the bedroom. She had taken a long, hot shower before collapsing in bed.

Azis and Omar sat straight up, which alerted the other guard Montoya had posted outside her door. She knew they were watching her walk. If she had more time, she would have turned and reminded them of who had trained them, and that their lives depended on her.

At this moment, Salma ignored them as she fast-walked barefoot on cold Saltillo floors to the other end of the long hallway. Three of Montoya's guards stood by the entrance to the residence's master bedroom.

Six hours ago, the drug boss had asked her to his bed after they had finished the bottle of 1965 Macallan. Albeit tipsy and quite attracted to the ruggedly handsome cartel chief, Salma had followed her instincts and her training, and decided to hold back one of her primary weapons for a better occasion.

Montoya must have talked to his guards, because they not only moved out of her way, but one even opened the double doors for her, ushering her through, before gently closing them behind her.

The bedroom was as large and opulent as his office. A bar and a sitting area faced a massive television screen hanging on a stucco wall. Dimmed accent lights cast a peaceful twilight in the Tuscany-style room, revealing his bulky shape beneath pearl-colored silk sheets. It rose and fell to the rhythm of light snoring.

She approached the round bed, recessed in the middle of the room, and sat at the edge.

"Miguel," she whispered, nudging his arm. "Wake up."

A soft grunt, followed by incomprehensible mumbles in Spanish, and his face emerged from between two pillows for a moment then sank out of sight again.

"Miguel. It's me. Salma. Wake up." She nudged him again.

"Salma?" he said, yawning while lifting his head and slowly sitting up. The silk sheets dropped to his waist, exposing a chest draped in dark hair.

Rubbing his face with the edge of his hands, he added, "What . . . what time is it?"

"Time to go," she said to this bear of a man, pointing at the satellite phone.

Blinking, he finally laid eyes on her and was unable to keep his gaze from dropping to her nearly exposed breasts.

"You look incredible in that." He grinned.

"I'm up here!" she snapped, grabbing a clump of hair on his chest and gently tugging it. "And I'm dead serious!"

"Don't stop," he said, still smiling, a hand now on her thigh, slowly shifting beneath the robe.

She tugged harder and pushed his hand away.

"No games!" she scolded, an edge now in her voice.

"No?"

"*No.* Atiq just sent me a warning. The Americans are coming."

The smile didn't vanish, but it turned from playful to a deadly leer. "Are they, now?"

"Yes. We need to move quickly."

His leer widened as he leaned closer, took her hands in his, and said, "Then let them come, my dear Salma."

Kissing the top of her hands, he added, "Let the bastards come."

61

Making a Difference

The Old Ebbitt Grill had been around.

It first opened as an unnamed restaurant in the Ebbitt House Hotel in 1827, before becoming a stand-alone business in 1926. It then moved locations twice, finally settling in its current quarters at 675 Fifteenth Street NW in 1983.

Its famous long mahogany bar dominated the establishment, sporting mounted animal trophies beneath ceilings adorned with murals and stencils. Patrons could sit at the bar or at the rows of booths surfaced with green leather and separated by etched-glass dividers. The place was always loud and packed with locals and tourists—all spending a small fortune to dine at one of Washington's most historic establishments, making it one of the highest-revenue restaurants in the United States.

And today, in the wake of the New York attack, it appeared unchanged. People had come to the historic bar in droves, but for a very different reason: information.

The place catered to Washington's best connected, from aides to congressmen and senators to lobbyists, White House staff, Pentagon brass, and members of various federal agencies. Whenever they weren't sharing their latest intel, their eyes were glued to the images on the multiple television screens, each tuned to a different media outlet.

Drinks flowed while conversations ranged from the very personal—trying to get news on friends and family in New York—to the very official. Chiefs of staff gathered to form a better picture for their superiors than those streaming down their own intelligence channels. Or those painted by the likes of CNN and Fox News. From updates on the death count to the latest EPA estimates on radiation fallout, the conversations churned endlessly. It made this establishment and several others like it into unofficial information-gathering enclaves during what all considered the worst national crisis in history.

Tristan had selected a private room in the rear, out of earshot of representatives from pretty much every part of the government. He had hosted small dinners and gatherings here in the past, both private as well as for his nonprofits and more recently to entertain U.N. dignitaries.

But today he sat alone with Ambassador Patras Dham. A bottle of 2009 Sequoia Grove Cambium iced between them as they conversed at one end of the table.

"Your prime minister realizes we still need to punish Pakistan?" Tristan asked after reading the information on the piece of paper Patras had just handed to him.

The old diplomat closed his eyes and slightly bobbed his head. "We understand, Mr. Ambassador. A proportionate response is in order. But we hoped this would . . . soften the blow . . . somehow . . . perhaps choose targets with minimal long-term impact?"

"It is a start," Tristan agreed, reading the information on Monterrey as well as a set of GPS coordinates for an undisclosed location in Pakistan along with timetables. "But this—assuming it checks out— will *not* be enough."

There was a knock on the door and a waiter stuck his head in.

"Just checking in, Mr. Lavastede. Anything we can do?"

Tristan smiled. "Thanks, Jimmy. We're good for now."

Patras waited for the door to close and said, "We know that . . . but, like you already indicated, it is a start . . . and we hope it will do some good for my country."

Tristan read the information again while taking another sip. If the intelligence were accurate, then perhaps President Vaccaro would consider a reduced version of the strike package. Maybe. But he certainly wasn't going to suggest it. At the moment it was quite difficult, perhaps impossible—even for a humanitarian like him—to feel any degree of compassion for Pakistan. The images monopolizing pretty much every television set around the globe had a way of bringing out the worst in him.

"My family . . ." Patras added.

"Yes?"

"They are in . . . Islamabad. Is that on the list of—"

"I don't have that information," Tristan said. He tilted his head and added, "But even if I did . . ."

Patras closed his eyes while downing the rest of his wine, then setting the glass down. "I understand, of course. There is nothing you can tell me officially. But if there was anyway way *unofficially* that—"

"Not possible."

"I see . . . but in full disclosure . . . you should know that . . ." Patras paused and looked away.

"Please," Tristan said, motioning for him to continue.

"You should know that . . . well, our prime minister has placed our military on high alert. Anyone entering our airspace without permission will be . . . shot down."

Tristan sipped wine, before pouring Patras some more and then serving himself.

"Thank you," the Pakistani mumbled, picking up his glass and bringing it to his lips, closing his eyes as he drank.

"We expected as much," said Tristan, noticing the slight shake in Patras's hand. "But in the end, no amount of military preparation on your side will make any difference."

Patras lowered the glass, his eyes widening as he mumbled, "N—no?"

Tristan slowly shook his head, frowning.

The Pakistani diplomat set down the glass, tears welling in his eyes.

Holding the piece of paper in front of him, Tristan added, "But *this*, my friend, and many, many *more* like this . . . just might."

62

EMP

Captain Frank Bertolotti, commanding officer of the Ohio-class submarine, stood next to his executive officer in the rear of the control room.

The diving officer of the watch, or "dive," sat in between the two submarine pilots facing the ship control panel. The left pilot, or "helm," steered the vessel with the rudder and also managed the bow planes. The right pilot, or "outboard," controlled the angle on the ship with the stern planes. Together, they brought the *Jackson* to a depth of 130 feet to carry out an order that Bertolotti had prayed for years would never come.

But he was ready. His crew was ready. His submarine was ready. They had trained endlessly for this moment. They had drilled to the point of obsession week after week, month after month. And the time had come to put their preparations to the test.

His country had been attacked, and the *Jackson* was the tip of the sword that would deliver the initial dose of American justice to the perpetrators.

The launch code had been received, authenticated, and concurred by all the right personnel. The launch keys had been retrieved from the safe and used to arm the system.

All that remained was for Bertolotti to give the final order to fire, which he did before swinging the periscope toward the stern. A moment later a blast of air bubbles preceded the long projectile as it left its tube and soared toward the surface.

The Trident II D5 ballistic missile, one of twenty-four carried by the *Jackson*, broke the water surface. The first stage ignited for sixty-five seconds, propelling it to the stratosphere before the second-stage motor accelerated it to eighteen thousand miles per hour in another sixty-five seconds.

The nose fairing separated from the missile as it reached low Earth orbit. There, the third-stage motor burned for forty seconds, thrusting it along the Earth's curvature to the targeted area before the post-boost control system jettisoned it.

The stellar sighting navigation system oriented the MIRV and aligned it with the guidance flight plan before aiming the first of three MK4 reentry vehicles at the mesosphere over the Port of Karachi.

The MIRV continued on its northern trajectory while the first hypersonic RV shot toward the Earth. It pierced the atmosphere with the ablative shield protecting its delicate cargo: a single W76 one-hundred-kiloton nuclear warhead.

Unlike the ten-kiloton warhead that caused the Manhattan ground-burst, the W76 detonated at an altitude of 150 miles, too high for its fireball, radiation, or shock wave to cause any damage to the vast port city.

But the gamma rays from the high-altitude detonation released high-energy electrons that interacted with the Earth's magnetic field to trigger a powerful electromagnetic pulse. All unshielded electronics were instantly fried in a three-hundred-mile radius directly below the blast.

Five minutes later, the MIRV shot its second RV into the atmosphere over Quetta, three hundred miles north of Karachi and home of the largest ISI training complex in Pakistan. It triggered a second wide-area EMP.

A third EMP followed five minutes later over Islamabad, silencing all electronics across 70 percent of the country.

63

Sitting Ducks

"Bloody hell? What was that?"

Gorman regarded Maryam in the moonlight filtering through the single window of the bungalow the moment the lights went out immediately following a high-altitude explosion.

He peered outside and saw nothing but darkness across the port city.

"Shit," he said, turning around. "EMP. I think it's the prep before the big one, which makes perfect sense, but very bad timing considering what we're doing."

She made a face and whispered, "Shit indeed. We're . . . what do you call it, sitting chickens?"

"Ducks," he replied, unable to control a grin while putting a hand to her face, finding it adorable when she got her slang mixed up. "And you're absolutely right. We *are* sitting ducks."

For the past two hours they had been interrogating Naveed Lari, Atiq's right-hand man in Karachi. He was a thin individual in his fifties with horn-rimmed glasses and a goatee who lived alone in a bungalow-like house in a suburb just northeast of the port area.

Gorman and Maryam had been questioning, threatening, and finally getting him to talk by offering him money and safety for his family. Though they still kept his wrists and ankles flex-cuffed to a chair.

Maryam was a great interrogator, with the possible drawback that Pakistani men were mostly dismissive of women. So they had decided to use straight-up custom and need. Chai tea was served, and Gorman and Maryam both waited on the ISI analyst and tried to get him to relax. In exchange for political asylum they did get critical information that added to what they already knew, or at least suspected. Lari painted a more complete picture of the ISI nuclear operation and goal, including the revised timeline for the attack, the new target, and even the delivery vehicle.

But as Gorman had walked to a separate room to use his satellite phone to call Lisa Jacobson, an air explosion had boomed high up in the sky.

All power, lights, and background noise of traffic, air conditioners, radios, television—the stuff of our electrically connected lives—went dark immediately.

Damn, Gorman thought. *The president is moving fast.*

He made an educated guess that if it were indeed an EMP, then bombing raids would soon follow.

He was about to return to the main room when Maryam rushed back in, holding a candle. "It's happening, isn't it?"

He nodded. "Tit for tat. Pakistan took out one of our port cities, and it looks like we're about to take out one of yours."

"We have to move now," she said.

"I know, but nothing with a battery is going to be working for many miles."

"We need old-fashioned leg power," she replied, "on the best bikes we can find, and get out of this blast area and then find transportation."

"What about them?" he asked, referring not only to Lari but also Manish, who was unconscious in one of the bedrooms following a far less civilized interrogation session.

Her brown eyes glistening in the moonlight, she said, "Let them burn."

64

Trust But Verify

"I said it before and I'll say it again: we simply *cannot* afford to wait," insisted Roman Dalton. "Montoya is moving the terrorists north in three hours, and as soon as the sun goes down our window is gone."

Monica sat across from him in the small conference room, staring at the satellite phone in between them.

"And I strongly recommend that we give Colonel Stark and his team time to land and get eyes on the ground before we get anywhere near that compound," she stated. "To make sure this isn't a setup."

"Hold for a moment," came the reply from the White House, where Porter, John Wright, and Lisa Jacobson were huddled in Wright's office to take this emergency call that Monica had initiated.

She sat back in her chair and just stared at her current superior. Dalton didn't seem as upset as she had expected, given that she had initiated the call and then invited Dalton to participate, essentially going over his head.

But she had no choice. Ten minutes ago, Lieutenant Alfonso Domingo had shared intelligence that the terrorists were shortening their planned stay in Monterrey.

"ASAC Cruz." A female voice cracked on the small speaker. "Do you recognize my voice?"

Monica and Dalton leaned forward simultaneously. "Yes, Madam President," she said.

"Do you not trust the GAFE forces deployed by President Gutierrez at *my* request?"

There it was.

It truly all boiled down to that simple question, which the president of the United States had just asked while Dalton leaned back and raised his palms in an I-told-you-so motion.

Realizing that the rest of her government career rested on her next words, Monica took a moment to think before replying, "To quote Ronald Reagan, Madam President, I want to 'trust, but verify.'"

President Vaccaro leaned back and considered what the young FBI agent had just told her, and for a moment Monica Cruz reminded Vaccaro of herself.

She stared at John Wright and saw a glistening in his stare that conveyed understanding and even a bit of dark amusement. Because of the past they shared in country, John Wright would always know her better that anyone else in the White House, and Vaccaro knew that Wright knew that the Reagan quote was one of her all-time favorites.

A long pause, followed by, "So do I, ASAC Cruz. I also wish we had the time to verify, but we simply can't take the chance. And I have just got off the phone *again* with President Gutierrez, who has assured me that the GAFE troops he's deployed are his finest and most trustworthy."

Monica held Dalton's gaze before closing her eyes.

For reasons she could not explain, Monica suddenly felt a strange connection with President Vaccaro, something she could not put her finger on, but it was there, floating somewhere in the static connection.

"And that means we go," added Vaccaro. "But we understand your hesitancy in trusting the locals, so we leave it to your discretion to delay as much as possible but remain *within* the new operational window. We don't want to show up late for the party, understood?"

Monica and Dalton replied in unison, "Yes, Madam President."

"Good," Vaccaro said. "We have also tasked two satellites for your use, so communications and photos are available to you on demand. We're giving the same information to Colonel Stark."

Monica sat back, still not liking this, even when directed by the president, but she held her tongue.

"ASAC Cruz," Vaccaro added, apparently reading her thoughts. "You were picked to be on this mission because you are the best of us. I know this situation is not optimal, but as my father used to say,

'Figure it out and make it happen.' To say your country depends on you would be understating what you're doing. Okay?"

"Yes, Madam President," she replied, staring at Dalton while the feeling in the back of her throat increased from a light scratch to a rake.

65

Karma

FIFTY THOUSAND FEET OVER THE INDIAN OCEAN

They were flying works of art, menacing yet graceful, massive yet invisible, dashing through the stratosphere like silent birds of prey. Four General Electric turbofans with reduced acoustic and infrared signatures stealthily propelled them to just below the speed of sound. Carbon-graphite composites covered their skins, stronger than steel yet lighter than aluminum. They absorbed most radar energy rather than reflecting it back to the source, allowing them to remain undetected.

The three stealth bombers flying in a standard delta formation maneuvered around the tip of Sri Lanka and turned to the northwest while remaining one hundred miles from the coast, per their flight plans.

Major Will "Sake" Sakai sat in the left seat of the lead Northrop Grumman B-2 Spirit on this star-filled night. He scanned the array of displays wrapped around him and his copilot, Captain Les "Fester" Adams. The two were currently stationed at Andersen Air Force Base in Guam, and they had logged over two thousand hours in the B-2, flying missions all over the world.

Past sorties included Kosovo, Iraq, and also the grueling bombing runs in support of Operation Enduring Freedom. The latter had required Sakai and Adams to fly forty-plus-hour sorties from White-man Air Force Base in Missouri to Afghanistan and back, including multiple air-to-air refuelings. Compared to that, this sortie was a cakewalk.

Sakai turned his eyes to the west.

Somewhere out there, beyond the range of his radar, cruised the United States Seventh Fleet, including Carrier Strike Group Five, centered around the USS *Ronald Reagan* aircraft carrier. Recently replacing the aging USS *George Washington*, the *Reagan* was home to the Carrier Air Wing 2 (CVQ-2). It consisted of nine squadrons, a deadly mix of F/A-18C Hornets, F/A-18E and F Super Hornets, plus E-2C Hawk-eyes and EA-6B Prowlers for electronic warfare support.

But Sakai and Adams would not make contact with the fleet. Their mission was stealth all the way—in and out of Pakistan while dropping enough conventional ordnance to level the equivalent of a third of New York City. Each of the bomber's two internal bays housed forty five-hundred-pound GBU-38s plus two two-thousand-pound GBU-31s, for a combined total of forty-eight thousand pounds of high explosives. The number was eight thousand pounds beyond the official limit, but Sakai knew they could carry even more, as he had in many missions. In addition, all bombs featured the bolt-on guidance package known as JDAM—joint direct attack munition—meaning Sakai could place them anywhere with ridiculous accuracy.

And tonight his "anywhere" started with a raid over the Port of Karachi before hitting in-country HVTs—high-value targets.

"Five minutes, Sake," said Adams on the intercom.

"Roger," replied Sakai as his GPS marked the location of the port city, though darkness enshrouded the entire horizon. No lights were visible on the ground.

"Effective EMP, I would say," said Adams.

"Roger that, Fester. Assholes are blind, deaf, and dumb."

"Two minutes," stated Adams.

"Roger, two minutes," came back into his earpiece.

The chatter stopped as his fingers moved automatically over the controls of the bombing system. They were led on a retaliation strike that was long overdue. The duplicitous nature of the Pakistani government had finally come home to roost in the form of the United States Air Force doing what no one in the world could do better. It was precision, finality, and destruction that would look as if the fist of God had slammed into the ground.

The formation approached the coast from the southeast, holding altitude as payload bay doors opened, slaved to algorithms running within the silicon fabric of the targeting computers. HVTs had been preselected by the finest strategists at the Pentagon to incur the greatest damage to military and terrorist targets per pound of explosives. But while minimizing civilian casualties.

Not quite an eye for an eye, he thought, but such decisions were beyond his pay grade.

In an instant each B-2 released a preordained number of GBU-38s, each earmarked to hit a specific target within a one-hundred-square-mile area. The onboard navigation and control systems compensated for the sudden drop in weight, close to ten thousand pounds per bird, holding altitude to within ten feet.

And just like that the Karachi bomb raid was over, at least for the B-2s, which continued in a northwesterly course while their smart munitions followed their computerized trajectories.

Less than a minute later the ground pulsated with bursts of light as military targets were hit with surgical precision. They included the Pakistani Air Force Base Masroor, home to half of the fighters making up their Southern Air Command, a mix of Mirages and F-7P interceptors, the Chinese version of the MiG-21.

"Those planes will never see the sky again," said Adams after getting electronic confirmation that the bombs had pretty much obliterated the base.

"I hope that hurt as intended," Sakai continued.

A village-like encampment between the base and the industrial port city, which the CIA had long earmarked as one of the largest IED—improvised explosive device—factories in the region, burst into light. The direct hit triggered a chain reaction of secondary explosions of large caches of munitions and explosives.

"That's some village," Adams commented, watching the pyrotechnic display.

"Looks like a fireworks factory on steroids."

"Too bad one of the bombs didn't drift and hit the port itself," said Adams. "Bastards hit *our* port. Those chemical plants and oil refineries down there would have burned for weeks."

"Ours is not to reason why," replied Sakai.

"Yeah, yeah, ours is but to do—" Adams started to say when suddenly an oil refinery less than a quarter of a mile from the IED factory vanished in a massive explosion.

"What the hell?" asked Sakai.

"Secondary explosions from the IED factory," replied Adams. "Plus maybe a little karma."

Sakai looked back and noticed what looked like dozens of rockets, probably Chinese 107s, blasting off the factory in every direction, including toward the refineries.

As the B-2s headed for the second target, an unexpected chain reaction began on the ground, with the oil refinery causing an adjacent chemical plant to catch fire. The resulting blast engulfed three city blocks.

"Yeah," Sakai said as they left the city behind them. "Karma can be a real bitch."

66

Out of Time

KARACHI, PAKISTAN

The world seemed to catch fire around them.

Gorman and Maryam rushed out of the bungalow as the chemical plant next door vanished behind a towering sheet of flames licking the night sky.

Nearly blinded by the inferno just over a block away, Gorman followed Maryam outside as the bungalow collapsed, trapping Lari and Manish. The heat grew intolerable and the floor trembled from the shock wave.

"Don't look back!" he shouted, perspiration filming his face—and hers—from the skyrocketing temperature as he grabbed her hand and ran away.

They covered almost one quarter of a mile in a couple of minutes before finding a bike shop amidst people screaming and crying. Some were frozen in apparent shock while staring at the incoming wall of fire.

Without breaking stride Gorman grabbed a trash can, threw it through the front window, and jumped in, followed by Maryam.

They found the tallest two bikes and were out of there in under a minute, riding as fast as they could. They were both strong and, if they were being honest, both scared of being fried in place. However, no way were they going to cover the distance they needed, given the size of the explosions. Just behind them, massive refineries and chemical plants vanished in an inferno that got dangerously close to the colossal holding tanks used to service the oil supertankers.

He pedaled as fast as he could side by side with Maryam, maneuvering in near-darkness around people yelling and running in every direction, other bicycles, and hundreds of abandoned mopeds, cars, and trucks—their electronics fried by the EMP.

It was chaos on a grand scale.

Gorman did the math and guessed that if those storage tanks went off, the blast would swallow at least a third of the city.

So after a mile they started looking for a way to get below ground.

Karachi was dead, no lights, no vehicles, and hordes stampeding in every direction under the flickering glow of flames consuming this neighborhood. Almost no one, except the two of them, seemed to realize what was coming next.

The firestorm obscured the first of dozens of holding tanks lining the southern end of the port. The moment one went off, it would trigger an apocalyptic chain reaction.

"We need a large building!" she screamed.

"Or a deep basement!" he added, wading through the mob of panicked locals.

They maneuvered through several back alleys and down another crowded avenue. And that's when Maryam pointed at a building site.

A large downtown station of the Karachi subway system was under construction. A billboard indicated it would include a large multilevel shopping center, market, office space, and parking garage. But most importantly, it would connect to the existing line between the Jinnah Airport and the Karachi Expo Center. It had a twenty-floor façade of steel and concrete and what he hoped would be multiple levels below. Being the middle of the night, there were no workers in sight, and because of the EMP, it was shrouded in darkness.

They ditched the bikes, climbed over the construction fence, and sprinted across a thousand feet separating them from the rising building.

Halfway there, they heard a noise behind them.

"We've got company," Gorman said, pointing behind him. Some people had apparently realized what they were trying to do and had brought down a section of the fence. Dozens now raced through, past mounds of construction supplies and equipment, presumably also seeking shelter.

Gorman and Maryam pressed on, reaching the station nearly out of breath.

He looked back at the port area, now completely covered in flames that appeared to be at least five stories high. Towering fire forked skyward. Above it hovered clouds of burning ashes.

"Come!" he screamed, tugging her as a river of people stampeded through the breach in the fence toward the construction site in full panic. "We don't have much time!"

They moved inside as fast as possible, using feel, though their eyes began to adjust to the darkness.

"There!" he said, pointing beyond piles of bricks, sand, and equipment. A wide set of stairs headed down into darkness, hopefully to the underground system.

Taking the steps quickly but carefully, they reached the lowest level under the dim glow of a handful of emergency lights that apparently had been deep enough below ground that they weren't affected by the EMP. The place reminded Gorman of a New York subway platform, running for nearly five hundred feet alongside a train track.

They raced to the north corner, past crates packed with white subway tiles and stacked bags of cement, finally settling beneath a massive steel beam in case the building above them collapsed.

Sitting down on the floor facing each other, they took a moment to catch their breath as they heard the commotion of people a few floors above—

Blinding clouds of dust and an eardrum-breaking noise that consumed their world followed the blast, incomprehensible in its shocking power. Dust rained from the ceiling, from the sides, and even radiated from below, as everything was made from concrete.

The massive explosion that started in the harbor traveled to Gorman and Maryam in all the waves of energy: light, acoustic, overpressure, and heat—a complex tsunami, building in power as it washed over the construction site.

The vibration, powerful and deep, reverberated down to the basement, shaking the foundation with such force, Gorman feared his teeth would come loose from his gums.

The concrete-and-steel cavity trembled as the energy from the blast permeated through the construction site. Flashes of light pulsated down the stairs as the explosion exhaled through it like a massive windpipe, shooting fire and burning debris to the middle of the platform.

"Bill!"

He jumped over Maryam, shielding her, as the world collapsed around them.

67

Live from New York

SOUTHERN PAKISTAN

"Jesus. What the hell was that?" asked Sakai as the sky almost fifty miles behind them lit up in what appeared to be an explosion of nuclear proportions—only he knew it couldn't be, because their ordnance was all conventional.

But they didn't have time to worry about it, as they had to get ready for their next target, which they reached ten minutes later.

This time they released almost half of their ordnance in Quetta, demolishing known ISIS training camps, key weapons depots, and also PAF Base Samungli. It made up the second half of the Pakistani Southern Air Command, consisting of more F-7Ps as well as an entire wing of Aerospatiale Alouette III helicopters.

The delta formation then turned to a northeasterly heading, reaching the city of Sargodha, sixty miles south of Islamabad, in twenty minutes. They unleashed most of the remaining munitions on top of the PAF Base Mushaf, Pakistan's Central Air Command and home of their premier fighters, mostly F-16s, Mirage 5PAs, and even more F-7Ps.

But each B-2 saved two GBU-31s for the final act of the evening.

They turned north toward Islamabad, but left the capital untouched. They could see sporadic ground fires burning for lighting since electricity would be out until they could replace the generators damaged by the EMP strike.

The stealth bombers continued north for twenty-five miles, until reaching the town of Abbottabad, home of a large Pakistani military academy as well as an ISIS stronghold.

And the place where the Pakistani government hid Osama bin Laden for years.

"Best for last," Adams said as they approached their target.

"Attention Abbottabad shoppers," Sakai said. "There is a nice message from the president of the United States coming your way from aisle up-your-ass."

"Ha," Adams grunted as the computerized system released the payload. "But I have a better one: Live from New York, it's the United States Air Force Show."

Within one hour, three B-2 stealth bombers had obliterated over 70 percent of Pakistan's air force and other military compounds. They had also destroyed a number of ISIS strongholds plus had indirectly devastated most of Karachi's refineries and chemical plants—along with a third of the city.

Before turning east, toward India, and heading back to Guam per the flight plan, Sakai circled the city twice. The two-thousand-pounders detonated in massive blasts of yellow and orange. But in his mind he saw the images from New York, the death toll already approaching two hundred thousand. He saw factories on fire, ships capsized, ports destroyed, and city blocks upon city blocks reduced to ashes.

But tonight the ashes belonged to Pakistan, to ISIS and its black-clad fanatics, to gutless terrorists and the nation that harbored them.

Tonight it was America's turn to retaliate.

And we're just getting warmed up.

68

Gideon

NORTHERN PAKISTAN

Their moon shadows shot across the mountainous terrain at dizzying speed. They were sleek, alien to their stark surroundings, slaved to the squadron of camouflaged Israeli Air Force F-16Is from Ramat David Airbase, southeast of Haifa.

Chief Commander Maya Behrman led the sortie, holding one hundred feet while flying at just under the speed of sound to conserve fuel.

Just aft of her right wingtip flew Captain Ben Sammet, her wingman. Like Maya, Sammet was a veteran pilot with countless sorties during his ten-year military career.

Her squadron of eleven "Netz" fighters—the Israeli nickname that meant "Falcon" in Hebrew—had left Ramat David six hours ago. They had jettisoned their external fuel tanks over the Red Sea and refueled twice from American KC-135 flying tankers—once over the Arabian Sea near the coast of Yemen, and again prior to entering Pakistani airspace, within sight of the imposing U.S. Seventh Fleet. Then they had continued northeast into the still-darkened country, its power infrastructure crippled by the American EMPs.

At twenty kilometers from the reactor complex, Maya climbed to two thousand meters. The Khushab facility, with its five weapons-grade-plutonium-producing reactors, covered most of the long valley. Perimeter fences under the yellowish glow of emergency lights surrounded massive domes, cooling towers, and endless structures, pipes, buildings, and cranes.

At a distance of ten kilometers from her assigned target, Reactor 1 on the northeast side of the complex, Maya inched the control stick forward, commanding the Netz into a forty-degree dive.

Sammet followed closely while the rest of the squadron broke up into pairs, one per reactor plus a solo fighter to eliminate the heavy water production plant in the southeast.

At an altitude of one thousand meters, Maya began to release her load of Mark 84 general-purpose bombs at six-second intervals. She then climbed to five thousand meters to lead their escape run into India, less than two hundred kilometers away.

The facility lit up the valley as dozens of two-thousand-pounders detonated on target. The containment domes of all reactors vanished in multiple fireballs of orange and yellow-gold, before secondary explosions propagated across the rest of the complex.

Maya's squadron resumed its formation while flames pulsated in the desert, reflecting their glow on the steep walls of surrounding mountains, turning the remote valley into a nuclear wasteland.

Breaking silence for the first time since entering Pakistani airspace, she recited a passage from the Book of Joshua.

"On the day the Lord gave the Amorites over to Israel, Joshua said to the Lord in the presence of Israel, 'Sun, stand still over Gideon, and you, moon, over the Valley of Aijalon.' So the sun stood still, and the moon stopped, till the nation avenged itself on its enemies."

Her squadron replied in unison, "There has never been a day like it before or since, a day when the Lord listened to a human being. Surely the Lord was fighting for Israel!"

69

Jade

It had never been done before, but it didn't mean it couldn't be, and Lieutenant Commander Jacob "Jade" Demetrius had argued its probability of success given enough accuracy and serial penetrating power.

So his air wing commander had gone up the chain of command, involving not just the Pentagon but also the CIA and the White House. The green light had arrived from an unexpected channel: via satellite phone from John Wright, the president's chief of staff.

The munitions retrofitting had begun in the middle of the night. Four F/A-18F Super Hornets from his strike fighter squadron, VFA-154, known as the Black Knights, were loaded with a pair of Enhanced GBU-28s, the laser-guided version of the "bunker-busting" bombs used during the First Gulf War and affectionately nicknamed "Deep Throat."

One hour later, the catapult shot kicked Demetrius in the back.

While in full flaps and full afterburners, the Super Hornet accelerated to its minimum maneuvering speed of 135 knots in three seconds with less than ten feet sink off of the bow. Dark ocean projected beyond his canopy.

Demetrius waited patiently as the Super Hornet picked up speed, reaching 370 knots before nudging the control stick back. He entered a forty-five-degree full-power climbout while maintaining 250 knots, leveling out at FL200—flight level 200 or twenty thousand feet—in one minute.

Easing back the throttles, he settled the F/A-18F at 450 knots, heading zero two zero, to wait for the rest of his team.

The veteran navy pilot, having accumulated over two thousand combat hours in the Super Hornet and its predecessor, the Hornet, accomplished this almost on automatic. Fingers moved with practiced ease, controlling the sixty-foot-long carrier-based multirole fighter with the grace of a ballet dancer.

Pakistani airspace, still silent from EMPs and B-2 strikes, gave him complete air superiority, almost making him feel sorry for the enemy.

But the images from New York quickly erased any emotions caused by a sortie he had conceived, planned, fought for approval of, and now led in its execution.

"All set back here, Jade," reported his WSO, weapons systems operator, Lieutenant Rolando "Speedy" Gonzales.

He sat directly behind Demetrius.

In command of their AN/APG-79 AESA radar, capable of executing multiple air-to-ground or air-to-air attacks, Gonzales's job was to place their Deep Throats dead on target.

Recurrent accuracy was key to the mission's success. To that end Demetrius had picked his team carefully, selecting the most experienced pilots and WSOs among the Black Knights brotherhood.

"Roger," he replied as the other Super Hornets caught up to him and assumed a diamond formation.

They headed north just as the tip of the sun broke the eastern horizon, streaks of orange and yellow staining the indigo sky, washing out the stars.

That was the beauty of proficiency, of having flown combat missions with these guys for so long: four pilots and their respective WSOs becoming one, reading each other's minds, operating with minimum chatter. Each did his job with quiet precision, matching airspeeds and altitudes, holding spacing, and executing maneuvers to an accuracy rivaling the finest air show performance.

"Cruise speed," Demetrius informed his team, advancing the throttles beyond the détente into full afterburner, accelerating the Super Hornet to 777 knots.

He felt the typical mild bump when going supersonic before easing back throttles to cruise setting. Coastal plains gave way to mountains and the final stars yielded to a glowing sun looming above the horizon.

At that speed, it took them less than fifteen minutes to cover 250 miles to the GPS coordinates of their target two miles outside Nawabshah, a city of just over a million people, roughly in the middle of the country.

To the untrained observer, their objective seemed little more than a couple of weathered buildings flanking a patch of desert off National Highway N-5, which connected it to the port city of Karachi. Intelligence reports, however, marked the site as Pakistan's largest depository of nuclear weapons, buried deep beneath a few hundred feet of desert, rock, and reinforced concrete.

On paper, the underground facility was placed beyond the penetrating power of the Deep Throat. But the dilapidated buildings housed the key to Demetrius's plan: large freight elevators connecting the surface to the underground complex.

In some strange way—and oddly enough Demetrius had even included it in his argument—the strike was not unlike that of the fictional *Star Wars* character Luke Skywalker. The legendary space warrior had guided a pair of proton torpedoes down a thermal exhaust port to destroy the original Death Star.

But unlike the famous starfighter, the U.S. Navy pilots would not be relying on supernatural forces to help them deliver their munitions to the target. At least not when the APG-79 system could accomplish the task with unparalleled precision.

Demetrius engaged the virtual speedbrake. The Super Hornet lacked the hydraulically deployed upper-fuselage speedbrake of its younger sister, the Hornet. But it accomplished similar results through the use of contrasting flight control surfaces, increasing drag without jeopardizing flight control, roll, or pitch.

As they slowed down to three hundred knots while maintaining FL200, Gonzales engaged the APG-79 and commenced the attack, painting the laser in the center of the southern warehouse. Within a couple of seconds, the large display showed a single track to target, marking the spot for their first GBU-28.

The eighteen-foot-long weapon dropped from its underfuselage mounts and guided itself to the precise location illuminated by the laser. Demetrius maintained leveled flight over the area, with his wingman following just behind and to his right. The other pair of Super Hornets began their dual bombing run on the southern warehouse to double their chances.

The blast, powerful, lit up the ground with orange flames as its five thousand pounds of explosives tore into the shaft. The warehouse imploded from within, a fireball of fire and debris the size of a football field.

As he made a wide turn to start his second run, Demetrius's wingman released his first Deep Throat precisely over the same coordinates where he had dropped the first one, now a deep crater of smoldering rubble.

The second bomb dove to its target as he finished his turn, getting a clear view just left of the Super Hornet's nose. The GBU-28 punched deeper, burrowing down the shaft before detonating several seconds later. The blast visibly lifted the surrounding desert as the second pair of Super Hornets dropped their first bombs, vaporizing the second warehouse.

"What do you think, Speedy?" asked Demetrius.

"Not bad," he replied. "But I think we could go deeper."

Demetrius nodded to himself. He figured that even if they couldn't get down to the nuclear arsenal, worst case the Pakis would have one hell of a time reaching their underground facility with both elevators demolished.

He waited with his wingman for the other pair of Super Hornets to drop their second set of Deep Throats, one per shaft, pushing deeper.

Secondary explosions erupted from the shafts, like volcanoes vomiting columns of fire and smoke, topping five hundred feet.

Then something unexpected happened. The ground between the elevator shafts swelled up like a balloon. It reached almost a hundred feet high before collapsing into itself, creating a massive crater at least two hundred feet deep.

"I think we got them, Jade," Gonzales said. "Want to hit them again just for shits and grins?"

As Demetrius considered releasing the final two Deep Throats down the middle of this new crater, he received the most peculiar order from his air wing commander.

A moment later, as the other set of Super Hornets turned back toward the coast, Demetrius punched in a new set of GPS coordinates. It pointed the pair of F/A-18Fs toward the northern section of Pakistan's Federally Administered Tribal Areas.

70

Ibrahim

**KHAR. FEDERALLY ADMINISTERED
TRIBAL AREAS. PAKISTAN**

They had once called him Ichabod Crane because of his prominent nose, wiry build, and mild disposition. Though it also didn't help that he was born Ibrahim al-Crameini. But the native of Baghdad never cared for the nickname given to him by his schoolmates at Oxford a lifetime ago.

Dressed in black, Ibrahim looked up from the speech he planned to broadcast to the world, for an instant remembering those humiliating times. The experience had sparked his hatred for the infidels—a hatred that grew in breadth and depth over the following decade when the Americans deposed Saddam Hussein. Ibrahim had been raised in prominence alongside his younger brother, Hassan. Their parents had been strong members of the Ba'ath Party.

Tightening the grip on the pen in his right hand, Ibrahim recalled the night the bombs fell over Baghdad. The night his parents died forever eliminated his way of life, forcing him into the mountains with his younger brother. It was there, as the unbelievers invaded the capital, that the siblings joined the radical Islamic movement. They worked their way through the ranks of the likes of al Qaeda, Hamas, and eventually ISIS, where Ibrahim reconnected with Atiq Gadai, his old roommate at Oxford. Together, they masterminded the plan to smuggle nuclear devices into America.

Ibrahim sighed, forcing his thoughts back to the task at hand. He was putting his degree in literature to the test as he went over his speech again, silently praying to Allah for divine inspiration.

Ibrahim needed to write an even more powerful global punch than his two prior speeches, released shortly after each detonation. This one would go online soon after Atiq's third detonation took place, sometime in the next few days.

America was already on the verge of anarchy, with riots and civil unrest sparking everywhere. He hoped this would be the coup de grâce.

But unfortunately, the right words would not come this night, even after five hours. Perhaps he needed a distraction, maybe his secret channel to vent off steam and find inspiration.

He had already left his bunker and walked the perimeter of the compound overlooking the ridges connecting his nation to Afghanistan. Most of Pakistan lay in darkness from the American attacks, but the tribal areas had been spared so far. He had electricity, communications, which he had used in the prior days to activate dormant cells in America to clear the way for Salma's readjusted mission, per Atiq's instructions.

But his stubborn writer's block still remained, requiring something more stimulating than fresh mountain air.

Ibrahim stood and stretched. His frustrated gaze landed on two women sitting on the edge of his bed, their faces cloaked in black veils, or *hijabs*. They were girls, really, barely fifteen and virgins both, gifts from Atiq.

He sighed, thinking of the many orphans his old schoolmate had assigned to him, especially as his position grew over the years in the turbulent ISIS leadership.

Ibrahim had enjoyed their silent fear as much as peering into their terrified innocent stares as he ravaged them.

But today the virgins would be his dessert, the cherry on the cake.

Ibrahim's main course was chained on her knees on a small stage in front of a pair of video cameras bathed in yellow lights. Her name was Priya Foster, a BBC news correspondent of Indian descent picked off the streets of Islamabad the night before while covering the war.

Priya was young and certainly beautiful, like so many newswomen, making his task all the more delightful to the cameras controlled by two of his men, also clad in black. But Priya was also a Christian, which always made the videos that much more interesting to watch.

Ibrahim reached for the knife and the pliers on a table next to her.

"Please," she said, lips trembling, her wet stare on him. "I haven't—"

Ibrahim slapped her before another one of his men held her steady.

He had done this many times, to men and women of every age.

He had done it to anyone who dared stand in the way of his Islamic jihad, just as this woman had for challenging Sharia Law, for turning her back on the only religion in the world by being a Christian.

"State your faith," he said.

She hesitated, her brown eyes wet with tears, blood dripping from her lower lip.

"I said," he repeated, leaning close to her while forcing her chin up to face the cameras, "state your faith."

"I'm . . . Catholic."

"I will ask you one more time. What is your religion?"

After a moment of hesitation, she repeated, "Catholic."

"Very well," Ibrahim said, and nodded to the man holding her from behind, who forced her mouth open.

Priya struggled but to no avail. The inevitability of what was about to happen, the helplessness, the despair—the overwhelming fear—made her cry while mumbling incoherently.

Ibrahim looked at the tools of pain he had before him with determination and a blackness that was soulless.

"Do you renounce Jesus Christ?" he asked her.

This was the last time he would ask her a question. The rest of the evening he would test this woman's ability to stand pain, and his ability to inflict it.

And that's when he heard it—the faint noise of jet engines amidst her cries.

Before fire engulfed him.

"Nice shot, Speedy," Demetrius commented as secondary explosions foretold the destruction of the bunker on the outskirts of the city.

"And here comes the double tap," Gonzales replied as their wingman released his final Deep Throat on the location his superiors had pinpointed as the current hideout of Ibrahim al-Crameini. The intelligence report had been verified a couple of hours earlier by one of the dozens of RQ-4 Global Hawks blanketing the Pakistani airspace to record the retaliatory strikes. The high-altitude UAV had captured the most-wanted terrorist mastermind walking the compound. Facial recognition software had provided final confirmation.

"Always a pleasure helping ISIS motherfuckers reach the land of a thousand virgins," Gonzales added as the Super Hornets turned back toward the coast.

"It's actually just seventy-two virgins, Speedy," Demetrius said.

"Really?" Gonzales replied. "You read that in the Koran?"

"Nah. WikiIslam. Says that believing men will be rewarded with seventy-two virgins with swelling breasts."

"Do they come with a bottle of Viagra? I can barely keep up with *one* crazy girlfriend."

Demetrius grinned, though he seriously doubted these crazy bastards would see any damn virgins in the afterlife, but only the deepest and hottest level of hell.

71

Twilight

KARACHI, PAKISTAN

Heat surrounded him, sweltering and suffocating, as if he had descended into hell itself. But it was the hands on his shoulders that awoke him.

Plus her screams.

"Bill! Wake up! Bill!"

Stunned from the blast, Gorman blinked, trying to clear his sight as he lay on his side, a throbbing pain stabbing the back of his head and in between his shoulder blades.

"Bill . . . thank God!"

In the twilight of emergency lights, through the dusty and sweltering air hovering above the platform, he saw her eyes on him.

Slowly, with some effort, he sat up, breathing once, twice.

"Are you all right?" he asked.

She simply hugged him tight. "Me? The question is, are *you* all right, love?"

"I think so," he said, remembering the shock wave kicking him in the back just before he had jumped on her.

"Thank you. Again," she whispered in the semidarkness, kissing him on the lips. "But you have to stop saving me."

He shrugged. "I'm old school. Ladies first. How long have I been out?"

"I think we were both out for about an hour. I came around a minute ago and for a moment thought that . . ."

"You won't be getting rid of me that easily," he said, brushing dust off her face.

"That was . . . some bloody explosion," she said.

"Yeah," he added, her eyes glistening inches from him. "Now we know what millions of gallons of oil going off a mile away feels like."

"Bill," she said, looking toward the stairs near the middle of the platform, "the people up there . . ."

He understood immediately. There were no more sounds coming from above. No screams. No cries. Just . . . silence.

"Are we the only ones who . . ." She let her voice trail off.

"Only one way to find out," he replied.

They stood and dusted each other off before walking toward the exit sign. Two of the emergency lights had survived the blast, casting a dim glow across the platform.

They reached the foot of the stairs and headed one level up but stopped halfway.

Dear God.

The entire stairwell had collapsed, blocking their way.

But that was not what froze him.

Before them stood a scene from Dante's *Inferno*, a sight that made Gorman bend over and heave once, feeling bile rising in his throat.

The yellow light from the platform reached the wall of rubble sealing the exit.

Only it wasn't just rubble.

Body parts protruded through the pile of bricks, subway tiles, concrete, and twisted rebar. Most were burned beyond recognition, fingers stretched, pleading silently in the dark.

As he lowered his gaze to the twenty or so feet separating him from the macabre sight, he recognized the others in front of the wall. The people who'd made it through the wreckage didn't get far. He recalled the blast of fire shooting down the stairs before he'd passed out. It had consumed their bodies. Charred figures littered the floor, incinerated in what became a brief but intense combustion chamber. The stench of burnt flesh was nauseating.

Gorman took a deep breath and fought the urge to vomit, summoning his training. Maryam heaved once but also held it back.

"Bill . . . those poor people," she said, the tips of her fingers covering her mouth.

"I know."

They stood side by side staring at the scene while realizing just how damn lucky they had been.

"Now what?" she said, pointing at the blocked exit.

He was about to reply when a distant blast rumbled through the station, like a rolling earthquake, stopping as soon as it began.

"Bloody hell! What was that?" she asked.

"Secondary blasts," he said. "I'm guessing that the port area is still—"

Gorman stopped, feeling a low and deep vibration, like a freight train leaving a station, but from above—far above, and rippling down the structure.

And that's when he remembered the stories of the survivors when the towers fell.

"Bill? What's wrong?"

But he was no longer listening, in an instant recalling their tales, their horrid descriptions of events from that day, as the world dropped over them. And it all began with a distant growl from high above, the rhythmic tremors, the pulsating roar of floors collapsing on top of each other.

"Bill?" Maryam asked again.

But he was staring at the ceiling, noticing the faint but sporadic wisps of fine white powder oozing from the subway tiles as the successive crumpling of floors broadcast shock waves to the bottom of the structure.

For reasons he couldn't explain, Jeannie's face loomed in his mind, urging him to run away.

Lacking the time to explain, he grabbed Maryam's hand and took off towards the north end of the tunnel. He had not been able to save his wife, but he sure as hell was determined to do everything in his power to save Maryam.

"Bill! What is—"

"Trust me!" he screamed as the ceiling trembled, releasing veils of dust over them to the beat of the collapsing building.

Squinting through the haze, he kept up the pressure, running as fast as he could while holding her hand very tight. They took less than fifteen seconds to reach the end of the platform before jumping to the tracks and scrambling into the tunnel.

And that's when the ceiling collapsed in an explosion of steel and concrete, the sound deafening, earsplitting. The shock wave crashed against the floor of the station and bounced back up, colliding with the avalanche of rubble crashing down. It pounded the foundation, triggering an earthquake-like energy wave and kicking up a boiling cloud of smoke, fire, and debris that engulfed them.

72

My Fellow Americans

WASHINGTON, D.C.

"Madam President," started the current head of the Department of Homeland Security, Jonathan Miller. "We have deployed all regional assets to New York. We have food, clothing, communications, trucks, potable water, and the ability to make more. We have to be able to move waste of all kinds away from the city and we are using portable burning units to—"

"Please stop, Mr. Miller," Vaccaro interrupted. "You need to understand my intent. I want *all* of FEMA's assets deployed to New York City now. I understand it's a logistical nightmare, but this government has two things to do today: protect the nation from further attacks, and rebuild lower Manhattan. You have the full authority of this office to carry out that intent, thank you." And she hung up the phone while John Wright, sitting across from her in the Oval Office, pointed at his watch.

Vaccaro nodded absently, deciding she would never get used to how many people, from members of her committees, cabinet, and staff, to the press and the public, knew exactly what the president of the United States should say. And if she did not say the exact words that all wanted, then they all would jump, leak, cajole, and comment on what she did and did not say. Or what it did and did not mean.

What she was *not* going to do was allow this bloated and out-of-control system she had inherited ruin the very thing she took an oath to protect. She knew one thing all the way down to her bones: the time for talking was done. She would continue to act, and ask permission later. Right now, as her chief of staff had just pointed out, her action was to update the country and the world as to what had happened in the past twenty-four hours.

Vaccaro stood and followed Wright to the lawn just outside the Oval Office, where a podium had already been set up. She had decided that the speech she had to give would be short and to the point. She had to spell out directly what had happened and what the country was doing and would continue to do, and that they, as a nation, would make it through this. She had to continue to lead, not hide or listen to advisors about legacy, politics, or any other distraction. It was not ego; it was necessary and the job, nothing more and certainly nothing less. Two nuclear devices had been exploded, one in New York City. The time for political consideration was long gone, hopefully forever, though that was not likely. The time for leadership was at hand, and the president of the United States prayed she was up to the task.

"Good afternoon," she began, facing a crowd of reporters. "The reason I did not start this speech with the familiar phrase 'My fellow Americans' is that although this speech is for the American people, I also wanted the world to know what has happened and what we are doing and will continue to do about it. Seven days ago a three-kiloton atomic bomb was detonated outside the Bagram Air Base in Afghanistan. Four days later a second atomic bomb was set off in Lower Manhattan. The death and injured tolls are still coming in, but hundreds of thousands of innocent people were killed and wounded. The loss of life and limb is heartbreaking. We have also suffered massive industrial and commercial damage. This assault on the United States of America is not going unpunished. I have directed—and it is being carried out as we speak—a retaliatory bombing raid on the infrastructure of Pakistan. The Pakistani Inter-Services Intelligence, or ISI, knowingly participated in two nuclear attacks, here in New York City and at Bagram Air Base. We are destroying their communications, electric grids, power centers, intelligence centers, and any capability for them to attack us or anyone else for a very long time. We are doing this because it is the right thing; it is the only thing—the righteous thing. In addition, I have signed what I will call the Recovery Act, empowering various agencies with executive powers to minimize our exposure to further acts of terror, as well as ordering all law enforcement—local, state, and federal—to employ any means possible, including deadly force, to maintain the peace. While I will do everything in my power to minimize the damage to our nation's supply chain, I also want everyone to be perfectly clear: riots and looting will not be tolerated on my watch.

"I want all to know that we did not ask for this attack. Nothing we did caused this attack . . . but we are responsible for what comes next. May God bless the United States of America and those who support us . . . and may God *damn* those who would do us harm."

73

Blinded by the Light

MONTERREY, MEXICO

"I still don't like it, sir," Monica replied, hands on the wheel of their black Chevy Suburban as the streets of Monterrey rushed by. "We needed eyes on the ground around the compound to make sure we're not walking into a trap. I know the president is giving us extra looks with the satellite overheads, but you and I know we need to have our own people looking at this place before *and* as we go. We also have little in the way of medical support . . . and I can go on."

"You've made your case, Cruz," Dalton replied. "And to the president, for crying out loud, but we're simply out of time. And for the record, I don't like it either, which is why I delayed it as much as we could, and I'm letting them go in first."

He sat next to her in the front seat of their SUV while pointing at the lead Suburban, where Captain Franco Lamar led the raid. Lieutenant Alfonso Domingo followed in the second Suburban, whose rear tires kicked up dust and dirt straight onto her windshield.

They approached the outskirts of the city, headed toward Montoya's place, nestled in the foothills of the Sierra Madre Oriental. Three more Suburbans plus a troop transport truck packed with GAFE soldiers followed them closely, along with a pair of GAFE Bell helicopters, looking ahead.

"And, albeit not ideal, we do have eyes closer to the ground . . . up there," Dalton added, pointing at the sky. A pair of ASACs occupied the rear, staring at the images on their laptops. They were connected to three U.S. Air Force MQ-1 A/B Predators circling the area at two thousand feet, confirming the target's location, including the number of armed guards that Alfonso had reported.

"Everything looks clear from here to the compound, sir," reported one of the ASACs.

"And the guard count inside the perimeter also looks as it should," added the second ASAC.

"See? Relax, Cruz," Dalton said, staring straight ahead. "It'll be over soon and we all get to go home."

Monica frowned while keeping a prudent distance from Alfonso's SUV. Everything looked as it should indeed, and that was *precisely* what bothered her: it looked too damned good.

Nothing ever was.

She had already argued—twice—that they should just have the drones fire their Hellfire missiles at the compound and be done with it. But if she was right and terrorists had hidden a nuclear device somewhere inside the place, the explosions from the missiles could likely turn it into a dirty bomb. She had also argued that the daylight attack eliminated the element of surprise and could prompt the terrorists to detonate the nuke. But Lamar and Alfonso had contended that Montoya was not the suicidal type. Once surrounded, he was likely to turn over the terrorists and the weapon in exchange for being left alone to go about his own business.

"And besides, Cruz," Dalton had whispered to her back at the conference room, "if the damn thing is going to go off, I'd much rather it blew up here than in Texas. And don't forget that this compound is almost a mile from the city, so damage should be minimal. This may be our best chance ever."

So she went along with it, even though her inner voice screamed at her that it was wrong on so many—

"Ah, sir," one of the ASACs said from the backseat while looking at his screen. "There's people on the rooftops just ahead of—"

She caught the flash off the corner of her left eye from the top of a four-story building near the edge of the city. The light arced toward Lamar's SUV, which blew up an instant later, almost in slow motion. Tumbling on its side, it slid across the street while exploding. Glass, metal, and flames nearly engulfed Alfonso's Suburban, which managed to veer out of the way.

Before she could react, gunfire peppered her vehicle. Armed men had emerged from nearby buildings and opened fire on them. The bullet-resistant glass momentarily protected them. Multiple rounds grazed off the glass, leaving tiny cracks that began to propagate across the windshield like spider webs.

We're fucked, Monica thought, as everything around them seemed to catch fire.

We are so fucked.

74

FUBAR

WASHINGTON, D.C.

"Could someone tell me what the *hell* is happening?" shouted Vaccaro, slapping the conference table in the Situation Room the moment the main screen opposite where she sat went blank. A moment ago it had shown a view from the hood-mounted camera of the Suburban driven by Cruz, which captured a couple of explosions. Then it had stopped transmitting, reminiscent of the final seconds of the Manhattan groundburst.

For a moment, Vaccaro thought the terrorists had detonated their weapon. But the feed from the circling drones on the side TV screens showed what appeared to be a conventional attack in progress against the convoy.

"An ambush," said John Wright. "Our guys have driven straight into a damn ambush."

"John, please tell me we have Hellfires on those drones."

"We do, Madam President," replied Wright, standing up and pointing at the screen, where people—presumably civilians—were running for cover amidst the attack. "But I don't recommend using them. Those men are firing from the rooftops of apartment buildings with civilians probably inside. And those armed men in the street are too close to innocent bystanders and to our guys in the other vehicles."

Vaccaro tried to control her rising anger as her people were being slaughtered, and she finally said, "Where the hell is Stark?"

"Final approach."

Staring at the screen, she asked, "Isn't there a large military academy in Monterrey?"

"Yes, Madam President," replied Secretary of Defense Leon Ford. "Three, actually. And the closest one is only fifteen minutes by land and one minute by helicopter."

Pointing at the screen, she said, "Then get Gutierrez on the line and get those troops the hell over there now!"

75

Kill Zone

MONTERREY, MEXICO

"Get us out of here!" shouted Dalton as another explosion rocked the street, this one from behind.

Ignoring the civilians running away from the attack, many disappearing inside buildings, Monica stomped on the brakes and put the Suburban in reverse.

Flooring it while looking over her right shoulder, she steered them away from the kill zone.

Two more blasts, and she watched flames swallowing the three SUVs trailing them. Doors swung open and people on fire jumped onto the street, screaming, collapsing on the asphalt. In an instant the calm city block had become a war zone, triggering memories from Baghdad and Kabul.

290COLONEL DAVID HUNT AND R. J. PINEIRO

And those old memories also kindled old instincts, which resurfaced with unexpected clarity, focusing her efforts.

Monica kept her eyes on the street behind them, left hand on the wheel and right foot on the gas, swinging the vehicle toward the sidewalk. People ran inside buildings as the truck packed with GAFE soldiers went up in flames from two more hits. Her mind registered them as RPGs fired at the convoy from unseen vantage points along multiple rooftops.

"Cruz!" Dalton screamed, pointing ahead, but she could not afford to take her eyes off the rear windshield as she pushed the Chevy in reverse as fast as she could.

She cruised past the flames and the smoking wrecks, steering back into the center of the street just as an arc of light flashed past Dalton's window.

And that's when she risked a forward look. A man dressed in a GAFE uniform lowered an RPG launch tube a couple hundred feet away.

The projectile slammed into a car parked on the sidewalk a dozen feet away, flipping it upside down. The blast shattered her Suburban's passenger-side windows as well as the rear windshield, bathing them in glass while lifting the right tires off the blacktop.

The scorching heat from the explosion filled the vehicle and she lost control, unable to counter the lateral shock wave from the powerful explosion. The Suburban overturned. Her world rotated upside down. They slid another fifty feet before crashing against parked cars across the street while gunshots struck the exposed side of the vehicle like a dozen hammers.

Blood splattered on her when bullets ricocheted off the asphalt and found their marks through the shattered passenger-side windows.

76

Acapulco

President Vaccaro stared at the main screen in silence, where the closest Predator feed depicted the carnage in high resolution. The bastards had ambushed the convoy and were now systematically shooting anyone who had survived. Some of them were on fire, crawling out of their vehicles before getting shot like animals amidst columns of smoke billowing skyward. And the dead included most of the contingent of GAFE soldiers, except for those in the second SUV. They were joined by at least two dozen armed men exiting buildings or climbing out of trucks and sedans reaching the scene.

"Where the hell is Stark?" she asked Wright.

"The airport, Madam President. Getting in their Humvee."

Vaccaro shook her head as the street executions continued. "Might as well be on the damn moon. Did you get ahold of Gutierrez?"

Wright shook his head. "He's traveling to . . . Acapulco, but his aide said they are contacting the bases right now."

Acapulco?

Vaccaro pinched the bridge of her nose, took a deep breath, and said, "Get those damn troops off their damn ass this minute! I don't care what you have to do!"

77

Counterstrike

The smell of gasoline filling her nostrils and the nearing gunfire woke her up.

Choking, her eyes burning, Monica stared at the street upside down.

Jesus.

Instinctively, she reached for her seat belt and tugged on the release lever. It gave, and she cringed as her head struck the ceiling before she landed on her side.

Blinking rapidly, she looked about her, trying to hold her breath from the fumes. Her mind screamed to get the hell out of this vehicle, away from gasoline pooling around her, from a vehicle that could ignite at any moment.

Roman Dalton hung upside down, blood dripping from multiple wounds to the head and neck, dead eyes staring straight ahead. His massive body, encrusted with broken glass, had shielded her.

The intense gas vapors stinging her throat, she struggled to think, to hold it together—to find a way out. The ASACs in back were also dead, their bullet-riddled bodies bleeding out, arms hanging over their heads.

Move.

Now!

Gunfire continued as she peered through the windshield, looking at three men firing against a handful of GAFE soldiers who had survived and were trying to run from their burning truck.

Reaching up for her sound-suppressed MP7A1 still secured between the front seats, she scrambled to the back of the SUV, crawling past the two ASACs, and into the trunk.

Clambering through the shattered rear windshield, she scraped her way out, finally rolling away on the pavement.

Monica took a deep breath, ignoring her burning eyes, coughing and breathing deeply again, clearing her airway. She looked for the incoming threat, spotting their legs a hundred feet on the other side of the SUV, their attention still on the burning transport truck, searching for more survivors.

They haven't seen me, she thought, certain that otherwise those men would be firing in her direction.

So, let's keep it that way.

Rising to a deep crouch, she looked about her, scanning the deserted streets.

Not a soul in sight, except for the termination team sent after them. Just like in Iraq or Afghanistan, the locals knew exactly what was going down and wanted no part of it, vanishing from sight.

She set the MP7A1's lever selector to semi-auto to conserve ammo before scrambling away behind a row of parked cars. Keeping her head down, she reached the sidewalk, spotting a few faces staring at her from inside a restaurant.

Monica brought a finger to her lips before starting in the opposite direction from the ambush, still in a crouch, reaching the corner before checking her six o'clock again.

The trio finally approached her Suburban, surrounding it, peering through the broken windows. One of them stood up abruptly and looked about him.

They know I got away, she thought, in the same instant recognizing none other than Lieutenant Alfonso Domingo walking toward the three men and barking orders in Spanish.

You piece of dog shit, she thought, aiming the MP7A1 at the SUV's metallic roof, which was surrounded in gasoline.

Exhaling slowly, she squeezed the trigger. The bulky sound suppressor absorbed most of the sound, allowing Monica to hear the metallic action ejecting the casing.

She was rewarded an instant later with a mushroom of fire as the round ricocheted off the pavement and sparked through the sheet metal by the puddled gas.

The fire spread around the vehicle, engulfing the three men. The shock wave pushed Alfonso and everyone else onto their backs.

78

Lone Survivor

"Is that one of ours?" asked Vaccaro.

"Looks that way, Madam President," replied Porter, walking up to the screen as the drone's HD camera zoomed in. Turning to face his commander in chief, he added, "Yes . . . definitely one of ours . . . and it looks like . . . I'll be damned . . . it's ASAC Cruz!"

"We need to get her the hell out of there," said Wright.

"She's armed with an MP7A1, her Glock, and concussion grenades. Plus extra ammo," said Porter. "That'll buy her a few minutes tops against a force like that one before she gets overrun."

"Get her coordinates to Stark ASAP," said Vaccaro.

"Yes, Madam President."

"Where are the Mexican contingents?"

"They've been notified, given the coordinates, and they're supposed to be airborne any moment."

79

Hide-and-Seek

Monica disappeared around the corner and ran full speed now, trying to gain as much distance as she could. Backtracking her way to the busy downtown area, she caught glances from pedestrians. Some got out of her way while screaming. Others used their phones, presumably calling the police, which by now she knew really meant Montoya and his guns.

Realizing that her MP7A1, as well as all of her SWAT gear, was an asset and also a liability, Monica stepped out of the street and into a deserted alley in between buildings. Racing toward the other end, past several garbage Dumpsters, she hid behind one near the sidewalk.

Reaching for her satphone strapped to the side of her FBI SWAT vest, she speed-dialed Ryan Hunt. The line rang in the Bluetooth earpiece wedged inside her right ear.

"Hey, we're on our way," he said after the third ring.

"Mission went FUBAR."

A pause, followed by, "We heard and we're hauling ass toward you. What the hell happened?"

She heard people screaming, running.

Risking a peek over the edge of the Dumpster, she spotted the surviving Suburban reaching her street. Alfonso, along with five armed men wearing civilian clothes, jumped out and shouted for everyone to get off the streets. She also saw people running on the street beyond the other end of the alley, which could only mean more armed men. She was being surrounded.

"Went in early. Long story," she whispered while keeping an eye on the nearing threat. "Ambush. Trying to shake them off."

Another pause.

"Cruz," came the deep voice of Colonel Stark.

"Yes, sir?"

"Larson has a fix on you," he said, referring to the large master chief who was also the communications and electronics expert on his team.

"Doesn't look good, sir," she replied as the street was suddenly devoid of people minus Alfonso's posse of armed men making a sweep.

"Keep moving," he said. "And keep the channel open. We'll get to you. What's your weapons situation?"

"MP7A1 and Glock, two extra mags each. Four flashbangers," she said, referring to the M84 stun grenades clipped to her vest.

"You know what to do, Cruz. Be there in twenty."

"*Twenty minutes?*" she hissed, trying her best to squeeze her slim frame into the narrow recess between the Dumpster and a brick wall as Alfonso and his men approached her position. "Colonel, this thing is going to be over in *twenty seconds!*"

80

On Their Own

WASHINGTON, D.C.

She remembered being in a similar spot a couple of lifetimes ago. After she'd been shot down over mountains controlled by the Taliban, the bastards had hunted her like a damn dog for two days.

Only her training, her guts, and a little luck had kept her from getting captured, though Captain Laura Vaccaro had been ready to eat a damn bullet. No way she was letting those bastards lay their filthy hands on her.

Hang in there, Monica, she thought as the conversation between

Stark and the FBI agent echoed in full surround sound in the Situation Room.

Drones tried to get a visual after she disappeared in a narrow alley.

Vaccaro stared at the screens to her right, where two Predators now circled the Mexican military bases, which showed absolutely no sign of activity.

Bastards, she thought. *You useless bastards.*

81

Flashbangers

MONTERREY, MEXICO

She killed the volume to the phone as the threat reached the alley, not wanting to miss one single sound. Two men ventured into the narrow passageway in between buildings. Shoes splashed over puddles of stinking water, almost reaching her position before doubling back to the street.

Slowly exhaling, Monica counted to thirty before coming out, quietly, swiftly, in a deep crouch, MP7A1 pressed against her right shoulder. She scanned the other end of the alley through the weapon's sights, making sure it was also clear before emerging around the corner. She caught her attackers walking down the street as sirens echoed in the distance.

"Hey!"

Monica swung the weapon around, aiming it at the opposite end of the street, realizing Alfonso had left a spotter by the Suburban covering that street corner.

"Shit," she said, lining him up from a hundred feet away and squeezing the trigger before rolling back inside the alley. Alfonso and the rest of his men turned around and raced after her.

Reaching for an M84, Monica counted to three and tossed it around the corner.

Men ran and screamed just as the magnesium and ammonium nitrate pyrotechnic mix detonated. The blast triggered immediate flash blindness, deafness, and disorientation within its ten-foot impact radius.

She stepped onto the street and caught two men down, hands over their eyes, rolling on the asphalt. The other crawled on all fours, vomiting, including Alfonso.

Hello.

Monica shot them all, except for Alfonso. Grabbing him by the vest, she forced him on his back while pressing the bulky sound suppressor against his neck.

"Where are they, you piece of shit?"

Obviously disoriented, Alfonso tried to speak, but instead vomited all over himself.

Monica grabbed the back of his vest, dragged him into the alleyway, and propped him up against the wall.

"You have five seconds to tell me where they went," she said, pressing the MP7A1 against his groin.

This time his eyes regained their alertness, settling on hers.

"Four . . . three . . . two . . ."

"Wait," he whispered, coughing. "They . . . they're gone."

"Not in the compound?"

He shook his head slowly, his eyes losing focus again.

"Where?" she demanded, slapping him.

He blinked, coming around again. "I . . . I don't know . . . and I wouldn't . . . tell you . . . if I did."

"Then wave bye-bye to your little pecker," she said, pressing the gun even harder and placing her finger on the trigger.

"Go to hell."

"Last chance."

He inhaled deeply, a hand against his right ear, which was now bleeding, as was his nose. He stared at the long barrel and back at her before hissing, "Do . . . what you have to—"

"¡Jefe! ¡Ya vamos!" a man screamed at the other end of the alley.

Monica swung the MP7A1 down the long corridor toward the distant figure and fired once.

The man jumped out of sight but three more appeared, weapons in hand. They shot high to avoid hitting Alfonso on the ground, their rounds thundering in the narrow passageway, striking trash, brick walls, and concrete.

She shifted, racing out of the alley and onto the street, away from the incoming fusillade.

Sprinting past the men she had just shot, she continued down the street; no panic, just deliberate. Reaching the corner and looking around, she verified it was clear and ran halfway down.

Three men appeared at the other end wielding weapons, swinging them in her direction.

Monica dove as bullets peppered a parked car.

She landed hard behind it, rolled up the sidewalk, and started to double back when spotting Alfonso and more of his men coming from the opposite direction.

She was trapped. Cartel soldiers covered both ends of the street, shouting obscenities and threats. Monica moved tactically, clambering toward the recessed entrance to a tall building.

Tapping the volume on her phone, she said, "A little help, guys!"

"Hold tight!" Stark replied. "We'll be there in ten."

Jesus.

Monica heard more vehicles reaching both ends of the street, more men getting out, at least fifteen or maybe twenty. She couldn't really tell. Then even more tires screeched to a halt, followed by more footsteps, shouts, and threats.

It's a fucking army, she thought, reaching for the double glass doors behind her, but they were locked.

Just as the incoming threat was about to overrun her position, she fired twice into the glass, shattering a panel, and squeezed through.

Facing the choice of a corridor leading to first-floor offices or a flight of stairs, she chose the latter.

Tossing an M84 stun grenade toward the street, she headed for higher ground.

Monica had been in quite a few gun battles, mostly in Iraq and

Afghanistan and a handful with the Bureau. Any experience in a gun-fight was helpful for the next one—the main help being the knowledge that you didn't want to be in another gunfight.

The damn things were so random. Ricochets, jammed guns, loose clothes catching on things, civilians showing up and getting in the way—the randomness of the universe followed all sides in a shootout. Those who survived them were the ones that could change direction and plans quickly and had a lucky charm stuck up their ass.

There was some technique to what she did, like checking corners, weapon positions, and the type of weapons. There was the area of the gunfight to consider: indoor, outdoor, street or woods, day or night, plus the damn weather.

Monica was now deep into a one-sided affair.

She was on borrowed time and lucky to still be standing, thanks in part to some training and skills.

The problem for her was that this was not TV or a movie; the bad guys could actually shoot. They were being paid well. Their weapons were modern and they knew how to use them. The way they moved told her they also had paramilitary training.

She had to be very good and hope that Stark and company would get there sooner rather than later—later she would be dead; Monica preferred that not to happen.

The shock and noise of a gunfight could be unnerving, an assault on mind and body. Shooting a gun indoors would hurt your ears and knock you off balance. Going from inside to outside could lessen shooting skills. How much sleep you had, food, booze, drugs you were on or took the night before—all had a direct effect on your hand-eye coordination and your ultimate survival.

Monica raced up the stairs and reached the roof, eyes searching for a vantage point to make her final stand.

82

Enough

She'd had enough.

Vaccaro had been in the military long enough to know when it was time to stop observing and start acting, irrespective of the consequences.

She stared at that small army of bastards crowding the street and approaching the building where ASAC Cruz had chosen to make her final stand.

Turning to her secretary of defense, the American commander in chief said, "Fire at will, Leon."

It took the Predator a moment to maneuver into position, but the familiar crosshairs suddenly appeared on the screen, centered on the vehicles and their armed passengers on the north end of the street.

They were there one moment and gone the next in a flash of light.

The crosshairs shifted south a few seconds later, catching the other group just as they realized what was happening and were attempting to flee.

Another flash.

"Hit them all again," she said, frowning at the men who had managed to get inside the building. "And where the hell is Colonel Stark?"

83

Operators

They made another systematic check of all the gear on them: primary weapon, backup weapon, ammo, medical kits, and night vision. Plus the communications gear, both for the team as well as the satellite phones that Stark and Larson carried.

The idea behind the gear was complementary, secondary, and tactically useful—all to support the most violent action these men of war could and were about to bring to those who were attempting to do harm to Monica Cruz.

The training required to drive a car to its maximum speed came from attending driving schools, like the Secret Service course. U.S. Marshalls, CIA, and also many in the Special Operations community attended such private driving schools. Once the basics were learned, its practice typically involved renting cars and driving them like your life depended on it.

The skills required the excellent hand-eye coordination that Chief Larson displayed while shifting lanes. The bulletproof Humvee passed cars as if they were standing still, as the streets of Monterrey blurred past them.

Larson turned the wheel firmly as they approached an intersection, achieving the perfect weight transference. He maneuvered the armored vehicle's mass and speed to steer smoothly around the corner. His feet worked the gas and brake pedals at the maximum capacity of the Humvee.

In other words, he drove so damn fast it scared everyone around them.

"Monica, we're closing on you! ETA six minutes! Status?" Ryan said as Colonel Stark spoke on the satphone with D.C. to get anything and everything that was available now to her position.

"Hope you brought lots of body bags! I'm piling them up as fast as I can, but they have me pinned down on this damn roof!"

"Colonel," said Ryan from the backseat while pointing at the GPS display in his hands. "We're about two kilometers from Cruz. Let me out at the next building that's more than four stories tall. I'm better use to everyone on this long gun than closing with you guys."

"Agreed," said Stark before turning to Larson. "Hey, Evan—"

"Got it, sir," the chief said while shifting lanes again. "Drop off the playboy so he doesn't get his pretty face scrapped."

Ryan thrust his right hand toward the front seat, middle finger up, while Stark shook his head.

"Actually, scars on your face would help," the chief added while steering the Humvee toward one side of the street as they approached what looked like a tall apartment building. "Curbside service for Romeo, coming up."

84

Pincer Movement

MONTERREY, MEXICO

This wasn't her first rodeo.

This wasn't the first time she had been surrounded, outnumbered, and on the verge of succumbing to a relentless enemy closing in, tightening the noose.

This wasn't the first time everyone around her perished while she fought back, unwilling to stop, not knowing how to quit, refusing to let fate claim her life without a fight.

And Monica did fight, just as she had done everywhere she'd ended up, from the mountains of Kabul to the deserts of Iraq, from the streets of East Los Angeles to the bazaars of Islamabad—even in that stupid bar in Scottsdale.

The MP7A1's hot muzzle coiled smoke as she controlled and directed fire only at sure targets: cartel soldiers emerging single file through the access door.

She focused on this choke point, her final stand on this rooftop she was forced to defend in a country not her own, in a war not of her choosing. But one she was determined to finish tonight, one way or the other.

She was wondering where the hell Ryan and Stark were as spent casings landed in pairs three feet to her right and back, littering the white gravel floor of her Alamo, her line in the sand.

Monica concentrated her energy on that narrow doorway, where the enemy's numbers meant nothing, where she could control the fight—for as long as her ammunition lasted.

She dropped the MP7A1's spent magazine, keeping the weapon trained at her target, and inserted her last one. She paused sporadically, making it last as long as possible, forcing the enemy to remain hidden within the shadows of the stairwell, waiting her out, believing time was on their side.

She had learned in Afghanistan not to count bodies unless they were friendly, but rather to be aware of how many rounds you were firing. In her current situation, where she was outnumbered, how many rounds she had left versus how many assholes were trying to kill her . . . well, that she understood.

No anxiety, just methodical movement: up, down, sideways, crouching, lying flat—she was trying not to shoot from the same position, changing after each engagement.

The cartel's men were trying to move out beyond the doorway, trying to pin her down. She estimated there were at least twenty of them when the fight started, which meant they still had at least ten or so able to—

A man rushed out, MAC-10 in hand, firing blindly.

Monica put him down with a headshot just as her left shoulder suddenly stung, the momentum of the bullet's impact spinning her around.

"Aghh!" she screamed in pain as she fell, as she heard Ryan calling her through the earpiece.

"Cruz, pick up! Cruz, status! Monica!" Ryan shouted as Larson pulled over to drop him off.

"Sounds like they got her," Stark said.

Ryan ripped the headset off his head. "Damn it!" he shouted to no one, flinging the door open while Larson was still slowing down. "We need to be there now!"

"My bet's she's down but not out," said Stark. "Now get the hell up that building!"

Still holding the MP7A1, Monica tore off her sleeve and frowned at the chunk of flesh missing from her shoulder.

Missed the bone.

Two things filled her mind in the following second, as blood spewed from the wound: inevitability—too many trained men with lots of guns against her—and anger that they got her.

The hit would slow her down.

She reacted by tossing a grenade at the entrance to buy herself a few seconds.

Reaching in her vest, she grabbed an emergency pack.

She squirted a combination of honey and an antibiotic cream with a bonding agent right into the flesh wound, before slapping an adhesive tape . . . no time for anything else.

She knew she could be in shock soon, and that the next one that hit her could be the end.

So fuck these assholes, and fuck Stark and Ryan for not getting here soon enough.

Keeping the MP7A1 focused on the doorway, she rolled to a new vantage point.

She might be going down, but not without a fight, and she still had plenty of that in her.

Sniper rifle strapped across his back, Ryan was out and running into a dark alley. The Humvee's tires burned asphalt while it fishtailed, accelerating toward the gunshots echoing in the distance, suggesting that perhaps Stark was right. Perhaps Monica was still in the fight.

He drew his custom Colt .45-caliber pistol that was standard issue to Delta Force operators and pointed it at the closest window of the tall apartment building.

Pulling the trigger, he was inside in seconds, taking the stairs two at a time.

He needed the fourth floor, now—and needed to be shooting in less than twenty seconds in order to make a difference. While in the car he had checked his batteries for the radio, ammo, primary and backup weapons, and small medical kit.

Ryan shot the door handle and lock of the nearest north-facing apartment on the fourth floor and kicked it in.

No one screamed, which he hoped meant the apartment was not occupied.

Rushing straight into the small dining room, he removed his backpack, rifle, and shooting pad. He pulled the table back from the window, quickly opened it, had his earplugs already in, and he could see weapons flashes on the distant rooftop.

Quickly sighting targets that were 1,100 yards from him, he exhaled, relaxed, and began.

Three hundred yards out from Cruz's building, all the doors swung open.

Stark's team hit the ground almost as one, weapons up, rounds always chambered, safeties off, and muzzles following the eyes. Trotting forward in tandem, they moved to the sound of gunfire.

All heard the MAC-10's distinct sound and one MP7A1. They all knew the latter belonged to Cruz.

They did not stop—did not hesitate. Hagen was point, closely followed by Danny Martin and Larson, with Stark bringing up the rear, shifting his weapon in every direction.

One hundred yards and closing.

The sound of a .50-caliber round going over your head was unmistakable, the air being parted by 660 grains of mayhem.

It was followed by "Three one way," which was Ryan Hunt's way of alerting all that he was in position and doing all he could do to make a difference in the fight.

His second round rode in the same air space, then a third, with remarkably short time between each trigger pull.

Her MP7A1 finally ran dry, but three rounds from somewhere behind her hammered the doorway, keeping the cartel soldiers inside.

Ryan!

Dropping the rifle, she clutched the Glock 22, her back to the wall. Steadying her weapon on her bent knee, she pointed it at the opening, aware of her fate if anyone made it through the choke point and into the open.

They would flank her, surround her, trap her—and hurt her real bad before killing her in an even worse way.

Monica had heard their threats, their warnings, bellowed in the streets and from the confines of that stairwell. She knew they were not empty words, that they meant everything they shouted.

So she kept careful track of her ammunition while using the cover of a large AC compressor. From this vantage point she emptied her first magazine of .40-caliber Smith & Wesson hollow points, placing them exactly in the middle of that doorway.

She fired one every four to five seconds, like granules of sand squeezing through the hourglass, counting down to her impending demise. There was no place to run, no place to hide, no higher ground to reach.

Two more rounds blasted the doorway.

Ryan again. He was helping. But would it be enough? She really needed Stark and team here. Now. Coming up behind those assholes in the stairwell.

She dropped the spent magazine and inserted another one within her five-second window, sustaining her rate of fire. She protected her safety zone for as long as she could, round after round, recoil after recoil. Ryan fired sporadically as well.

But the numbers didn't add up.

The slide ejected the last spent casing, and she dropped the empty magazine and inserted her final ten rounds.

Bracing herself for what could be the last minute of her life, she counted them slowly, trigger pull after trigger pull, knowing she would have to stop on nine.

She could only fire nine.

The last one would be for her, to leave as little of her head as possible for those bastards to put on one of their fucking sticks.

Four.

Five.

Six.

Monica suddenly paused, lips compressed, her shooting eye fixated on the sights centered on that rectangle of darkness, choosing to wait, to try to bait them.

If she could make them think she was out—

A shadow shifted from within, a hand, in and out before she could react, tossing a canister, blue smoke oozing from it as it rolled away from the doorway.

Damn.

Three men emerged, short, dark, agile, clutching MAC-10s, swinging them in her direction while shooting blindly.

Before she could fire, a round found the lead cartel man, taking out half his back, almost cutting him in half. Then the head of one of his shooting partners disappeared next. The third one's right leg was severed at the hip just a few feet from her; he bled out in seconds, lips moaning a prayer only he could hear.

Go Ryan!

She tried to fire as a fourth figure tried his luck beyond the door, but his head exploded in a burst of crimson splattering the door frame. He dropped from view, but not before releasing two more smoke grenades.

Damn, she thought, realizing that the smoke would likely block Ryan's line of sight.

Focusing her attention back to the doorway, she peered through the thickening smoke oozing from the canisters, but two figures had already run outside.

Before she could react, they leaped over their fallen comrades and spread out, one right, the other left, enveloped by smoke, invisible to Ryan, just as she had feared.

Four rounds left.

Probably at least ten men hiding in the stairwell.

Impossible math.

Plus they were about to place her in their cross fire.

Momentarily ignoring the two on the rooftop, she watched as two more men attempted the same feat, and she fired three times. Three shots. Two kills.

The rest remained huddled in the darkness, beyond the smoke and the doorway.

A distant gunshot and a man screamed to her far left—Ryan taking out one of the cartel men riding the periphery of the cloud while trying to flank her.

Good, but not good enough.

She only had one bullet left, and she had a decision to make: eat it, or . . .

Monica raced toward the doorway, using the bluish haze to her advantage to hide from the one still alive on the rooftop searching for a safe vantage point.

Trained fingers pulled the safety pin of her final M84 grenade as she cruised through the protection of this sapphire cloud, counting to three before pitching the flashbanger into the open doorway.

Hiding around the corner, her back pressed against the wall, she waited.

The pyrotechnic boomed inside the enclosure, its walls amplifying its effect.

She sprinted into the darkness a second after it went off, smoke and the smell of cordite engulfing her. Holstering her Glock, she grabbed the MAC10s from two of the dead men piled up by the entrance.

The interior still echoed from the blast, mixed with the cries of men scattered down the staircase.

Monica fired indiscriminately, first at the floor, ripping through the fallen cartel men, and then into the stairwell, clearing her way to—

The cylindrical object flung up from beyond the landing at the bottom of the flight of stairs skittered toward her.

Monica backed away from the concussion grenade, trying to distance herself, reaching the top of the landing, the doorway.

The blast pushed her out into the hazy rooftop, punching her squarely in the middle of her vest with savage force.

She landed on her back against the gravel. Stunned and disoriented, she felt dizzy and nauseous at the taste of her own medicine.

Stark's team reached the building with precision and coordination. But then Ryan's voice broke their tactical silence.

"I don't have eyes on her anymore! Rooftop full of smoke—and full of cartel!"

Just then they heard another grenade go off above them.

Hagen suddenly shot up the stairs, leaping them three at a time, vanishing from sight as Larson, Martin, and Stark struggled to keep up with the nimble former SEAL.

Rolling over, thick smoke blinding her, Monica started to vomit, catching a brief glimpse of a boot swinging toward her.

It hit her in the gut, powerful, lifting her light frame, flipping her in midair, tossing her into the bodies of those she had just killed.

"*Puta!*"

The curse was distant, muffled by the intense ringing from the concussion grenade, muted by the pain raking her.

She curled up, hugging her stomach, eyes closed in agony.

A second kick against her torso nearly made her lose control of her bladder as she rolled away from the impact.

She tried to scream but the blow had just taken the wind out of her.

Somehow she managed to reach for her Glock, fingers wrapping automatically around the handle, freeing it from the holster, aiming it not at the incoming figures but her right temple.

She squeezed the trigger, but not before another boot kicked her shooting hand up. The round was deafening, hammering her eardrums, but it struck metal behind her.

A powerful slap followed, nearly tearing her head from her shoulders.

"That would be too easy, Miss FBI," came a familiar voice through the thick smoke as someone kicked the Glock she still clutched.

Alfonso.

She jerked her empty shooting hand back, throbbing from the blow, fingers trembling. The coppery taste of her own blood filled her mouth. A massive headache clouded her thoughts. Monica tried to see him but couldn't through the haze and the tears blurring her world.

But she still recognized his figure looming over her, leaning down. She could smell his stinking breath as he cupped her face with his left hand and forced her to look at the sharp wooden stick he held in his right hand.

"Before we fuck you with this, you should know that my boss and our friends from Pakistan are boarding a plane to Texas within the hour. "

Unseen hands pulled down her pants, and she kicked and screamed.

Someone slapped her across the face again, the strike overpowering. Punch-drunk, unable to speak or cry out, she tried to fight the dark figures holding her down. But they kept her back against the gravel while Alfonso positioned the stick in between her thighs.

Just before gunfire erupted all around her.

Stark followed Danny and Larson onto the rooftop, but the clearing smoke revealed that the firefight was already over.

Though someone had to inform Hagen.

Surrounded by dead cartel bodies, the former Navy SEAL stood above the body of a man next to Monica. Hagen was stabbing him repeatedly with a spearlike wooden stick.

"Chief," Stark said, tilting his head toward Hagen. "You mind?"

Larson shrugged and began to talk Hagen off the corpse as Stark and Danny knelt by Monica's side and pulled up her pants.

The faces came in and out of focus. There one moment and gone the next.

She felt their hands on her, lifting her, carrying her across the rooftop, down the stairs, and into the back of a large vehicle.

She tried to move but everything hurt, her ribs protesting even the slightest motion as she lay there facing the ceiling of an SUV accelerating in the night.

But somewhere in the twilight surrounding her, somewhere beyond the pounding headache and the shifting shadows of streetlights forking through side windows, she thought she saw his face.

The camouflage cream covered features that could not be hidden—not from her. She recognized his prominent cheekbones, his strong chin, aquiline nose, and the green eyes that had captivated her a lifetime ago in Arizona.

"Hey," was all he said.

Her lips parted but she could not produce a sound as her thoughts, her vision—everything started to go dark.

But she couldn't afford to pass out again, not now, not while those bastards were headed for an airfield.

Mustering savage control, Monica found the strength to say, "Ryan . . . the terrorists . . . north . . . airfield to fly to . . . Texas."

85

Rules of Engagement

WASHINGTON, D.C.

"I want every available unit from the army, marines, navy, and air force to coordinate with Border Patrol and comb every last square inch of desert between our border and Monterrey! And ladies and gentlemen, I do not want to hear or see the words 'rules of engagement' anywhere! If those bastards so much as twitch on one of our radars, I want that area hit with everything we have. And I want enough drones up there to count every last damn scorpion and snake crawling around in that fucking country."

John Wright, Defense Secretary Leon Ford, and other cabinet members conveyed the directive to the right channels.

"What about President Gutierrez?" Wright asked.

"What about him?"

Ford said, "We're about to send jets, tanks, and infantry across the border of a friendly nation."

Vaccaro stood and looked around the room. As had been the case since this mess began over a week ago, all eyes were on her, from her immediate staff to the Joint Chiefs and selected cabinet members.

"The moment the people that President Gutierrez *personally* assigned to the joint task force *turned* on us, then *vanished* from sight in the heat of battle and *refused* to deploy soldiers . . . well, he signaled that he is certainly *not* with us, meaning he is *against* us."

Vaccaro paused before adding, "And so help me God, if that weapon makes it inside our borders and it is detonated, I will punish Mexico just as I'm currently punishing Pakistan."

86

Under Attack

NORTHERN MEXICO

Salma heard the explosions in the distance, echoing off the towering Sierra Madre Oriental, distant yet significant. They marked the end of the FBI posse and the beginning of a clean slate, a fresh start alongside her new allies.

Montoya sat next to her in the rear of the lead Mercedes SUV, talking on his phone in machine-gun Spanish. He spoke it so darn fast that she could barely make out a word here or there.

A landscape of tumbleweeds, stunted bushes, and rock formations projected beyond her tinted window. It was all backdropped by a mountain range bathed in shades of crimson and gold as the sun touched the jagged rim rock.

Hanging up abruptly, he turned to her and said, "That was Daniel. We got most of them. But a few got away. We lost several men in the process . . . including Alfonso. He was a good asset."

"I'm very sorry," she said, placing a hand over his.

"Don't be," he said, kissing it. "They all did what I pay them very well to do."

"Is the mission in jeopardy?"

He slowly shook his head. "It continues per our plan."

"Any news from home?" she asked. Since the bomb raids began, she had lost contact with her network.

"I am sorry, Salma. Still no word from Atiq, only what's coming through the news channels. Your country is under attack."

Salma nodded, crossed her arms, and looked away, eyes narrowed in an anger she knew she would have to control. But to be completely honest with herself, she also knew this moment could come. Her country had kicked the mighty bear that was the United States of America. Although Atiq had taken immense precautions to make it all look like the work of ISIS, she had always feared that sooner or later the Americans might figure it all out. Now Pakistan would have to endure the full force of what she reluctantly acknowledged was the best armed forces in the world.

Now more than ever, she had to make the enemy suffer the agony of her own retaliation. Before the bombs had silenced her country, Atiq had ordered the weapon to Washington, to the head of the beast. To that end, he and Ibrahim had made arrangements with dormant ISIS cells along her planned route. Men and women long recruited, trained, and deployed under the assistance of her own intelligence network had now been activated.

And those assets waited for her beyond the border, across Texas, Louisiana, and the rest of the states on her route.

But first she needed to get past the forces deployed along the Rio Grande by an enemy who was well aware of her presence—aware of her efforts to detour via the Texas-Mexico border.

"Let them attack Pakistan," she finally said, as the first stars appeared along the eastern horizon. "It changes nothing."

Montoya nodded as the lead vehicle turned off the highway and continued down a gravel road that snaked its way through the mountains. Halogens pierced the night, washing the barren desert in yellow light. They cruised past endless fields of dead trees and cacti, finally reaching a remote airfield nestled in a canyon thirty minutes later.

"Welcome to one of my secret airports," he said.

She pointed at the sky. "Not *that* secret."

Montoya grinned. "If the gringos bother to probe this narrow gap in the mountains with their fancy satellites and drones, all they're going to see are those rusted relics over there," he said, tilting his head at a pair of weathered crop dusters adjacent to a large but equally battered hangar. It appeared just one storm away from collapsing.

They drove the Mercedes SUVs inside the hangar.

To Salma's surprise, the shelter was quite pristine on the inside, in sharp contrast with its exterior walls of rusting corrugated metal. It housed three large and shiny Cessna Caravans and four smaller Cessna 182s. Fueling crews and several mechanics readied the planes.

"Impressive," she mumbled.

"We don't fight their technology," the large cartel boss said before getting out. "We simply deceive it."

"When do we leave?" she asked, filling her lungs with the arid air that reminded her of home. It was mixed with the smell of fuel and lubricants.

Azis, Omar, and the rest of the team got out and started to move their gear to the Caravans.

Before he could answer, four men approached Montoya, all carrying pilot bags and headphones. He turned to Salma and said, "I need a moment."

Salma gave him the space while inspecting this covert operation, which she could only guess was used to smuggle drugs into the United States.

But what really caught her attention was the almost ritualistic aspect of Montoya's discussion with his pilots. He told them each something she could not hear but that was apparently significant. Embraces followed before all four headed for the smaller Cessnas.

As he walked back to her side, Montoya said, "We leave soon . . . and they'll never see us coming."

87

Hero

KARACHI, PAKISTAN

It had probably just been instinct, though his training likely had something to do with the way he'd grabbed Maryam, embracing her firmly in front of him. Pressing her against his chest, he had jumped into the tunnel while the world became unhinged behind them.

His back once again took the brunt of the expanding swell of heat and debris punching him with savage force, knocking the air out of his lungs. It lifted them off their feet and tossed them into the tunnel as torrents of dust rained on them.

And Gorman had reacted again, this time drawing from his high school sports days, protecting the football, hanging on to Maryam with all his might while rolling in midair.

Gorman had landed on his back, like his coaches had drilled in him a lifetime ago, shielding his precious cargo. He hugged Maryam like he had never hugged anything in his life.

Train tracks punched him on the back, arresting his momentum, until all motion ceased. Until silence replaced the angered roar of collapsing metal and concrete.

Slowly, Gorman relaxed his grip, letting go. His back throbbed, his limbs trembled, his vision tunneled, and his thoughts faded.

But then he saw her at the end of this narrowing shaft. Her face smudged with dust and grime, yet beautiful in the yellowish glow of their subterranean world. Her lips moved but he could hear nothing beyond the intense ringing from the blast, deep, intense, reverberating inside his cloudy mind.

It was Jeannie, smiling that amazing smile of hers.

Damn, I've missed you, he thought, staring into her hazel eyes.

And I'll always love you, Darling. But it's time for you to move on.

Slowly, Jeannie's face faded in the hazy darkness, replaced by a pair of wet brown eyes, tears running down the sides of the high cheekbones on a light-olive face.

Maryam.

My beautiful Maryam.

She turned him over, gently, exposing his throbbing back to the warm air.

Gorman cringed, his skin feeling on fire. The pain was arresting. His mind grew foggy, dark, like his narrowing vision.

He tried to speak, to scream, but his body was shutting down, taxed beyond endurance, until everything faded away.

88

Talons

WEST OF ISLAMABAD, PAKISTAN

He was the first to leave the bunker, and he insisted on doing it alone.

He needed to be alone, if only for a little while, after being holed up like a rat in the massive underground systems of tunnels and facilities built by his government to protect its leadership against precisely this kind of attack.

Field reports were few, and those that made it through to his command center were unclear, disjointed, like loose pieces of a massive puzzle. Each provided a glimpse into the hell being unleashed by the Americans.

But nowhere in the fragmented news did he see anything remotely resembling a direct nuclear attack.

The Americans had blinded his nation with massive EMP strikes just prior to destroying most of his country's air force, navy, and many army installations. They had bombed bases in Karachi, Quetta, and Sargodha. They had even demolished a number of ISIS training camps as well as some of his ISI network's operations. Plus they had erased Abbottabad off the map.

But the enemy had not used nuclear weapons, besides those detonated in the stratosphere to trigger the EMPs. The Americans had chosen not to fight fire with fire, and the result was bittersweet for the ISI chief. On the one hand, a nuclear attack by the United States would have sparked a massive wave of sympathy for Pakistan, condemning the Americans for using nuclear weapons against a weaker nation. But on the other hand, the lack of a nuclear retaliatory strike would allow Pakistan to recover quickly. It also broadcast to the world that America was weak, that its president was incapable of making the hard decisions. He would use his country's survival as another weapon against the U.S. and its president.

And that suits my purposes just fine, he thought, walking through the wide tunnel leading to the side of the mountain.

He had arrived the day before with Prime Minister Korai and the heads of the various government agencies and the military, as well as Parliament and the judicial system.

Atiq inhaled the cold mountain air and stared into the distant fires of the military bases in the valley south of Islamabad. His spies in Tel Aviv and New Delhi reported that the attack on the bases near the capital was not the work of the Americans. The Indian Air Force, along with Israel, had publicly joined the United States in the sorties across most of the country.

"Sat com is still down, sir."

Atiq didn't turn around, listening to the wind whistling as it swept across the face of the mountain. A lonely white-tailed eagle screeched overhead. Its long-fingered wings rode the thermals in wide, lazy circles as it searched for prey. "Keep working the problem."

"Also, sir . . ."

"Yes?"

"Prime Minister Korai asked for you. He said they needed to finalize the list."

"Tell him I'll be there in a moment," he replied, staring at the eagle before dropping his gaze to the valley. But his mind went farther to the south, to Karachi, where Ahmed and Manish had last reported seeing his daughter and the CIA man by a train station.

Then radio silence.

Did my guys survive the explosions?

Did Maryam and Gorman?

The sketchy reports from around Pakistan suggested massive destruction in the port city, with tens of thousands dead, if not more. But he felt certain that Gorman would have known of the attacks in advance and escaped them.

If so, I will find you, he thought, confident that either his men or the army of mercenaries were still on the chase. But he was unable to verify it. At the moment Karachi was one big black hole. No information coming in or out.

Frustrated, he cursed the Americans' EMP attack, which in many ways was worse than the actual bombs. But above all, Atiq cursed the day his daughter was born.

He gazed at the fires raging in the distance, their reflection flickering against the mountains across the valley.

Maryam was responsible for all of this. She had betrayed the ISI and in the process had placed Pakistan squarely in the crosshairs of the United States of America.

The eagle suddenly contracted its wings and dove fast, unseen by its enemy, swooping past a protruding rock. It momentarily vanished from sight, before winging skyward, its small and furry prey writhing in its talons.

I will find you and I will kill you.

The eagle clutched its prey without mercy, without remorse. It squeezed out its life, ripping the creature with razor-sharp hooks until it stopped struggling, until it died while disappearing in the clouds.

Kill the unbelievers, wherever you find them.

Fight against them until there is no dissention.

Fight until no other religion exists but Islam.

Atiq watched it through his tears.

89

The Tracks of My Tears

KARACHI, PAKISTAN

Her features came in and out of focus, slowly resolving, as did the interior of the tunnel, dark, quiet, even peaceful.

Gorman took a deep breath, lungs filling with stale, dusty air.

He coughed and blinked, inhaling deeply again, his mouth dry, having difficulty swallowing. But it was his back that rose above all other feelings, throbbing, stinging, and sore. Yet, it reminded him that he was still very much alive—that he had not only managed to survive but done so while protecting Maryam.

Her appreciative gaze regarded him, glistening with affection, tears filling the corners of her eyes. Trickling down her welcoming smile, they formed tracks of clean skin on a face filmed with soot.

"Hey, love," Maryam said, a hand on his cheek. "We have to stop meeting like this."

Gorman stared at her; an angel hovering over him, beautiful, surreal—a comforting sight in a world turned upside down.

"Hey," he whispered, feeling his strength returning, flexing his hands, his arms.

"You gave me quite the scare," Maryam said, lowering the hand to his right shoulder and massaging it gently. "And you saved our lives. Again."

He sat up and she hugged him, head pressed against his chest. He hugged her back, just as he had done when . . .

"How . . . long?" he asked. "How long was I out *this* time?"

Maryam leaned forward to check Gorman's Rolex. "About six hours. I need to get me one of these. Takes a beating and just keeps on bloody ticking."

"You've got it. As soon as we get home," he said, staring at the scratches he'd managed to carve into the watch's supposedly scratch-proof sapphire glass. Though he had a feeling that the good people at Rolex probably never meant for it to be put through this kind of wringer.

Slowly, with her help, Gorman stood, breathing deeply again, wearing only his jeans and sneakers, before looking back toward the station. A wall of rubble had closed that end of the tunnel from the vertical force of the collapsing building above, the roar that had given him enough warning to race just beyond its grip.

"We got lucky," he said.

"No, Bill," Maryam said, cupping his face and kissing him softly on the lips. "We've got *you*."

Before he could reply, Maryam added, "What do you say we get out of here? The exit is that way, about a half kilometer. It's another subway station under construction next to a bazaar. Mostly everything is burned down."

"You found a way out?"

She smiled. "I found a lot of things while you were sleeping, love, including a first aid kit."

Gorman noticed the bandages on his shoulder and also felt them on his back. They hurt, but it was manageable. And besides, after sleeping for so long, he felt good.

"When did you—"

"You have your talents and I have mine. I also found this." She reached for a bag by her feet. "No husband of mine is going anywhere dressed like that," she added, digging in it. She produced cream-colored Punjabi pants, a *thawb* or ankle-length tunic, a pair of leather sandals, and two bottles of water.

He set his Beretta on the floor and went for the water first. Then he slipped out of his jeans under her amused stare.

"Enjoying yourself?" he asked as he put on the baggy pants, which had a drawstring that allowed him to secure them at waist level, tight enough to tuck his Beretta in at the small of his back.

"You have no idea," she replied.

He finished off with the dark tunic and sandals before standing straight and extending his arms to the sides. "Well? Do I look Muslim enough?"

"Not quite," she said, grinning while offering a *keffiyeh*, the local male headdress fashioned from a square of cotton scarf. "Now stand still," she added while draping the *keffiyeh* on his head.

He complied, in a strange way enjoying the moment as she stood right in front of him but with her eyes focused over his head while arranging the headdress. He put his hands on her hips and pulled her closer.

"Stop that!" she said, tapping him on the nose, before smiling as she finished. "There . . . *now* you look like the man I fancied in my dreams."

"Yeah, quite the fashion statement," he said, pulling her close and giving her a kiss.

They ventured down the tunnel, reaching the station in ten minutes. It was similar to the one that had collapsed and it was devoid of people.

Climbing two flights of stairs, they reached the street. The explosion had leveled everything in sight except for the building's concrete and steel façade, which, being farther away from the blast, had stood up to the shock wave.

Fires burned everywhere. Anything made of wood or other combustive material—houses, restaurants, trees, shops—was ablaze or was missing altogether.

But it was the stench—an overpowering acrid brew of fresh asphalt, burnt wood, plastic, and God knew what else—that struck their senses, enveloping them.

And that's when Gorman realized that at least for now he didn't need to look like a local. While the streets had been packed with people before the blast, now there wasn't a single human being in sight.

90

The List

"We had a problem in Monterrey," Tristan said while stepping away from a black Ford sedan in an underground parking garage a mile from the White House.

The man standing by the shadow of a concrete column shifted his weight uncomfortably, arms crossed.

"I don't understand," Patras whispered, stepping into the light. "The intelligence came from—"

"The information was somehow leaked back to the terrorists," Tristan said. "They knew we were coming."

"How do you know this?"

"That is not important . . . only that we know someone alerted them."

"I . . . my prime minister acted in good faith. I will notify him of this . . . issue. It will be fixed . . . I assure you."

Tristan just stared back at him.

"Was the other information useful?"

Tristan nodded. "It's the only reason I am back. But know this: I don't care what you need to do. All future intelligence must be bulletproof. No more surprises. Find the mole and cut it off."

Patras nodded and handed him a folded piece of paper. "The prime minister thanks you for sparing Islamabad."

Tristan ignored him while reading the note once, looking up, and reading it one more time, before staring Patras in the eye. "If this is . . . accurate—"

"The list is good. Minister Korai is acting in good faith."

"There will be repercussions," Tristan said, reading the list of targets, which included descriptions and GPS coordinates. "ISIS will know this had to come from inside Pakistan . . . from your own ISI."

"Probably . . . yes, most likely. But if you do your job right and cut off the head of the snake . . . the body should die along with it."

"Yes," Tristan said. "But not before making a fuss . . . and assuming this is good enough to achieve a clean cut."

"Then let's pray that we all do our jobs right."

91

Nap of the Earth

SOUTH TEXAS

She never imagined anyone could fly so damn close to the ground.

And at night.

The bleak land beneath the Caravan's belly seemed so close she could almost touch it. Endless plains of sand, crumbling rock, cracked mud, and sparse vegetation rushed past at nauseating speed under a silvery moon.

The border had come and gone in a flicker of dark waters snaking between canyon walls and wind-worn rock formations. Montoya's pilot had cleared them with inches to spare, before dropping over the desert like a ghost. Its moon shadow dashed over some of the harshest terrain Salma had ever seen.

A wasteland. Desolate. Bare.

And most importantly, void of enemy forces.

Just as Miguel had planned, she thought, recalling the four Cessna 182 pilots he had deployed an hour before their departure to draw the American forces away from his planned route.

Her heartbeat still pounded excitedly in her chest, and she wasn't sure why. Maybe it was the nap-of-the-earth flying, as the Caravan followed a dry creek bed flanked by towering walls of sandstone. Or perhaps it was because she had just crossed into America.

Montoya snored annoyingly peacefully on the seat across the narrow aisle—and so did Azis and Omar one seat behind her.

Salma put a hand on the Bluetooth remote control detonator clipped to the end of a chain beneath her T-shirt, nestled between her breasts. From now on she could ignite the device, safely secured behind the last seat. And the blast would be heard around the world, even if it resulted in minimal loss of life.

The effect of a second nuclear explosion anywhere on American soil would send formidable waves of fear across this large nation. It would trigger a devastating swell of terror in an already frazzled society, pushing them ever closer to total chaos. She had read the reports, heard the news as panic spread in cities, suburbs, towns, farms, ranches, and even the most remote communities. Rogue militia groups had formed and were clashing with law enforcement to sack stores and hoard goods in anticipation of shortages.

The home of the brave was rapidly becoming the land of the frightful.

From sea to shining sea.

And she could pull the trigger at any moment, even as she spotted the distant lights of the remote Texas town of Carrizo Springs, their next stop on her way to Washington, D.C.

The knowledge washed away the anxiety of failure that had gripped her from the moment she had set sail off Karachi. The apprehension had only increased after the African rebels had attempted to steal her weapon. And it only got worse when Malik detonated his weapon early, placing her mission in jeopardy, forcing her to improvise, to adapt and overcome. She had used every skill to keep the mission alive, even forging an alliance with this man who seemed genuinely interested in helping her succeed.

And who also wishes to unzip my jeans.

Salma had felt his hungry stare from the moment they'd met. She had managed to hold him back with grace, biding her time, waiting for the right moment to play this critical card in her arsenal. Montoya might be powerful. He might be ruthless. He might be richer and better connected than anyone Salma had ever met before. But he was still a man, and that meant he could be enchanted, charmed, forced to fall under her spell, just like the Norwegian captain and so many others before him.

The Caravan suddenly dropped even lower—if that was possible.

Salma held back a scream, gripping the edges of her seat as tires scraped the rough terrain, shaking the airframe, rattling it.

The pilot throttled back the single-engine plane, quickly slowing down. He taxied toward two parked vans on the opposite side of what she now recognized as a dusty airfield in the middle of nowhere.

Montoya opened his eyes and leaned forward.

Yawning once, he glanced in her direction, winked, and said, "Welcome to Texas."

92

Diversion

WASHINGTON, D.C.

"What do you mean there were no terrorists aboard any of the planes?" asked Vaccaro. She stood at the front of the Situation Room with the chief of the U.S. Border Patrol on the video feed.

"That's correct, Madam President," replied the tall man in the center of the screen, his face washed with hues of green, as it was still nighttime. "We spotted and intercepted four single-engine planes. They were spread all across the border from Nuevo Laredo to Juarez, but there were only pilots aboard. And all claimed they got lost and entered our airspace on accident."

Accident my ass, she thought, realizing what this was.

John Wright said it first. "Damn diversion."

"Also, we just received reports of planes landing outside Carrizo Springs, a town a couple of hours southwest of San Antonio," added the chief. "We're deploying all personnel as we speak."

"You said *planes*, as in plural?"

"That's right, Madam President. At least two . . . maybe three."

"Any way we can confirm that, or track them?"

"Ah . . . no, unfortunately our drones and satellites were all pointing to northern Mexico per the instructions we received, so we had no eyes in that part of Texas at that time. Plus it was at night, though we did spot some abnormalities in the radar but dismissed them as ground clutter and went after the four small Cessnas."

"Of course," Vaccaro mumbled, arms crossed as she turned to Wright and added, "Get the coordinates for Carrizo Springs to Colonel Stark. I want him personally leading this. I don't want a repeat of Monterrey."

93

Not Enough

WEST OF ISLAMABAD, PAKISTAN

He had been caught, but he still maintained his trained façade.

Once again, Atiq sat alone with Korai in his office in their mountainside emergency compound. The bombs had ceased falling for now—at least as far as they could tell. Many parts of the country, however, were still under a blackout and therefore unable to send damage reports to the capital.

An undercurrent of antagonism washed across the prime minister's face.

"So you deny alerting Salma in Mexico?"

"I do. Besides, even if I wanted to, how could I with the existing blackout? Our networks are—"

"Don't," Korai said, raising his right hand. "It happened *before* the attack. Our IT people discovered the message . . . sent from *your* BlackBerry, which has now been disabled."

Atiq reached in his coat's pocket and produced the offending gadget, tossing it across the desk. "All yours. Just like the computers you probably already took from my office."

"So you admit it?"

"I do not. Anyone could have sent that message and made it look as if I did. *Anyone.*"

Korai briefly closed his eyes before leaning forward, resting his forearms on his desk and saying, "I'm trying to help you . . . because of our friendship. But you are making it very difficult. There are many in the government looking for someone to blame, for a scapegoat, and their eyes are converging on you."

"Then let them come," Atiq said, raising his hands. "They have nothing on me. Nothing. I followed the process and presented the plan, and Parliament voted on it, Vijay. I also explained the risks. Remember? Even with all of the precautions we took, there was always the chance of a leak. I just thought that it would come from ISIS, not from our own damn network."

"From your own daughter, Atiq. Your *own daughter.*"

"Yes! Yes, I know! How many times must I hear that? But it doesn't change the fact that those cowards in Parliament *voted* for the attack. And now, when the chips are down, they . . . they . . ."

Atiq stopped, took a deep breath, sat back and crossed his arms.

The prime minister chewed on a thought for a moment. He looked tired, dark circles lining each of his bloodshot eyes. His voice was soft and low. "I need the location of the bomb. And no more games . . . no more warnings."

"What happened? Your IT guys were unable to pull that from my hard drive?"

"We got plenty of information on ISIS locations, their training camps, underground hideouts, even those belonging to al Qaeda, but not on—"

"You would betray our allies?" Atiq said, trying to control his anger.

"Terrorist organizations are not the allies of Pakistan."

"ISIS—as well as Hamas, al Qaeda, and the other warriors of Islam—fight a fight that must be fought, a fight that your government is too afraid to fight for fear of reprisals."

"Where is the bomb?" Korai insisted.

"I'm afraid it is out of my hands."

The prime minister stood, visibly frustrated, though Atiq could feel the fear pumping off his old friend, like the smoke spiraling skyward across their nation.

"Isn't New York enough to avenge your family?" Korai asked. "Isn't that enough destruction? So many have died in New York! Their financial system is in ruins! And what of the destruction in our own country? In forty-eight hours we have been pushed back years—if not decades—especially in our military, in our nuclear research. How much are you willing to have Pakistan punished for your damn pride?"

Atiq sat there contemplating his response, and in the end he chose silence. The destruction in New York—and Bagram—was certainly a good start, but it wasn't enough. Even Salma's bomb, detonated at the very front steps of the White House with the president in the Oval Office, would not be enough. Nothing short of the complete extermination of all infidels would satisfy him. But there was no use arguing about it with this man who had already turned his back on Islam while making a pact with the enemy to save his own skin.

"Atiq . . . last chance."

He could now even smell the stench of desperation oozing from his old friend. Korai waited, visibly nervous, for Atiq to come around.

Atiq waited longer.

"Then . . . I'm afraid you leave me no choice," Korai finally said, his face flushed with anger, or was it fear? He tapped a button on his desk.

A moment later a pair of guards walked in, followed by four men in business suits.

"Dr. Gadai is no longer in charge of the ISI," he announced. "Please take him to a holding cell until further notice."

Two thoughts ran through Atiq's mind as he was escorted to the basement. The first went to Salma, hoping that all of his preparations, including anticipation of problems she might encounter and their corresponding contingencies, would be enough to get her to Washington.

And the second thought was of his daughter.

94

Whitewater

SOUTHERN PAKISTAN

He wasn't sure how it happened.

Only that it did.

Despite their best precautions, including stealing two more bicycles and using side roads to leave the port city the night before, someone had caught up to them at dusk sixty miles northeast of Karachi.

The side roads had led them to the national highway, which skirted the eastern bank of Kalri Lake while connecting Karachi to Hyderabad. They had followed it for almost twenty miles, before cutting east toward the mountains leading to India.

It was here, along a narrow road bordering the Hub River at the bottom of a narrow canyon, that Atiq's posse had caught up to them. And it came in the form of a silent bullet buzzing his ear, splintering the wood of a tree bordering the road.

Gorman reacted first, dragging Maryam with him off the bikes and down the steep hill. Vegetation scraped them as they shifted from tree to tree, dropping down the heavily forested canyon wall, managing their downward momentum as best they could.

Too fast and they could lose their footing, tumbling out of control to a certain death a few hundred feet below, where the rocky foot-hill bordered the Hub River's roaring rapids.

Too slow and they risked a bullet to the head.

But it was Maryam who made them stop halfway the moment the terrain leveled off for a few feet, forming a narrow ledge before it dropped again at an even steeper angle.

"See anything?" Gorman asked, catching his breath, huddled next to her behind a fallen log, the Beretta in his right hand. He gave the near-precipice a respectful glance before inspecting the woods above them. He somehow hoped to remove the threat and return to the road.

"Not a damn thing," she replied, also clutching a 9mm Beretta, but with both hands, long and thin fingers wrapped around the handle.

A shadow shifted some fifty feet above them, dashing nimbly in between trees. Then another figure positioned itself to the right of the first one, and a third person appeared off to their far left.

They were being hunted, encircled.

The one in the middle was big and bald, with powerful shoulders, holding a rifle with a bulky silencer. For an instant a beam of dying sunlight forking through the canopy touched him, before he vanished behind a towering pine. Too quickly to fire but long enough for Maryam to mumble, *"Ahmed?"*

"What?" Gorman whispered.

"Ahmed," she repeated. "The other operative with Manish . . . in Karachi."

"How the hell did he—"

"You are surrounded by bounty hunters! There is a price on your heads!"

The voice boomed through the murky woods, echoing off the op-posite wall of the deep ravine a few seconds later.

"There is no escape!"

In the twilight of their world, Gorman stared into her eyes, which widened with fear. If they were captured, the ISI could kill him, though more likely they would hold him hostage for a future trade. They might beat him up some and probably interrogate him extensively. But in the end, he was a valuable asset worth saving for a future exchange. It was just the way the game was played, especially with someone as powerful as Pakistan's Inter-Services Intelligence.

But Maryam . . . the things those assholes would do to her.

In his decades managing foreign nationals spying against their own governments, Gorman had seen his unfortunate share of assets caught in the act of treason. It was the stuff of horror novels.

And he would be damned if he was going to let that happen to Maryam.

He put a hand to her face, feeling her breath on him. "*Nothing* will happen to you. You hear me?"

She placed a hand over his and slowly nodded.

"Follow my lead," he whispered, before giving her a kiss.

Looking back at the cluster of trees above them as darkness rapidly overtook them, he shouted, "Okay! We give up!"

And he slowly stood.

It was an old trick, and he didn't really think it would work.

But what did they have to lose?

A pair of shadows broke the vertical edge of the trunks by just a few inches.

But it was enough.

Maryam fired, the shots thundering as bark exploded in clouds of splinters.

Agonizing screams—high-pitched cries—came a second later, as the reports echoed off the opposite canyon wall.

They slid downhill on their backs, using their feet to slow themselves, keeping their hands free. Rocks, exposed roots, and fallen branches scraped them, but they were out of options and persisted, finally reaching the bottom of the canyon.

The sandy shore, broken up by clusters of stunted trees and waist-high vegetation, led to the river. It was a splashing mess of whitecaps colliding with boulders as the last of the day's light gave way to an indigo sky.

Gorman paused a moment, realizing how bad the swollen river looked, especially without life jackets and at night. For a second he recalled a whitewater rafting trip down the Colorado a lifetime ago.

A silenced bullet ricocheted off a rock in a burst of pulverized limestone. It provided the required motivation for Gorman to tug Maryam alongside him.

They jumped feetfirst into the dark rapids as another bullet sparked off to his left.

But all he heard was Maryam's scream just before the shockingly cold waters swallowed them. A current stronger than the worst riptide swirled them at dizzying speed. He managed to keep hold of her while trying to look ahead in the turbulence. He was under one moment and surfacing the next, trying not to swallow water, holding his breath as long as possible.

"Don't fight it!" he shouted the instant they surfaced in unison, her wet hair all over her face. "Float . . . feetfirst!"

And she did, holding his hand, trying to remain clear of the rocky bottom, the angered water blinding them, making it nearly impossible to breathe as he tried to maneuver them in between—

Suddenly realizing they were rushing straight toward a boulder slick with algae, Gorman pushed Maryam out of the way. He shoved her as hard as he could into the current gushing between the incoming massive rock and another one.

"Bill!" she shouted as he let go of her hand.

But in an instant, she was gone, floating downstream.

Right before he crashed into the boulder.

95

Spring Cleaning

WASHINGTON, D.C.

Tristan Lavastede stepped into the corner office of John Wright, located down the hall from the Oval Office on the first floor of the White House's West Wing.

"Tristan," Wright said from behind his desk, where rain tapped at the windows overlooking manicured lawns. He stood and walked around it while extending an open hand.

"Hello, John," he said, shaking hands with the chief of staff.

They went through small talk, asking about each other's families, while an aide poured coffee and they settled on a sofa opposite Wright's desk.

The moment they were alone, Tristan reached into his suit and produced the note from Patras, handing it over.

Wright read it once, looked up in surprise, and read it again, before leaning back and whispering, "Jesus Christ."

"Exactly," Tristan replied.

"I mean . . . we always had our suspicions about their hideouts, including Ibrahim's brother, Hassan. But these areas are supposed to be . . ."

"Anything but ISIS strongholds . . . I know. And that's why we can never eliminate them. Bastards know we have eyes everywhere, so they opt to hide in plain sight . . . or underground in those damn caves."

Wright shrugged. "I guess I would do the same in their shoes. Now, I have to ask . . . how good is this? How do we know we're not being set up to blow up innocent civilians? Or worse, have our people walk into another ambush?"

"I've known Patras for a long time, John. He's scared out of his mind—and from what I can tell, so is Korai. I think they want the bombing to come to an end. But there's another factor in play here that makes me believe the list is for real."

Wright raised his brows and just stared at him.

"I think Korai wants to clean his house. But he can't do it when ISIS and al Qaeda have such a strong presence, not only in Pakistan but also across the border in Afghanistan. And he can't direct what's left of his military to strike them because of the strong political repercussions. In the eyes of his people, ISIS and al Qaeda are fighting a holy war."

"But *we* can."

Tristan slowly nodded. "Everyone wins."

Wright stared at the list again. "Everyone wins. We would shift from punitive strikes to the surgical removal of ISIS and al Qaeda, which helps the president gain the trust of the American people."

"While we help Korai rebuild Pakistan without the political backlash of direct strikes against those terrorist organizations."

"All right, Tristan. I get it. Now, what about the runaway bomb?"

The ambassador slowly shook his head. "Patras hasn't given up, but there's a chance we may be on our own."

Holding the piece of paper, Wright stood and said, "Let's go grab Lisa. I think we need to head downstairs and brief the president."

96

Souvenir

TEXAS-MEXICO BORDER

The vibration awoke her. Powerful. Deep. Shaking her into unwanted consciousness.

Monica opened her eyes slowly, with effort, and found herself in his arms, cradled like a mother does a baby, tenderly. His features slowly came into focus through the pain stabbing her temples. She noticed the needles in each arm connecting to tubes running up to bags of some medical cocktails, probably fluids, as she was likely dehydrated.

"Hey, Miss Cruz. Been a while."

Monica grimaced, the coppery taste of blood in her mouth bitter, nauseating, and she had difficulty focusing through the lightheadedness clouding her thoughts.

"What . . . have you clowns . . . got me on?" she whispered as Ryan helped her sit up next to him in the rear of what she now recognized as a Black Hawk helicopter.

"Oh, you know," he replied. "Just the normal lifesaving stuff one would apply to anyone who just got her ass shot and kicked while fighting a cartel army."

She ignored him while gazing out the side window, breathing deeply. Mountains devoid of vegetation extended beyond the glass.

Her tired eyes wandered back inside the cabin, blinking. She recognized the backs of the figures in front, a towering man with massive shoulders sitting next to an equally wide though not as tall man.

Stark and Larson, she thought, before spotting a muscular figure sleeping across the aisle. Mickey Hagen, the quiet one in the group, deadly with guns, knives, and even bare knuckles, if her foggy mind was not failing her. In the cockpit she spotted just the very top of a blond head wearing a pair of headphones. Danny Martin, always in the pilot's seat.

And there was Ryan, of course, the handsome sniper with those damn green eyes, whose mere touch had a way of melting through defenses erected by a lifetime of dating assholes.

He offered a canteen and she took it with both hands, enjoying the warm, flat, metal-tasting water swirling inside her dry mouth. Closing her eyes while swallowing, she took another sip, and another.

Inhaling deeply, she put a hand to her side, grimacing at the shooting pain.

"They're just bruised," he said.

"And the bullet?" she asked, feeling the patch on her shoulder.

"Flesh wound. Lucky for you we got there when we did."

"Yeah," she said, dropping her gaze to the metal floor. "Happy-fucking-go-lucky me. Now can you get these fucking needles off me? Had enough of your damn cocktails."

Ryan removed the IVs while she flexed her hands, feeling quite good considering what she'd been through.

"I see some things haven't changed," said a commanding voice over her, thundering above the engine noise.

Lifting her eyes, she looked at the imposing figure of Colonel Hunter Stark.

His bald, mean, and downright craggy and scarred face stared her down with those penetrating and ice-cold blue eyes of his.

"Colonel," she mumbled.

"Cruz. Exactly which part of *hold tight* did you not understand?"

"Yeah . . . about that . . ." She frowned and just shrugged.

Stark grunted, reached on the side of the seat across the aisle, and produced a wooden stick roughly four feet long with a very sharp end smeared in dry blood.

"Here," he said, handing it to her. "Your Mexican souvenir. I took it from the bastards who had pulled down your pants and were going to fuck you with it."

The colonel returned to his seat, whispered something to Evan Larson, and then just gazed out his window. The giant chief looked over his shoulder straight back at her, stood, and came over.

"Hey, kiddo," he said.

"Hey," she replied as the massive soldier towered over her. She had forgotten just how damn big the man was, with linebacker shoulders and muscular arms as wide as her thighs.

"Been a while," he replied.

"Sure has," she said. "Still playing with your little radios?"

Larson smiled. "And I see you're still hanging out with this loser."

Ryan gave him the bird.

"Next time listen to the man, would ya?" he added. "Just might allow you to keep that pretty face attached to that pretty neck."

"So I've been told." She held up her souvenir. "Glad you made it when you did."

"Wasn't hard. Just followed the trail of bodies. You did all right, kiddo." He tossed her hair and winked before returning to his seat, but not before punching Hagen on the shoulder.

The SEAL sat up abruptly with the massive knife already clutched in a gloved hand, squinting at Larson, ready to strike. Stark shook his head and Larson laughed out loud before stretching a thumb back toward Monica.

Hagen slowly lowered the serrated blade and looked over at her. Narrowed eyes on a camouflaged face sized her up, shooting her the look that had always made her damn glad he was on her side.

Gradually, he lifted his chin ever so slightly at Monica in his typical, wordless version of hello, before going back to sleep.

She shook her head. "I see it's still like pulling teeth to get a word out of that man."

Ryan leaned closer and whispered, "Mickey was point, and shot up those stairs like a damn rocket. He beat everyone to the roof by nearly fifteen seconds." He paused, then added, "By the time Stark made it up there with Danny and Evan, he had already shot them all and was stabbing one of the bastards repeatedly with the same stick they were going to use to . . . well, you know. The chief had to literally drag Mickey away. Never seen the man so . . . pissed."

Monica stood, went up to Hagen, and put a hand on his shoulder. The veteran warrior slowly raised his gaze. Bending down, she kissed him on the cheek and whispered in his ear, "Thanks."

Hagen managed a very rare half smile, just the corners of his mouth bending up a little as he patted her on the hand.

Returning to her seat next to Ryan, she gazed at the window and stared at the landscape for a time before looking at the stick again and then at her pants.

Breathing deeply, she whispered, "Ryan . . . did I get . . ."

"No," he replied. "But the boys told me about your bikini cut. That's new."

Monica elbowed him on his side. "Perv."

"Hey, that's what I was told, anyway. I was a couple of klicks away, covering your pretty ass on that rooftop."

"That you were," she said, patting his forearm.

"But seriously," he added. "I missed you . . . we all have."

Staring outside again, she asked, "So, where are we going?"

"Airfield in South Texas. Got word that some planes landed there a couple of hours ago. Maybe our guys. Maybe not. But it's the best lead we have, so we're following up. Meanwhile, local cops and the Guard are setting up roadblocks from the border to eternity while all commercial and private air traffic has been shut down in Texas. There are more fighter jets and drones covering the Lone Star State than we had in both Gulf Wars, with presidential orders to shoot down anything that flies without permission."

"I'm assuming we're good flying into that?"

Ryan smiled his amazing smile. "You're always good hanging out with us, Miss Cruz."

"I wish you'd stop calling me that . . . Where are we now?"

"Just crossed the border east of Eagle Pass."

Monica blinked at the mention of her hometown, and her eyes and mind drifted to the world beyond the window while Ryan kept talking. But she was no longer listening, the mountains in the distance stirring old memories. It had to be at least five years since she had visited her two brothers when her mother passed. They had buried her next to her father under a large oak tree.

A wave of nostalgia filled her as she wondered how everyone was doing at the old ranch. Last time she checked her Facebook account—

which she did as often as she thought prudent, once or twice a year—her younger brother, Michael, had married some local girl. And Monica was on her way to becoming Auntie Monica. Her older brother, Marty, was divorced and too busy running the ranch to date anyone.

She smiled at the thought of her brothers. Her parents, Mike and Melinda, had a thing for M-names, but her memory of them faded as she noticed Ryan staring at her with a where-the-hell-did-you-just-go look.

"Sorry . . . what were we talking about?"

Slowly shaking his head, he said, "That we're in the middle of nowhere. But that would be us, always in the middle of no-fucking-where."

"Figures," she said. "What's the middle of nowhere to the rest of the world happens to be my home."

"Oh," Ryan said. "I forgot. You were quite the cowgirl back in the day."

"Yeah. Hee-fucking-haw," she mumbled.

The terrain transitioned from mountainous to flat. Very flat and also very dry, with cacti outcrops amidst rocks, and vast fields layered with soil fractured by the lack of rains. It was desolate yet beautiful, barren yet serene, quiet, peaceful, bringing back long-lost simple times working her father's ranch alongside her brothers.

They had tended cattle, tamed horses, spent days reading the terrain and tracking stray calves. They had mended fences, stocked ponds, and enjoyed the most incredible sunrises. For a moment it all made her question her decision to ever leave.

For reasons she couldn't explain—perhaps because she had nearly died a terrible death, or maybe because she had just turned forty—Monica even recalled the face of a boy from school. She thought of his wonderful smile and wondered what her life would have been if . . .

Shaking the thought away, she chastised herself for allowing the distraction, returning to the reality of the moment. The brutal truth was that she should have pushed back harder to allow Stark and team the time to assess the situation in Monterrey before engaging the enemy. But how could she? Monica had even gotten the president involved.

Still . . .

"Stark's right. I screwed this one up, didn't I?"

"Don't," Ryan said, taking her hand. "You of all people should know just how many different ways these things could play out." Leaning closer, he whispered in her ear, "And don't be so hard on yourself. In spite of all his precautions, the colonel walked us straight into a damn ambush in Paki a few days back. And the joke's that we even had a good spook—guy named Gorman—and an excellent SOG team led by another spook named Harwich. They coordinated all of the intel with Danny and Evan. And we still almost got our heads handed to us. Shit happens. I'm just glad we got to you when we did."

"Yeah . . . well, speaking of heads, tell that to the guys who got theirs on one of these by now," she replied, clutching the stick in both hands, realizing just how damn close she had come to . . .

"Our profession is very unforgiving, which is why the colonel is so damn hard on all of us. The man is just trying to do a job while keeping us alive."

"Speaking of your boss," she finally said, gazing at a forsaken landscape that at the moment seemed so damned wonderful.

"What about him?"

She stared at the stick in her hands and said, "That man . . . he's still one hell of a motivator."

Sitting next to Larson, Colonel Hunter Stark stared out the window of the Black Hawk helicopter and exhaled heavily out of pursed lips.

He considered how close Monica had come to "buying the farm." The intense nature of the rescue, Ryan's quick thinking and world-class shooting, combined with Hagen's nimbleness and practiced violence, had probably saved her life.

Stark was once again curious and appreciative of how quickly apparent normalcy returned to those who survive the violence.

He knew, as did those with whom he served and now led, that no one truly survived combat without emotional if not physical injuries. The fear, action, close calls, bloodletting, wounds, good luck, bad luck, unforeseen moments, and fate all combined to touch those involved in ways few can imagine, but none could avoid.

The wounded, like Monica, tended to the immediacy of their physical needs and fought off the guilt of surviving or the anguish of one who caused the violence.

Monica was probably more the latter; she was seriously aggressive—even irresponsible—but her country's survival was at stake. To her credit, she had gone over her FBI superior's head and tried to get the White House to listen. But in the end, Stark, Ryan, and the rest had to come in to help and save her. She probably hated that fact and was thankful at the same time.

Though he would never dare show it, Stark empathized with the FBI agent, as he lived with the capricious nature of war and still could not sleep without the meds that helped keep his demons in check.

97

HVTs

USS *RONALD REAGAN*. INDIAN OCEAN

The light stung his eyes, and he just rolled away from it while mumbling his best attempt at an obscenity.

"Jade. Wake up."

"Go away, Speedy."

"Sorry, man. But something's come up," said Gonzales, shaking his shoulder.

"Yeah, my foot in your ass."

"I'm serious, man."

For the love of . . .

"Got new intel on ISIS . . . same source as the last time."

Slowly, Commander Demetrius rolled back over to face his WSO already in flight gear. His narrow face under closely cropped dark hair peered down at him. He held a mug of steaming coffee like a peace offering.

"What time is it?"

"Time to go kick some ass, *amigo*."

"I ain't nobody's *amigo* at this fucking hour," he grumbled.

Sitting up, he rubbed his eyes before staring at the watch hugging his left wrist.

Just past one in the morning, meaning the U.S. Navy was only going to let him get four hours of sleep between sorties.

Yawning, he took the coffee and began to sip it while inhaling deeply, letting the caffeine reboot his brain.

"Well? Speak," he finally said.

"Word is that we got twenty-three HVTs, all confirmed, spread across Syria, Iraq, Afghanistan, and Paki. The U.S. takes sixteen and the rest are split between the Israelis and the Indians. The Black Knights own one of them. Munitions are already being loaded up. Briefing starts in less than an hour, and we head out an hour later. We're going to hit ISIS simultaneously across four countries. They're calling it Operation Sunrise, because by the time the sun comes up ISIS would have gone bye-bye. Ain't that freaking amazing?"

Demetrius did have an appreciation for his young WSO's enthusiasm. But at the moment he needed to supply his body with copious amounts of coffee before anything could be remotely considered in the vicinity of amazing.

"So, *ándele, ándele, Señor Gato*," Gonzales added. "Wheels up at three. We hit our HVT at four."

"Yeah, yeah," he replied, slowly getting up and reaching for his flight suit, trying to get his mind and body ready for what looked like a very long, long day.

98

Hitchhikers

SOUTHERN PAKISTAN

He was at the rear of the stack, right hand holding the Beretta.

Harwich was in front along with Zarmani and Abdel, the FNG.

The weapon swung in his direction before he could react, clutched by the man Zarmani said could be trusted.

But the traitor's head didn't explode. It didn't vanish behind a cloud of blood.

The gun continued pointing toward him, muzzle aimed at his face. Before it went off.

Gorman jumped, hands shielding his face, cringing as he touched the left side of his forehead.

"Easy there, love."

Slowly opening his eyes, his throat dry, his mouth pasty, he breathed deeply once, twice, and saw her face, backdropped by a sea of stars.

"Welcome back," she added. "Thought I lost you back there."

The throbbing behind his left eye nearly unbearable, Gorman managed to sit up, coming around, remembering the gunshots, the jump, and the cold river.

The boulder.

"What . . . where are we?"

"A few miles downriver, where you washed up. Dead."

It took a moment for that to register.

"What do you mean, *dead*?"

"As in not breathing. No pulse. Stone cold. You know . . . dead? Gave me a bloody heart attack."

Now he was awake, a hand on his chest, feeling his heart beating. He checked himself, flexing his arms and legs, not seeing or feeling evidence of anything broken except for the pounding headache and the soreness of his chest.

"Did you . . ."

"Took a little while . . . but you came back . . . though I had to get the water out of your lungs and then pound you quite a bit," she replied, a finger on his chest. "You have big bones, love. I almost broke your sternum."

"Jesus," he said. "How long was I out *this* time?"

"Five hours, according to your watch."

He stared at the Rolex, still ticking, and stood with difficulty, holding on to her, fighting the dizziness, inhaling deeply again as she embraced him.

"I take it we lost the bastards?" he said, returning the hug.

"Aye. But that's not all we lost. Guns are gone. Washed away, along with everything else. And all I've got are these five very wet twenty-dollar bills I managed to tuck away for an emergency."

"Tuck away? Where?"

"None of your bloody business, love," she replied.

Gorman tried to laugh but his ribs hurt. He glanced over at the waters of the Hub River gurgling beyond the edge of the woods. They were much calmer down here than upstream.

Pointing at his throbbing forehead, he said, "Do I look . . . as bad as I feel?"

"Much worse, love."

He laughed and immediately regretted it as the stabbing intensified, like someone driving a pencil through his left eye.

"But consider it an asset," she added. "Makes our refugee story more believable."

Looking to their left, she said, "There's a road two kilometers that way. Heads up the mountains. Checked it out while you were sleeping. Looks safe."

He nodded.

They had their clothes, some money, their training and wits—and not much else. It took them thirty minutes to reach the road around midnight, though it was so dark they almost missed it. The night sky was the only light they could see.

When the pickup truck came around the corner, it almost hit them, swerved, ran off the road, and came to a stop by a cluster of trees.

Maryam ran to the truck, seeing two men and a woman in the cab, and three children, two goats, and a chicken in the back.

In her native tongue she asked if all were okay. One of the men answered by aiming a weapon at her face.

She motioned to Gorman to stand back—not that he was in any shape to assist as he was feeling tired again and could barely stand up after trekking through the woods to get here.

Maryam offered the driver money for a ride, explaining her need to get to the border with her husband to join her family, who was waiting for them.

Fortunately for Gorman, the hundred dollars and the sincerity in Maryam's voice did the trick.

Before he knew it, Gorman was lying down between her and a goat in the rear of the truck under the curious brown-eyed stare of two girls and a boy.

He noticed that the sky was full of stars as he rested his head on her lap while Maryam spoke to the kids, who seemed fascinated by them. But his mind was too tired to translate Urdu into English, so he just let that go, ignoring them, their voices fading in the background while the damn chicken jumped on his chest.

Seriously?

His tired vision tunneled on the two-legged farm creature. It was brown with some white on the tips of the ruffled feathers on its neck, and it clucked in a tight circle while Gorman thought he heard the kids and Maryam laughing in the very distant background. The chicken's little brown head turned sideways to him and jerked back and forth, apparently checking him out while taking a shit right on his sternum.

The smell reached his nostrils, but that also faded away as he fell into a deep sleep the moment the truck steered back on the road.

99

Honor System

They were supposed to work in thirty-minute shifts.

But no one was really timing them.

The first responders headquartered in massive tents on Liberty Street had set it up as an honor system. After all, who would be crazy enough to remain in the radioactive pocket a second longer than the hazmat rating of their suits?

But it really didn't matter to NYPD Sergeant Ray Kazemi.

His body had already received a deadly dose, so what was the harm of piling up more rem. It was no different than giving more life sentences to a convicted felon already serving one or more life terms.

The comparison wasn't ideal. But it was the only one floating through his head at the moment.

Ray worked alone, venturing up the next flight of stairs of an apartment building on Barclay Street, four blocks north from where he had lost his partner and his cruiser four days ago.

None of his fellow first responders had been able to make it this far up before their dosimeters, which measured the amount of radiation that had permeated through their thick vinyl suits, told them their shifts were up.

The time limitation made it impossible for anyone to check the floors above the fourth or fifth level of any building in this ten-block-square hot zone—the only one on this side of town, according to the EPA.

There were two other hot zones, but further south, in areas where no survivors were expected due to the excessive heat and the strong pressure wave that had leveled all standing structures.

So this was the premier spot to find survivors, just below Chambers Street but above Fulton, the zone where the pressure and heat waves had turned benign for anyone hiding inside and away from windows. But as luck would have it, this area was also the lucky recipient of a radiation deposit. And city officials could not begin to clean it up until it was cleared of all survivors, because "cleanup" meant tearing it all down to foundations. It meant leveling what the bomb did not. It meant bulldozing millions of tons of contaminated rubble onto barges to be taken to wherever the U.S. government took such radioactive waste for proper disposal.

And that's where Ray came in.

He was not under the immediate time pressure of the rest of the first responders. Everyone else had to spend seven minutes running to the site from Chambers Street in those bulky rubber boots and another seven minutes to return. That left them with sixteen minutes of actual search and rescue—all while being stuffed inside the very thick and very hot vinyl hazmat suits. And while constantly checking the readings in the dosimeters strapped to their rubber gloves.

Ray's time pressure was on a different scale. He had to find as many survivors as possible before his own meter ran out. If the good Dr. Victoria Gorman back at Madison Square Garden was anywhere close to being right, symptoms should start to present themselves in another twelve hours. But Ray was a large man, strong and muscular, requiring a double-X suit to fit his bodybuilder frame—a physique he hoped would buy him more time than predicted.

He reached the fifth floor and began to walk down the long hallway flanked by rows of closed apartment doors. Filling his lungs with the strong vinyl smell of the yellow suit, he ignored the sweat dripping down the sides of his face, stinging his eyes.

A wounded firefighter had given Ray the five-minute crash course on the use of the Halligan tool in combination with a standard fire axe to rip open deadbolts or break into locked doors. It was simple, reminding him of the physics courses he had taken back in school. The trick was to apply the right amount of force on the right spot.

Ray knocked on the first door while screaming, "First responders! Is anyone inside?"

After waiting a few seconds, he inserted the fork end of the Halligan just above the lock but with the bevel side of the fork touching the door. He then angled the tool toward the ceiling before hammering the end of the Halligan with the back of the axe, driving the fork deep inside the doorjamb.

Then it was all physics and some elbow grease.

He grabbed the opposite end of the Halligan tool and pulled. His large biceps exerted enough force through the thirty-inch-long tool to pry the door open, revealing a narrow foyer leading to a dark living room.

"Hello! Anyone here?" he called out, venturing inside the small apartment.

He went into every room and closet, verifying it was empty before stepping back into the hallway. He shoved the door back in the jamb and secured it with bright yellow duct tape. Finally, he marked the door with yellow chalk to let anyone know it had been inspected and cleared.

Blinking to get the sweat out of his burning eyes, Ray looked down the long hallway. At first he had been skeptical about the value of this door-to-door search. After all, who would willingly remain behind—unless they were hurt, of course?

But the same firefighter who had trained him had also told him not to underestimate the number of people who would rather remain inside their homes to keep them from being looted.

So he continued on to the next door.

He had seen experienced firefighters clearing an apartment in less than two minutes, including breaking down the door and also marking it. Ray was working his way below four.

He continued down the hallway, spending nearly an hour before reaching the second to last apartment on the floor.

And that's where he found them: two girls on the floor. Early teens.

Kneeling down, he felt for a pulse and was relieved to find it on both.

Weak, but still there, he thought while trying to wake them up, but all the response he got was a brief fluttering of eyelids.

Securing the Halligan and the fire axe to his suit, he hoisted the girls over his shoulders just as he had done with those Israeli kids and made his way down the stairs and up to Chambers. He walked past mounds of rubble pushed aside the day before by an army of bulldozers to create a narrow corridor for first responders.

Flanked by towering walls of piled-up debris rising almost three stories high, Ray walked through this surreal world while controlling his breathing. The weight of the kids taxed his endurance.

Slowly, he made his way to the sea of tents, where he passed the girls over to a pair of NYC cops.

Sitting on the sidewalk, he removed his helmet, wiped his face with a wet rag, ate a protein bar, and downed it with two bottles of water.

He used the same rag to clean the ashes off his face mask before heading back into the hot zone.

100

Tomahawk

SOUTHERN AFGHANISTAN.
FIFTY MILES NORTHEAST OF KANDAHAR

A solid-propellant rocket had launched it ten minutes ago from the deck of the USS *Princeton* (CG-59), a *Ticonderoga*-class Aegis guided missile cruiser patrolling the northern edge of the U.S. Seventh Fleet.

It now flew through the darkness like a phantom, subsonic, grazing 550 miles per hour, thrust by its quiet Williams International F107-WR-402 turbofan.

The BGM-109 Tomahawk missile's small cross section made it nearly invisible to the radar-based ground-to-air defenses protecting a compound that didn't exist—at least according to NATO high command.

The Tomahawk's terrain contour matching (TERCOM) radar system compared the map stored in its electronic brain to the images captured by its digital terrain scanner. It then cross-checked them with the GPS receiver, keeping the missile on target.

As it reached fifty miles from its objective, terminal guidance switched to the optical Digital Scene Matching Area Correlation (DSMAC) system. It overlaid the high-resolution video captured by its looking-down cameras to a three-dimensional image of the target stored in memory. Issuing fine adjustments to its control surfaces, the DSMAC ignored the large encampment spread along the valley, steering the Tomahawk over a hill and into the roof of a compound a mile away.

The thousand-pound warhead vaporized the two-story building and everyone in it. But the blast went deeper, boring through both floors and a basement. The outward ball of fire and debris the size of a basketball court that erupted an instant later shot sizzling rubble in a radial pattern for a quarter of a mile.

The flash over the hill and the explosion that followed made the desert floor tremble under his sandals.

Rattled, Nasseer jumped to his feet, nearly tripping on the .50-caliber machine gun he manned on the southern perimeter of the encampment.

What is happening?

For months he had sat here, behind the handles of a weapon left-over from the days the Americans had been their ally, arming the mujahideen to combat the Soviets. His father had fought the Soviet pigs back then with this very weapon. In time, long after they had driven them out, he had passed it to the young Nasseer, who became proficient during the endless battles in the mountains.

In his twenty-seven years of life, Nasseer had killed four American soldiers in those distant peaks, along with many more who were not sympathetic with the sacred beliefs of the State of Islam. And that included not just Afghan and Pakistani men but also women and children. This was a holy war, and those who didn't believe were destined to die like the rats they were.

Like the infidels in New York City, he thought while trying to figure out the reason for the blast.

This area had been quiet for nearly half a year now, as the governments of both Afghanistan and Pakistan pretty much left them in peace. He didn't know the details of the agreements, which involved the powerful Pakistani ISI. But he knew enough to know that the explosion painting the night sky with splashes of yellow and orange should not have happened.

Just like the two dark shapes that suddenly loomed over the horizon.

Nasseer reacted when spotting the incoming jets, illuminated by the fire consuming the home of the chief of his ISIS caliphate and his family.

Pushing all thought aside—and as alarms broke out across the valley—Nasseer focused on the inbound threat. Trained fingers clutched the handles of the machine gun while pivoting it toward the enemy.

"There goes the head," Lieutenant Gonzales said as the ISIS headquarters in this section of the country lit up the night sky.

"And the body's next," Demetrius replied, tilting the Super Hornet ten degrees to the north while skimming the desert floor just below the speed of sound.

"Target's coming up in five, four—"

Ground fire broke out of the southern sector, the tracers' phosphorous heads brushing the sky in front of them.

"Three, two, one . . ."

A few rounds hammered the right wing, punching through as they approached a machine gun emplacement. Warning lights flickered on Demetrius's control panel.

"They're off!" Gonzales shouted.

Demetrius pushed full afterburners and cut hard right, escaping the ground fire as six CBU-87 cluster bombs continued in a parabolic trajectory toward the large camp. Dozens of permanent structures, some two and three stories high, surrounded endless tents and campfires under a star-filled sky.

Demetrius climbed back up into the night while momentarily ignoring the warning lights. He was focused on his wingman, also releasing his munitions before scrambling after him in full afterburners.

The free-falling CBU-87s spread evenly over the encampment. While spinning, each released two hundred BLU-97/B Combined Effect Bomblets through sheer centrifugal force in radial patterns that blanketed the entire site.

Each bomblet, two inches long and a half inch in diameter, consisted of a shaped charge, a steel fragmentation cylinder, and a zirconium disk for high-temperature flammable effects.

Proximity fuses detonated thousands of bomblets in deadly synchronization at an altitude of twenty feet.

Absoluteness engulfed all in their path.

Nasseer watched the jet exhausts vanish over the horizon as long cylindrical shapes floated overhead.

Dancing above him, they ejected countless smaller objects that blocked the stars, like a descending plague, just as a blinding fire consumed him.

He tried to scream, to cry out into the night, but the rain of metal shards and flames had already robbed him of this ability. Temperatures soared across the encampment like a curse. The combined munitions obliterated buildings and shredded tents, skin, muscle, and bone. The attack spared no one, turning everyone and everything within its kill radius into smoldering carnage.

Nasseer felt the heat, seething, penetrating, and followed by darkness and total silence.

Then a force that felt beyond this world carried him away from a headless torso lying ten feet from his severed arms—hands still clutching the .50-caliber machine gun.

For an instant the macabre sight vanished in a dense fog, replaced by spectacular fields of green amidst the whitest clouds and brightest stars.

He felt the most wonderful warmth engulfing him.

Paradise.

At last.

But it didn't last long.

A stronger force suddenly dragged him down, pulling him below this glimpse of what felt like heaven and into darkness beyond anything he had ever experienced.

And it was here, as the heat returned, overwhelming him, that the wails and cries of countless souls smothered him. Nasseer felt the presence of the many warriors of Islam who had fought alongside him and perished, killed by the infidels.

As the blaze scoured him, the visions came, materializing within the flames—visions of his life, of all the people he had killed. He recalled the men he had castrated in front of their wives and daughters, before raping and maiming them. He remembered every instance when he had taken a life. He recollected every act of torture, when he had violated women and even girls and boys while his comrades cheered him on. Visions of him, clad in black, beheading their enemies in front of video cameras surrounded him as the fire closed in.

The disturbing images came and went in an instant, but it was long enough for him to understand, to realize the lie that had been his life.

But it was too late now.

So Nasseer did the only thing he could do: cry out into this endless inferno, joining those howling around him.

He cried in anger for having been deceived, for having believed in his superiors, for following a path that was anything but righteous.

And then he cried in raw fear, as panic gripped him, as the sizzling pain of terror tore into him with the crushing realization that it would be . . . *forever.*

The munitions lit up the sky even from ten miles away as Gonzales did a damage assessment while Demetrius kept an eye on engine parameters.

"We got lucky, Jade," his WSO reported. "Nothing vital."

"Good shooting, guys," Demetrius replied as he eased back the throttles and leveled off the Super Hornet at twenty thousand feet. Pushing Mach 1.2, he pointed the nose straight for the *Reagan* two hundred miles away. "Tonight we made the world a safer place."

"Yeah," Gonzales replied. "And it looks like we're just getting started."

Demetrius inspected his radar and noticed the blips a hundred miles north of their position, which his system told him were friendlies headed for their HVT.

101

Hassan

JALALABAD, EASTERN AFGHANISTAN

The Saudi prince had arrived in full regalia with not one or two but *three* shiny business jets, identical in their opulence and gleam. They reflected the ramp's floodlights like mirrors in the night.

Hassan al-Crameini, brother of Ibrahim and leader of the ISIS caliphate in this section of the country, had greeted him and his large party of royals on the tarmac, all dressed in traditional Saudi fine-cotton clothes. Gold watches hugged their wrists. Diamond rings adorned manicured fingers. Half of them were on their eighteen-karat gold iPhones.

Hassan had escorted them to his villa nestled in the mountains northeast of the city, where he treated his guests to the pleasures of the flesh.

He personally kicked off the festivities, as fine wine and local food flowed amidst music and dance. But he didn't linger in the loud plaza, nor did he spend much time in the main hall. He retreated to his secluded top-floor penthouse along with his most honored guest, walking past corridors leading to private chambers. Visitors engaged young virgins beyond closed doors. Moans of pleasure from the men mixed with the typical cries of girls.

"Your generosity is appreciated," said Prince Khalid al-Saud, royal descendant from the ruling Saud dynasty.

"As is yours," Hassan replied, reaching his office and opening the door for the Saudi.

Walking straight for the large glass doors behind his desk, he drew back the curtains, revealing a large encampment stretching the length of the valley.

"Impressive," the prince said, standing next to him.

"And that's just what's on the surface, my good friend."

"You mean caves?"

"A whole system of them beneath the valley and in the mountains, far beyond the reach of American bombs—and all thanks to *your* generosity."

He opened the doors and stepped onto a third-story balcony with a spectacular view of snow-topped mountains flanking the valley under a blanket of stars.

"My task is the easier one," Prince Khalid said, following him outside and joining him by a round table set up with wine and food. "I'm simply shifting excess funds to achieve better returns . . . like New York. I'm afraid you have the larger challenge of recruiting, training, and deploying."

"Ibrahim and I shall humbly continue devoting our lives to liberating the world from the grip of Christianity and Judaism."

"How is Ibrahim?" Prince Khalid asked, obviously aware of the ongoing retaliatory strikes.

Hassan shrugged. "Communications are still down across most of Pakistan. I'm sure we'll hear from him soon enough. Last we spoke he was working on a new video."

The Saudi smiled. "The first two broke all records."

"So it seems," Hassan said, rolling his eyes. "Ibrahim the YouTube star. Who would have guessed?"

They toasted to the future, which the prince had just secured with a new infusion of oil money laundered through a scheme of fake corporations. A third of the funds had already been deposited in offshore accounts. A third had arrived in four large suitcases packed with dollars, euros, and bonds. The last third was in the capable hands of his younger sister, Princess Lisha al-Saud, aboard a large Cessna Citation jet headed for Paris. There, she would hand it off to Hassan's agents while visiting the City of Lights during another one of her shopping trips.

And the irony of it all was that the funds came primarily from the West, from American and European pockets. They came from hundreds of millions of infidels at gas pumps across two continents.

The two men laughed, drank, ate, and laughed some more.

Until they heard the sound of distant helicopters.

Only they weren't helicopters.

102

Mack

The United States Marine Corps master gunnery sergeant stood in the rear of the V-22 Osprey tilt-rotor aircraft, motivating his men. Those around him would call it screaming. And those who thrived in the world of political correctness would call it bullying.

Problem was, Mack "Truck" Johnson believed that political correctness would not spare the lives of his soldiers when the bullets started flying.

Every one of his men had to shed all thoughts of normalcy, of civility, and replace them with the detached indifference of a trained killer.

And it was Mack's job to light such intense fire under their collective ass in order to expedite this lifesaving mental shift before the rear gate dropped.

Everyone aboard had the training, the skill to kill—and, most importantly, to *avoid* being killed. Some even had prior experience. But it was those fragmented remnants of benevolence, of religious beliefs, of compassion that had to be eviscerated for the sake of the mission. Once outside there could be no hesitating, no wavering, not the smallest inkling of doubt. Out there it was kill or be killed, and Mack would be damned if he or any under his command would fall to the latter group.

So the gunnery sergeant screamed. He shouted and attacked as loud as he could. He threw everything he had at his men. He reminded them in his own colorful language of New York City, of the many lives lost to the bastards they were about to hit. He stared into each set of eyes, into each camouflaged face, and squeezed their humanity, casting it out. He exorcised them of everything good in their lives for the sake of their very own survival—if only for the next hour, until the job was done.

The harder job, he knew better than most, would be to help them find a way back to civility after fighting the good fight.

But that wasn't his job, though he wondered if those in charge of the mental well-being of America's fighting warriors knew what the hell they were doing. After all, in the past few years, more soldiers had died from suicides than had been killed in combat.

Mack pushed that last thought aside as the Osprey's pilot arrested its forward motion a mile from the large encampment. The twin thirty-eight-foot-diameter rotors tilted skyward, transitioning the sixty-thousand-pound troop carrier from horizontal flight to a hover.

"Why are they stopping?" the prince asked, his voice cracking while Hassan spoke hurriedly on the phone, commanding his troops, deploying their air defenses.

"Get me out of here, now!" the Saudi demanded.

Hassan ignored him while staring at the wide void between towering mountains at the far end of the valley. It was filled with those infernal machines that were neither aircraft nor helicopters, resembling the bastard offspring of the devil, a reminder of the evil that was America. The flying beasts were indeed ugly, with engines that looked like horns when pointing at the sky. Plus those dark windshields that reminded him of the eyes of a shark: black, dead, indifferent.

And they had indeed stopped, remaining a safe distance from the north end of the training camp, beyond the range of their machine gun emplacements or their RPGs.

As he continued to disregard Prince Khalid and kept barking orders, a shadow flew overhead. Skimming the mountain peaks, it was massive, shaped like a vampire bat, dark and sinister, there one moment and gone the next.

And then Hassan understood.

"Let's get out of here, Sake," said Captain Les Adams.

Major Will Sakai turned the B-2 bomber thirty degrees to the east while climbing back up to fifty thousand feet, starting his long flight back to Guam.

"That's two this week, boss," Adams added. "Where's my fucking overtime?"

"Tell me you got them, Fester," Sakai said as he engaged the autopilot and dropped his gaze to the monitor slaved to the under-mounted cameras. They provided him with a wide-angle view of the valley, where they had been ordered to drop their entire load of precision munitions.

"Oh, I've got them," replied Adams.

The explosions began at the north end of the encampment, distant groundbursts of orange and yellow peppering the valley, swallowing tents, vehicles, structures, and his warriors. The flashes arrived seconds before the blasts, resembling thunder, only this was no act of God.

At least of the God he believed in.

"You must take me back to the airport!" Prince Khalid demanded.

As Hassan set his phone down and was about to reply, he spotted a parachute blossoming near the ground, by the perimeter fence of his compound.

"I must leave immediately!" the Saudi insisted, his voice pitched with fear.

Hassan saw more parachutes opening all around them. And he noticed even more men dropping from the skies. Helmeted figures dressed in black, silent, ghostly, their canopies popping for mere seconds, before they scurried out of sight.

HALO insertions.

As the explosions neared and the silent army from hell descended right on top of his villa, and while the Ospreys resumed their approach to drop off troops in the wake of the explosions, Hassan said, "No one is leaving tonight . . . at least not on the surface."

Wearing night-vision goggles as well as webcams mounted on their helmets, Mack led his men down the rear ramp of the Osprey and toward their objective.

The two-story structure that NATO intelligence had reported as the southern command post was already on fire by the foot of the mountains.

But it wasn't really a command post—at least not according to the briefing two hours ago.

Every other team had a very simple mission: secure the compound. Anyone with a weapon was the enemy.

Mack, however, had been given a special assignment: the termination of Hassan al-Crameini, Ibrahim's brother and the commander of this region's ISIS caliphate. And to that end, he had not only memorized the man's face, but he had also made sure the man's image was etched into the minds of every one of his men.

"Single file!" he shouted over his left shoulder.

Other V-22s unloaded their troops close to their respective targets before soaring into the night under the power of their dual Rolls-Royce Allison turbines.

The Ospreys swooped down like massive birds of prey, never quite touching down, grazing the desert floor. They hovered in place while kicking up a small sandstorm for the seconds it took the soldiers to rush out, before lifting skyward, vanishing in the darkness.

But the V-22s were no longer Mack's concern.

The master gunnery sergeant had his mission, and that meant he had his priorities, had his blinders on. He'd learned long ago, during his first tour in this forsaken country, that everyone had a job. Every man, every platoon, every division, even every damn air force jock and navy sailor. Each had a task, and the coordination of those tasks, as orchestrated by people with much higher pay grades, was what got the job done.

And that meant trust.

Trust the guy next to you as much as you trusted the platoon operating a mile away. Trust the missile cruiser launched from the Indian Ocean or the drone operator on the other side of the world.

So Mack forced everything from his mind, choosing to trust the same system that had kept him alive in dozens of battles, and commanded his men to engage.

They blew the front door and entered in pairs, firing at everything that moved. Half-dressed men scrambled in the dark, trying to reach their weapons. Some even opened fire. But his well-trained force quickly put everyone down before heading to the stairs leading into what was supposed to be the basement.

Only it wasn't.

"Red is in position," Mack spoke into his throat mike, reporting to his commanding officer.

"*Red hold*," came the reply, and Mack lifted his left arm in a fist.

The motion instructed his team to take a defensive stance all around the wide entrance to the cave.

He waited. Forty-five seconds and they had secured his initial objective. Not bad for inheriting this mix of experienced men and newbies a month ago and shaping them into a unified fighting force.

"*Roto-Rooter, Red. Roto-Rooter.*"

"Roger. Red is Roto-Rooter."

Mack positioned his men accordingly. Two of them were armed with M32 grenade launchers, aiming their weapons into the cave and firing incendiary rounds before stepping away from the entrance.

"Fire in the hole!" Mack shouted as the shells flew down the tunnel a couple hundred feet before detonating, filling the length of the passage with fire and acoustic energy.

"Lock and load!" he called out the moment the fire cleared.

Mack headed the charge, the muzzle of his M16A4 leading the way as the noise subsided, replaced by agonizing cries.

He stormed in, trusting his PVS-14 night-vision goggles, leading his team toward the first corner in the cave. He stepped over dozens of charred bodies and didn't bother wasting bullets on the ones who were still alive and burning. The images from New York flashed briefly in his mind, stripping every last ounce of compassion from him.

Pausing just short of the corner, ignoring the smell of burnt flesh, he pressed his back against the wall while reaching for a concussion grenade on his vest.

Two of his men did the same. They removed the pins in unison and silently counted to two before tossing them around the corner. The technique prevented the enemy from tossing them right back at them.

The blasts were powerful, deep, dazzling, and followed by more screams and cries.

"Now!" Mack shouted while rushing around the corner and immediately spotting several figures less than twenty feet away. Some rolled on the ground holding their heads, others were on all fours, disoriented. Two vomited. All were dressed in traditional black ISIS uniforms, their AK-47s on the rocky cave floor.

Mack and his men fired twice into each head, double-tapping them before jumping over them and reaching the next corner.

"Good luck with those fucking virgins!" shouted one of his soldiers, a kid from Brooklyn whose father worked the docks and was presumed dead during the groundburst.

And that's when Mack heard the grenade skittering toward him.

Hassan led the way with three of his best warriors while six more assisted the prince and his guests. Some of the Saudis were shirtless, other shoeless. All wore the same mask of terror as they were pulled from their private party and forced down the underground passage. And Hassan had managed it just in time. The villa—his villa—had already been overrun by the soldiers he had seen dropping from the sky. But nothing could get them down here. They were now beyond the massive and hidden metal doors already locked in place. They were isolated from the surface in a vast underground city connected by a system of tunnels that rivaled the ones below New York City.

"We will take you and your guests to the airport now," he told the Saudi prince as they reached a garage-like cavity lined with a dozen vehicles.

But before Prince Khalid could respond, fire shot from one of the tunnels connecting the underground garage to the southern command post. The blaze was followed by multiple detonations and the cries of wounded men.

The rookie from Brooklyn saved them.

The kid, barely nineteen years old, had shown more courage in two seconds than many men show in two lifetimes, jumping on the grenade.

The blast lifted him off the cave floor, tossing him about like a rag doll. But not before his body absorbed the brunt of the blast, allowing it to inflict just flesh wounds on two of his buddies.

The rest of the team counterattacked, drowning the enemy with a deadly mix of fragmentation grenades and automatic fire.

Mack peered through the haze, the smell of cordite thick in the air he breathed while sweeping his weapon at chest level. He neutralized three more ISIS rebels while the rest of his men spread across the underground garage.

His briefing had claimed this spot would be directly beneath the villa of Hassan al-Crameini.

If everything was going according to plan, a team of parachuting Army Rangers should have already flushed the mastermind terrorist and his cronies into the caves—straight into the hot muzzles of his team.

Hassan spotted the American soldiers at the other end of the garage and did his best to hide the shock.

How did they find this place?

Someone somewhere had betrayed him.

But he couldn't worry about that just yet.

He ordered his men to mount a defense perimeter while ushering the Saudis into two large Ford vans.

Hassan climbed into the driver's seat of the first one, with the prince sitting next to him, eyes wide in fear.

Gunning the engine, tires spinning, rubber burning, he steered the vehicle toward the exit that would lead them away from the valley.

A fierce firefight ensued behind them, but Hassan kept his focus on the corner of the garage that led to the tunnel's entrance. His men would battle the Americans so he and his wealthy guests could reach safety.

Mack saw the people getting in the vans just as more ISIS rebels dressed in black and wielding AK-47s put up a wall of fire.

Shifting his gaze to the corner of the garage, he noticed an oval-shaped entrance to what looked like a tunnel—the escape route in his briefing.

Signaling three of his men holding M32s, Mack provided covering fire. He mowed down two rebels, clearing the way for his men racing across the far end of the garage and leveling their grenade launchers at the tunnel.

Hassan stepped on his brakes when the tunnel's entrance exploded in a blinding sphere of concrete and fire as part of the ceiling collapsed a dozen feet away.

"What now?" the Saudi prince demanded. "What happens now?"

The answer came a moment later, when he saw more grenades launched in their direction, a couple of them skittering under his van.

Mack moved quickly, guiding his men around the vans as grenades went off, six of them, three per van, rocking the vehicles in deafening blasts.

He raced to the first van as the driver jumped out, pistol in hand.

Hassan al-Crameini.

The master gunnery sergeant leveled his rifle at the ISIS chief while his webcam recorded his face to confirm the kill.

Hassan looked directly at Mack, but he never got the chance to bring his pistol around. His chest exploded from three well-placed rounds while Mack's team cut down everyone else exiting the vans.

Mack eyed the dead terrorist mastermind before shifting his weapon to the man getting out of the front passenger seat of the van. He was a man of short stature dressed in white cotton, reminding him of wealthy Arabs.

"Stop! I am not armed!" he shouted in a strong British accent.

Mack paused, sizing him up, keeping his weapon leveled at the middle of his chest.

"I'm Prince Khalid al-Saud from Saudi Arabia!" he cried. "I am a good friend of your president!"

"Not tonight you're not," Mack replied.

"Please! I beg you! I have money—suitcases full of money in the back of the van!"

Mack frowned. Everyone knew the Saudis had been involved in funding the attacks on September 11. His intelligence service had also long known that the Saudis were funding ISIS. But to see its ugly form right in front of him just made him want to vomit.

Instead of shooting an unarmed civilian, especially since everything was being recorded with their webcams, Mack struck him across the head with the butt of his rifle, knocking him unconscious.

"Charges!" he shouted, stepping away from the van.

His team made a final sweep of the place, making sure there were no other survivors, and set up C-4 charges on timers on a dozen support columns.

"Five minutes!" he shouted as they started their retreat.

Turning to three of his men, he pointed at the unconscious Saudi prince on the floor. "We're taking this piece of shit with us. And get the damn suitcases from the back of the van!"

They reached the surface in under a minute, where their Osprey reappeared out of nowhere as if on cue.

They loaded up the wounded first and then the rest of the men, plus one unconscious Saudi and three large suitcases full of cash and bonds.

Mack kept watch and was the last one to board the V-22.

They took off a full minute before the ground swelled beneath them, collapsing in an explosion of concrete, dirt, and fire that swallowed Hassan al-Crameini's villa.

103

Long Shot

SOUTH TEXAS

They advanced noiselessly in the dark, covering the mile of desert from the drop zone near a high school on the outskirts of Carrizo Springs under a cloudy sky.

The desert air was cool and dry. Invigorating. Monica filled her lungs with it while doing her best to keep up. Ryan was point, just like in the old days, searching for the perfect vantage point to set up his massive sniper rifle.

Stark and Larson covered the rear while Hagen and Danny were somewhere off to their right, hidden in the darkness painted in palettes of green by the night-vision goggles everyone wore.

They approached the airfield from the south, where a pair of hangars flanked a single dirt runway. A detachment of U.S. Army Rangers from the 3rd Battalion, 75th Ranger Regiment out of Fort Benning, Georgia, were getting into position to secure both ends of the runway as well as access roads. Two UAVs providing eyes in the sky had confirmed thirteen armed men by the larger hangar before the sun went down. Infrared imagery continued to track their movement. Most of them patrolled the front of the metal structure, which everyone believed could be the current location of the nuclear device.

Clutching a sound-suppressed Heckler & Koch MP7A1, Monica ignored the pain in her side and remained on Ryan's tail. She had been offered the option to sit this one out given what she had gone through. But there simply was no way she would go for that. This was what she did, what she was trained to do, what she was born to do—what she was willing to die doing. So she had told Colonel Stark to count her in.

They continued all the way to the perimeter fence in a deep crouch, staying low, knowing this could be the real thing, or a trap, or a diversion.

Or just nothing more than a fucking airfield used for the drug trade, she thought.

The intelligence brief indicated it belonged to a crop-dusting firm from El Paso owned by a bank in Mexico City with suspected ties to the Sinaloa Cartel. And if she could still believe what she was told in Monterrey by the GAFE, that meant it had ties to Miguel Montoya.

It was a long shot, but it was also all they had.

Ryan produced a pair of wire cutters and made an L-shaped opening in the chain link, pulling it toward him and letting Monica go through, followed by Stark and Larson. Hagen and Danny were going to make their own way into the compound from somewhere else.

Once inside, Ryan grinned at her before disappearing inside the compound.

Ryan knew the Rangers would also deploy snipers and that the water tower would be a possible perch. He also realized that once up there, he would not be able to shift quickly to an alternate firing position. So as he moved, he scanned the area and sure enough saw four Rangers, all wearing the newest combat load.

He stopped and, knowing they would have seen him as well, flashed the prearranged hand and arm signal, receiving the countersign.

Time to pick another nest, he thought, finding a series of mounds that were four hundred yards from the target.

Ryan selected four positions about twenty yards apart and settled in the best one, glad that he had done the map and aerial photo recon before getting here.

He hit the Send button on his radio twice, signaling he was in position.

Through his rifle's scope, he tracked Stark's team plus Monica moving with the shadows, weapons up less than a hundred yards from the target.

He checked the wind, ranged the first cartel soldier, and began to relax his body and breathing.

Monica watched Stark and Larson off to her far right vanish behind a clump of boulders. Following his instructions, she hid in between two gas trucks. The stench of fuel made her grimace. It suggested recent use, and reminded her of her close encounter in Monterrey.

Focus.

Inching her way under one of the vehicles, she removed her night-vision goggles because they always got in her way, plus there was enough light this close to the hangar.

Letting her eyes adjust, she sized up the two figures standing a dozen feet from her, in between the truck and the side of the hangar. They were young, certainly Hispanic, and well armed, MAC10 pistols in hand. They also had large revolvers secured cowboy style in leather holsters hanging from thick gun belts opposite machetes in sheaths. Both wore baseball caps. Off to their left, four more men stood similarly armed.

Wait for my signal, Cruz, Stark had told her.

What signal?

But he had already rushed off with Chief Larson.

So she paused, probably longer than she would have liked, her MP7A1 aimed at the closest figure, waiting for whatever it was that she was supposed to—

It happened fast.

One of the four men to her far right went down, his head splitting.

Ryan.

Her two marks turned toward their comrades under attack.

Monica fired, scoring a direct headshot, switching targets and firing again. But the second man was fast, agile, scrambling out of sight. The round punched through the corrugated metal wall where he had been an instant earlier.

And then he was gone.

Damn, she thought, rolling out from under the truck, MP7A1 aimed at the last place she had seen him.

She shifted in the direction of Stark and Larson, who had already killed the rest of their targets and were also gone.

And that's when she spotted the glint of a shiny revolver, still holstered, briefly reflecting light from an unseen source. It had been there one moment and gone the next, but long enough for Monica to go in pursuit.

In a deep crouch, MP7A1 aimed at darkness, she bided her time, waiting for another chance to—

A shadow surged in the night, suddenly, quickly, shifting directions, a hand raised above his head, the long shape of his machete descending on her.

She instinctively lifted the MP7A1, metal hitting metal, sparking as she blocked the incoming machete while falling on her back.

But she lost her grip on the submachine gun, watching it fall out of reach.

Ryan! Now would be a good time!

The man lifted the machete again, ready to deliver a fatal blow.

Monica realized that the fuel truck had to be blocking the view from Ryan's direction.

Sweeping her right leg under her enemy's, Monica kicked the back of his knees, forcing him to the ground. But he managed to land on top of her, a hand on her throat, the other raising the long blade again.

Monica grabbed his lapels, smelled his breath of beer and tobacco; his face was round, dark, eyes glinting in controlled anger.

She jerked her right leg up, driving it in between his.

Her knee struck his groin hard.

He trembled, grimaced, but remained in place, the machete high above her.

She tried to stop him but saw the sharp edge falling toward the middle of her face.

When she shifted her head to the side, the cold steel brushed her ear before striking gravel.

Monica kicked him again, even harder, and this time he fell on his side, gasping, releasing the machete. Both hands on his groin, he curled into a fetal position.

She surged to her feet and kicked him in his solar plexus, shocking a web of nerves. The man vomited.

Flex-cuffing his wrists and ankles, she left him there and scrambled up the side of the hangar. Running past the bodies of the men Stark and Larson had killed, she reached the front of the structure, next to the open hangar gate.

She paused, her back pressed against the corrugated metal wall, MP7A1 pointed at the night sky, shooting finger resting on the trigger casing.

In an instant, she rolled inside, ignoring her throbbing ribs, rising to a deep crouch while sweeping the weapon at—

"Cruz, what took you so damn long?" Stark asked, standing next to Larson in front of the bodies of five more men. "We could have used some help here."

Before she could reply, Danny and Hagen suddenly materialized off to her right, weapons over their shoulders.

"Got three more dead guys back there, Colonel," Danny said.

As they walked by Monica, Hagen put a gloved hand over the bulky silencer of her MP7A1 and pushed it down.

"Muzzle control, Miss Cruz," Danny said. "We only shoot the bad guys."

Monica frowned while lowering her submachine gun, staring at an empty hangar. No planes, no vehicles, and certainly no damn bombs.

"Place is secure," Ryan said, also walking inside the hangar, his long camouflaged sniper rifle over his right shoulder. A half-dozen Army Rangers accompanied him. "Our pals here took care of several guys trying to make a run for the other side of the . . . hey, you're bleeding from your ear."

"It's nothing," she said, growing annoyed, rubbing a finger over the place where the sharp blade had nicked her earlobe. "I decided to capture a live one . . . you know, so we can actually fucking *talk* to him?"

The group exchanged glances before following her to the side of the hangar, where Monica showed them the cartel guard she had flex-cuffed moments ago.

Only he now had a bullet hole in between his eyes.

"Is this your idea of fun, Cruz?" Stark asked. "Cuff and shoot?"

"No, wait," Danny said, smiling. "Maybe she shot him and *then* cuffed him."

Ryan punched him on the shoulder while trying not to laugh.

"I'm just saying," Danny mumbled, rubbing his shoulder.

"Screw ya'll," she hissed, standing there staring at the dead man.

"Maybe we missed one," Stark said.

"If we did," Ryan replied, "he's long gone, sir. The field's clear. Rangers got it surrounded."

Monica stepped away from everyone, fuming. She needed to clear her head, which had been nearly severed by that machete-wielding son of a bitch, shot by another bastard to keep him from talking.

Walking to the middle of the airfield, she just sat there on a shallow sand dune and simply stared at the stars while wondering where the hell these clowns were.

Who seem to have Lady fucking Luck on their side.

104

Surprises

They had not stopped moving.

Not to eat, sleep, or even to use the restroom.

First the Cessna Caravans had dropped them off in that dusty South Texas field while keeping the engines running, taking off in separate directions, disappearing in the night sky.

Then they had boarded two Chrysler minivans and driven to the town of Uvalde, an hour north of Carrizo Springs, before turning east toward the outskirts of San Antonio. There, they dropped off the minivans with a local ISIS cell, went on foot around a police checkpoint, and loaded everything in a pair of old but reliable Nissan SUVs. Then it was north, to Austin, where another cell helped them avoid the areas of the city packed with protesters and rioters, exchanging the SUVs for three sedans of different colors, makes, and models. They had reached Waco along the I-35 corridor, where another cell got them through another checkpoint, this one run by the National Guard. And they switched vehicles again.

Salma had kept the device close to her at every turn, as the group carried it across parks, forests, and ravines and around roadblocks. She kept her hand always on the Bluetooth detonator, ready to end it if discovered, if she found herself without options. But her network of cells had come through at every turn, guiding them around the hot spots, keeping her mission alive.

Along the way Salma had met members from four separate cells— men, women, and children planted by ISIS with assistance from her intelligence network many years ago. They had been instructed to blend in with the American society, to attend their schools, to work in their businesses, to pay taxes and vote in their elections. They married the infidels, and even prayed in their churches and temples—all thanks to America's benevolent laws when it came to immigrants.

The quiet warriors she had met, if only for the hours when transitioning vehicles to get around checkpoints, were now American citizens. But they had all been uprooted from places like Kabul, Islamabad, and Karachi to live in neighborhoods with manicured lawns and white picket fences. Some even had dogs in their yards. Most had never killed, much less fired a weapon, even in practice. But that was not their purpose, their mission. They were doctors and lawyers, engineers and construction workers, businessmen and industrialists. They were bankers, housewives, and students; three were even police officers and local politicians. Their objective was far more important, complex, and powerful than simply wearing a vest packed with Semtex to a shopping mall. Their mission was strategic in nature, long term, nurtured to fruition over many years. They slowly but steadily infiltrated the very fabric of a society that must be brought to its knees.

Salma tried to remember all of their faces, their greeting smiles. They had encouraged her, fed her, and even clothed her. They had helped her team blend in and made them look like average Americans.

She gazed out the window from the rear of her black Lexus SUV following Highway 31, which cut to the northeast corner of the state from Waco toward the border with Louisiana. A Ford sedan with Azis, Omar, and two of Montoya's men—all dressed like Texas A&M college students headed for the casinos in Shreveport, Louisiana—led the nondescript caravan. Two more sedans carrying the rest of the team followed them from a respectful distance, so as to not appear to be traveling together.

She looked down at the bouquet of white roses that the daughter of a nurse in Waco had given Salma after helping them switch vehicles again.

"I have seen many things in my life, my dear Salma," Montoya said while sitting next to her after getting off his phone. "Many of them terrible but necessary . . . and some good, of course. But I have never seen so many people willing to help a single cause, so passionately united behind a common goal."

Salma turned to face this very odd man who was taking an

enormous risk by being in this country. His face was on the FBI's top-ten most wanted list.

Montoya was a modern-day Pablo Escobar. Folk hero in his native homeland of Colombia as well as in his adopted country of Mexico, he was wanted on two continents. His crimes ranged from murder, illegal drugs, and money laundering to human trafficking. In America alone he was charged with the deaths of a dozen DEA agents and twice as many Border Patrol officers in the past five years. And that didn't include the group of FBI agents his people had slaughtered yesterday in Monterrey.

Yet, here he was, telling her how proud he was to be with her in this historic mission.

And this is why Salma knew Allah was on her side.

Everything was falling into place now, including her alliance with this man and the manner in which Atiq and Ibrahim had activated cells to facilitate her safe transport, especially in such perilous times. Riots were igniting in every city, propelling this society to the verge of anarchy.

And I'm the one who will push it over the edge, she thought, placing a hand over Montoya's and squeezing it gently.

As the drug lord was about to reply, traffic stopped in the middle of town.

"What is this?" Montoya asked the driver.

"Riots, *Jefe*," he replied without turning around. "Up by that Walmart."

"Can we get around it?"

The driver shook his head while pointing at the people crowding the street between the line of cars and the sidewalk, blocking the way.

Montoya turned around, frowning at the traffic and the people piled up behind him.

105

Daryl

This was only his second year with the Tyler Police Department.

But today he wondered if there would be a third.

Dressed in full riot gear, Officer Daryl Brown, a native of the South Side of Chicago, stood shoulder to shoulder with his fellow officers, protecting the entrance to the Walmart Supercenter in the center of town.

Daryl was born and raised in the Windy City, a nickname earned eons ago not because of Chicago's gusty winds sweeping in from Lake Michigan but because of its full-of-hot-air politicians. He had seen his share of violence, in particular during his troubled teens. Back then he had a knack for making the wrong choices, eventually joining a gang and nearly losing his life when fighting a rival group.

Daryl was a true believer of the saying "What doesn't kill you makes you stronger."

He had miraculously survived his gang experience by following a girl to Texas. There he applied for the Tyler PD at the insistence of his girlfriend, now his wife and an expectant mother. She taught him the value of making better choices. Daryl earned his badge two years later.

He would never understand what she saw in him, but he was thankful every day that she did.

But as he stood today facing a mob many times larger than the forty-five officers deployed to protect the largest business in town, Daryl dreaded the choices that he might be forced to make.

The Recovery Act from President Vaccaro empowered the National Guard as well as all federal, state, and local law enforcement to use any means required to prevent looting and maintain the peace.

Word had gotten out two days ago about the borders being temporarily closed. It meant a breakdown in the nation's supply chain, which made the produce and products crowding the shelves of the large store behind them suddenly priceless.

Priceless and to be sold according to a set of rationing rules that would be delivered to each grocery store manager directly from the mayor's office by this evening.

But those rules meant nothing if rioters were allowed to sack the stores today.

And that's where the Tyler PD came in, hopefully soon to be assisted by the National Guard, already en route.

The TPD had a force of 194 sworn officers. But there were just too many stores to be protected while also keeping some semblance of a police force patrolling the streets in twelve-hour shifts. They needed the promised 250 National Guardsmen now, not by their scheduled arrival time midafternoon.

Might as well be next year, he thought, as it was only ten in the morning.

None of those future reinforcements made any difference at the moment to Daryl or his fellow officers forming this defensive wall.

The lieutenant in charge warned the incoming group of hooded rioters armed with bricks, baseball bats, knives, crowbars—and very likely concealed firearms—to disperse and go home.

Daryl looked to the officers on either side of him, who he knew would have his back as he would have theirs, steeling himself for what was about to go down.

He was not new to death, having seen more than his share of it during those turbulent years back in the day, when the choice had been simple: kill or be killed. So he had chosen the former, using every conceivable weapon—some too brutal to be among the ones wielded by the incoming crowd—to take lives, seven in total.

He had been lucky to get away clean, leaving that life and then becoming the very thing he had loathed as a teenager: a cop.

But at this particular moment, as the lieutenant ordered tear gas against the wall of humanity heading his way, Daryl felt anything *but* lucky.

"We need to get out of here," Salma hissed while the mob approached the police line a couple hundred feet from the street.

"Can't do it without drawing attention to ourselves," Montoya replied. "It should be over soon."

An instant later a dozen officers fired canisters at the front of the line, light gray clouds engulfing them, forcing them to slow down. Many fell to their knees coughing, hands on their faces.

But others pressed on, running with rags tied over their noses and mouths, emerging through the mist.

"Grenade launchers," said Salma, watching the show.

Several officers armed with M32s fired at the horde.

The concussion grenades skittered across the pavement and detonated in bursts of blinding light. Their SUV shook from the acoustic energy, discouraging nearly half of the rioters, forcing them to their knees. Many clutched their ears or eyes, some vomiting. Others ran off crying.

But the rest persisted, breaking into a run toward the police line.

Daryl cringed at the incoming rioters, now less than fifty feet from where he stood, holding ranks, riot shields held tight, evoking images of the Spartans at the Hot Gates.

Behind them—and behind other police lines deployed across the city—was the very essence of their survival as a society, as a nation. No one knew how long it would be before the eighteen-wheelers arrived again with goods. It could be days or weeks, unlike after the riots of Los Angeles, Ferguson, or Baltimore, where the surrounding communities came to their rescue in the wake of burning and looting.

Daryl frowned. No one was coming to Tyler, Texas, with supplies to replenish the shelves of his city if they were sacked—at least for the foreseeable future.

The governor had stated it clearly in his press conference the day before. Each community had to do everything and anything possible to protect their own reserves of food and drinking water.

So Daryl got ready to do just that. He would hold his line in the sand, shoulder to shoulder, as the looters who cleared the first two obstacles charged at them.

Rubber bullets stripped the determination of another dozen, sending them scrambling for cover. But the rest clashed against the shields, swinging bats and crowbars, thrusting knives and even prison-style shanks.

But the disciplined officers held the line. The wall of shields took the abuse before they pushed the hoodlums back. Using their standard-issue batons, the officers landed a barrage of blows, cracking skulls and bones. The unexpectedly brutal response forced the rioters back into the stalled traffic. Many limped, most bled. All screamed obscenities. Many shouted accusations of police brutality.

The wave of angry and wounded people pushed back by the police now surrounded them, some banging on the windows of the SUV. Four of them began to rock their vehicle.

Salma had had enough, and before Montoya could react, she lowered her window and fired twice at the crowd, which broke into a stampede.

"What are you doing?" he screamed.

"Making a hole!"

"What?"

"Trust me! The police won't care!"

"We're moving out! Now!" Montoya shouted into the radio, and a moment later the lead car also fired at the surrounding horde, triggering panic as they stepped on the gas, creating their own lane between the line of stalled traffic and a sidewalk packed with rioters.

The SUV followed the lead car while Montoya also pulled out a gun and discharged it in the air.

Daryl was momentarily confused. Someone had opened fire.

One of us?

He doubted it, plus the shots had come from the crowd, from the street, though it was difficult to see with everyone running.

Glancing down the cop line, he saw none of his officers down, and he returned his gaze to the commotion in the street.

And that's when Daryl noticed handguns being withdrawn from

behind the windows of a sedan followed by an SUV trying to get through the stalled traffic. Their bumpers pitched pedestrians out of the way, rolling over some, sparking even more panic as the mass dispersed in every direction.

The havoc created by the departing vehicles, which included two more sedans squeezing through the maddened horde, somehow reinvigorated the rioters, turning them away from the street and back toward the police line.

Daryl wanted to go after the vehicles but could not break ranks. The store had to be protected at all cost. It was the priority, so he remained in place. His left hand firmly clutched his shield and his right hand gripped the hardwood baton, which he used a moment later against two rioters trying to get past him, scoring five solid blows.

And there's more where that came from, assholes, he thought, catching the runaway vehicles disappearing around the corner, heading northeast on Highway 31.

"I'll be damned," Montoya said as they left the havoc behind.

"It was the only way, Miguel," Salma replied, rolling up her window and putting away her Beretta.

"You were right," he replied, looking through the rear windshield. "No one's following us."

"And they won't," she said.

"How . . . did you know?"

She shrugged. "They don't care about us as long as we're not a threat to their supplies."

The drug lord slowly nodded, put a hand over hers, and said, "Balls *and* brains. You definitely need to come work for me."

Daryl kept thinking about the people in the vehicles that had fired above the crowd as he dispensed more blows, pushing rioters back, and holding the line. But he couldn't do a damn thing about it now, as the crowd kept coming at him. He remembered the very different clashes he had endured a lifetime ago back in Chicago's South Side.

He noticed that some of his fellow officers seemed quite agitated, sweating, a few even trembling.

But as he stared at his own right hand holding the baton, he noticed it was rock solid. And so was his head, clear, thinking, under control.

He was fully aware of the need to ride the fine line between controlling a crowd and coming across as mass murderers on some damn YouTube video. Just because they had been given permission to use deadly force, it didn't mean they had to—at least until there was no other choice to protect the invaluable asset behind them.

For now Daryl had choices, good choices. And he used them a dozen times in the next hour, pushing back wave after wave of rioters. They arrested several after each round and kept them flex-cuffed—wrists and ankles—behind the police line.

The tactic was a simple one: thin out the herd a little at a time. With every counterstrike, a few predesignated officers grabbed the closest and most impaired of the retreating rioters and pulled them out of the fray. They slowly reduced their numbers until there were far more of the idiots sitting by the steps to the Walmart than their even dumber associates still trying to figure a way through.

By two in the afternoon they had immobilized over a hundred protesters, and the rest soon vanished as ten Humvees from the National Guard finally made their way downtown to provide relief.

By three P.M. the mayor announced that the police department had clashed with looters at thirteen different locations. He was pleased to report that not a single store had been looted but over eight hundred rioters had been apprehended. They were being held at the local high school football stadium until further notice. But best of all, not a single life had been taken in what many thought would be the bloodiest day the city of Tyler had ever seen.

By three thirty P.M., Daryl had placed calls to the Texas and Louisiana state troopers and their respective National Guards to report the vehicles he had seen firing their way through the crowd. He reported that they appeared to be headed northeast on Highway 31, presumably toward the largest city within fifty miles: Shreveport, Louisiana, one of the busiest port cities on the Mississippi River.

His call resulted in several additional deployments of state troopers and National Guard platoons to put up additional roadblocks across northeast Texas and northwestern Louisiana. But for reasons that would be never understood, Daryl's sighting, as critically as it was treated at the local and state level, died a quick death beneath the piled paperwork of an overworked FBI agent in the Shreveport field office.

106

Alone

ISLAMABAD, PAKISTAN

Fucking cowards.

That's what Atiq thought of everyone in that room.

Damn gutless cowards, born without a backbone, too quick to succumb to pressure from the Americans.

Leading this witchhunt was none other than Minister Vijay Korai. He sat opposite Atiq across the long table in the main conference room of the mountain facility, anger flashing in his eyes.

"You have betrayed our trust," Korai began, flanked by the top generals of the Pakistani Army and Air Force. Present also were the heads of both houses of Parliament, the chairman of the Senate, and the speaker of the National Assembly.

The Supreme Court chief justice as well as the chief justices of the High Courts of Islamabad and the Federal Shariat Court also sat across the table.

In contrast, Atiq sat alone, on trial, glaring at his inquisitors with defiance. Even his colleagues in the intelligence services and the internal police were distancing themselves, sitting at the ends of the table.

Looking down at his notes, Korai continued, "We have lost over sixty percent of our fighter jets, two-thirds of our army bases, and . . ."

He shuffled a few papers and said, "Seventy thousand dead so far and the numbers are likely to increase in the coming days and weeks, especially from the destruction in Karachi. Our reactors at Khushab are destroyed, and we've just received an unconfirmed report of an attack against our underground facility in Nawabshah."

Atiq raised his brows in obvious surprise. That complex had been buried deep enough to survive a direct nuclear strike. Yet, the Americans had found a way to get to it.

Korai droned on and on about their military and industrial losses since the attacks began, reading out reports from various agencies, including the Department of Energy, which was slowly bringing the country back online.

Finally, the prime minister stood, pointed a finger at Atiq, and said, "You stood before all of us and guaranteed that the responsibility would fall on ISIS, not us. You have weakened our position against India . . . against our enemies. I'm here today, in front of the heads from all branches of our government, accusing you of the highest treason against Pakistan. Do you have anything to say in your defense?"

Atiq stared at them and once again chose silence. Their minds were already made up, and he would not give them the pleasure of hearing him beg for his life.

"Do you still refuse to tell us the location of the third bomb?" Korai asked.

Atiq continued looking at them with indifference.

Looking about him, Korai added, "Very well . . . all who find Dr. Gadai guilty of high treason, please raise your hand."

In unison, everyone in the room not only raised a hand but also stood.

107

Extinction

"My prime minister sends his gratitude for refocusing the strikes."

Tristan regarded Ambassador Patras Dham crossing his legs as they sat across from each other in the same rear room at the Old Ebbitt Grill. The man looked terrible, dark circles under his eyes suggesting a lack of sleep.

I probably look just as bad, he thought, having slept little since the New York blast, which had shaken his office at the United Nations complex near Forty-Fourth Street, almost four miles from ground zero. But unlike the madness that had engulfed the tip of Manhattan, the worst thing that happened to him was a temporary loss of electricity. It had required him to climb twenty stories to reach the helipad and board the Black Hawk that President Vaccaro had sent for him.

He had definitely been among the lucky ones, as had his wife and two young girls, who lived on the Upper East Side, even farther away. But Tristan felt anything but lucky as the reports from New York continued to stream in. He had just met with John Wright to discuss the recent strikes. The chief of staff had mentioned that the death count had already topped two hundred thousand.

Tristan had closed his eyes, trying to wrap his head around that figure, and he still couldn't. That was almost twice the number of American casualties in World War I, and almost half the number of American deaths in World War II. And it had all happened in a very short time.

Nuclear warfare had come full circle.

"I hope the information was useful," Patras added.

Tristan slowly bowed.

Reaching into his suit, the Pakistani ambassador produced another sheet of paper. "I hope this is also helpful."

Tristan read it twice and frowned.

"What is wrong? That is the rest of the targets, yes?"

"And they will be dealt with," he replied. "Just as we have dealt with your prior lists. But Ambassador, what we *really* need . . . what is *most important* to my country now, is the location of the bomb."

"We have identified the man responsible for the . . . collaboration with the al-Crameini brothers. His name is Dr. Atiq Gadai."

"Your chief nuclear scientist?" Tristan said, pretending surprise. Wright had already briefed him on Bill Gorman's findings.

"Correct," Patras said. "We believe he knows the location. Prime Minister Patras has arrested him. He will be questioned and—"

Leaning forward, Tristan interrupted, "*Will be* questioned, Mr. Ambassador? *Will be?*"

Tristan paused for effect. Patras appeared to shrink in his chair.

After a moment, he added, "A terrorist group assisted by *your* government has smuggled another bomb into our nation, and you have not yet interrogated the one person who could identify its location?"

"Mr. Ambassador, I—"

"For the sake of your *country*," Tristan interrupted him, "for the sake of your *people*, of your society, you must find a way to tell us *yesterday* where it is. You need to be doing everything possible and impossible to extract the information on its location before it's too late. I can't begin to describe to you what would happen to Pakistan if that bomb is detonated anywhere on our soil."

Patras began to sweat, and he produced a handkerchief from his suit, dabbing his forehead.

Tristan stood and pocketed the list. "Time is running out, Mr. Ambassador, so I'll leave you to it. Please, tell your prime minister that he needs to do whatever is necessary to spare his country . . . from extinction."

108

The Grab

PARIS, FRANCE

In his thirty years with the CIA, Glenn Harwich thought he had seen everything. Ten years in Colombia were followed by another decade in Moscow. Then the past ten years floating between Europe and the Middle East. He had been shot, stabbed, beaten, left for dead, and once even electrocuted while fighting America's war on terror.

Harwich thought he had seen everything . . . until this evening.

The field directive had reached his station in the basement of the American embassy, located a block from Place de la Concorde at the southern end of the Champs-Élysées. It had been . . . well, poetic, ironic, and not without a sense of humor.

But it didn't change how serious it was to execute the grab without a hitch, and while keeping the principal unharmed.

The exclusive boutique on Avenue Montaigne catered to the rich.

The very, very rich.

Harwich could not even pronounce its name without drawing laughs from his French assets impersonating paparazzi covering the front of the establishment.

Princess Lisha al-Saud arrived in a fleet of four limousines, accompanied by an entourage of bodyguards, secretaries to manage schedules, assistants to carry packages, and bookkeepers to settle accounts.

The plan was simple, devised by Harwich. It relied on the fact that people such as the princess had a goddess-like complex. She believed herself to be above all reproach, that the laws of this world did not apply to her. And this particular noblewoman certainly lived the regal brand with a well-publicized history of excess. Weeklong parties costing *millions*. Monthlong stays at five-star Parisian hotels topping *tens* of millions. Shopping sprees in the eighth arrondissement, the favorite destination of wealthy Saudis.

The limos arrived an hour late, past the shop's regular closing time, another sign of rebellion against established business etiquette and simple courtesy. But to the party dressed in black exiting the shiny limousines under the yellow glow of streetlights, businesses existed to cater to them. And as far as courtesy . . . well, that just wasn't in the royal vocabulary. In the case of the good princess, neither was paying her bills. She already owed this particular store over eleven million dollars from a trip six months ago. She had purchased more clothes, hats, shoes, and handbags than any woman could possibly wear in a lifetime, plus jewelry—lots and lots of jewelry.

Princess Lisha exited last, in full regalia, a diamond-studded tiara adorning her head, sparkling in the evening lights, like the goddess she believed she was. More gems accessorized her very white gown. It contrasted sharply with the dozen black-dressed men and women surrounding her—she'd unknowingly made Harwich's job easier.

"Target in white. Repeat. Target is in white," he spoke into his hidden microphone from across the street to his SOG team, the same group who had accompanied him to Islamabad last week.

"Copy that. Teams ready," came the reply from his lead man.

The CIA officer's eyes momentarily shifted from his mark to the last limousine. Three men hoisted large suitcases from the trunk, rolling them behind the entourage, ushering the princess to the front of the boutique.

"Now," Harwich said.

It happened fast.

A sedan slammed into a parked vehicle a block away, drawing the attention of pedestrians and a pair of police officers away from his mark.

While the distraction worked its intended magic, two technicians in a utility tunnel beneath the cobblestone street disabled all street cameras with line of sight of the boutique.

Three Renault vans with local plates appeared around the opposite corner, screeching to a halt by the boutique. The store's doors were locked, as arranged with the owners, who didn't need much convincing after being promised full payment for their cooperation.

Harwich eyed his digital stopwatch. Ten seconds.

The princess and her staff were caught by the front steps of the boutique. While her assistants slapped the glass doors, the paparazzi impersonators emptied the contents of small gas canisters into the faces of the bodyguards, who collapsed around the shocked princess.

Seventeen seconds.

The side doors of all three vans slid back. Tasers fired from the lead van found the men towing the suitcases. They immediately released them while thrashing on the sidewalk, urinating in their designer suits.

Twenty-two seconds.

While agents grabbed the suitcases and threw them in the lead van, three hooded agents jumped out of the middle van. They shoved the paralyzed secretaries and accountants out of the way, stepped over the unconscious bodyguards, and put a bag over the princess's head—tiara and all. Flex-cuffing her wrists and ankles, they tossed her royal ass inside the van.

Thirty-three seconds.

The crew in the third Renault, there for backup, did nothing but enjoy the show. They took off after the first two vans, precisely thirty-nine seconds from the moment Harwich gave the order from across the street.

But Harwich didn't leave. He blended among the Parisians and tourists that were quickly shifting away from the distraction, many with phones in hand trying to film the departing vans.

He waited for confirmation from a fourth Renault crew working the alley behind the store. His best team had just bagged the two top ISIS chiefs of the French caliphate deployed by Hassan al-Crameini to collect over 195 million dollars in cash, bonds, gold, and diamonds from the princess.

As his final act, Harwich inconspicuously dropped a backpack by his feet and stepped away from the crowd. He walked the required distance and pressed a button on a remote control, activating a powerful magnet that trashed all electronics within a hundred feet, including the phones of one of Princess Lisha's secretaries who was trying to call for help.

And that's how he left everyone: staring stupidly at their dark screens as a black Fiat 500 pulled up at the end of the block to take him to the American embassy.

Harwich climbed in the front passenger seat and was about to hit the speed dial on his encrypted phone to update Lisa Jacobson in Washington when the unit started to vibrate. The caller ID indicated it was from New York.

"Harwich," he said.

"Glenn, it's Vic."

Harwich stared at the Parisian streets rushing by as memories filled his mind. He had dated Gorman's sister for about a year in New York a lifetime ago. She was a very independent, driven, and quite tough Brooklyn girl turned paramedic. But the affair had dwindled the moment he was sent overseas.

"Vic. This is a surprise. How are—"

"Where is my brother, Glenn? I just got a text sent *two days* ago. He's not answering his phone."

"How did you get this number?"

"Bill gave it to me in the same text message. Now, why don't you cut through the crap and tell me he is out of that fucking country."

He spent a minute bringing her up to speed, realizing that in the process of doing so he was illegally releasing enough classified information to send him to prison for life.

"So you just left him there?"

Harwich took a deep breath. "I told him it was a stupid idea, but in the end it was his decision, Vic. He's a big boy."

"So you don't know where he is."

"Like I said, last I heard he was headed for Karachi to follow up on some lead."

"Glenn, now you listen to me. We're going to hang up and then you're going to make whatever phone calls you need to make to set whatever wheels in motion you need to set to find him and get him the fuck out of there. Got it?"

Harwich nodded, said, "Got it," hung up, and hit the speed dial.

"Do you have the package?" asked Lisa at the other end.

"Yes, but there's something else. Bill Gorman. Any word on him?"

"He's missing . . . as well as his key asset," Lisa said.

"Damn it. I told him it was a dumb idea," Harwich said, remembering last seeing him and Maryam disappearing inside the train station in Islamabad.

She briefed him on how he'd made his way to Karachi to interrogate an ISI analyst before losing contact after the bombing started.

Harwich slowly shook his head as they reached the embassy gates. "You mean to tell me Bill was in Karachi and you guys didn't give him a fucking heads-up?"

Silence, followed by, "Fell through the cracks . . . look, too many moving pieces and too little time. But your phone call is timely. We were wondering if there's a chance that he may have gathered more intel on the third bomb, and assuming he managed to survive the attack . . . well, we think he might be on the run . . . and you are familiar with the area and know how Bill thinks."

Harwich sighed and closed his eyes, realizing where this was headed.

109

Two Jobs

WASHINGTON, D.C.

"Madam President, knowing you do not want us to get 'into the weeds' on these briefings, I will highlight actions and let your questions and decisions guide the rest of the meeting," said John Wright. He stood on the side of the Situation Room, which was packed to the brim with every federal agency director and Pentagon chief.

Vaccaro regarded her chief of staff, who looked as tired as she felt, and motioned for him to continue.

"Bad news first," he began. "We have not located the third bomb. We believe the group that Cruz and Stark are chasing has it with them."

"How is she?"

"Agent Cruz is walking wounded but still very much in the fight and has linked up with Colonel Stark's team. They are in pursuit of the terrorists that came ashore in Monterey thirty-two hours ago. That's the update for now."

Wright paused for a few seconds, and then said, "We have had very successful bombing missions in Pakistan, Afghanistan, Syria, and Iraq. Due to State and CIA contacts we have significantly diminished ISIS's forces and are planning to hit them continuously when and wherever they appear."

Vaccaro stood and crossed her arms. "Okay, everyone. We need to use every resource we have to find the missing bomb. I want everything that flies, drives, goes on top of or under the water that is not in New York to be looking at Texas and its neighboring states. Oh, and here is the hardest part . . . all of that terrorist-chasing activity will be under the direct control of either Colonel Stark or ASAC Cruz, whoever answers the phone first or makes the request. We screwed up at least twice, people, once by the shores of Mexico and again in Monterrey. We also missed them in Carrizo Springs. We fell for their decoys multiple times. We are not being smart enough to act quickly and decisively. So now I'm placing the control stick in the hands of the only two individuals who seem to care more about finding the bomb than how their actions might affect their careers."

A half-dozen people, including the head of Homeland Security, leaned forward, their faces telegraphing their intention to object.

She raised a hand and cut them off while adding, "Before the sounds of protest leave your mouths, allow me to elaborate. I am fully aware of all the chains of command, centers of power, and personal and professional issues. What I'm ordering challenges it all. I do not care. Let everyone in your teams know that the first organization that tries to 'end run' me on this order, the first organization that says no to a request, the first organization that slows down a request, well . . . the head of that organization and all those we can find will be fired and possibly prosecuted."

Slowly, she raised the index and middle fingers of her right hand.

"We have *two* jobs right now: find the third bomb, and rebuild Lower Manhattan. If anyone in this government has another agenda or issue, they will be fired immediately. We have no choice but to get this right. I am responsible for what is happening, so save your phone calls for the press and your donors and get back to work saving this nation." The president then stood up and left the room, followed by Wright and Lisa Jacobson.

"Have we located Gorman yet?" she asked both as they headed for the stairs to go up to the Oval Office.

"No yet, Madam President," replied Lisa. "And we're doing his search only with Agency assets plus assistance from the navy . . . we cannot trust anyone else."

"Lisa . . . I don't care what you need to do. We're going to find him and get him the hell out of there."

110

Barnes

HOUSTON, TEXAS

Houston PD Senior Officer Seth Barnes had been in the force for over two decades. Most of his old graduating class from 1995 had moved up to become detectives, sergeants, lieutenants, or even captains. Some had left the force altogether to join agencies like the DEA and the FBI, or the more lucrative private security business.

Barnes remained in uniform and in the streets, where he could make a difference, where he belonged. His patrol car was his home. His partner of twelve years, Officer John Parker, was the closest thing he had to a family after his wife died in a car accident four years ago because some asshole couldn't wait to return a text.

Barnes, who'd stopped smoking a year ago and now constantly chewed nicotine gum and wore patches, drove while Parker sipped from a paper cup of steaming coffee.

They cruised by the large parking lot belonging to the Compass

BBVA Stadium at the intersection of Dowling and Texas Streets, in the heart of the downtown area. The lot was leased on weekdays to accommodate commuters, but today was Sunday afternoon and there was no game scheduled, meaning it was supposed to be empty.

Only it wasn't.

"What do you think?" Barnes asked while pointing at the large white van parked in the middle of the lot next to a blue sedan.

Parker put down the coffee, peered across the street, and shrugged. "They shouldn't be there. But after the week we've had, are you really going to worry about issuing a couple of fucking tickets?"

Barnes sighed. His partner had a foul mouth, but he also had a point.

Thanks to President Vaccaro's Recovery Act, this was the first day since the bomb went off that the downtown area was clear of anything resembling an angry crowd. And thanks to the city's efficient cleanup crews, most of the mess had been swept away. Only a few boarded-up windows remained. And now with the National Guard also patrolling the streets in numbers, he hoped the city would return to some semblance of normalcy by tomorrow, when businesses and schools were due to reopen. The mayor and the governor seemed quite aligned with President Vaccaro's message to get everyone back into their routines as soon as possible.

Your job is doing what you were doing the day before the bomb. Do your part to get the nation back on its feet. My job is to catch those who did it while doing everything possible and impossible for the people of New York City.

Barnes stared at the two vehicles, recalling the quote from the president while she stood on a podium at the edge of the quarantined zone around ground zero. The day before the bomb he had been patrolling these streets, responding to typical dispatches, from domestic disturbances to traffic accidents.

And issuing parking tickets.

"You fucking kidding me?" Parker cursed when Barnes turned the cruiser around and stopped at the corner.

"It's our job, Johnny."

"Whatever, Mr. Nicorette. Though I speak for the whole department when I say we all liked you a heck of a lot better when you were smoking."

"Don't start. I'm still the same *damn guy*."

"Yeah, in your *damn mind*. But hey, why don't you call this one in? Maybe the Guard can assist since they're 'Always Ready. Always There.'" Parker made quotation marks with his fingers.

Barnes frowned. Sometimes his partner could act like such an idiot. "Do you really think we could have brought this city under control without them?"

He sipped more coffee and slowly shrugged. "All right, all right. Look, I love the Guard. I just don't want someone pissing in our pond. And I'm still a little on edge after . . . Hey, look." Parker pointed at the parking lot.

Barnes turned back and saw a man getting out of the van and into the passenger side of the sedan, before it accelerated toward the exit.

"Well," Parker added, "I don't know about you, partner, but I can't imagine a scenario where *that* can be any good."

Barnes floored the cruiser while Parker tossed the coffee out the window and turned on the lights and siren. He then called it in, both on the standard HPD channel as well as the channel preselected for National Guard emergencies.

Rather than decelerating when spotting the incoming patrol car, the sedan, a Toyota Camry, tried to outrun them. It reached the street and fishtailed while heading straight for the highway entrance ramp two blocks away.

But the Camry was no match for the police cruiser.

Barnes easily caught up to it within a half block and hit the Camry's rear quarter panel with his heavy-duty front bumper push bar, sending it into a spin.

The Camry whirled twice across the wide street, its driver obviously not experienced enough to know how to counter the rotation. The passenger-side wheels struck the curb, the car nearly flipped, then crashed against a large oak.

Barnes stopped his car a couple dozen feet from the Camry's front grille. He jumped out seconds later along with Parker, weapons drawn, using the open doors as shields.

"Show me your hands!" he shouted, his Colt .45 semiautomatic pistol aimed at the passenger while his partner covered the driver.

The men inside seemed in shock, dazed, almost nonresponsive. But they appeared conscious. He could see their eyes blinking, their heads moving.

But he could not see their hands.

"Your hands!" Barnes shouted again.

MAC-10s materialized out of both windows. Their muzzle flashes pulsated with gunfire, the sound cracking down the street.

Barnes reacted quickly. He jumped back in the front seat as a barrage ripped into the door, shattering the window, peppering metal with the sound of a dozen hammers. Parker was pushed back by the fusillade, his figure vanishing from view as he fell back on the street.

Instincts took over.

Barnes put the cruiser in gear and floored it while remaining below the windshield. The heavy patrol car leaped forward, tires screeching, accelerating, building momentum. It rammed the much lighter Toyota, crushing its hood, shattering the windshield. The momentum lifted the sedan and tossed it sideways against another oak a dozen feet away, the frame nearly wrapping itself around the wide trunk.

Rolling out, Barnes aimed his gun at the wreck. Steam hissed from the radiator, a rear tire still spun, and the men no longer moved. One of them had fallen out the side window only to be crushed by the weight of the car when it landed on its side, limbs twisted at unnatural angles. The second gunman lay on top of his comrade, his face covered with glass. But his right hand still held the MAC-10, and he began to turn it toward Barnes.

For the first time in almost a decade, Barnes fired his service weapon. Three times, all shots hitting the man in the face.

He ran back to Parker's side as two Humvees from the National Guard turned the corner, accelerating toward them. Barnes reached his partner, noting blood pouring from a shoulder wound, as soldiers leaped out, surrounding the Camry. One of them was a medic who knelt next to Barnes, opening his kit and applying pressure to the injury.

"That Ford van!" Barnes shouted, stepping back to give the medic room to work just as a young National Guard lieutenant rushed to his side. "They were trying to get away from that van!"

Within fifteen minutes a dozen more Humvees, twice as many HPD patrol cars, two ambulances, three fire trucks, and probably a combined hundred soldiers and police officers arrived at the scene. The city's best bomb squad had cordoned the entire parking lot. TV crews set up shop beyond the police perimeter as three black Suburbans drove up to the bomb squad. Men and women in FBI SWAT gear as well as in business suits jumped out and conferred with the bomb squad chief, the captain of the Guard, and two HPD captains.

While paramedics tended Parker's wound and Barnes held his partner's hand, the low, pulsating sound of a helicopter echoed off the surrounding skyscrapers.

A Black Hawk materialized over the parking lot. Its camouflaged silhouette hovered off to the side, landing softly on the asphalt near the FBI SUVs.

A woman jumped out first, tall, slender, her light olive skin suggesting a Hispanic descent. She also wore an FBI SWAT uniform. Her long hair swirled in the downwash as she ran from the chopper directly to those who appeared to be in charge. Five men dressed for warfare and wielding sound-suppressed MP7A1s followed her. Their camouflaged faces blended them with their dark battledress. One of them, a bald and stocky man with hard-edged features, appeared to be in charge, and he engaged the heads of the other groups.

Before long, a pair of bomb disposal robots maneuvered to the sides of the white van. Their tall booms positioned cameras to provide clear views of the interior to the personnel behind laptops a hundred feet away.

Barnes watched from a distance as paramedics sedated his partner, patched him up, and rolled him into the rear of an ambulance before speeding away.

Sighing, he joined a group of HPD uniformed officers and detectives in suits gathered just beyond the Black Hawk, his captain among them.

"Good reaction, Barnes," HPD Captain Pete Dawson said while several colleagues patted him on the back. "Saved your partner's life."

"Thank you, sir. Will our boys get a chance to work this one?" He motioned toward the detectives conferring in a circle a dozen feet away.

"Nah," Dawson replied, pointing at the group that had just arrived via helicopter. "This one's for people with a higher pay grade than us."

"But it's our city," Barnes said.

"Not today."

"Who are they, anyway?"

"Hell if I know, Barnes," Dawson said. "Hell if I know."

———

"This is bullshit! We're wasting time with those stupid toys," Monica said, standing next to Colonel Stark and Hollis Gallagher, the ranking DHS officer. He happened to be the same guy running that ill-fated cross-agency task force at the Port of Houston that she'd walked away from three days ago.

For Monica it was hate at first sight. Gallagher was tall and well groomed, wore expensive suits and shoes, and probably spent more on haircuts than she did.

The three of them observed the bomb squad robots humming around the van. Ryan, Larson, Danny, and Hagen stood to the side but were obviously within earshot, because they seemed amused at her outburst.

"Why's that, ASAC Cruz?" Hollis asked.

"Because if this was the *real* thing, we would be standing in the middle of a fucking crater the size of three football fields surrounded by square miles of smoking rubble. *That's* why."

"So . . . you don't think this thing—"

"If this thing were going to go off, it would have already done so. My gut's telling me this ain't it."

"Last time we listened to your gut we lost a dozen agents, so if you don't mind, this time we will—"

Gallagher found it hard to continue when his throat was being squeezed expertly.

"Let him go, Cruz," Stark said.

Monica released him and said, "If you ever say that again, I will put a bullet in both your knees and you will forever remember who did it and why you'll never walk right."

Gallagher stepped back and massaged his throat while Stark slowly shook his head. Ryan whispered something to his buddies along the lines of Monica making new friends. She ran a hand behind her back and flipped him the bird.

"ASAC Cruz," Gallagher said in between coughs. "You *cannot* . . . put your hands on and threaten . . . a federal agent, and *this* . . . this is the best lead we've got since you lost them in Mexico."

"Wrong," Monica replied. "I did just assault and threaten a federal agent, and this event where we are all standing and jerking each other off . . . is a *diversion*, and meanwhile the bastards are taking the *real* bomb to the *real* target."

"Yeah? And where's that?"

"Disney *fucking* World for all I know. But we sure as hell aren't going to figure it out standing here . . . and I don't have the time to prove you wrong again."

"That's enough. Both of you," Stark said before Gallagher could retort. "Let's just see what the man has to say," he added, pointing to the bomb squad chief walking toward them.

"Bots detected radiation inside the van," the chief reported. He was a man in his early fifties with a raspy voice that suggested years of smoking.

"I knew it!" said Gallagher.

"But . . . that's the problem," the chief added. "The levels are wrong."

"What do you mean?" asked Gallagher.

"It means," interrupted Stark, "that a real gun-type device based on uranium-235 would not give out much radiation in its predetonation form, certainly not in any harmful levels, and most certainly not enough to be detected outside a van."

"That's correct," said the chief.

"And what does *that* mean?" pressed Gallagher.

Faced with the choice of slugging this idiot or counting to ten, Monica chose the latter. She parked her tongue and waited for technicians to access the rear of the van and expose an opened yellow barrel marked with a radiation hazard symbol under the words:

MD ANDERSON CANCER CENTER
MEDICAL RADIATION WASTE

And it was surrounded by plastic explosives.

"Need everyone to move back another two hundred feet," said the bomb chief after estimating the blast radius based on the amount of explosives.

"Still think it's a *diversion*?" asked Gallagher as the bomb squad secured the lid back on the barrel and went to work on the bomb section.

Monica shot an exasperated look at Stark and Ryan. As she was about to put the DHS man in his rightful place, Stark put up a hand.

"Mr. Gallagher," said the colonel while Monica crossed her arms and turned away, unable to even look at him. "We're in the middle of a massive parking lot. We were just asked to move back a couple hundred extra feet, which still puts us over a *thousand* feet from the closest street." He paused and looked around for effect, before adding, "*Meaning* that even if it goes off, all that would be damaged or contaminated is . . . well, asphalt."

"What about the explosion releasing radiation into the atmosphere?"

"Minimal," said Stark. "Certainly nonlethal, and again, contained pretty much to this parking lot. So yes, we're being played."

As Gallagher was about to reply, his phone rang. He answered, listened for a minute, hung up, and said, "Just got word of another van parked illegally in downtown Austin. Perhaps ASAC Cruz is right after all and that's the real one."

Before anyone could reply, Gallagher's phone rang again. This time he listened for thirty seconds, hung up, and, leaning closer to Cruz and Stark, he lowered his voice and said, "May I speak with you both privately for a moment?"

When they were out of earshot, Gallagher said, "That was John Wright saying that everyone in on this effort, including me, is now taking orders from you both."

Stark exchanged a brief glance with Monica before facing the Homeland man again, who added, "I don't know what that means, but I'm not about to try and figure it out right now . . . so, what do you want me to do?"

"Perhaps we can just all do our jobs and find the damn bomb," Monica said quietly, before turning to face the group again and adding, "but my money is that Austin, just like this one, is another diversion. Otherwise it should have also already gone off."

A moment later the bomb squad chief approached them, holding an electronic gadget in one hand and something resembling a ball of plastic explosives in the other.

"Dummy trigger . . . just a remote control . . . for a toy car," he said. "And . . . well . . . twenty pounds of Play-Doh."

"Toys," Monica hissed. "That's all this is. Toys R *fucking* Us."

Flanked by his team while Monica, Stark, and the Homeland agent discussed whatever it was he needed to discuss in private, Ryan did everything in his power to control his temper while whispering to Larson, "It takes real talent to put up with this bullshit. The world is literally falling apart around us and this dickhead wants to argue about whose agency swings the biggest stick?"

The large chief, arms crossed while watching the show, nodded and replied in his tenor voice, "I'm amazed she has survived in this shithole this long. I need to recommend to Stark that he hires her."

"Yep," added Danny. "She's always been a fighter, and in the last hours more than proved her value. Isn't that right, Mickey?"

Hagen stood to the side smoking a cigarette. He exhaled through his nostrils while nodding once.

"Plus it's great to see her again," added Ryan, grinning.

111

Guardsmen

NORTH OF SHREVEPORT, LOUISIANA

They appeared out of nowhere.

Three National Guard Humvees blocked the country road connecting Shreveport to a secret airfield a few miles away. Montoya's planes waited to take them through the mountains of Arkansas, Tennessee, Kentucky, and into Virginia for the final leg of Salma's trip into Washington, D.C.

Traffic was stopped in both directions. Guardsmen looked inside each vehicle, checking documents and inspecting trunks while chatting amiably with passengers before waving them through.

"They're not supposed to be here," said Ebra Janwari, head of the

ISIS cell in western Louisiana. She drove her own Honda minivan while Salma sat next to her. Azis and Omar occupied the middle seats. The third row of seating had been removed to accommodate the trunk, always within range. "I *specifically* checked with my husband."

Salma placed a hand on her chest, feeling the remote control under her shirt. She frowned at the thought of being forced to detonate here, ten miles north of the city, in the middle of nothing but a forest of towering pines.

Ebra was married to a Shreveport police officer who had provided his wife with all planned afternoon roadblocks for the area so she could avoid getting stuck in traffic while picking up the kids from a birthday party. Apparently he had missed this one.

"Now what?" Ebra asked.

Salma stared calmly at a dozen Guardsmen wielding standard-issue M16A4 assault rifles with thirty-round detachable magazines. They let another car go through before inspecting a Ford SUV now four vehicles ahead of them. In a few minutes she would be facing the wrong end of 360 5.56mm NATO rounds, which could be fired at a rate of fifteen rounds per second per rifle in full automatic mode. Between Montoya and Salma they had eleven men armed with a mix of UZIs and MAC-10s—almost an even fight.

At least on paper.

Salma, however, seriously doubted those Guardsmen were as battle hardened as her team and Montoya's.

Ebra moved up slowly as the soldiers let the Ford through.

"We discussed this possibility," Salma said, three cars now separating them from the checkpoint. She had reviewed potential scenarios with Montoya, who was in a white Buick sedan right behind her, and they had agreed to a plan if the situation arose.

Although slightly outgunned, Salma had the element of surprise and the benefit of experience on her side, and also her charming smile. She hoped it would be enough to put the soldiers at ease before she killed them.

"So . . . you have a plan?" asked Ebra, visibly nervous. Like so many other dormant cell members, she was an unarmed civilian, a nurse, in her case. Her mission was to infiltrate, provide transportation support, and even medical care should a member of Salma's team require it. But the woman had never held a weapon in her life.

Salma nodded. "Keep driving, don't forget to smile, and hide under the dash when I tell you."

Ebra, a native of Quetta brought here as a ten-year-old by her parents, and who shared Salma's skin color and her good looks, slowly bobbed her head in response.

Salma glanced over her left shoulder at Azis and Omar and said, "Follow my lead. Be ready."

She felt reassured by the determination in their eyes as they nodded their heads.

Reaching for her own UZI in the foot well between her legs, she verified it was set in full automatic mode, and kept it just out of sight while rolling down her window. Azis and Omar also lowered their windows.

Two cars to go.

Salma breathed deeply while scanning the roadblock, going from guard to guard. Although she had counted twelve, only five seemed engaged in the inspection. The rest stood together in a group to the side, in almost perfect position to be taken by Omar and her through the open windows. Three were even smoking, their M16A4s hanging loosely, and therefore uselessly, from their shoulders.

She brought the two-way radio to her lips. "Ready, Miguel?"

"Oh, yeah," he replied. "Won't take long."

Salma put the radio down and fought the urge to smile at his confidence even though they were about to face a group of armed soldiers in hostile territory.

Montoya would have made a great jihadist leader in another life.

One car.

"We're . . . next," Ebra said, her voice cracking.

Salma put a hand on her shoulder. "Relax. We are trained for this. It's going to be fine."

Ebra swallowed and whispered, "Are you certain?"

"I am," replied Salma.

The soldiers inspected the small red coupe in front of them before waving it through and signaling them over.

"Here we go. Easy now," Salma said, smiling at the soldiers. They smiled back.

Ebra inched the minivan forward, her eyes on the closest Guardsman on the driver's side. He was still smiling.

One instant his face was there, a young man with ash blond hair and blue eyes, kissed by the sun's waning light. And then it was gone, vanishing behind a cloud of blood before his body fell on the road, already a corpse.

"Get down, Ebra!" Salma shouted, aiming her UZI at the group of guards in a circle. The staccato gunfire pounded her eardrums as she kept her left hand under the muzzle, preventing it from shooting high. Shell casings flew all over. The smell of gunpowder filled the air.

The soldiers died quickly, cut down by her accurate bursts as well as Omar's. Their combined fusillade robbed them of a chance to fight back.

Shadows moved past Ebra's window, beyond Azis and his UZI tearing down the guards on the opposite side of the roadblock. It was Montoya and the rest of the combined teams, machine guns in hand, rounds finding their marks. Soldiers' chests exploded, peppered with bullets, wide-eyed stares glaring back in surprise and horror.

Leading the charge was the drug lord himself. A MAC-10 in each hand, he sprayed a deadly shower of .45-caliber rounds on an unsuspecting enemy caught in the monotony of the moment.

The Guardsmen, who didn't even wear protective vests, died before realizing what had taken place.

Only one soldier managed to return the fire, releasing a few rounds over Montoya's head. The large Colombian dropped and rolled with unexpected agility while firing back, bullets exploding through the soldier's neck and abdomen.

It was over in less than fifteen seconds.

Salma watched Montoya walk slowly by the corpses, guns in hand, the sun reflecting off his fair skin. He asserted his command, firing a round into each head to ensure no survivors, ordering everyone to clear the road while he surveyed the area. Making certain they were in the clear, he calmly walked over to Salma's window, blood staining his shirt and face.

"Everyone okay here?"

Salma had already traded seats with Ebra, who shook uncontrollably.

"Good call. You'd better drive the rest of the way," he told Salma, before looking back at the road and adding, "The people around us. They drove off in a hurry, probably calling the police."

"This country is on high alert, Miguel, and although we had to do this today, we have just given our exact location to the enemy."

"I agree," replied Montoya. "This means nothing except that it helps those hunting us."

Salma drove past the Humvees, following Montoya for the next five miles. They veered off a gravel lane that snaked its way through thickening forest, leaving behind the chaos they had created. The distant sirens of emergency vehicles eventually faded away altogether.

They drove for another twenty minutes as night finally fell, reaching a private airfield owned by one of Montoya's associates near the Arkansas border, truly in the middle of nowhere.

Two Cessna Caravans waited for them.

112

Seizures

ISLAMABAD, PAKISTAN

Atiq knew they would be coming for him soon. And when he failed to answer their questions, they would follow the process that he had established to interrogate enemies. It focused around the concept of inflicting the highest amount of pain while keeping the subject alive.

They would start easy, waterboarding him for a couple of hours, before removing his fingernails, then his molars. They would finish the first session by torching his testicles with a disposable lighter. When that didn't work, they would begin the second session by peeling the skin off his feet before immersing them in salt. But the real pain would begin on the third session.

Atiq shook his head. Prime Minister Korai wanted to know the itinerary, the route to deliver the bomb, as well as the delivery vehicle—information the former ISI chief planned to take to his grave. The only other soul besides Salma and Montoya with that knowledge was Lari, and he had likely perished in the dead zone that was Karachi. His bungalow had been right next to the chemical plants.

Atiq would indeed take the knowledge to his grave. But he intended to do so while sparing himself the suffering he had inflicted on so many of his enemies, some lasting as long as a week before succumbing to unimaginable pain.

They would be coming soon indeed, but he would not give them the pleasure of torturing him.

They had removed every object from his cell that Atiq could have used to end his life . . . except one.

On his knees facing Mecca, Atiq said his final prayers as he prepared to fight back for the last time by preventing Korai from jeopardizing his final act of vengeance against the Americans.

Kill the unbelievers, wherever you find them.

Fight against them until there is no dissention.

Fight until no other religion exists but Islam.

The words of the Koran echoed in his mind as he whispered them again and again. He sought and found in them the strength to bite hard into one of his rear molars, cracking the tiny capsule surgically implanted for this very occasion.

He stared at the wall as the chemicals were released. The capillaries lacing the ceiling of his mouth absorbed them, injecting them into his bloodstream.

He waited while whispering those simple words that had defined his life from the moment he watched his family burn alive.

Kill the unbelievers, wherever you find them.

Fight against them until there is no—

The cyanide worked quickly, inducing seizures. Histotoxic hypoxia set in when his cells were no longer able to absorb oxygen, followed by cardiac arrest and death seconds later.

113

Bad News

Tristan sat in Wright's office reviewing the list of targets and the results from the multiple surgical strikes against ISIS in Pakistan, Afghanistan, Syria, and Iraq. To date, dozens of training camps no longer existed. Multiple caves had been cleared and sealed, and most of the ISIS leadership had been eliminated. In addition, many computers and hard drives had been captured, yielding a wealth of intelligence on dormant cells in America as well as bank accounts around the world. At the last count, they had seized nearly a billion dollars in assets from the terrorist organization. But they both knew that ISIS had at least three times that amount, so the search continued.

As they sat there, the FBI and local law enforcement were raiding the homes and businesses of hundreds of American citizens that had been planted by the terrorist organization years ago. In operations conducted under the umbrella of the Recovery Act, suspected terrorists were being ushered to undisclosed locations around the country.

And it had all started with the intelligence reports that Tristan had obtained through his back channel into the Korai administration.

"It's ironic, you know," Wright said.

"What is?"

"That it took something like New York City for us to get this kind of intel. We've been after these bastards for what? Four decades? Then within a week, we wipe out most of their strongholds, freeze a third of their cash . . . plus we now have some ammunition to go after the Saudis."

Tristan grinned at the mention of the captured royals and their cash. "Yeah . . . that was most unfortunate for them, but very fortunate for us. I only wish the good prince and his sister had any knowledge of the whereabouts of the third bomb."

"Our people are still squeezing them . . . but after two straight days of interrogations, I'm starting to believe that ISIS didn't share that kind of knowledge with either of them."

"Of course. It would have been too convenient if they had."

"Yeah," Wright said. "That stuff is for the movies. In our world everything is difficult. Though Khalid did confess that Kuwait and Qatar also funded Ibrahim and Hassan al-Crameini."

"Now *that's* ironic."

"What do you mean?"

"We attacked Iraq in order to liberate Kuwait from Saddam Hussein. Now the bastards are helping the rise of his successors."

"Yeah," Wright said, leaning back. "We've known for some time that the Kuwaiti banking system is a major channel for funds fattening the coffers of the Sunni Muslim extremists that form the core of ISIS in Syria and Iraq."

Tristan nodded. After the fall of Saddam Hussein, the Sunni Muslim community—longtime loyalist to his Ba'ath Party—came under heavy fire by the invading Americans and also by the rival Shia Muslims. Together, they chased the Sunnis to the mountains. Many escaped to Syria, where they suffered atrocities under King Assad's regime. Eventually, they formed the core of ISIS through secret funding from countries like Saudi Arabia, Kuwait, and Qatar, who felt the need to protect the Sunnis suffering in both Iraq and Syria.

"And look at the monster they've created," Tristan finally said.

They remained quiet for a while. Then Wright asked, "What about our Paki friends? Are they squeezing Dr. Gadai?"

"That's the plan. Still waiting to get word from my channel."

Wright rubbed his eyes. "We're running out of time and out of options, Tristan. When are you meeting with the Saudi ambassador?"

"It's been arranged. We're speaking in a couple of hours."

Given the success of Tristan's back channel to Prime Minister Korai, President Vaccaro had decided to take the same approach with the Saudis. The United States now had irrefutable proof of their direct involvement with Hassan al-Crameini. A soldier had captured it in high-resolution video during the raid in Afghanistan, pushing Saudi

Arabia into the circle of those directly responsible for New York. And based on the confession of Prince Khalid, it looked as if Kuwait and Qatar might be right behind them.

"Good," Wright said. "Though to be completely honest, if Khalid and his sister don't know where the damn bomb is, chances are no one else in Riyadh does . . . but we still have to put the fear of God in them. They need to know that we know they were involved, and that we're beyond pissed. Worst case, we should at least get more targets to finish erasing ISIS off the face of the planet."

"I'll take care of it," Tristan replied. "I'll make sure that—"

Tristan's iPhone chimed twice, signaling a new text message. It was from Ambassador Patras Dham.

A.G. TOOK HIS LIFE BEFORE WE COULD INTERROGATE HIM.

He showed it to Wright, who sank into his chair, closed his eyes for a moment, then said, "Let's go down the hall. The president insists on hearing bad news immediately."

114

Controlled Crash

USS *RONALD REAGAN*, INDIAN OCEAN

"So you don't really know where he is, or even if he's still alive?"

Harwich could see the commander's point of view, of course. Why would he risk placing any of his men, or himself, in harm's way when there was a damn good chance that Gorman and Maryam could have been killed in Karachi?

The CIA officer knew it was a long shot. No, scratch that. It was the long shot of *all* long shots.

But he still had to try.

"Look," Demetrius said. He was sitting next to his WSO, Lieutenant Gonzales, in the rear of the mess hall, sipping coffee. "You didn't see what we saw over there. Tell him, Speedy."

Gonzales leaned forward and placed both arms on the table. He was a very wiry man with an even thinner face, wearing U.S. Navy shorts and a white T-shirt. "Our sortie was right on the tails of the B-2s from Guam. Part of their mission was to take out the military assets in Karachi and an IED factory. Well, we now think the IED factory had more than IEDs. Maybe Chinese 107s like the ones they used at Bagram. The video we saw showed rockets shooting in every direction, all over the damn place, and we think some hit a nearby refinery or something. Whatever it was, it triggered one hell of a chain reaction. I mean it was nuclear-level shit the way the sky lit up a hundred miles away."

Demetrius was taller than his WSO, with a receding hairline and a face that appeared as haggard as Harwich felt.

He'd flown nonstop aboard three separate military transports to get here in a record twelve hours since speaking to Victoria and Lisa—including that gut-wrenching landing on the *Reagan*.

A controlled crash, the pilot had called it.

Controlled my ass, Harwich thought. The only thing he had managed to control had been his bladder as the pilot rammed the plane onto the deck before the arresting wire tugged it back with eye-popping force.

"We think," Harwich said, "that the same EMP that fried his gear may have given him a warning to get the hell out of Dodge." Then, almost under his breath, he added, "Which is more warning than he got from our own fucking people."

Demetrius exchanged a glance with Gonzales.

"What do you think, Speedy?"

The officer rubbed his narrow chin while considering that for a moment before replying, "I mean, it's possible, Jade . . . but only if they found a place to hide. That secondary blast covered almost five square miles."

Turning back to Harwich, Demetrius said, "To put it in perspective, Mr. Harwich—"

"Glenn, please."

"Okay . . . Glenn, look, the New York blast was just under a mile in radius. This was at least *four* times the size . . . but, you said your man is . . . resourceful?"

"If someone can survive that, it would be Gorman. And if there is a chance—even a very, *very* small one—that he may have gotten intel on the whereabouts of that runaway bomb . . . well, you see why the White House sent me halfway across the world to take a joyride on your ship."

"Very well, Glenn," Demetrius said. "What do you have in mind?"

Twenty minutes later, Harwich found his way up to the ship's main deck to watch the amazing navy show. Hornets and Super Hornets took off and landed to the rhythm of ground crews moving about the flight deck with the precision of a masterfully orchestrated ballet.

The sun slowly sank in the western skies, its dying burnt orange blaze giving way to a star-filled indigo sky.

His eyes shifted north, toward the unseen coast of Pakistan one hundred miles beyond the horizon.

He felt it in his bones that somewhere beyond the waves, the beach, and the mountains, Bill Gorman was running for his life.

Somewhere.

115

A Simple Plan

SOUTHERN PAKISTAN

It could have been the High Plains desert of Colorado, or Death Valley in California, or the mountains of Peru.

It just happened to be Pakistan, near Hyderabad.

Because without the right equipment, without the right clothes, and with an entire terrorist organization plus a nation's intelligence service hunting you . . . it almost didn't matter where you were.

The truck had dropped them off by a small village at the foot of the mountains, where Maryam had managed to get warmer clothes, some food and drink, plus a couple of old bicycles to head into the mountain range—all in exchange for Gorman's Rolex.

Parting with the watch had been difficult, but as he handed it over to the village elder, a man in his eighties who smiled a smile of a handful of brown teeth, Jeannie's face filled his mind.

And I'd always love you, Darling. But it's time for you to move on.

And Gorman did, walking away with the hope that the last thing connecting him to his former life would buy them a chance at a new life.

A day later they were climbing past eleven thousand feet—"climbing" meaning trying to ride bikes up twenty-degree inclines on trails goats would have trouble with. Plus they had no lights, water limited to one bottle, and other than that only some smelly bread and even smellier cheese.

While his lungs sucked air like a vacuum cleaner, Gorman regretted that he did not do more hill training. Maryam seemed in far better shape, or perhaps she was just more resolute, aware of her fate if captured.

Stopping to take a break, they were alerted to the sound of vehicles coming toward their resting spot. They had decided that heading north and then moving east was crude but effective and also practical, as neither had a map or technical device to help them. What they both had was their training, and both knew how to read the sky at night. Plus they were keenly aware that they had a better chance of survival by only moving at night.

Gorman thought there was an outside chance that some form of overhead drone, satellite, or aircraft might see them. However, without the ability to electronically talk to anyone, they were going to have to improvise . . . and be luckier than they had ever been in their lives.

Their plan was simple: get a truck or car to stop, convince the driver or take over the vehicle, and drive like hell to the border. They walked their bikes now, as at this altitude and as tired as they were, it was all they could do.

Maryam was first to crest the ridge, placing her bike in the middle of the road, and Gorman was next, setting his down forty feet away from Maryam.

The truck driver had been on the road for days. He almost did not see the first bike, swerved left toward the mountain from which the road was cut, saw the second bike, and swerved right while braking.

Coming to a stop, he was surprised to see his door swing open and a large man grab him rather harshly.

116

Instincts

AUSTIN, TEXAS

It was the same story.

Another van. Another commotion. Another disappointment.

Monica sat against the open side door of the Black Hawk on the edge of a parking lot watching the show and drinking a terrible cup of coffee brought to her by Danny Martin. The rest of the gang conferred with the local heads of the FBI, the National Guard, the Texas state troopers, and the Austin PD.

"They forgot to invite the Boy Scouts of America," she said more to herself than to Danny. "What a mess."

"They don't seem to mind," he replied, indicating the media trucks and the row of reporters thrusting microphones toward press officers from the various agencies.

"Shouldn't you be over there getting your fifteen minutes?" she asked. Although Danny also handled intelligence, his friendly disposition had long ago earned him the honor—or the curse—of dealing with journalists to make sure no one mentioned Stark's team.

He smiled. "I'd rather fly this chopper into the middle of an ISIS ambush. At least with them I know where I stand."

"We should be ashamed of ourselves, Danny. Playing right into their hands. So pathetic."

"Don't worry. We're gonna catch them. It's just a matter of when. Sooner or later they *will* make a mistake, and when they do, we'll be right there hiding in the bush ready to expedite their journey to meet their damn virgins."

"No, Danny," she said. "The question is not *when* but *how*—how many Americans will have to die before we—"

"Cruz! Martin! Huddle!" shouted Stark, running toward them holding his satphone and followed by Larson, Ryan, and Hagen.

"What's going on?" asked Monica.

"Dallas," Stark said. "Another van. Initial reports from the bomb squad suggest this might be the real thing. Homeland's routing all available resources there as we speak. They've even begun an evac of the—"

"*Seriously?*" Monica interrupted while the rest of the gang stared at her as if she had three heads. "How long are we going to keep beating this fucking dead horse before—"

Stark whacked her on the head with the phone's long antenna.

"Or," he continued while Monica frowned and rubbed her head, "we can follow up on this call I've just received from the Louisiana National Guard up in Shreveport. A group of cars shot their way through a checkpoint. Homeland's prioritizing Dallas instead, thinking Shreveport's probably another rogue militia group hoarding goods, but my head's with Cruz . . . minus the attitude."

Stark watched Monica hit the speed dial on her satellite phone and put it on speaker so everyone could listen.

"Yes, ASAC Cruz," came the voice of Lisa Jacobson.

"We are running out of time," Monica said. "And we have two real choices: go to Dallas or Louisiana. I'm betting on Louisiana."

"The president has ordered all agencies to support you and Stark, so it's really your call," replied the coordinator of the national security apparatus.

"Then we go to Louisiana, and you can send the rest to Dallas," Monica said, terminating the call.

Colonel Stark pointed at her with the same antenna and said, "One, you made the right call. Two, you saved us a nasty fight, as I was concerned you would fold under the pressure. And three, you have come a long way, Cruz."

Monica stifled a wiseass answer and just nodded.

117

Akbir

**TWO HUNDRED MILES FROM THE
PAKISTANI-INDIAN BORDER**

Akbir was the truck driver's name.

He was simply bored and tired, and took Gorman and Maryam on his truck for the entertainment value. But Gorman was certain that Maryam, even as exhausted as she looked, was probably the best-looking woman Akbir had ever seen not in a magazine or on TV.

Gorman and Maryam knew that a cooperative, relaxed companion/helper was much easier to handle than someone who needed to be forced to assist. So they engaged Akbir—well, mostly Maryam talked to him and in fact sat next to the large truck driver, while Gorman pretended to be sick while listening to their fast-spoken Urdu.

The entire cab smelled as expected, like no one in it had seen a bar of soap in days. Akbir offered his guests tea and fruit that was stored in a cooler in a compartment behind his seat. Both tried not to eat too fast; they were terribly hungry and, thanks to their new friend, the edge had been taken taken off.

As they relaxed a few degrees, Akbir began to sing.

118

Gut Feeling

Anticipation led to reality, followed by disappointment with a sprinkle of anger and a squeeze of frustration.

The site was truly a massacre, bullet-riddled bodies piled on each other, all shot in the head; kids mostly, early twenties. Based on the ammo still in their magazines, they were caught by surprise, slaughtered before they could mount a counterstrike.

"I doubt any of them saw combat," said Larson in his baritone voice, standing next to Monica. Stark and Ryan spoke to local authorities and another detachment of Guardsmen. Hagen stood by himself near the police tape, smoking. Danny tinkered with the Black Hawk.

Beyond the yellow tape a dozen media trucks and a small army of reporters did their thing, thrusting microphones into the faces of those in charge.

"Doesn't look like it," she replied.

"Pups," Larson said. "Probably at the local college last week before all this shit happened."

"Never had a chance," she said, before stretching an index finger toward Hagen. "Still smoking, huh?"

"He tried quitting once," Larson said.

"And?"

"Not good. Drove us crazy. The colonel bought him a carton a week later."

Smiling, she stepped away.

"Where are you going?"

"To think," she replied, arms crossed.

"Don't go too far, kiddo. We'll be on the move soon."

She didn't reply, walking past the group near Stark, ignoring a wink from Ryan, and continuing to the edge of the police tape.

"Those things will kill you, Mickey," she said as she came up to Hagen.

The former SEAL, dressed in black like the rest of the team, his MP7A1 strapped across his back, turned to her and tilted his head with a frown.

"Yeah," she said. "I think we could all use a smoke about now."

Hagen pulled out a pack of HBs from a pocket on his vest and offered her one.

She smiled, remembering the very strong German brand of cigarettes he used to smoke back in the day. "I tried one, remember? Turned green."

He sighed, perhaps even smiled, though it was hard to tell, and put the pack away before taking another drag and looking at the woods.

"Bastards' luck is bound to run out, Mickey," she said. "Sooner or later."

Hagen nodded once, exhaling smoke through his nostrils.

"You know," she added, "I know this isn't the best of times, but I sure missed you guys."

Hagen stared at her, and this time he did smile. But even then he still seemed menacing. Then he looked away again and continued smoking.

Monica patted him on the shoulder. "Glad we had this little talk," she said, walking away.

She followed the police tape for a few hundred feet, staring at the surrounding woods, tall pines mostly, flanking both ends of a road that continued north to Arkansas and endless mountains. Eyewitnesses had seen the four vehicles and provided descriptions to the authorities. APBs had gone out, of course, and this road as well as every artery connecting it to any populated area in a two-hundred-mile radius swarmed with law enforcement. Two of the vehicles had already been found, one in the town of Springfield, on the Louisiana-Arkansas border, and the second one in Hope, Arkansas. Both abandoned on the side of the road, where authorities believed the terrorists swapped vehicles.

But as was the case before, there was no sign of them.

Monica half listened to several motorists gathered by a pair of Louisiana state troopers standing next to their Harleys. She looked absently at them and at their shiny bikes, for a moment missing her Ducati. She had left it parked illegally in front of the J. Edgar Hoover Building.

Hopefully Porter took care of that, she thought, her mind replaying the events she'd heard from eyewitnesses over the past hour again and again.

It all boiled down to several men and maybe one or two women opening fire on the Guardsmen. It had been over in seconds, before the four-car caravan continued north.

Three hours ago.

Bastards could be anywhere by—

Something caught her attention . . . the manner in which one of the men speaking to the state troopers made a sweeping motion with his hand. He had shaped it like an airplane, keeping his middle, index, and ring fingers together while extending his thumb and pinky. He appeared somewhat agitated, like someone trying to convey a point that has fallen on deaf ears.

She walked closer to them.

"Sir," the older of the two troopers said while writing on his notepad, "according to the FAA, the closest airfield is twenty miles to the south. I'm not sure how you could have heard a plane taking off. Plus, all nonessential air traffic is still grounded. You sure it wasn't a boat? There's lots of lakes around and it's fishing season."

"Two planes," the man said. "I said *two* planes taking off, not one . . . Look, I was in the air force. I know what planes taking off sound like, and I heard two of them roughly an hour after the shooting . . . coming from over there." He pointed to the northeast.

"There are no airfields that way, sir."

"And they were single-engine turboprops," the man insisted.

"And I have written it all down, Mr. . . . Bergeron," replied the trooper, checking his notes. "We will collect all eyewitness accounts and present them to the task force this evening."

Are you fucking kidding me?

Monica's head nearly exploded at the mention of another task force. The likelihood of more PowerPoint slides, all properly formatted, nearly made her go postal. For a moment she imagined overworked staffs and their bosses, and perhaps even their bosses' bosses, going through them. And it probably was happening all across this country. Politicians arguing endlessly as to what had merit and what didn't while jockeying for position, playing the Washington game in its most ugly form, just as she had seen it in Houston.

And all the while the terrorists are getting closer to detonating another bomb right under their fat bureaucratic ass.

Before she could help herself, Monica crashed the troopers' interview.

"Mr. Bergeron," she said, walking up to them. "Exactly where and when did you hear those planes?"

Before he could reply, the older trooper turned to her. "Ma'am, thanks, but we've got this. We're taking statements and—"

"I don't have time to deal with you," she said, flashing her ASAC badge. "Now, move along."

The troopers shared a glance before stomping away toward their superiors gathered by Stark and the other chiefs. The older one hissed, "We'll *fucking* see about that."

Bergeron, a man in his early fifties with a scraggy white beard, dressed in plain jeans, sneakers, a T-shirt, and a New Orleans Saints baseball cap, turned his wide-eyed stare to her, a mix of surprise, amusement, and even admiration.

"You don't see that every day," he mumbled.

"You from this area, sir?"

"Yep. Lived here all my life."

"Okay, sir . . . please tell me *everything*."

"Is it possible that you collectively and individually do not comprehend the danger?" Stark said to everyone, rhetorically.

He was surrounded by the National Guard captain, sheriffs from three different cities, and the Shreveport chief of police. There were also agents from various Homeland Security stations, plus more FBI—all while a dozen camera crews filmed the event from behind yellow police tape.

These people simply did not get the danger they were in. Stark was disappointed with the Louisiana National Guard for letting the assholes slip right past their roadblock. But he was enraged at the FBI guys from Shreveport for not relaying the call made by a Taylor PD officer earlier that day. He had reported four vehicles with armed men shooting their way through the crowd during a riot by a Walmart in Tyler, Texas.

How could you not relay that information to Washington? Stark had asked.

You realize how many reports we've gotten every day since New York? the local G-man had retorted.

Stark had nearly blown his head off.

He breathed deeply and continued. "If we capture or kill the terrorists we're all supposed to be hunting, then and only then will I even consider . . ." He paused when he lost the attention of three guys from Homeland. They started chatting with two FBI ASACs from Shreveport, including the one who had ignored the TPD officer.

"Fuck this," he said, walking away from them and hitting the speed dial on his satellite phone.

"Yes, Colonel?" answered Lisa Jacobson.

"We're wasting time again, Lisa. Get my location from the phone GPS and clear a path for us. The locals here, and I mean everyone with a badge and a gun, either has not heard of the president's order or has and does not care."

Stark hung up, and thirty seconds later heard five phones ringing near him.

His eyes gravitated from the federal agents answering their phones to his team standing by the Black Hawk, all accounted for except . . .

"Where the hell is Cruz?" he yelled.

119

Hog Ride

NORTH OF SHREVEPORT, LOUISIANA

It took a while to find the gravel road Bergeron had shown her on the GPS map on her phone, veering to the east from the main road.

Roughly eight miles beyond it she came up to a closed gate with a large sign warning:

PRIVATE PROPERTY

VIOLATORS WILL BE SHOT

SURVIVORS WILL BE SHOT AGAIN

She had gone around it easily with the Harley, but when she finally reached the clearing, the place didn't resemble an airfield but more a flat and grassy meadow. It was roughly a half mile square with a large camouflage canvas stretched at one corner, hiding from the sky a pair of fuel trucks similar to the ones back in Carrizo Springs.

She checked her phone, noticed the half-dozen calls and texts from Stark, and ignored them while accessing the online FAA sectionals for this region. There were no wind socks, hangars, or anything that would remotely associate it with an airfield—at least from the sky.

So it's not on the map.

She inspected it from the edge of the gravel path before deciding to text the GPS coordinates to Stark along with BRING EVERYONE!

She considered waiting for the colonel and team but a little voice kept screaming at her that every second mattered. So she chose instead to walk the perimeter, scouting the place, making sure it was empty.

Satisfied, she stepped onto the deserted field, walking it twice in each direction. She inspected the camouflaged hangar and the fuel trucks. The smell of gas suggested very recent use.

Already breaking a sweat in the late-afternoon sun, she wiped the perspiration from her brows with the sleeve of her SWAT uniform and stared at the ground. It had not rained in the past few hours, allowing her to see the tracks of four vehicles driving to the sheltered hangar and back out.

Bastards were dropped off and the vehicles driven to different locations as decoys, she thought.

Anger swelled in her gut at their cleverness, ruthlessness, and nimbleness—and at the gullibility of her country's combined law enforcement. Some of them were still screwing around in Dallas. The rest either tracked down the abandoned vehicles or prepared Power-Point slides for—

"Focus," she whispered, shaking the frustrating thoughts away.

Next to those tracks she noticed wider ones that could belong to a pair of airplane main landing gears with a narrower track in between made by the smaller nose wheels. They had arrived from the south. The planes made deep tracks when touching down, before decelerating and taxiing into the camouflaged hangar.

They aligned with the tracks from the fueling trucks, before the planes taxied out of the camouflaged hangar and down the wide field in an easterly direction.

Takeoff runs.

She followed the tracks all the way to the edge of the field. At first they were deep—more so than on the way in—carrying the entire weight of each plane plus fuel, and passengers.

Plus one nuclear bomb at large.

The tracks became shallower as wings picked up the load during takeoff, before disappearing altogether a couple hundred feet before the tree line.

And that's where she stood, staring at the eastern sky as the sun sank below the horizon behind her, when the Black Hawk arrived. It circled the field twice before landing fifty feet from her while kicking up a cloud of dust.

Stark emerged through the swirling haze looking large and mean, a sound-suppressed MP7A1 clutched in his right hand and his satphone in the left. Ryan and Larson materialized behind him, also holding their weapons of choice, but remaining a respectful distance from the obviously very pissed-off colonel.

"So, taking in the local fauna, maybe picking damn blueberries while I'm . . . right in the middle of a hunt for a terrorist group with a nuclear bomb!" he shouted over the noise of the rotor, his craggy face twisting in rage.

"Colonel, I—"

"Tell me you found the device! Tell me some fucking thing that helps me understand why I don't leave your ass here and finish this without you!"

"Well, as a matter of fact, I—"

"Oh, and you stole a man's hog! A guy's ride! What the fuck, Cruz?"

Ryan and Larson stood behind him, making faces at her while trying damn hard not to laugh out loud. A few steps behind them Hagen lit up a cigarette, exhaling through his nostrils while watching the show.

"Just *borrowed* the hog, sir. Put it to good use." She pointed at the Harley parked by the edge of the road.

"All right, Cruz," Stark said, lowering his voice. "Make all of this worth my while. What the hell's going on?"

"They're airborne, Colonel."

"Airborne? How? We checked all of the airports and airfields in a—"

"Not this one." She pointed at the camouflaged hangar on the other side of the field.

He glared at it a while, before staring back at her, frowning. "I'll be damned. We didn't even see it during the flyover."

"That would be the point," she replied, turning to the tire marks disappearing where she stood. "Bastards are definitely airborne again . . . and there's no wind, so based on the direction they took off, I think they're heading east."

As they headed for the chopper, Ryan Hunt walked past her and whispered, "Looks like it's your world, Miss Cruz, and we're just living in it." And he didn't turn around, knowing Monica was already giving him the middle-finger salute.

120

Rush

TENNESSEE MOUNTAINS

She knew it would happen sooner or later.

Perhaps it was because of the way he talked or handled himself, or commanded his men, or even killed.

With power.

With resolution.

Without remorse.

Just like Malik.

Or it could be the overarching effort he had orchestrated toward her mission, going beyond Atiq's financial compensation. He had acted without regard for his own safety. He had formulated and executed a strategy of diversions that had allowed them to get this far, and possibly even make it the rest of the way.

Salma wasn't exactly sure why.

Maybe she longed for the touch of a real man one final time, someone who could please her. But somewhere in the middle of the mountains, as darkness engulfed them, she had given herself to Miguel Montoya.

This wasn't love, and it certainly wasn't gratitude. But it wasn't pure lust either, or the use of the best weapon in her arsenal to accomplish a higher goal, like when conquering that Norwegian captain.

Perhaps it was a form of friendship, forged by the unyielding desire to destroy a common enemy—an enemy far more powerful, that he had managed to outfox with elegance and strength. And done so while operating in their territory with the entire nation on high alert.

Salma felt that strength enveloping her as they moved as one, the constant droning of the turboprop the only reality in the rear cabin of the Cessna Caravan. For a moment she forgot about the risks, about the enemy in close pursuit—about the countless Pakistanis who had been killed in the past days at the hands of the enemy.

She shut it all out while lowering her hips, hands on his chest, fingers tensed as shadows rushed past the windows. The pilot hugged the treetops lining the bottom of unseen canyons as Montoya grabbed her shoulders, her breasts, squeezing, eyes closed.

They shifted, bowed, and shifted again, clasping each other as the plane turned and dipped, before climbing and pitching once more, constantly adjusting, twisting, tracking the narrow rift between towering peaks.

Neither uttered a word, moist skin sliding, aware not of the danger of flying in a gorge at night but of their own passion, of their labored breathing. They let everything else go as they tensed, climaxing, arms wrapped around heated bodies, shivering. They gradually relaxed, quietly falling, chests heaving as he hugged her from behind.

Salma placed her hands over his as they embraced her chest, warm, tender, remaining like that for a long time, half asleep and half awake, spooning, cuddling just as she used to do with Malik.

Moonlight grazed the rushing vegetation beyond the windowpane, casting trembling shadows over them.

"Come back with me," he whispered after a while.

"I . . . I can't," she mumbled. "I—"

"Let them finish," he added. "They can finish it."

"But—"

"Your job is done."

"Miguel, I—"

"You are too valuable, my lovely Salma. Too important . . . to me."

"But I can't abandon my—"

She gasped as he entered her again, his hands dropping to her abdomen as she reached behind her, eyes shut, clasping his hips, his breath caressing the back of her neck.

"Please," he hissed in her ear as she shuddered, as she swallowed and panted and swallowed again, breathing through parted lips. "Please come back with me."

But she was no longer listening, no longer aware of anything but the rush of sensations boiling through her, blanking her thoughts. They propelled her beyond her control, shattering years of detachment, pulling her back from muscle memory and into the reality of a moment she wished would never end. But it did, and she collapsed, exhausted.

And so did he. His heavy breathing slowly steadied, and he quickly fell into deep sleep.

Salma took far longer before her heart stopped racing.

Her mind finally regained focus, transcending passion, and facing her reality.

In the twilight of the cabin, mountains dashing past like silent ghosts, Salma sat up and held the remote control in between her breasts while staring out the window.

"I'm sorry, Miguel," she whispered in the dark. "I just . . . can't."

But he was no longer listening.

121

Kelnor

PAKISTANI-INDIAN BORDER

In his long CIA career, Bill Gorman had seen his share of desolate areas. But as they approached the border he decided this rocky and mountainous terrain was truly the land that God forgot.

Ten hours, two stops to refuel his truck, three to pee, and one to nap for thirty minutes.

There were no gas stations in these mountains. Akbir, like everyone else who drove this range, carried everything he needed.

"Where will we cross the border?" asked Maryam.

"A shithole called Kelnor," Akbir replied, scratching the thick beard running down his throat before adding, "Where I pay the guards to let me cross. Today the payment will be cigarettes and winter parkas . . .

but the payment will not be enough to get you and your American across."

Gorman frowned at Akbir's tone, which could be interpreted in a hundred different ways.

"Figured you were smart, Akbir, and a survivor," Gorman started in his heavily accented but fluent Urdu. "Both are necessary to drive this truck up here between these dangerous borders. My name is Bill Gorman. I work for the CIA and I need to get my wife and myself across that border. War is on us and I have information that can make it less damaging to your country and mine . . . but we must get to the American embassy in New Delhi or to a phone to make a call."

Akbir pulled the truck over, reached down, and grabbed a Makarov pistol. He didn't point it. Just held it in his left hand.

Maryam relaxed, knowing what she would do if the weapon or Akbir moved in the wrong direction.

"My family was killed by the Taliban," Akbir said, his eyes sunken in his weathered face. "I have worked for your country indirectly, Mr. Gorman, smuggling goods . . . contraband for your soldiers, mostly cigarettes and alcohol, plus marijuana and some opium."

Gorman didn't reply.

"That is correct," he continued. "I am a black market smuggler. A little risky but it is quite profitable. And if I don't do it, others will. Your people have always paid me well, not always been honest but they always paid."

Gorman continued regarding this very strange man.

"I believe you," Akbir continued. "Something about you and your wife rings true—enough that I believe no one would admit to be CIA on this night of nights. Even up in this range, the explosions I observed in the distance . . . I imagined who dropped those bombs."

As Gorman waited for the Pakistani to make his move, Akbir handed the weapon to him, handle first.

122

Saudis

Tristan rode with the Saudi ambassador in the rear of his silver Mercedes stretch limo with diplomatic plates, sitting across from him.

He looked about the luxurious custom-made interior—lots of rosewood, leather, and the latest in electronics—the very best money could buy.

It was classy, it was expensive, but above all, it was ostentatious—the Saudi way.

The ambassador, Prince Assad bin Saud, a direct descendant of the king, had always leaned toward Western clothes. Tonight he was dressed in a tailored gray suit, Italian shoes, and a gold Patek Philippe watch, which he checked absently before crossing his legs.

Tristan had first met the Saudi royal during his nonprofit days, when Tristan had attempted to set up a shelter for abused women in Riyadh after Saudi authorities failed to manage their own safe houses. Prince Assad had been minister of interior in those days. He had genuinely tried to help Tristan's cause after his sister was severely beaten by her abusive husband. But Assad got caught between trying to do the right thing and his government's traditional views on the subject. In the end, Assad was forced to throw every conceivable roadblock to keep Tristan from obtaining the required permits. Meanwhile, women of all ages in the Saudi capital continued to be abused, neglected, forced into unwanted marriages for the benefit of their fathers, and beaten when uttering the slightest protest. So Tristan had done the only thing he could do: he had devoted a full chapter of his book *A Trail of Tears* to the cruel way women were treated in Saudi Arabia. And in doing so, he created quite the stir among the Saudi royalty.

"Well?" the prince asked. "What was so important that it couldn't wait for normal working hours?"

"This," he replied, pulling out his iPad and handing it to him.

"What am I supposed to—"

"Just press Play."

The prince watched the video. It included all of the incriminating evidence from Prince Khalid being caught in an ISIS encampment plus the footage from the grab in Paris, and the interrogations of the prince and the princess.

"What . . . what is the meaning of this?" he asked. "Where is Prince Khalid? And where is the princess?"

"They're both safe . . . with us," Tristan replied.

"Where?"

"Like I said. They're safe with us, just like these videos are also safe with us . . . or the fact that your government funded the very individuals who attacked New York City."

Prince Assad leaned forward. "Wait a minute! That is—"

"The ugly truth. And at this moment my government is reviewing a Saudi Arabia strike package similar to the one our coalition has been delivering against Pakistan and ISIS."

Color drained from Prince Assad's face. "What . . . hold on. My government—"

"Your government has much to answer for."

"I . . . I need to process this. I need to discuss it with Riyadh."

"Yeah . . . you do that," Tristan replied. "You have two hours."

"*Two hours?* But . . . it's the middle of the night in Riyadh . . . everyone is—"

"You either interrupt their beauty sleep . . . or the bombs will . . . and then you'll have no one left to discuss anything with."

"The world will never condone an attack against—"

"The world will keep its head down, just as it has for Pakistan. You have financed the terrorists who attacked us—who destroyed New York City. The world won't care what happens to Pakistan or Saudi Arabia as long as it also doesn't happen to them. Face it, Assad: no one really likes the Saudis, with all of your extravagance and arrogance . . . except the Saudis. So you won't be missed, though we will be sure to avoid hitting the oil fields and the refineries so we can run them afterwards. You know . . . to the victor belong the spoils."

Tristan let that sink in a moment, before adding, "Your country is responsible for financing the New York and Bagram attacks, just as it is responsible for funding the bastards who have smuggled another bomb into this country."

"Another bomb?"

Tristan paused again. For as far back as he could remember he had wanted to make the Saudis suffer for their role in 9/11. He wanted to stretch the moment for as long as possible.

"You have two hours to give us its location," he finally said. "Or I'm afraid the video will go viral, followed by a White House press conference announcing your government's involvement . . . and by the time we're finished with you, Saudi Arabia will be little more than a pile of fused sand."

123

Just One More

LOWER MANHATTAN

He had fallen into a routine. Climbing stairs, breaking down doors, clearing rooms, and occasionally finding a survivor, always unconscious. Ray would hoist the victim over his shoulders and head back down as many flights of stairs as necessary—typically below the sixth or seventh floor. There, he would pass the victim to one of the growing number of rotating first responders in shiny yellow vinyl suits. And then it was back up again, using the Halligan and the fire axe now as walking sticks.

His thighs burned.

His lungs could barely keep up with an effort that grew steadily more difficult with each passing hour.

He had already vomited twice. The last time blood mixed in the bile.

It was happening. As large and muscular as he was, molecular cells were no longer reproducing. His body was no longer replacing the ones that perished to the radiation. And the symptoms would only get worse—much worse.

But he persisted.

Floor after floor.

Apartment after apartment.

Hour after hour.

He pushed all other thoughts aside except for saving one more soul. Just one more.

An elderly woman collapsed on her kitchen floor; a kid unconscious in bed; a man who'd fallen down the stairs and knocked himself out.

One by one Ray carried them down to a safe floor, depositing them in the hands of the other first responders, their eyes meeting briefly across clear plastic masks. They all knew what he was doing and why. And they let him because no one else really could—at least not without knowingly or willingly signing their own death sentences.

He only had one floor left—the penthouse level on the thirty-eighth floor.

But he passed out just as he was about to reach it.

124

Trust Me

PAKISTANI-INDIAN BORDER

The plan was weak, but there were few options.

Gorman and Maryam would be dropped off close to the checkpoint. Akbir would continue to the border and negotiate as he always did. But this time he would cause an argument, creating a distraction so they could walk around the checkpoint and meet a mile or so down the road.

The truck slowed around the final bend in the road before reaching the border guard station. A few yards from the searchlights just beyond the turn, Gorman jumped out, followed by Maryam. They rushed across the narrow road and around a mound bordering the turn, stopping in twenty yards and pausing to observe.

The truck continued, tires kicking up gravel and dust visible in the intense yellow lights that quickly engulfed it.

Indian border guards dressed in light brown uniforms and armed with AK-47s blocked the way as Akbir brought his truck up to the gate.

The Pakistani smuggler got out, holding up his usual bribe, but as the guards lowered their weapons, he started to shout, picking a fight, per the plan.

Maryam moved out first now, in a deep crouch. Gorman followed, taking advantage of the distraction to attempt a border crossing roughly five hundred yards from the military post. They used the cover of darkness, the sparse vegetation, rocky outcrops—and Akbir's screams—to mask their movements.

They paused after a minute as the shouting intensified, though it appeared as if the guards were trying to calm down the agitated smuggler.

Surveying the sloping terrain as it rose toward the hilltop marking the border, Gorman stared at the commotion down by the road, under the intense lights. He hoped those same searchlights that allowed the soldiers to guard the road would also kill their night vision, preventing them from spotting him and Maryam.

Only one way to find out, he thought, contemplating the final three hundred yards.

Maryam's brown eyes flashed understanding. From here to the border there were just a couple of outcrops and no shrubs—nothing to provide cover. But then again, that was the whole point of Indian authorities setting up the outpost at this location. It provided the guards with a good vantage point and line of sight.

They moved as quickly as possible, but without enough stealth.

Shots rang out thirty seconds later, just as they reached the first clump of boulders. A pair of rounds bounced off a rock and whistled skyward.

Gorman pushed Maryam down, but he didn't return fire, believing that the guards were shooting in their direction but could not—

The 9mm round spun him around to his right, smacking him in the left shoulder.

Damn.

He fell on his side, his shoulder numb.

Maryam began to scream but Gorman stopped her, motioning her to stay low while cringing in pain and whispering, "Trust me."

Slowly, and while inhaling deeply, Gorman rose above the cover of jagged rocks, only to be hit again, this time in the left leg.

And he still didn't shoot back.

"Bill!" Maryam screamed as spotlights converged on their hideout.

Instead, Gorman dropped the gun and put up his hand.

125

Farewells

OUTSIDE LYNCHBURG, VIRGINIA

Farewells had never been her thing.

As thick-skinned as she was, hardened by the sacrifices she had to make in body, mind, and soul for the greater good of Pakistan, saying good-bye for the last time had always been a weakness.

And this time around it felt worse than seeing Malik standing by the gangway connecting the dock to the supertanker. They had smiled, embraced, and kissed. They had whispered final words of love and encouragement, realizing they would soon be rejoined in paradise.

But as she stood alone with Montoya by the side of one of the Cessna Caravans, his face somber, sadness shadowing his eyes, Salma realized she would never see him again, in this life or the next.

Mixed feelings whirled inside her mind for this man she hardly knew, yet who knew her better than most men in her turbulent life. There was something about him that could not be explained—something beyond his looks. Maybe it was his power, his confidence. Or perhaps the way he'd made her explode in that rear cabin. Montoya had ripped through her layers of training and pride, and stared straight into the eyes of a little orphan girl from Karachi.

But she still told him no.

She still watched him get in his plane and fly back into the mountains.

Closing her eyes as forested hills swallowed the distant sounds of engines, Salma steeled herself for the final phase of her mission. She thought about how far she had come, sailing halfway across the Atlantic and facing near disaster at the hands of African rebels. She remembered escaping the American Coast Guard inspection zone by diverting south, taking over the tanker, even battling that crazy American helicopter.

The images of the past week flashed in her mind, from the treacherous mountain pass into Monterrey to her initial meeting with Montoya. The flight across the desert had been as memorable as the ride through Texas and Louisiana before the unforgettable crossing of the Tennessee mountains.

She turned her back to the distant peaks over her right shoulder, just as she had turned the page on the supertanker when setting foot on that Mexican beach. Salma stared at the sun rising over the eastern horizon, marking the dawn of a new day—of her final one in this world.

And the start of a new life with Malik.

She walked toward the large delivery truck and two sedans parked by the dirt road at the edge of the meadow. Azis and Omar waited for her, along with the rest of the warriors who had accompanied her halfway across the world in this historic journey.

She put a hand on the large man's shoulder, gazing into his eyes.

"Are you ready, my brother?" she asked.

"We are," he replied while Omar and the rest of the men mumbled prayers.

A man dressed in a business suit minus the tie walked up to them. He was tall and handsome, with a closely trimmed beard and dark, intelligent eyes that reminded her of Malik. Three men, similarly dressed, followed him. One had a slight limp and wore a brace on his left wrist.

"Welcome to Virginia, Salma," he said. "My name is Amir Dham, a dear friend of Dr. Gadai and your local support for the remainder of your journey. I also own this land. Those men over there are part of my cell and will remain behind to cover our tracks in case Uncle Sam is watching." He pointed at the sky.

Salma nodded while two dozen men hauled RPGs and machine guns to the tree line on the western end of the clearing.

"And those gentlemen by the vehicles are my most trusted friends." He pointed to the men standing by the driver's side doors of the truck and three sedans. "They will drive you and your team the rest of the way."

126

Fertile Valley

LOWER MANHATTAN

By the time Ray Kazemi came around, he was facedown on the stairs between the thirty-seventh and thirty-eighth floors.

Slowly, with considerable effort, he rolled over and managed to sit up, breathing, wincing as pain stabbed his shoulders.

He had vomited inside his mask again—more blood and bile—and this time he had been damn lucky not to drown in it.

Removing it and clearing it while taking a deep breath, he looked up and realized he had fallen almost a full flight of stairs from the landing above him.

Albeit in a world of hurt—from his head to his ankles—nothing seemed broken.

He thought about securing the mask back on, but the stench was unbearable.

And what's the fucking point?

He had been exposed to lethal radiation for over four days since walking out of Madison Square Garden, and in the past twelve hours it had been nearly impossible to keep anything down.

He was weak. He was tired. He was terribly dehydrated, and short of getting himself hooked up to an IV, there was no way he could replenish his lost fluids.

But doing so meant abandoning his task, capitulating. It meant turning his back on the reason God had given him a few extra days.

Certainly not to wither away on some Red Cross cot.

"You survived for a reason," he mumbled, stretching each limb before standing, right hand reaching for the Halligan, left hand clutching the metal railing for support.

How long have I been out?

He checked the dosimeter, ignoring the massive amount of radiation it displayed, and stared at the digital clock.

Three hours.

And not surprisingly, no one had come to his rescue—and no one ever would.

Ray had been on his own the moment he'd crossed the seventh-floor threshold, the highest level that any of the other first responders could ever reach, given their thirty-minute curfews.

He reached the top floor and spent the next hour checking each apartment, finding them all empty.

Too hot to keep wearing the vinyl suit, he unzipped it and walked out of it, wearing only a pair of gym shorts and a plain white T-shirt.

Enjoying the cool air, he snagged a couple of bottles of water from the pantry of the last apartment. Deciding he needed to rest before heading back down, Ray climbed the last flight of stairs leading to the roof.

The landlord had landscaped it to resemble a park, including benches overlooking the Manhattan skyline in all four directions.

Light-headed, he almost collapsed on a bench facing south, but managed to sit up as a wave of nausea swept through him.

Leaning forward, he vomited blood and bile between his legs, heaving uncontrollably. His throat burned and his eyes clouded with tears.

Slowly, he sat back, taking a few deep breaths. He opened a bottle of water and poured its contents over his head before drinking the second bottle.

His mind grew cloudy again, like the cumulus hovering over the demolished section of the city. Fires still burned in many areas, their billowing columns of smoke still shifting west, toward the Long Island Sound.

Minutes passed and he tried to stand but lay sideways on the bench instead, unable to hold up his head.

And that's how his mind recorded the final minutes of his life—sideways.

He stared at the burnt façades of buildings amidst columns of smoke. It was all gray, dark, and lifeless. Even the sky was the color of gunmetal from the haze slowly blowing in the breeze.

He stared at it as his heart gave, as his vision tunneled.

The stark, desolate skyline with its charcoal spirals of smoldering ash and smog slowly faded away. It was replaced by vivid hues, by the greenest green and the bluest blue, sharp, with infinite detail. Demolished buildings morphed into lush mountains and fertile valleys; barren streets into meandering rivers and meadows.

In the middle of it all, he saw the warmest of lights, soothing, comforting, and welcoming.

Ray Kazemi closed his eyes as it enveloped him.

127

Footing the Bill

"They admit to the funding, but he claims they don't know the location of the bomb," Tristan said after an aide showed him to Wright's office and closed the door.

"And you believe him?" Wright sat behind his desk, fingers interlaced on his lap, as if he were praying.

"Not sure what to believe," Tristan replied, shrugging before sitting down and crossing his legs, smoothing his tie with two fingers. "But I am sure *they* believe we're going to hit them. The ambassador was scared out of his mind."

"Good," Wright said. "That was the idea. Put the fear of God— or *Allah*—in them."

"Now what?"

"Now nothing. Don't answer his calls for a while. Keep him and the rest of his kind looking at the sky for a while, waiting for it to fall on their pompous ass."

"So we make them sweat it out . . . then what?"

Still in the prayer position, Wright pursed his lips, before leaning forward and staring Tristan in the eye. "Okay, look, here's the deal. We didn't expect the Saudis to know much besides admitting funding ISIS. I mean, they've done it for years to keep those fanatics from blowing up their fancy palaces and pretty skyscrapers, right? But now we've caught them with their hand in the cookie jar. So first we make them believe we're going to turn their beautiful capital inside out. But when this is over—and one way or another it *will* be over pretty damn soon—the president will call a very nervous Saudi king and present her . . . demands."

"Demands?"

Wright shrugged. "If they can't help us find the missing bomb, then we're going to hit the bastards where it really hurts."

"Hit them?" Tristan said. "But I thought you said—"

"We're going to make them pay for rebuilding everything that was destroyed."

Tristan opened his eyes wide.

"You mean . . ."

"They'll foot the bill for rebuilding New York. And that's just the beginning."

"The beginning?"

"At the risk of sounding crude, Tristan, from now on Saudi Arabia, Kuwait, Qatar, and whatever's left of Pakistan, are going to be . . . our bitches."

128

Making Friends

KENTUCKY-VIRGINIA BORDER

They had spotted the Cessna Caravans cruising in tandem at 180 knots deep in a rift heading west, well below radar. Hidden in the ground clutter, they were invisible but to the cameras of a fleet of Predators looking down at the mountainous terrain from various altitudes. Their discerning digital eyes possessed the resolution to spot the nearly invisible dark silhouettes against a sea of dark green—just barely.

But they had located them.

F-22 Raptors from the 27th Fighter Squadron out of Langley Air Force Base, Virginia, forced them to land in a field outside the town of Big Stone Gap, nestled in the middle of the Jefferson National

Forest. Unfortunately, the actual Pakistani terrorists and the bomb were not aboard.

Stark jumped out of the Black Hawk first, followed by Monica, Ryan, and the rest of the group. Bending slightly under the rotor downwash swirling the tall grass, the group ran toward the Cessna Caravans.

Cruisers and bikes from the Virginia state troopers, Humvees from the Virginia National Guard, and FBI SUVs and two helicopters surrounded the planes.

F-22s continued circling overhead.

"Chance to make new friends, Miss Cruz!" Ryan screamed over the rotor noise.

She ignored him, following Stark to the law enforcement assemblage standing by the planes next to a row of men on their knees, wrists flex-cuffed behind their backs.

To her utter disappointment, the DHS lead was once more Hollis Gallagher, and he was once again dressed as if he were headed for the opera. She kept her finger on the White House speed dial button and let Gallagher see it.

Monica exchanged a glance with him before leaving Stark dealing with the clown and the rest of the chiefs. She was more interested in the Hispanic men on their knees, and immediately recognized the face of Miguel Montoya.

"Hey, asshole," she said, standing in front of him.

Slowly, the stocky drug lord lifted his gaze, regarding her with indifference.

"Where are they?"

Montoya slowly shook his head, apparently already bored with her.

"You have no idea who I am," she added.

The drug lord had already looked away, toward Gallagher and team.

"I'm the motherfucker who killed Alfonso and the rest of that sorry-ass group of men you sent after us in Monterrey."

That got his attention. Montoya glared at her and clenched his jaw. But still, he said nothing.

"Yeah," Monica added. "You're pissed off now, aren't you, cartel boy?"

Leaning down and locking eyes with him, she said, "I'm going to ask you nicely one more time: Where . . . did . . . you . . . *fucking* . . . take . . . Salma?"

Montoya blinked at the mention of the name, but grunted and spat by her feet.

She pulled out her gun and shot him in the right knee. Actually, her round just grazed it, but still inflicted a painful flesh wound.

Montoya screamed, falling on his side.

"One more time, asshole," she said, kneeling next to him. "Where is Salma?"

"Hey!" shouted Gallagher, running to her, followed by Stark and the chiefs of the Guard, the troopers, and even some FBI ASACs she had never seen before, probably from the Lexington field office. "You can't do that!"

"Yeah?" Monica said, pointing the gun at the other knee. "Watch me."

"Stop right there, ASAC Cruz," Gallagher insisted, "or I'll have you removed. Mr. Montoya has requested legal counsel and full immunity in exchange for his cooperation."

"Are you fucking kidding me?" she asked as a National Guard medic rushed toward them hauling a case. "This guy dropped off nuclear-armed terrorists somewhere in the area and you're going to fall for this bullshit delay tactic? How many times is it going to take before you get your head out of your—"

"That's enough, Cruz," said Stark while the medic bandaged Montoya's knee. "We're getting the White House on the line now. Go help the chief." He pointed at Larson, who stood with Ryan, holding his electronics gadgets by the steps to one of the Caravans. Danny stood behind the colonel, looking concerned, while Hagen stoically regarded the show from a respectful distance while smoking one of his German cigarettes.

"But—"

"The White House will sort these asswipes out," Stark said, dropping his voice, signaling the end of his patience. "You stay focused. Remember, because of you we have gotten this far . . . Do not lose your shit now. I'll handle this. Now go."

Cursing under her breath while holstering her Glock, Monica stomped toward Larson, who handed Ryan a crisp twenty-dollar bill.

"Who's the loser now?" Ryan said, winking at Monica while pocketing the cash.

"Shit," mumbled the chief. "Guess you were right, lover boy."

Monica regarded them for a moment. "Right about what?"

"Romeo here bet me you wouldn't last a minute before stirring the pot," added Larson.

"Fuck you both," she said. "Bastard's getting lawyered up while those terrorists are on the loose and that DHS clown is falling right into their plan—and you two are—"

"About to do some real damage, Miss Cruz," said Ryan as Larson stepped inside one of the Caravans. "Come. Let's go kick some ass."

Confused and downright frustrated, she took a deep breath and stomped inside the plane after them and into the cockpit. Ryan sat in the copilot's seat. Larson pointed Monica to the pilot's seat while he knelt in between them, powering up the avionics.

"What are you doing?" she asked.

"Bypassing your new friends," said Ryan.

"What?"

"Just zip the chatter for a moment, kiddo," Larson added, hands reaching under the control panel and freeing a bundle of wires. His fingers ran through them, selecting three of them. He clipped the alligator leads of probes to connect them to one of his gadgets, which resembled a thick tablet computer but with lots of buttons on the sides.

The Caravan's dual Garmin GPS screens came on in vivid color, displaying their current location. Larson began to push buttons on the control panel of the Caravan's top GPS unit, pulling up different menus, before glancing over at his partner in crime.

"Sneaky bastards," whispered Ryan.

"Told ya," Larson said, thrusting his right hand at him, palm facing up.

The sniper frowned, reached in a pocket, and produced the same twenty-dollar bill, slapping it onto the chief's hand.

"Could anyone tell me what the hell is going on?"

"The chief," Ryan said as Larson pocketed the money. "He bet me a twenty that the pilots would have deleted their GPS track to keep anyone poking into their system from knowing where they had come from. He was . . . well, right."

"Of course, lover boy. It's electronics. You need to stick to matters of the heart with your little girlfriend."

"I'm not his fucking girlfriend!" she snapped, before asking, "So . . . after all that we still don't know where the hell they came from?"

"Not exactly," Ryan replied. "The assholes were trying to be smart."

"But not smart enough," added Larson, switching his attention to the bulky tablet connected to the bundle of wires, fingering the touch screen.

"I'm still not following."

Larson ignored her, and so did Ryan. They worked on the unit, touching this and turning that, plugging and unplugging connectors in apparent random fashion while whispering tech jargon back and forth.

Monica grew more annoyed. She hated being ignored, and especially being fed information piecemeal. And these guys knew exactly how to do it, just as they had back in Afghanistan, controlling information to the point that her head would explode.

Just as her blood pressure rose in her temples, throbbing behind her eyes, Larson's screen displayed a GPS map of their current location. Only this time a light purple line connected it to a spot just outside of Lynchburg, Virginia.

Ryan turned to her and grinned. She wanted to slap him but the man was just too damn handsome.

"See, Miss Cruz," he began while Larson continued fiddling with the gear. "When you delete something from a GPS unit—or any computer or smartphone for that matter—the system doesn't really clear the contents of that memory location, only the *pointer* or link to that location. You need to write *over* it by programming a new destination to erase it. So I just read it back out, loaded the coordinates into my tablet, and *voila*. We now know the last location where those clowns flew out of."

"Which has to be the place where they dropped off the terrorists," said Monica, finally understanding.

Ryan looked over at Larson while standing up. "See, I told you there was a brain inside that pretty head."

"Yeah," the chief replied, stowing his gear. "Too bad she's got that damn attitude."

"I know, but she's so damn cute," said Ryan. "And there's that bikini cut you guys keep telling me about that—"

"Hey, motherfuckers, I'm right here and this is a real gun."

But they were already out of the cockpit and walking down the center aisle while arguing about whether or not Monica looked like some exotic dancer in Colombia last year. Reaching the exit hatch, they jumped out.

She scrambled after them but chose to remain by Hagen so she could decompress a bit. The former SEAL was on his third cigarette while Larson and Ryan walked up to Danny and the colonel, the latter on his sat phone, probably still talking to the White House.

"Safer from here, Mickey?"

Hagen nodded ever so slightly, taking a drag and exhaling skyward.

The group conferred for a while with Gallagher after Stark hung up the satphone and went over to speak with Montoya. The cartel boss no longer wore flex-cuffs and stood with obvious effort by the DHS lead. A deal had obviously been brokered, and that just made her blood pressure rise back up to the point that her eyeballs hurt.

"I should just gut that no-good bastard right now. And as for Gallagher, I'm going to chop off his balls for the benefit of mankind. People like him shouldn't be allowed to procreate."

Hagen pulled out his massive blade and handed it to her. Before she knew it she was feeling the weight, which approximated that of a machete, taking a few swings. It was certainly one hell of a wicked weapon, very balanced. The serrated edge and hooked tip were designed to latch on to organs and entrails to inflict more damage on the way out. Once again, she was glad this man was on her—

"Too big for you, Cruz," said Stark, holding his satphone in his right hand as he walked up to them with the rest of the team in tow.

Gallagher and some FBI agents escorted a limping Montoya to one of the FBI helicopters while the rest of his cartel gang remained in place by the Caravans.

She frowned and handed the knife back to Hagen. "What's the word?"

"Montoya got a presidential pardon in exchange for the whereabouts of the—"

"Seriously? Are you—"

Stark lifted his phone, antenna pointed at her head, and she quickly shut up, crossing her arms.

"Montoya claims he dropped them off at a field near Charleston, West Virginia, and they boarded a couple of large Chevy vans. Black, he said, headed for Maryland. He won't say more until his attorneys draft the official papers, which will happen within the hour. But we can all guess the target is probably D.C. The president is boarding Marine One headed for Andrews, where she and selected members of her cabinet will be on Air Force One until the matter is resolved."

"But—" Monica began to say before Hagen put a hand on her shoulder, which caused her to pause.

"That being said," Stark continued, "I think there's a pretty good chance the bastard is playing us, and the chief here may have confirmed my suspicions." He pointed to the tablet computer in Larson's hands.

"So," Monica said tentatively, her eyes on Stark's phone. "What are we going to do?"

Stark looked over to the FBI chopper as its main rotor turned into an invisible disk before it gently took off toward the northeast.

"Divide and conquer, Cruz," he finally said, before heading for the Black Hawk. "Divide and conquer."

As she slowly followed the group and Danny got into the pilot's seat and engaged the turbines, Monica couldn't help but wonder who exactly was dividing and conquering whom.

Stark hit the speed dial button and briefed the national security advisor, who wanted to send the entire U.S. government to the location Montoya had provided.

"Not a good idea, Lisa," Stark replied. "What *is* a good idea is to have everything you've got just over the horizon on listening mode, not in talking-and-asking-questions mode. The people who have this bomb have proven themselves to be very smart, cunning, and to have considerable assets. They will be looking for a large crowd to chase them. They also have to be getting tired and on edge and suspect that we would make a deal with Montoya to get at them."

"So, Colonel," Lisa asked. "What are you going to do?"

"I'm splitting off with my team to chase the best information we have—which, by the way, contradicts Montoya's. I will have Chief Larson call you on this number in thirty seconds to brief you. What I really need is help standing by fifteen minutes away, and I mean help that *really* matters."

Before she could reply, Stark hung up, tossed the phone to Larson, and said, "Hit redial and brief whomever answers on what we're doing."

129

The Right Thing

MARINE ONE. WASHINGTON, D.C.

President Vaccaro knew leaving was the *smart* thing.

She just wasn't sure if it was the *right* thing.

What the hell is the point if the leader of the free world takes off and runs to a deep hole while the rest of the country burns?

Looking over at Wright in the seat across from her, she said, "John, turn this helicopter around. I'm going to work in my White House. This president and this country will not run and hide. We will stand and fight. We all have our jobs to do, and mine is to be in D.C. leading the nation . . . not hiding in some plush cabin at thirty thousand feet, monitoring activities."

Wright tried to suppress a smile.

"What's so funny?" she asked.

He didn't reply, tapping the flight attendant button on the side of his seat three times. Almost immediately, Marine One settled back down on the lawn.

Vaccaro dropped his gaze at him. "How did you do that?"

Wright looked away for a moment then back at her. "I told the pilot we probably weren't going anywhere, and to wait for my signal, just like I told the war cabinet to stay put."

"Stay put where?"

"Where we left them fifteen minutes ago, Madam President, in the Situation Room."

"So they're not in Marine Two or the other choppers headed for Andrews?"

Wright slowly shook his head. "Like I said, I told them to stay put, just in case."

"Just in case of what?"

Wright leaned forward and stared her in the face. "See, Madam President, you didn't abandon us in country—even got shot down in the process. No way you were going to abandon your nation now."

Vaccaro also smiled and mumbled out of earshot from everyone. "Jesus, am I *that* predictable, John?"

Wright leaned ever closer and whispered into her ear, "You are predictable, Laura, but only to me . . . and that's not a bad thing."

130

Incoming!

OUTSIDE LYNCHBURG, VIRGINIA

The explosion came out of nowhere, powerful and blinding.

One moment they were circling the open field, centered on Larson's GPS coordinates, and the next flames swallowed her world. The instrument panel lit up and alarms blared just as the turbines went out, and they were falling from an altitude of one thousand feet.

From the copilot's seat, Monica saw Danny drop the collective lever with his left hand while pitching the cyclic forward to increase airspeed. The freewheeling unit, a centrifugal clutch mechanism, disengaged the main rotor automatically when engine rpm dropped below rotor rpm. Driven solely by the upward flow of air through the blades, the Black Hawk entered an autorotation descent.

"Incoming!" shouted Stark as bullets hammered the exterior of the Sikorsky helicopter.

Hagen and Ryan opened fire toward the tree line. Larson was on the radio.

She grabbed her MP7A1 and rushed to the main cabin, joining Ryan, shoulder to shoulder. She focused her fire on the muzzle flashes at the base of the forest on the north side of the meadow.

Danny put them on a steep descent, quickly gathering forward airspeed. In an ideal autorotation, the chopper would move forward at a shallow angle as the pilot selected a clearing to set the bird down. But given the barrage of ground fire they were taking, landing anywhere on the field would place them in the middle of a deadly cross fire. So Danny glided over the treetops, away from the enemy's line of sight, toward a dry ravine a quarter of a mile away.

But the angle of descent was too steep, and she saw a sea of green rushing up toward them.

"Brace for impact!" Danny shouted as he tried to clear the top of towering pines, smoke rapidly filling the cabin.

The Black Hawk trembled as its belly trashed the canopy. Branches scored the craft's underside, bending metal, ripping the rear landing gear in a burst of splinters and sparks.

Monica lost her footing and almost went out the window, but Ryan grabbed her with one arm while holding on to an overhead pipe as the helicopter trembled.

Its belly sank in branches, the scraping noise deafening, threatening to rip the craft apart.

She grabbed on to the same overhead pipe as Ryan, dreading plummeting through the trees in a helicopter with its whirling blades. But somehow they pulled through, breaking free of the forest's grip, dropping over the ravine.

Danny aligned the chopper with the dry riverbed before flaring it. He used the kinetic energy stored in the rotor to decrease the rate of descent as they dropped ten feet above the rocks. The Black Hawk flared, landing far softer than Monica had anticipated.

Stark was out even before the helicopter had settled at an angle on the uneven terrain, its blades still rotating, smoke billowing from the side of the engines. He already had the phone to his ear, barking orders she could not hear.

Larson and Hagen jumped after him, followed by Ryan and Monica. Danny was last, ditching the headphones and clutching his MP7A1.

Controlled hard landings can be a bitch, thought Stark, deciding that Danny had saved their ass again. As he jumped out of the plane, he speed-dialed the White House.

"Colonel?"

"We need a new chopper standing by and two UAVs with Hell-fires and the pilot on my radio now!"

He hung up before the NSA could respond. The time for idle chit-chat was long since over.

"Chief, you got that?" whispered Stark, looking toward the clearing.

"Roger," Larson replied.

The beauty of a team working together was just that . . . it just worked.

Monica watched Stark split them into three groups of two, she and Ryan to the left, Hagen and Danny to the right, and he went up the middle with Larson, who was still on the radio.

"Get inside, hide, and wait for my signal!" shouted the colonel.

She was about to ask, "What signal?" but in classic Stark fashion he was already gone.

Annoyed at this cryptic man who seemed to be always right, Monica followed Ryan into the forest. They scrambled up the angled terrain, over loose rock and dirt, cruising through waist-high vegetation leading to the massive pines they had just escaped. Moving through in practiced synchronization, they covered each other while advancing from tree to tree. One looked ahead while the other shifted to the next column of bark, peering through the darkness. The massive canopy swallowed the sun, and the barrier of rising trunks behind them blocked the remaining daylight.

They paused, having gone deep enough, letting their senses adjust to the sudden darkness. Their night-vision goggles were stowed away back in the Black Hawk.

Slowly, his face materialized, green eyes staring at her, a hand on her shoulder. It was a gesture of recognition, support, and probably also affection. It was at once the touch of a close friend and of a soldier telling another soldier, "We've got this."

And suddenly Monica was back at that bar in Scottsdale, dancing with the Delta sniper after he had taken out those bikers, each larger than him. She remembered his smile, the way he'd looked at her. For a moment she had forgotten all of the rotten relationships in her life, including those she'd had while in the military, to L.A., to her early FBI career. Ryan Hunt swept them all aside as she glided with him on that dusty dance floor. The training school had been brief, as had their short-lived romance. But what they'd lacked in time together they had more than made up in intensity—a fervor that had reignited in Afghanistan.

Lady Luck had thrown them together in Kandahar, her as an FBI ASAC as part of a in-country joint counterterrorism task force with the CIA and the DIA, and Ryan . . . well, doing what Ryan did in those days and continued to do today: follow Colonel Hunter Stark on special assignments around the world.

Their second round had been longer but just as passionate, including an unforgettable night in a remote mountain cave overlooking an al Qaeda encampment. It had been terribly dangerous and it had been the most memorable and thrilling night of her life, even after Stark caught them at the end of the act.

A week later she had returned to Quantico and Ryan was gone to wherever his team was assigned to next.

But now the former Delta sniper was back, almost six years to the day, massaging her shoulder, those same damn eyes on her now as they had been in Arizona.

Before she realized what she was doing, Monica put a hand over his and smiled.

Ryan pulled her closer.

She wanted to resist but didn't—maybe couldn't—letting him kiss her, softly, like in the old days. The taste of him brought her back to that motel in Arizona, to Afghanistan, to steep mountains, narrow goat trails, and dark caves; brief moments of passion lost in between fierce battles.

Stark finished surveying the grounds, spotting Hagen and Danny already in place to his far right while he and Larson took up the middle. But he couldn't see his left team.

Where the hell are Cruz and Hunt?

Frowning, he whispered to Larson, "Chief, I'll be right back."

The large chief kept his eyes on the objective by the clearing while giving him a slight nod.

Stark moved in a deep crouch, silently, shifting from tree to tree.

He spotted them right away and sighed . . . soldiers; all soldiers would have sex at the drop of a hat when they were deployed. It had to do with fear, aggression, and lack of sleep.

Stark understood it, but he just couldn't allow it, certainly not now and not here.

"Ryan . . . what the fuck . . . are you doing?" Monica mumbled, lips brushing his. "The . . . enemy is just . . . around the—"

"When you two are done," hissed Stark, standing next to them, camouflaged face as stoic as ever.

Monica looked back and frowned. Ryan just stared at the colonel, who added, "And if it's not too *inconvenient*, I need you to move your ass another thirty feet, hold tight, and actually *guard* this flank. But stay well clear of the tree line. Think you can handle that?"

He was gone before either one could reply, vanishing like a ghost.

"Dammit," she mumbled while Ryan cleared his throat.

"Let's go," she added, half embarrassed and half angry, pushing the moment aside while leading the way.

Once again they shifted in the forest, quietly but swiftly. Her eyes had already adjusted to the murky surroundings, her boots sinking in the bed of fallen vegetation. They reached the desired spot, a few rays of light forking through the clearing thirty feet away.

They stopped, but this time she directed him to an adjacent trunk. He frowned before moving over to it, back pressed against the bark as they waited for whatever it was they were supposed to wait for.

131

Dials

KELNOR, INDIA

It was a six-year-old flip phone with a range close to nowhere, but Maryam got a number from their now cooperating Indian border patrol.

The station, nestled in the middle of the desolate mountain range, smelled of heavy cigarette smoke and curry. Lacking air conditioning, everyone was perspiring, even at dusk.

Everyone was also visibly nervous. After all, the United States had pretty much demolished Pakistan, and the last thing the young Captain Hindaru wanted was to focus any of that anger toward his country by killing an American agent.

She had patched up Gorman as best she could, given the limited first aid supplies in Hindaru's office, plus the gear Akbir had kept in his truck for emergencies. Her main concern was blood loss. She had stanched it but Gorman could really use an infusion to keep him from going into shock.

"This . . . could have been avoided," said Captain Hindaru in heavily accented English. He was a thin man with a wispy mustache. The rifle responsible for Gorman's two bullet wounds now strapped across his back, Hindaru nervously looked from Maryam to Gorman. Gorman was out cold on a small bed in the back of the captain's office while Akbir kept close watch on him to make sure the bandages continued to hold.

"What we *need*," Maryam explained, tossing the useless phone back at Hindaru, "is to reach the American embassy in New Delhi."

The Indian captain stared at the phone, and then motioned to his two-way radio operator, who went to work turning dials on the massive equipment on a plain wooden table next to the cot.

Static filled the room as he fidgeted with the knobs for what seemed like an eternity before he spoke in very fast Hindi, which Maryam understood. He finally got a response from a larger command post south of New Delhi.

Hindaru then grabbed the microphone from the operator and began to explain the situation to his superior officer.

132

Miss Cruz

OUTSIDE LYNCHBURG, VIRGINIA

She heard them an instant before they hit.

The powerful explosions boomed across the woods, shaking the ground beneath them. They stood with their backs pressed against rough bark, weapons ready, muzzles pointed at the stroboscopic glare forking through the trees.

Bursts of disintegrating forest followed the blast, splinters, branches on fire, flames, smoke, and . . . screams.

Lots of screams.

"I think that's our signal," Ryan said, waiting until the shock wave blew past them before hastening around the trunk.

Monica followed him through the pulsating light stabbing the darkness. Silhouettes stumbled about in flames, the smell of charred flesh mixed with the haze making her eyes water.

Blinking, squinting, she watched the blurred image of Ryan shooting the burning figures, one by one. They dropped where they stood, amidst flames quickly spreading across the thick and dry forest floor, kindling the inferno.

They ran around it, searching for any surviving enemy while

putting dozens of feet between them and the blaze. But somewhere along the way she lost track of Ryan in the thickening haze.

Damn.

She looked about her, confused, wondering where he had gone, finally deciding to press forward alone. Following her instincts, she walked in a deep crouch, slowly making a wide circle toward the tree line. Along the way she spotted three more men in flames, one already down and the other two stumbling, cries muffled by the roaring fire.

Monica put two bullets in each before moving on with added caution. The smoke receded as she distanced herself from the fire. The forest once more darkened in between sporadic glows casting ragged shadows across her path.

Where the hell did you go? she thought, frowning, searching for Ryan while standing next to a tree roughly twenty feet from the clearing and twice that from the blaze.

But he had vanished. There one moment and gone the next, like some ghost, and for a moment she wondered if—

A shadow detached itself from a tree trunk near the clearing. Its silhouette dashed across her path twenty feet away, following the edge of the meadow. A man held an UZI PRO at chest level, pointed straight ahead.

She stared at it a moment. It was just like the ones Amir's guards had used, including the bulky Gemtec sound suppressors and the Reflex scopes.

Raising her MP7A1, she aligned the head in her sights, hesitating for an instant, trying to decide whether to kill or to wound. Choosing the latter, she lowered her aim to the knees, index finger squeezing the—

The blow came from behind, silent but powerful, smacking her squarely in between the shoulder blades. Her back bent like a bow, and her grip on the MP7A1 loosened as the unseen force shoved her forward.

Her mind screamed that she had just been shot in the vest. The fact that she could entertain the thought meant the layers of Kevlar had done their magical work. Absorbing the slug's energy, the resilient fabric spread the impact across her back. The crippling force knocked the air from her lungs as her legs gave out.

Rolling on the bed of pine needles, eyelids twitching, lips quivering, she tried to breathe, gasping, swallowing, and wheezing again. Two figures loomed over her, followed by a third, who grabbed her by the hair. They dragged her deeper into the forest, away from the fire, from the clearing. She felt as if her scalp was separating from her head, the pain arresting, enveloping her senses.

She tried to reach for his viselike grip as the canopy overhead grew darker, but the kick to her solar plexus left her in a state of shock, lips wide open. She tried to breathe but instead started gagging on her own spit.

The hand clutching her hair suddenly let go and her head fell against the ground just as someone kicked her again, on the shoulder, then in her rib cage.

Monica rolled over and started to heave. Her mind flashed images from that rooftop in Monterrey.

Hugging her aching chest, she tried to catch her breath, the pain paralyzing. But she still discerned figures standing over her. There were three of them speaking, not in English but in what sounded a hell of a lot like . . . Urdu.

Fucking Pakistanis!

An unseen hand slapped her, momentarily blurring her sight.

Blinking, breathing, she came back around, noticing one of them with a cell phone pressed to his right ear. The other two slowly knelt by her side. One of them clutched a knife, long and serrated, like Hagen's, but without the hooked tip.

He pressed it against her neck. His partner dropped his knees on her shoulders from behind, hard, pinning her against the bed of needles, hands grabbing her wrists. Crossing them over her chest as if she were wearing a straitjacket, he immobilized her, making it impossible to break his hold.

"How many of you?" the man with the knife asked in a thick accent while sitting on her thighs.

"Enough," she replied, taking a deep breath. "Enough to . . . send you to meet your fucking virgins."

"Tell me!" the man with the knife hissed, slapping her, the blow disorienting her again.

The coppery taste of blood filled her mouth.

"Tell me! Or I will cut!"

Monica took the abuse while trying to listen to the third man on the phone. She forced her mind to ignore the brutes on her, catching the word *Richmond* amidst fast-spoken Urdu, followed by *Washington*.

"How many?" the man insisted. "Tell me!"

"Go to hell," she whispered.

And that was followed by more insults, by more blows, but she could only think of one thing.

Ryan, where the fuck are you?

She never left his side. Ryan had to move, firing and moving, moving and firing, checking on her as he did. Then she was gone.

Shit.

He doubled back, going to the last spot where he had seen her.

Movement to his left, weapon up, slow trotting, heading directly toward what he hoped was Monica.

He heard the anger. He heard it and then saw three men and Monica beneath them.

He fired twice, dropping the first. Taking three steps closer, he finished the second and third in rapid succession.

Why they bothered to use a knife was beyond him, but he was relieved they were that stupid.

Monica, however, was too still on the ground.

Fuck, he thought, *you'd better not be dead.*

The men surrounding her dropped from view. Her mind once more grew confused, eyes slowly regaining focus. She stared at the canopy overhead, at the layer of dark green slowly broken by a new figure.

It was his face.

"We have to stop meeting like this, Miss Cruz," he said.

"I . . . had this," she whispered.

"That's my girl," he replied, lifting her off the ground, cradling her, pressing her against his chest.

Monica threw her arms around his neck, burying her face in his chest, breathing, quietly taking the pain as light replaced darkness. The pulsating sound of an approaching helicopter boomed across the meadow.

"Ryan . . ."

"Easy, there," he replied. "Let's get you in that chopper."

"Richmond . . . Washington . . ." she said, breathing deeply, getting air in her lungs while ignoring her protesting ribs, anger displacing the pain. "The terrorist . . . spoke Urdu . . . but he said . . . Richmond . . . and Washington."

133

Rescue Party

USS *RONALD REAGAN*. INDIAN OCEAN

One moment he had been in deep sleep in some bunk bed several levels below deck, and the next he was wearing a pair of headphones linked to his satellite phone.

Glenn Harwich struggled to keep his balance and his dinner as the Super Stallion helicopter shot off toward the coast of India while Commander Demetrius led a pair of escorting Super Hornets.

The upward acceleration contracted his stomach while the massive carrier grew smaller in a sea of darkness broken sporadically by the lights from dozens of escort ships. Static sparked in his headset as he was patched to Jack Walch, the station chief at the U.S. embassy in New Delhi.

The information that had gotten him out of bed and thrown on this chopper had been sketchy. Something about an Indian border patrol captain claiming to have found an American agent who was badly injured. But apparently he was in possession of important information regarding the safety of his nation.

Following another dose of annoying static, a voice said, "Glenn?"

"Shit, Jack, that's Bill Gorman. Unbelievable, but it has to be."

"We're not so sure, Glenn . . . could be a trap . . . we haven't heard from him directly. Apparently he's unconscious at the GPS coordinates we provided. It's some border patrol shithole in the middle of no-fucking-where. And he's in the company of some Paki broad who claims to be his asset."

Maryam, Harwich thought.

"Give me the number," he finally said as dawn broke on the eastern sky. It would be daylight soon, meaning more exposure than he would have liked, but he took comfort in the Super Hornets flying overhead.

"Careful, Glenn. We've lost good people to these kind of ambushes," Walch warned. "We have no confirmation that it's legit, and by the time you get there it will be morning, so everyone is going to hear you *and* see you from miles away."

"I know," replied Harwich as the Indian coast loomed in the distance under the sun's wan light. "And Jack, thanks for doing this. Many would have done the safe thing. Logged it and forgot it. You did not. We owe you."

134

Familiar Face

KELNOR, INDIA

The connection was terrible, something to do with a two-way radio interfaced to a satellite phone, but somewhere in the noise cracking through the headphones, she thought she heard a man speak her name.

"Maryam?"

"Aye!" she shouted, startling everyone in Captain Hindaru's small office. "I have Bill with me! He needs medical assistance immediately!"

But all she got in response was static.

"Bollocks!" she yelled, listening for five more minutes to static while the operator fiddled with the dials, trying to reestablish the connection.

Frustrated, she removed the headphones and sat by Gorman, who was snoring peacefully.

She placed two fingers against the underside of his wrist and checked the second hand on the wall clock above Hindaru's desk. But as she counted the number of pulses, she sensed another type of pulse in the distance, slowly but steadily echoing against the wood structure.

Helicopter.

"Keep an eye on him!" she shouted to Akbir while running outside with Hindaru in tow. Three other soldiers joined her as she raced across the hill and turned south, spotting it just above the southern rim rock. It was large, white with red stripes, its rotor noise growing to an ear-piercing crescendo.

Waving her arms frantically as two jets flew overhead and began to make wide circles, Maryam guided the chopper to the rocky clearing, squinting as the landing craft kicked up a cloud of dust and debris.

She shielded her eyes but stood her ground, watching the massive helicopter settle in the middle of the hilltop field, touching down, its turbines decelerating as the entire craft vanished behind a veil of white.

A figure emerged through the haze moments later, like a ghost, running straight for Maryam, who recognized him immediately.

Glenn Harwich, one of the men who had helped Gorman rescue her back in Islamabad.

"Hiya, Glenn!" she shouted. "What took you so bloody long?"

135

Sons of Bitches

Everyone in the Situation Room listened to the woman with the thick British accent coming through the overhead speakers. Maryam Gadai conveyed the intelligence she had gathered in Karachi along with her CIA handler, Bill Gorman, who was still unconscious and in the hands of the Seventh Fleet's surgeons.

Vaccaro listened without interruption, and after the call, she stood and looked at her staff. This information, combined with what Stark had learned, allowed President Vaccaro to say, "John, get Porter to coordinate the blockade north of Richmond and let's get more drones in the area. We have a target vehicle. Now let's get the sons of bitches."

136

One Way or Another

The thoughts invading her mind were as unpredictable as the events that had unfolded this past week.

Salma sat on the heavy trunk secured to the rear of the delivery truck surrounded by an assortment of solar energy hardware destined for the Hay-Adams Hotel in Washington, D.C.

The Bluetooth detonator in her hands, she tried to visualize the destruction it would inflict for miles around, the moment she activated it.

Of all things she could contemplate at the moment, the layout of the city—which she had memorized back in Karachi to a level of detail rivaling the most veteran of D.C. taxi drivers—filled her mind.

Her twelve-kiloton device, detonated the moment the truck pulled up to the rear dock of the hotel, would unleash a fireball engulfing several city blocks, evaporating them in the initial milliseconds. The ensuing twenty-psi overpressure would level every structure within a quarter of a mile, including the White House, the Washington Monument, the Federal Triangle, and the National Archives. As the wave gradually receded to the five-psi contour, it would severely damage all Smithsonian museums and the National Mall. It would also collapse all residential buildings from Dupont Circle to Independence Avenue. A radiation dose of five hundred rem would reach as far as the U.S. Capitol and West Potomac Park.

Thermal energy powerful enough to inflict third-degree burns would reach a full mile from the hotel, encompassing the Supreme Court, the Library of Congress, the Watergate Center, George Washington University, and its adjacent medical center.

And that's not even the best part, Salma thought, a grin forming at the edge of her lips as she remembered the weather forecast. Winds were predicted to be light and variable over the entire D.C. area. Unlike in New York, radioactive debris would rain across the capital like an apocalyptic plague. It could even touch nearby Baltimore, turning the area into a nuclear wasteland for the foreseeable future.

The thoughts filled her with hope, reaffirming her discipline to stay the course, to control the desire to detonate the device at any of the cities she had already visited. And that included the one she was now approaching: Richmond, with its quarter of a million infidels.

She stared at the GPS device connected to the truck's rooftop antenna. It tracked her progress, counting the miles separating her from making history.

At her current speed, she should reach the I-495 outer loop in two hours, and the start of her acceptable detonation perimeter, the north end of the Theodore Roosevelt Bridge, thirty minutes later.

Once she'd reached this point, it wouldn't matter where she detonated. The blast would devastate the heart of the American capital in a fraction of a second.

She was covered in sweat, tired from the long journey yet energized by the prospect of completing her mission and joining Malik in the afterlife. Salma forced her mind to remain sharp, frosty, reviewing every aspect of the final hours of her carefully crafted plan.

She couldn't afford to fail this close to her objective.

Though if it came right down to it, she was prepared to detonate the device the instant she smelled trouble.

One way or another, the bomb would go off today.

137

Lucky Bastards

LYNCHBURG, VIRGINIA

She wasn't sure how much more abuse her body could take.

Thanks to the Percodan Ryan had given her, and the two energy drinks she'd washed it down with, Monica was suddenly up and about in the Black Hawk's main cabin as they cruised toward Richmond. Hagen slept, for a change, while Larson and Ryan played cards. Stark spoke on his satellite phone to someone from the White House.

But it was her mind having the most difficulty keeping up with current events, from the terrorists on their way to Washington to kissing Ryan in the woods.

Kissing Ryan in the woods?
Seriously?

The thought made her think of Porter.

What are you? Sixteen?

She frowned, checking her gear, including the .45-caliber SIG-Sauer that Larson had given her after she lost her Glock in the woods. It had a ten-round high-capacity magazine plus one in the chamber. And she had four more magazines—enough to do some damage when the time came for a little payback. Though based on where the terrorists could be by now, she could only hope they weren't too late.

Crossing her arms while the Virginia countryside rushed beneath them, Monica let out a disappointed sigh at the opportunities lost in the Gulf of Mexico, Monterrey, Carrizo Springs, north of Shreveport, and now Lynchburg. She cringed at the way everyone fell for those diversions in Texas. Even finding that hidden airfield in Louisiana plus Larson's ability to extract the coordinates of that clearing had only resulted in flying right into an ambush.

Lucky bastards.

But she knew better than to believe in luck. The terrorists had been better prepared. They had conjured ever more inventive ways to create diversions, to buy time, to get closer to their objective. They were focused, determined, and willing to give up everything to achieve their objective.

What about us?

Was everyone in the government prepared to do the same?

The president and her immediate staff certainly seemed to believe in Monica's passion for working outside the purview of the Constitution to get the job done. And certainly Stark, Ryan, and the rest of the guys shared the same conviction.

But she wasn't certain about the average law enforcement agent or officer's ability or willingness to step beyond their job descriptions, even in the face of certain annihilation.

Even capturing Montoya had resulted in nothing more than confusion, and perhaps even another diversion while Homeland and the FBI were sidetracked to West Virginia to check out his story.

And all the while, despite her best efforts and her supposedly good instincts—even after joining forces with Stark—the good guys always managed to stay one step behind.

"Behind the fucking eight ball," she complained, earning a curious glance from Ryan before he returned to the cards in his hands while Larson dealt.

She ignored him, for a moment wondering if perhaps she wasn't the right person for the job. The terrorists had managed to evade her at every turn in spite of what she thought was relentless focus and determination. And now, once more, she was a day late and a dollar short, having missed them in Lynchburg while nearly getting killed.

For the fourth time in four days.

But she had to control her growing frustration, perhaps learn a trick or two from Stark's veteran team. They didn't just fight hard but also quite smart. Plus they knew how to relax in between fights, how to recharge, as Hagen, Ryan, and Larson now did. Instead, however, she felt anger rising in her gut at their apparent lack of concern for the events rapidly unfolding before them.

How can they be so damn calm when terrorists are about to turn Washington, D.C., into a well-done steak?

But Monica wondered if they were relaxed or just saving their energy for the upcoming fight while she was simply high strung, falling victim to the same angst that had cost her so many promotions?

Probably the latter, she thought, accepting the reality that no one else on the team had a scratch on them, yet they probably had killed more bad guys than she had.

Monica, on the other hand, had almost lost her head in the Gulf of Mexico, in Monterrey, outside Carrizo Springs, and again an hour ago.

Stark got off the phone and motioned everyone over. Larson punched Hagen on the shoulder and earned the typical knife-in-hand reaction before the group gathered around the colonel in the rear of the chopper.

"Just got word that our man Gorman and that Paki girlfriend of his somehow made it to the Indian border in one piece. Pretty amazing, if you ask me. Based on their intel, it looks like the target is Washington and they're aboard a truck, and thanks to Cruz here, we think they may be trying to approach it via Richmond. The president has deployed UAVs all over the area to find anything that fits the bill, and they're setting up roadblocks between Richmond and Washington. But as you may imagine, there must be a million damn delivery trucks in the—"

"*Delivery* trucks?" Monica interrupted. Her gaze narrowed as it all suddenly came together. The UZI PROs, the Urdu the men spoke, and now delivery trucks—all roads, however circumstantial, certainly led toward . . .

Stark pointed at her with the phone's antenna, frowning. "Cruz? How many times are we going to have to do this?"

"Sorry, sir, but . . . but I think I know what kind of truck they might be in."

Stark had learned a long time ago that if you hired talented, smart, and aggressive people, you had to give them the time and space to be themselves, to figure it out and get it done. He loved his team, trusted them with his life, and now Monica was a part of it, and so far she had nailed it every time.

So when she interrupted him yet again, Stark looked at her, then at Ryan and the rest of the team.

Slowly, his gaze landed back on Monica and he said, "Please enlighten us, ASAC Cruz."

138

Managers of Violence

FREDERICKSBURG, VIRGINIA

They approached the clearing from the southwest, hovering fifty feet over a dozen police cruisers, FBI helicopters and black Suburbans, and a dozen Humvees—all surrounding a large white tent. Beyond them projected a rolling meadow flanked by I-95, roughly halfway between Richmond and Washington: President Vaccaro's line in the sand.

Danny set them down a couple hundred feet away.

Stark jumped out first, closely followed by Monica and the rest of the gang.

She did her best to ignore the pain and kept up with the massive yet agile man almost ten years her senior.

They reached a wall of soldiers and men in suits blocking the entrance to the tent, where she could see Gustavo Porter sitting at the head of a table surrounded by military men and other FBI suits.

"Sorry, sir," a marine told the colonel, blocking the way with his rifle. "Mr. Porter gave us strict orders. No one goes in there while he's on a conference call with the president."

Visibly frustrated, Stark got on the satphone, but neither John Wright or Lisa Jacobson was picking up.

Putting the phone away, the veteran colonel looked at the dozen or so men by the tent before turning to Monica and saying, "I can buy you around thirty seconds in there. Make them count."

Stark felt sorry for them.

The guards were simply not prepared.

Their lives were not dedicated to this craft of war. They were good men, good agents, cops, and soldiers, just not *managers of violence*, the very nature of his team.

Danny's movements were fluid. If watched from above, they resembled a dance as bodies dropped around him. Ryan was more linear, opting to go for the knees, ankles, and the occasional sternum. Stark and Larson simply threw people to the ground while Hagen used his massive knife to encourage them to stay down.

"We don't have time for this chicken shit!" he hissed at the last man standing in his way, a young U.S. Marine corporal, who quickly moved aside.

Monica cruised by the melee and into the command tent.

139

Party Crashers

President Vaccaro and her team were in the middle of a conference call with FBI DSC Gustavo Porter and local law enforcement teams on the ground between Richmond and Washington.

That's when she heard a woman's voice in the background shouting what sounded like, *"Gus, you're a fucking idiot! Thousands will die because you refuse to grow a pair!"*

Although Vaccaro was not new to foul language given her military background, she couldn't help but blink and lean toward the speaker box in the middle of the conference table.

"Porter? Who *was* that?" she asked.

"My name's FBI ASAC Monica Cruz, Madam President. We spoke once in Monterrey. I'm the one who's been tracking the damned terrorists since they steered the supertanker away from Houston. I've partnered with Colonel Stark and his team and we've been following the bastards all the way here."

Vaccaro saw her chief of staff leaning back and trying hard to suppress a grin while Lisa Jacobs raised her eyebrows.

"Ah . . . yes, Madam President," added Porter after clearing his throat. "She's just arrived with Colonel Hunter Stark and his team."

"About time they did," Vaccaro replied. "And we know who you are, ASAC Cruz. Now, about your comment?"

"If you put up roadblocks and start inspecting every truck, you're going to spook the terrorists into detonating the weapon right where they are, as was the case in New York. I passed on intel about—"

"Give us more credit, Agent Cruz," Vaccaro interrupted. "We got your message on Amir Dham's possible involvement, and in the past two hours—and in spite of direct objections from John Wright—we have accounted for every last one of his trucks."

John Wright muted the phone and whispered, "Madam President, Cruz has had it in for Amir for some time. But so far all the evidence has been inconclu—"

"I'm not surprised, Madam President," Monica replied, unknowingly interrupting Wright. "Amir is too fucking smart to make the same mistake twice."

Vaccaro stared at the phone and pursed her lips while staring at Wright and then at Lisa Jacobson before asking, "What do you mean?"

"We've already caught one of his delivery trucks running guns and explosives two months ago, so he isn't using one of his regular company vehicles."

"How do you know that?"

"Because after Porter suspended me for tailing Amir, I decided to use my time off to survey his headquarters in Manassas last week. Before I was nearly killed by his guards, I noticed three things. One, his guards were using the same type of guns that we confiscated from one of his Jasmine Company trucks two months earlier. Two, I saw a different truck at the yard that morning, belonging to a company called Solar Energy Group. And three, that company has something to do with Amir and his dealings with a couple of Saudi royals."

Wright suddenly leaned forward, surprising Vaccaro. "Cruz, John Wright. Exactly whom are you referring to from the Saudi royal family?"

"Prince Khalid al-Saud and his sister, Princess Lisha. Amir met with them at the Hay-Adams the morning after the attack at Bagram Airfield, and again in the hours before the New York blast at his corporate headquarters." Monica also told them what she'd witnessed at the Ronald Reagan National Airport private air terminal just before and after the detonation.

Vaccaro watched Wright's jaw drop an inch before she said, "You certainly have our attention, ASAC Cruz. What do you suggest?"

"Simple. Find the truck belonging to this Solar Energy Group and we find the bomb. We now know the route and the exact delivery vehicle. Focus our energy on that."

"Very well," Vaccaro replied. "And what do we do when we find it? How do we prevent the terrorists from detonating early?"

"I have a pretty damn good idea how to handle that too, Madam President."

140

Short Circuit

FREDERICKSBURG, VIRGINIA

The General Atomics MQ-9 Reaper unmanned aerial vehicle flew over the I-95 corridor forty miles south of Washington, D.C., at an altitude of five hundred feet.

A single 950-horsepower turboprop engine propelled its sleek gray shape to almost two hundred knots.

Its control surfaces and systems were slaved to the commands of a two-person aircrew from the 138th Attack Squadron at Hancock Field Air National Guard Base in Syracuse, New York.

As it approached its designated target area, the Reaper ejected a shiny bullet-shaped object roughly five feet long over the northbound traffic before breaking hard left and climbing away.

The device, a metal armature surrounded by a coil of wire—or stator winding—connected to a bank of capacitors and a core filled with high explosives. It followed a parabolic trajectory toward the ground.

At an altitude of just one hundred feet above a Solar Energy Group delivery truck cruising at the speed limit in the right-hand lane, onboard capacitors distributed an electrical current through the stator wires. The surge generated an intense magnetic field, triggering a fuse mechanism that ignited the explosive core.

The blast traveled as a wave through the middle of the armature cylinder and came in contact with the stator winding, creating a short circuit and cutting the coiled wire from its power source. The moving short circuit compressed the magnetic field, generating an intense electromagnetic pulse that fried all unshielded electronics in a one-hundred-foot radius.

Half a dozen vehicles on the northbound side of I-95, including the targeted truck, came to a stop as their computerized ignition control systems ceased to operate, as well as all onboard electronics.

141

Moment of Truth

FREDERICKSBURG, VIRGINIA

Monica moved out quickly the moment traffic stopped, as police helicopters swarmed the highway from the west. Their rotor noise echoing across the valley, they landed in the gap between the stalled traffic and the cars north of the EMP radius, which continued undisturbed toward the nation's capital.

Police cruisers and three SWAT vans rushed into the gap from seemingly nowhere, blocking the way. Doors swung open. Armed law enforcement officers jumped out, taking position, aiming a deadly mix of rifles, submachine guns, and semiautomatic pistols at the vehicles in the kill zone.

Another gap in the highway had been created south of the stalled traffic by two unmarked police cruisers. They had driven side by side well under the speed limit for the prior five minutes. In doing so, they forced everyone to slow down behind the targeted truck and its surrounding cars. More police helicopters and SWAT teams descended on this second quarter-of-a-mile space, further isolating the target vehicles, some expected to belong to innocent civilians.

The late-afternoon sun in her face, the breeze swirling her hair, Monica rushed across the edge of the tree line separating the highway, alongside Hagen. They covered two hundred feet of sloping terrain in twenty seconds, reaching the edge of the highway's wide shoulder. It was lined with clumps of boulders amidst knee-high brush skirting towering pines. Ryan Hunt and a pair of snipers from a D.C. SWAT team had already taken their positions on thick branches overhead with clear lines of sight into the kill zone.

Armed men exited the sedan directly in front of the truck, leveling their weapons—ironically mostly UZI PROs—at the north blockade. A second group jumped out of another sedan two cars behind the truck and turned their weapons to the SWAT team moving up on the southern gap. The driver of the truck and its passenger also leaped out of the cabin and joined the group facing the north blockade.

"They're trying to buy time," she said to Hagen as they reached a boulder outcrop a couple dozen feet from the rear of the truck.

The police used a loudspeaker to urge civilians to lock their doors and hide in the vehicles. Some did, but others panicked and sprinted away from their cars, running for cover.

The police ordered the terrorists to put down their weapons, but they answered by opening fire against the southern roadblock. Their rounds ricocheted off asphalt, pounding police vehicles, shattering glass, and puncturing metal. Some bullets even hit a couple of the civilians running away. Their cries as they rolled bleeding on the asphalt mixed with sirens and gunfire.

The second group also opened fire against the northern roadblock with matching intensity, their muzzle flashes stroboscopic, pulsating, deafening.

Porter arrived a moment later, huddling behind them as both blockades reciprocated, peppering the vehicles around the terrorists. Two police helicopters hovered somewhere off to their right, firing from above, forcing some terrorists to duck behind their vehicles.

A hundred feet north of them, Stark, Larson, and Danny also reached their position, covering the second group of terrorists.

The perimeter secured from all angles, Stark gave the signal and the group opened fire from the edge of the road. They flanked the terrorists, some caught by surprise, their heads exploding before dropping from view.

"Cruz! Get your ass inside that truck and finish this!" Porter shouted while firing his semiautomatic into a pair of terrorists hiding behind a sedan.

142

Out of Choices

FREDERICKSBURG, VIRGINIA

Salma knew it was still too far away, but the time had come.

Remaining in the truck while her team bought her time, she silently prayed that the winds aloft would at least carry some of the fallout from the groundburst over the outskirts of Washington.

Rounds pounded the truck like a hundred mallets; some punched through, striking furniture, zooming dangerously close to the device—and to her.

She leaned to her right as the truck suddenly fell to one side, then the other, as bullets ripped through the tires, deflating them.

She had to do this now. There was no choice, no escape. They were surrounded and soon the Americans would break into the rear of the truck.

Reaching for the remote control at the end of the chain under her T-shirt, she briefly glanced at the ceiling of the truck.

Closing her eyes, she took a deep breath, and pressed the button for the required five seconds.

But nothing happened. The device did not respond with the acknowledging beeps signaling the start of the short countdown.

Shocked, she opened her eyes at the continued rattle of gunfire, of rounds hitting the truck, of men screaming outside.

"No . . . it cannot be," she hissed, horrified, pressing the detonator again and counting to five, but the handheld device was dead.

And she suddenly realized that the same weapon—likely an EMP—that the Americans had used to disable the truck had also damaged her detonator.

Turning to the metallic trunk in the back of the cargo compartment, Salma entered the digital combination to open it, but the external electronic lock was also disabled.

"Oh, no . . . NO!" she screamed, eyes searching for anything that could provide leverage, her mind racing, her heart pounding, suddenly finding it difficult to breathe.

You can do this, she could hear Malik telling her, urging her to think, to focus.

Her eyes searched the interior for something, for leverage, finally settling on a red toolbox secured to the side wall.

Rushing to it, she snapped the twin metal clasps, rummaging through the top compartment, finding nothing sturdy enough to pry the trunk open. She lifted it out of the way to search the larger bottom section, her hand grabbing a yellow crowbar.

143

Hand-to-Hand

FREDERICKSBURG, VIRGINIA

Clutching her SIG-Sauer, Monica leaped over the guardrail, landing in a deep crouch on gravel. Keeping her head low, she ran toward the truck, eyes focused on the rear door, on the—

A terrorist swung toward her, bringing his UZI PRO around. Their eyes met for an instant before his head exploded from a sniper round, blood splattering by her feet as he fell.

She cut right, going around him, reaching the side of an abandoned SUV. Taking a deep breath, she realized that time was of the essence but that she also needed to be more careful. She had Ryan and the other snipers on her side, but they relied on line of sight to protect her. Next time she might not be as lucky if a terrorist waited for her hidden from their vantage points.

Running around the vehicle, the SIG leading the way, Monica inspected the dozen feet separating her from her target. Her eyes searched north and south, making sure she was clear, before sprinting again, approaching the rear of the truck. She scanned everything through the pistol's sights in quick sweeps as she reached the truck's rear quarter panel, noticing the blown tires.

Gunfire subsided from the southern blockade per Stark's instructions to avoid hitting her, but that meant giving the terrorists a short break.

And that's when she spotted them: three terrorists reloading their UZI PROs.

She fired in rapid succession. The semiautomatic ejected spent shells. She hit the first man but missed the other two, her bullets shattering the window of another empty vehicle.

The terrorists rolled out of the way behind the sedan. One tried to make a run for the woods when a silent round tore into his neck and he fell gasping for air, blood squirting about.

Deciding that she did not have the time to screw with the last terrorist at this end, she chose to trust Ryan and the other snipers to cover her back. Monica reached for the metal lever above the rear bumper and rotated it counterclockwise, unlatching the door.

Shoving it upward, she jumped out of the way in case someone waited inside with a weapon aimed at the opening.

Sunlight invaded her world as the loading gate slid open.

Salma didn't turn around, hands on the crowbar as it broke through the right hinge. Wood splintered, metal bent, and the lid gave on one side, partly exposing the device. Green LEDs blinked next to the manual activation pad. The layers of lead film designed to keep any radiation from leaking out had also protected its electronics during the EMP.

Filled with hope that the computerized trigger mechanism was not damaged, Salma shoved the edge of the crowbar into the gap on the other side, pushing down with all her might to rip through the second hinge.

Monica jumped inside, standing among crates and large solar panels stacked vertically and secured with lanyards to anchored points along the floor and walls of the truck.

A man shouted behind her. The third terrorist, emerging behind the sedan, UZI PRO in hand. But a silent round tore into the side of his head and he fell back out of sight.

Thank you, guys, she thought, breathing heavily.

Wood cracked, but not from the bullets still pounding the truck.

This was something else, coming from the interior—like someone hacking and splitting lumber up in front, beyond the crates, panels, and other hardware.

Time was quickly running out. Raw fear coiled in her gut. Any second now her world could vanish in a blinding flash of superheated air.

Monica charged straight to the front, around wooden crates, squeezing between what looked like power transformers and shiny solar panels.

And that's where she found her. A woman on her knees, a crowbar by her feet, hands inside a long metallic trunk. Her dark hair covered her upper back. A shiny Beretta was tucked in her blue jeans, pressed against her spine.

"Freeze! Hands up where I can see them! Now, Salma! I mean it!"

Salma stopped, momentarily startled at hearing her name.

She had entered less than half of the required activation sequence when noticing the shadow of the American woman cast by sunlight forking through the rear door.

Salma had two choices: she could ignore the warning and continue keying in the long password while risking a bullet in the head before she could finish, or . . .

The terrorist raised her hands.

Monica stepped closer, the SIG-Sauer aimed at the back of Salma's skull, hoping like hell she was not too late.

"Get up very slowly, Salma," she said. "And keep those hands up."

The terrorist complied, her back still facing Monica.

"Now reach down with your left hand and use just your thumb and index fingers to pick up the pistol by the end of the handle and toss it behind you."

The terrorist complied, the Beretta clanging on the floor by her feet. Monica kicked it under a large metallic case.

"You are too late," Salma said in heavily accented English, still facing the trunk. "It is done. It will all be over very soon."

A heavy sinking feeling descended on Monica as she recalled the final words of the Navy SEALs in New York. Bordering on panic, she stepped closer to take a look inside the trunk.

Salma pivoted on her left leg the instant the American's shadow telegraphed her being close enough. Bringing her right leg up and around, she struck the infidel across the left cheek. The impact was hard, decisive, forcing her to the floor. As she fell she dropped her pistol, which skittered to the side.

Jumping toward the fallen gun, which she recognized as a SIG-Sauer, Salma tried to grab it but felt a tug on her left leg, pulling her back.

The kick stung, but Monica was unfortunately getting quite used to it, allowing her mind to get past the shock and react quickly. Leaping toward the terrorist reaching for her .45 semiautomatic, she snagged her foot and jerked it back.

Salma's hand missed the weapon's handle by a foot. She surged to a deep crouch while Monica did the same. Turning sideways to the terrorist, Monica kept most of her weight on her rear leg and her arms curled in front, fists tight.

Salma faked with her left leg and threw a side kick with her right, aimed at Monica's midriff, heel extended and toes pointing down.

Monica stepped back, missing the attack while driving her right elbow down, hard, shoving it deep into Salma's ankle.

The terrorist recoiled, limping, face twisting in pain, surprise flashing in her eyes at Monica's nimbleness.

Monica followed by palm-striking her chest, the impact shoving Salma against a side wall, slamming her back and head, bouncing, and landing on all fours.

Monica went to kick her across the face but Salma rolled out of the way. Her legs scissored as she surged back up, chest heaving, arms in front, eyes glinting in anger.

The terrorist lunged, throwing a jab with her left hand while trying to land a punch with her right. Monica deflected them while sweeping her left arm counterclockwise in front of her.

She snagged Salma's wrist with her left hand before she could withdraw it. Stepping aside, Monica forced Salma's arm in between them and twisted it to expose the side of the elbow.

"No! Stop!" Salma screamed, apparently aware of what would come next.

Monica ignored her, palm-striking the elbow. The sound of cartilage snapping and bone cracking filled the truck's interior.

Salma screamed again while recoiling, wide eyes staring in disbelief at her bent arm.

Monica finished her off by punching her just below the right ear, knocking her out just as Stark and Porter jumped in the truck.

Scrambling past the stacked panels, shoving some out of the way, they reached the space where she stood in front of the terrorist.

Heaving, hands on her knees, trying to catch her breath, Monica looked toward the trunk. They knelt by it and looked inside.

"She . . . said," Monica started, wincing in pain from her throbbing ribs, before leaning down to pick up her gun. "Said . . . that . . . it was done."

Porter shook his head while pointing at the device. "Doesn't look that way, Cruz."

"Yeah," Stark added. "I don't think it's activated, but let's get the bomb squad in here ASAP to be sure. Then we can call it a day."

While Porter made the call, Monica stepped behind them to take a look at the fission-type bomb. It was smaller than she had expected, with the target at one end and the trigger mechanism and conventional explosives at the other.

"Doesn't get any simpler than that," said Stark.

"Simple . . . and pretty fucking deadly," Monica said, staring at it while thinking of the damage it could have done—the damage one just like this did to New York City.

Salma started to come around, moaning, a hand on her torso.

Stark and Porter exchanged a look.

"Keep an eye on her, Cruz," Porter finally said. "We need her alive."

Alive.

Monica briefly closed her eyes, thinking of all the people who were no longer alive because of these terrorist assholes. Those countless souls in New York, the crew of the supertanker, the agents slaughtered in the streets of Monterrey, and those Louisiana National Guardsmen. Yet, this sad excuse for a human being would get to live, probably get legal counsel, followed by months, if not years, of expensive court time. And to what end? So she could eventually get executed? Or even worse, maybe even get exchanged for some kidnapped American years into the future, like so many of her predecessors?

As Porter and Stark continued to inspect the bomb, Monica unceremoniously pointed the SIG at Salma's head and fired once, the sound deafening inside the enclosure, pounding her eardrums.

"Well, I'll be damned," whispered Stark.

"Cruz!" Porter screamed through the ringing in her ears. "What the hell? That was an *asset*!"

"Not anymore, Gus," she replied. "Not anymore."

Monica thumbed the safety on her weapon, removed the magazine, extracted the chambered round, and dropped it all by Porter's feet.

Along with her badge.

Porter looked at his feet, then back up at Monica. "Cruz, what the hell are you—"

"This time I don't want them back."

And simply walked away.

EPILOGUE

Six Months Later . . .

BAR HARBOR, MAINE

Gorman had fallen into a pattern, taking morning walks along rocky cliffs overlooking the ocean and gathering firewood in the snowy trails on the way back to the cabin. Filling his lungs with the pine-resin fragrance from towering trees and his mind with peaceful sea-scapes, Gorman turned his face toward the ocean.

The breeze sweeping in from the North Atlantic was cold, humid, and invigorating. It was certainly a far cry from the dusty Pakistan mountains that he and Maryam had traveled what seemed like a life-time ago.

He wasn't sure why this particular area was so full of former spooks. But he was glad, as this spot, besides being beautiful, had some of the nation's finest—albeit oldest—intelligence officers on the planet. They all still had connections to their former business, and they all knew to look out for Gorman and his beautiful wife.

Plus, come October, after the leaves changed, the cruise ships stopped visiting the harbor. The area settled into its near-hypnotic winter trance, providing the peace and quiet longed for by those who'd spent a lifetime in the grind.

The cabin was modest, old-fashioned, made of heavy logs and a metal roof, but still providing all of the modern creature com-forts, from central heating and plumbing to satellite television and Internet.

Gorman wanted seclusion, but he didn't want to rough it. He had opted for this place deep in the woods next to Acadia National Park, accessible by a long dirt road, yet only a twenty-minute drive to down-town Bar Harbor.

A network of cameras and infrared sensors surrounded it in case an old foe decided to pay him or his wife a visit. In addition to selecting foot-thick logs for the walls, capable of withstanding a fusillade of the heaviest caliber, he had replaced all of the windows with bullet-resistant glass and had built a basement panic room with a tunnel leading to the woods behind the house.

He dropped the load of firewood by the growing pile stacked next to the steps leading to the covered porch, where he kicked off his boots and slipped into a pair of wool-lined moccasins.

Maryam, four months pregnant, had her feet up on the sofa by a fire, reading a paperback next to a cup of steaming coffee and a 9mm Beretta.

She wore unbuttoned faded jeans and white T-shirt pulled up to her midriff. A hand rested on her exposed belly. A stainless steel Rolex hugged her left wrist.

She looked up, smiled, and returned to her reading.

He had declined witness protection for her, well aware of the potential leaks in the system as well as the vast ISIS and ISI reach and predictable thirst for retaliation. Instead, he had taken his early retirement package and gone hiding where many spies go when they wish to forget—and be forgotten by—their prior world.

He inspected the woods projecting beyond the front porch, wondering if it would be just a matter of time before their past caught up to them.

Feeling the reassuring cold steel of the Glock tucked in his jeans, against his spine, he closed and bolted the door before joining his wife by the fire.

EAGLE PASS, SOUTH TEXAS

The morning rides helped Monica clear her mind before starting her day at the ranch. After so many years, she thought it would be difficult getting back in the saddle, literally. But her body had remembered—though not without punishing her for the first couple of weeks with aches in the most unforgettable places.

The work never ended at the ranch. Cattle needed herding. Fences needed mending. She had to make sure each bull, cow, and horse ate and drank water every day. She repaired barns, dug irrigation ditches, killed coyotes, plus there was the endless tagging, vaccinating, and looking after all the calves and foals.

The work was hard but rewarding, physically draining her by the end of each day. It filled her with a strong sense of accomplishment that seemed to wash away her anger, her anxiety, and her attitude. She had even cut back on the profanity, though not as much as her brothers would have liked.

One weekend a month she would ride the Ducati a hundred miles to volunteer at the San Antonio Military Medical Center. The place was packed with New York burn victims, both military and civilian. She offered her services, reading, talking, and just spending time with soldiers who had sacrificed far more than she had, or civilians who'd simply been at the wrong place at the wrong time.

It was the least she could do after quitting the Bureau and spending the following three months immersed in ashes as just another civilian volunteer in New York City. She had joined the real heroes clearing streets and hauling rubble, doing anything and everything she could to help make amends for allowing this to happen, for not having fought harder when she'd had the chance. Especially when it came to Amir Dham, now in a detention center that didn't exist.

So day after day, she had gotten into a routine, working her way through the Financial District, through what remained of Battery Park. She had cleaned, dumped, and hauled, turning demolished square miles into a blank canvas. Teams of international architects and builders funded by Saudi Arabia and Kuwait, of all places, would soon commence the long process of rebuilding.

Then one day into her third month there she had received the most unexpected call from her younger brother, Michael, informing her that Marty, their older brother, had been diagnosed with prostate cancer. Although the prognosis was encouraging, the chemotherapy would likely keep him in bed for a few months.

New York still needed her, but charity started at home, so she had climbed on the Ducati and pointed it to Texas, trading in her yellow hard hat for her old Stetson.

Ranch work kept her grounded, focused, helping her forget the turbulent decades of her military and law enforcement career, the many lives she had taken—even if she did it for a noble cause, making the world safer.

She continued to decline the attempts by the Bureau to get her back. There was still much work to be done in the war on terror, but Monica felt the time had come for younger and brighter agents to step up.

She had also declined the multiple invitations to the White House. After what she had done to ISIS, the last thing she wanted was awards, medals, and her name in the damn papers. Although it was seriously wounded, she felt the global terrorist network still had enough fight left in it to at least seek retribution against those responsible for foiling their well-crafted plans.

Monica ignored everyone from her prior life and forced herself to work sixteen-hour days. And it wasn't just to help her brothers as much as she could—and in some strange way to try to make up for time lost. It was also to be completely exhausted, ensuring deep sleep rather than facing her demons in the middle of the night.

Though they were not all demons.

As Monica rode Marty's Mustang home one early evening, the sun started to set in the western sky, painting the desert in the most amazing of colors, from blazing red to burnt orange.

She thought of him, her Delta sniper with the green eyes and the amazing smile. She had hoped that their third round would have yielded something meaningful, especially since they were both in their forties. But Ryan had been Ryan and he had just said good-bye and boarded that Black Hawk helicopter shortly after dropping her off on the rooftop of the J. Edgar Hoover Building.

Monica looked toward the east as the first stars appeared, as a light breeze swept across the dusty plains bordering the northern bank of the Rio Grande, snaking its way to the Gulf of Mexico.

Somewhere in the darkness beyond the horizon, she had flown over from Mexico not long ago looking in this direction. She had wondered what life was like for her brothers at the old ranch. And now she decided that it was certainly good—filled with hard work but also with the promise of a future that could include someone to grow old with.

Maybe not today or tomorrow, but *someday*.

She hoped that special someone would become tired of the endless missions, grow weary of the chase, of fighting the good fight, of circling the globe in war machines.

Perhaps someday.

Monica inhaled deeply.

A moon in its third quarter replaced the dying sun, casting a grayish glow across this barren land she never knew she loved so much.

Coyotes howled in the distance. The desert wind whispered in her ears.

And Monica Cruz let the mustang take her home.

MARINE ONE. OVER NEW YORK HARBOR

President Laura Vaccaro still didn't want to interrupt the work.

She knew of the choking atmosphere that surrounded a presidential visit, even more so since the nuclear attack. But she still needed to be near the action and see the city, even if it was from a distance.

They flew above "the Zone," the section of Manhattan a block south of Chambers Street where bulldozers and earthmovers worked twenty-four/seven leveling the roughly one and a half square miles of the most precious real estate on the planet.

Or at least it will be once again when we're through, President Vaccaro thought, as the pilot followed the tall construction fence from the top of Rockefeller Park on the Hudson River to the foot of the Brooklyn Bridge.

New Yorkers being New Yorkers had already turned the stretch of land immediately north of the fence into a picturesque, long and narrow park with jogging and biking trails, trees, benches, ponds, gardens, and fountains.

At her request, work had also started on a memorial similar to the Vietnam Veterans Memorial in D.C. Though this one would be much longer—almost a half mile long—to capture the names of all those who'd perished on that fateful day.

What impressed Vaccaro the most was the speed at which the reconstruction work was progressing. It had taken almost a decade before Freedom Tower stood tall where the Twin Towers had fallen. Yet, the Zone looked almost ready to begin construction.

Freedom Tower was erected while surrounded by functional city blocks. It had required a large degree of finesse, both above and below ground, to avoid disrupting services to the busiest city in the world. The Zone, however, was a "blank canvas" accessible by water from three sides, making it relatively easier to clear out—though it still was an unprecedented task by any measure.

But there was plenty of funding, in particular from Saudi Arabia and Kuwait. The oil-rich nations had shocked the world by their willingness to shoulder most of the cost, and also assisting the San Francisco Stock Exchange in accelerating the economic recovery of the nation. On top of that, the Saudi government, which had always played a leading role in OPEC, had persuaded its allies in the region to join in the effort. Kuwait had stepped up first. Others followed.

Vaccaro knew that sooner or later word would get out about how she had circumvented every power center in Washington to get the job done. But she would not apologize if and when the time came. In fact, she would welcome the opportunity to tell everyone that it was not she but the men and women on the ground who had saved the nation. She would say that the true heroes were the ones who did not survive. The president would pray for them, and acknowledge the sacrifice so many made, for the rest of her life.

The helicopter continued hovering over the tip of Manhattan, where swarms of heavy machinery cleared out debris and dumped it on a fleet of docked barges to give way to what she had described as the finest financial and commercial district the world had ever seen.

Rising from the ashes of a painful victory.

She frowned. Even now some were questioning her every action to achieve this painful victory.

Let them, she thought.

The nation was more important than her or her mounting critics. She did not need or ask for adoration that also came her way. The city rising beneath her was all that mattered.

Marine One turned south, back to Washington, as her former brother in arms and chief of staff handed her the phone.